If you loved Conan Doyle's, *The Hound of the Baskerville*, prepare to be enthralled by KD Sherrinford's captivating follow-up, *The Whistle of Revenge*.

The deadly antagonist, Jack Stapleton, makes a spectacular return to the city of Milan in pursuit of his old nemesis, the celebrated Detective Sherlock Holmes.

Adopting the enigmatic persona of Janus, a vengeful Stapleton, along with the Italian mafia, wreak havoc on the Italian horse racing fraternity and fledgling car manufacturing industry, and kidnapping Holmes's beloved son as part of their evil and well-executed master plan — Operation Whistle.

Will Holmes, Irene Adler, and their trusted ally, Inspector Romano, crack the code, rescue the boy, and unmask the deadly Janus?

Set against the backdrop of modern Milan, mind games and misdeeds of the highest order play out as the story reaches its thrilling and memorable conclusion.

The unauthorized reproduction or distribution of this copyrighted work is illegal. Criminal copyright infringement, including infringement without monetary gain, is investigated by the FBI and is punishable by up to 5 years in federal prison and a fine of $250,000.

This book is a work of fiction. Names, characters, places, and incidents either are products of the author's imagination or are used fictitiously. Any resemblance to actual events or locales or persons, living or dead, is entirely coincidental.

The Whistle of Revenge
Copyright © 2024 KD Sherrinford
ISBN: 978-1-4874-4251-4
Cover art by Martine Jardin

All rights reserved. Except for use in any review, the reproduction or utilization of this work in whole or in part in any form by any electronic, mechanical or other means, now known or hereafter invented, is forbidden without the written permission of the publisher.

Published by eXtasy Books Inc

Extasy BOOKS

Look for us online at:
www.eXtasybooks.com

The Whistle of Revenge
Sherlock Holmes and Irene Adler Mysteries Book Four

By

KD Sherrinford

Dedication

To my dear friends, Tony and Barbara Waslin-Ashbridge.

Prologue

The advantage of any long-term relationship was that after settling into a stable and, at times, predictable routine, the man you adore can sometimes surprise you. That was how it was with my husband, the world-famous consulting Detective Sherlock Holmes. Eleven years after our first encounter, Sherlock and I finally found our inner peace. Our unconventional marriage and enduring love affair were fundamental to our happiness. As he often worked away in London, our acceptance of being apart was a form of intimacy that only enhanced our relationship.

There were many astonishing aspects of my marriage to Sherlock Holmes, alias Lucca Sapori. He agreed to my request to remove the word *obey* from our marriage vows. Instead, he asked that I love and honour him, and I had no problem with that.

"Why should I expect you to obey me?" he'd said. *"You're my wife, not my servant."*

When we reaffirmed our vows, I knew for the first time what it was like to be in a loving marriage.

Whatever people may think of Sherlock, he was never one to shirk his responsibilities. As a keen observer of human behaviour, my husband's ability to assess complex situations and discern pragmatic paths was extraordinary. Like others, I was frequently perplexed by his critical views and egotism, although I knew it wasn't because of selfishness or conceit. To Sherlock, it was impersonal. His honesty was often perceived as insensitive, but there was nothing callous about that honesty.

Even after being apart for long periods, we had this almost telepathic, physical connection, maintaining our double life as Signor and Signora Sapori like the tide ebbing and flowing.

Life could be complex, exciting, and stimulating until unexplained moments brought out the dark side of one's behaviour. My father, Alfred, used to say that disagreeable things happened to good people — and vice versa. Who could lecture us on what's good, bad, or indifferent? My husband might have something to say on the matter.

Over the years, I learned that the line between the present and future isn't a solid wall or a flimsy pane of glass. Life's curtain could be closed at any time. Loyalty and integrity were precious commodities. Have you ever wondered what betrayal looked like? I often asked myself that question, and in the summer of 1906, I was about to find out.

An incident was coming that would shake us to the core.

Chapter One: Nene Adler
Scherzi Veneziani — Venetian Frolics.

The year 1906 started with so much promise. A few weeks earlier, Sherlock and I took a long-overdue vacation at an idyllic villa in Venice overlooking the Adriatic Sea. Surprisingly, Sherlock's brother, Mycroft, extended the invitation.

The house belonged to an old acquaintance, Derek Hamilton, who worked alongside Mycroft in Westminster and used the villa as a holiday home. Mr Hamilton was away on business with the Foreign Office for the best part of a year and enquired if Mycroft wanted to use the place while he was away.

Mycroft politely declined the invitation, blaming work pressures, but he said he had friends in Italy who would likely enjoy a break. It was a lovely, thoughtful gesture, but I suspected Mycroft was still trying to make amends for his machinations eleven years earlier in Fiesole, which forced Sherlock and me apart for over four years. However, after a reconciliation at Christmas in 1904 at our farm on the Sussex Downs, relations significantly improved. That was also when Mycroft first met his niece and nephew, Nicco and Charlotte.

I felt excited when Sherlock accepted Mycroft's offer to use the villa. We deliberated over taking the children, but as my husband pointed out, Nicco had important upcoming exams. So we left them in the capable hands of our trusted staff members, including their governess, Hildegard, whom the children adored and held in the highest regard.

That was how I found myself on the first Friday in May,

setting out on my train journey from Milano Centrale on a perfect spring morning.

Sitting next to the window, I looked out at the changing landscape. The passing trees and distant localities shimmered in the glow of the morning sun against the backdrop of the vast Tuscan sky as the train gradually picked up speed.

I closed my eyes momentarily as the rhythmic tugging and hissing filled the air with bittersweet memories of nostalgia. It brought back poignant memories of a trip to Manhattan with my late father, Alfred, when I was eight. It was the first time I'd ever travelled on a train.

My father died in 1895, just a few months before Nicco was born. Unfortunately, he never got to see his grandchildren, although he left a canny proviso in his will. Touched by his kindness, I was determined to make my father's memory count. I set up a trust fund to honour him. The Alfred Adler Foundation was a charity and bursary that nurtured the skills and talents of musicians and singers from disadvantaged backgrounds and offered financial assistance.

Over the years, the foundation had helped countless performing arts members realise their dreams. My father helped shape the person I am today. He encouraged my love of music and taught me how to play the piano, supporting my love of opera. He was such a kind, generous, and thoughtful soul, possessing qualities I could only aspire to emulate.

Three hours later, I arrived at Venezia Santa Lucia train station to find my husband's familiar sight waiting for me on the platform. Sherlock was attired in an ulster and cap, holding his valise in one hand and a cigarette in the other.

I waved and smiled as those penetrating grey eyes fixed on me and gazed back with such warmth and affection. I walked towards my husband, the porter following close behind. I shook with delight as Sherlock wrapped his arms around me, holding me tightly. He kissed me gently on the lips, pushing the hair away from my face as I drank in his manly scent and the faint aroma of his cologne. Then he broke off our embrace, quickly summoning the porter to take care of our luggage as though nothing had happened between us.

We took the ferry from Santa Lucia to San Zaccaria, hiring a gondolier to take us on the last leg of our journey to Chioggia, known as Little Venice. It was a picturesque fishing town with colourful houses, narrow streets, and a bustling market. We could only get to the town by boat from San Zaccaria or Fusina, and to be away from the madding crowd suited Sherlock and me just fine.

We considered using the vaporetto to complete our journey, which Sherlock reasoned would have been much quicker. But I persuaded him that travelling by gondola would be far more adventurous and romantic. After checking with the gondolier to see if our luggage would fit, Sherlock agreed to my request. The gondolier was a diminutive, wiry fellow named Adamo with an engaging smile and a cheerful disposition. He navigated the boat effortlessly through the waterway of The Grand Canal, winding through the heart of the city, lined with historic palaces, churches and bridges, making it a picturesque route.

Finally, he docked outside our destination, located in its private and secluded setting. It was a quaint Venetian villa with Rigoletto charm that would be our home for the next two weeks. Adamo jumped out of the boat and took my hand to disembark before helping Sherlock carry our luggage into the villa. After receiving a handsome tip, the gondolier doffed his brightly coloured straw hat and waved goodbye before proceeding with his journey.

The house was bright, airy, and well-appointed. It offered a good-sized galley kitchen with a larder to its rear, fully stocked with bread, cheese, antipasto, olives, fresh fruit, sweetbreads, and biscotti. Jugs of fresh milk, homemade lemonade, sugar, tea, and coffee were all at our disposal. There was a welcome note from a lady identifying as Mariette waiting for us on the worktop. Mariette told us she would serve as our maid during our stay. We should expect her to come in daily to change the bedding and bring fresh towels.

The lounge was large and beautifully decorated, with white-painted walls dotted with paintings of Italian landscapes. Sherlock helped me open the heavy blinds, revealing two large picture windows boasting spectacular sea views. A tufted leather settee, a chaise lounge, and two hard-backed chairs furnished the room, along with an ornate coffee table and a gramophone set in the corner. Next to the sitting area was a drinks cabinet, fully stocked with whiskey, brandy, and port, and holding several bottles of Venetian red wine and champagne. We discovered a shelf underneath the cabinet having a fine selection of English cigarettes, shag tobacco and Tosca Nello cigars.

The main bedroom with en-suite was cosy and intimate. Its centrepiece was a four-poster, mahogany bed with matching furniture—the highly polished floors covered with handmade, richly coloured Turkish Kilim rugs. We entered the bathroom to discover panelled walls and a cork-tiled floor boasting a walk-in shower, roll-top bath, a separate toilet, and a comprehensive selection of towels and toiletries.

We walked outside, exploring the medium-sized garden with pots of spring flowers surrounding its borders. Next to several olive trees stood a raised area serving as a patio with a table and four comfortable-looking, stylish natural wicker chairs with linen cushions offering spectacular views over the commanding Adriatic Sea.

All of this, the glorious weather, and the sun beating down caused me to sigh and reminisce. It reminded me of our time together at La Sole in Fiesole all those years ago. It was picture-perfect, the ideal setting. A second honeymoon should differ from a more lavish or far-reaching holiday, staying in the grandest hotels. But here, in this humble yet exquisitely furnished villa in one of the most romantic cities in the world, my husband and I found the privacy we yearned for.

After Sherlock and I unpacked, we decided not to go out, as we felt a little tired from the journey. Instead, I made a platter of cold food for each of us from the larder, which I took outside onto the patio while Sherlock uncorked a bottle of champagne. At the same time, I placed a record on the gramophone. We sat gazing at the spectacular views, chatting quietly, eating our food, and sipping the delicious champagne with Beethoven's delightful minuet from his *Piano Trio* in C minor playing in the background.

We retired early, around nine, taking our champagne upstairs. Physical tension intensified during the evening, like the third and fourth movements of Beethoven's *Fifth Symphony*, which built up to a remarkable crescendo. A shy stare, a nod, a knowing look in that magnificent setting stirred our senses. Frankly, I'd been looking forward to being flirted with, anticipating the thrill of his touch.

Sherlock stroked the back of my neck, untying the pins in my hair, as he'd done countless times before until my hair fell loose upon my shoulders, and then he gently turned me around to face him, pulling me onto the bed. I leaned in to kiss him, but instead, in a golden moment of vulnerability, my lover, husband, and best friend cradled my face with his hands, lifted my chin and gave me a soft, lingering kiss. Then, he kissed me again, but the kiss was more urgent, making my head spin.

An overwhelming urge to touch him washed over me. I unbuttoned his shirt, tracing my fingertips over the contours of his skin, taking in his masculine scent. Our eyes met as we explored each other. His sensitive fingers mastered my body like a concert violinist, each stroke sending shivers down my spine. We spent the remainder of the evening in a romantic dalliance as my husband made love to me with a haunting intensity that was simultaneously natural and sensual.

Late, as dusk descended, Sherlock lay asleep on the bed. I listened to my husband's soft breathing against the backdrop of the waves crashing onto the beach. I didn't want the night to end. I felt safe, loved, and protected here.

I drifted into a delightful slumber with my husband's arms wrapped around me, my head upon his chest.

Neither of us stirred until dawn when we were awoken by the sun streaming in through the blinds, the chatter of the chaffinches and the melodious repetitive whistle of the blackbirds hopping from branch to branch in the olive trees.

When I thought things couldn't improve, Sherlock surprised me at breakfast with two tickets for Giuseppe Verdi's *Rigoletto*, to be performed at the La Fenice Grand Opera House later that evening.

After disembarking from the vaporetto at the Venice terminal, we took a cab to take us on the last leg of our journey to the theatre. As the coach rattled down the narrow, winding streets, the rhythmic clip-clop of the horse's hooves against the cobblestone was music to my ears. The early evening sun cast its warm glow upon the city, gilding every stone and shadow alive with a golden shimmering light that danced upon the canals. It caught the rippling reflections as we passed. The theatre rose before us as a masterpiece of ornate stonework, resplendent in its grandeur, and it beckoned us forward. The impressive sign above the main theatre doors, showing the rising bird above the gold words, *Gran Teatro La Fenice*, against a blue background, was a striking feature. After La Scala, La Fenice was my favourite opera house.

It was a scene perfectly orchestrated by nature and design.

The Whistle of Revenge

Venice at her most magnificent, her charm was intoxicating as the finest wine, and one could scarcely resist the allure La Fenice presented on that fine May evening. The faint scent of salt and sea lingered in the air, mingling with the heady aroma of blooming jasmine and freshly baked pastries from the remaining colourful market stalls still open nearby. Merchants were engaged in lively conversation, their voices rising and falling in the customary rhythm of negotiations.

Elegant Venetians strolled towards the theatre, their laughter and voices carried on the gentle breeze. Well-dressed gentlemen and ladies paused in their promenades to look with mild curiosity at our coach.

The crowd's soft murmur enveloped us as we descended and entered the theatre, blending with a violinist's harmonious yet faint low strains serenading outside a nearby cafe.

Over the years, I've had the privilege of treading the boards at the prestigious venue, following in the footsteps of the great and the good, those iconic performers who had walked before me.

Antonio Selva designed the opera house, which was classically elegant. Its grand facade featured stylish columns, a sweeping staircase, and ornate furnishings. Inside, visitors marvelled at frescoes, gilded mouldings, and crystal chandeliers.

Tragically, the Great Opera House burned down in 1836 due to a faulty heater. The fire brigade took three days to extinguish the fire, and the smouldering hotspots remained for fifteen days. La Fenice was rebuilt in record time and reopened just one year later.

Over the years, the opera house has hosted many renowned composers such as Rossini, Verdi, and Wagner. Its acoustics were amongst Europe's finest, making it a premier opera and classical music venue.

My husband looked striking that night in his tailcoat,

cummerbund, white shirt, black tie, and top hat. I wore an emerald green silk dress with a silver tiara, a matching bag, and shoes. The world premiere of the iconic opera *Rigoletto* was launched in 1851 at La Fenice, so it felt like the opera had come full circle. Judging by the polished performances of the ensemble cast, the production was still as fresh and commanding as it had always been. I marvelled at the humanity in that theatre as the power of the singers' bold tones soared into the rafters of the auditorium, and the thrilled audience shrieked with delight.

This dramatic journey of undeniable force has always been one of my favourites. The story is based on the controversial 1832 play *Le Roi Samuse* by Victor Hugo, the French writer and politician who became famous for such literary classics as *Les Miserables* and The *Hunchback of Notre Dame*. The play was banned from public performance for fifty years, as it was said to include insulting references to King Louis-Phillippe of France.

Our good friend Enrico Caruso made his American debut in *Rigoletto* on the opening night of the Metropolitan Opera House in New York in 1903, having made his London debut in the same opera at Covent Garden the previous year. Enrico played the Duke of Mantua and made best-selling recordings of the arias, *Questaquella* and *La Donna e Mobile*.

Rigoletto tells the tale of an outsider — a hunch-backed jester who struggles to balance the dual elements of beauty and evil in his life — writing splendidly during the most fertile period of Verdi's artistic life while at the peak of his lyrical powers, the opera resonates with a universality frequently described by many as Shakespearean. I've always thought that music's evocative power was most significant when heard in live performances. The ensemble cast did nothing to prove me wrong.

Tears streamed down my face as I sat spellbound,

watching this spectacular production and holding my breath as the emotionally charged dramatic ending neared its thrilling climax. In a scene-stealing performance, Rigoletto sang a heartbreaking duet with Gilda, his dying daughter. It was unbelievably tense, combining melancholy, serenity, and tragedy in one great improvisation that lingered in the memory.

Even though I knew what was coming and every word of the song, it was still a scene that got to me every time I watched it performed. So many of us have experienced immeasurable heartache and despair at some point in our lives, and to me, the magnitude of those feelings, that unbearable pain, was splendidly encapsulated into the sound of opera. Nothing compared.

Sherlock slipped his hand into mine, and tears of happiness rolled down my face.

"Thank you. What a treat," I whispered.

"My great pleasure," he replied, smiling at me gently.

The next few days flew by in a haze. We explored every corner of the city, feeding my husband's bohemian tendencies. Rather than booking into fancy restaurants, we preferred to make the most of our time together. We ate suppers outside, under the tranquil moonlight, with the sea almost on our doorstep. We enjoyed picnics during the day, walked barefoot on the beach, swam in the Mare Adriatic, part of the Mediterranean Sea, and drank copious amounts of wine, lying on a blanket in the sand by the shore, reading and chatting. We laughed as we observed the gulls flying overhead, screeching and singing in the glare of the afternoon sun, marvelling at the golden facade and the place's inherent beauty. I felt at one with the entire cosmos.

When we returned from the beach the following morning, we finally met our elusive maid, Mariette. She was a lovely lady around thirty-five, tall and slim, with twinkling brown eyes and blonde hair tied back in a ponytail. Mariette apologised for interrupting, explaining that she lived nearby and purposefully came in late mornings to avoid disturbing our privacy.

Two days before the end of our vacation, Sherlock and I embarked on a half-day lagoon boat tour of Burano and Murano. The former was famous for its colourful buildings, while Murano was renowned for glassmaking. Both were perfect locations to escape the crowds of tourists. After exploring the island streams, we visited the market square, where we watched the artisans at work and rummaged through the stalls where I bought gifts for the children.

Sherlock knew I wanted to visit the San Zaccaria Church and the corner museum. San Zaccaria's Church was on the waterfront southeast of Piazza San Marco. It was a former 15th-century monastic church in the Campo San Zaccaria and Saint Mark's Basilica. The church was dedicated to St. Zachariah, the father of John the Baptist.

Its apse was surrounded by an ambulatory lit by tall gothic windows, a typical feature of Northern European church architecture unique to Venice. Nearly every wall was covered with paintings by 17th and 18th-century artists. However, the most famous painting was from much earlier—the masterpiece San Zaccaria Altarpiece. It was an oil-on-panel painting by the Italian Renaissance artist Giovanni Bellini, who completed the stunning artwork in 1505.

Sherlock and I agreed that we would return with the children, if not later that year, then the following summer. We even talked about buying a holiday home in the vicinity.

Everything was perfect until we came home.

Little did we know that there would be a price to pay for our fleeting contentment, a painful reminder that nothing lasts forever, least of all happiness. And no one could have prepared us for what happened later that summer—the abduction of our beloved Nicco. As my husband said, the whistle of revenge blows long and cold.

CHAPTER TWO: NENE ADLER
Pensando al Rapimento-Thinking about the kidnapping

Sunday, June 3rd, 1906 —
It was a humid morning at our villa in Milan. The dusty street was silent, the tranquillity broken only by a dog barking in the distance. The yammering of the natterjacks and the chirping of the crickets woke me from a troubled sleep. The dawn sun crept above the horizon, casting a faintly purple haze across the landscape, a soft glow that bathed the scene in an ethereal light. It lent a quiet dignity to the surroundings, a beauty unadorned and stirring within me, a fondness for this Italian land and culture that I'd come to regard as my home over the years.

I slipped into my son's bedroom. But there was no welcoming smile or protestation about having to get up. Instead, the bed was empty, as it had been for the past two nights. Helen, our chocolate labrador foundling dog we'd brought from England, wouldn't stop whining. She was pining for Nicco and his sister, Charlotte. An overwhelming sense of grief washed over me, trying to make sense of the whole sordid situation. I was incensed that despite Inspector Salvatore Romano, Mycroft, Sherlock's brother and my husband's best efforts, my son's abductors still walked the streets with impunity.

"Please, God, bring my son safely home." I prayed, picking up Nicco's dressing gown and pressing it to my nose as I drank in his familiar scent. I couldn't cry because there were no tears left.

The Whistle of Revenge

Gazing around the room, I noted my son's cello and violin in the alcove, the new strings he'd ordered that arrived only yesterday, still wrapped in brown paper. His atlas, gramophone, and comprehensive collection of shellac records sat next to a bookcase overflowing with books on science, music, psychology, medicine, cyphers, and codes.

I picked up Nicco's battered old teddy bear, Rufus, from the pillow, and he stared at me accusingly. "I'll bring him home, I promise," I whispered.

After days of tears, prayers, and unwavering belief, I fervently hoped our son would soon be found and that Nicco would somehow feel our longing, the immense love that filled our hearts. I pictured him walking through the door a thousand times like nothing had happened.

My little man, albeit not so little now, Nicco, was tall for his age and darkly handsome. His beautiful face gazed at me from the photograph on the bookcase. My husband and late mother, Marianne, had endowed our children with the same thick dark hair and piercing eyes. Like Sherlock, Nicco was always outwardly confident in his abilities, although never arrogant.

The esteemed playwright William Shakespeare wrote King John when his beloved only son, Hamnet, had died in 1596 at age eleven. The cause of death was unknown, and he was the same age as Nicco. I do not doubt that *The Sweet Swan of Avon* was writing of himself when he penned the following sonnet in tribute to his son.

Grief fills the room up with my absent child,
Lies in his bed, walks up and down with me,
Puts on his pretty looks, repeats his words,
Remembers me of all his gracious parts,
Stuffs out his vacant garments with his form.
Then, have I reason to be fond of grief?

Of course, I'd lost others in the past. My parents, my first husband, Godfrey, my daughter, Rosemary, and then, although not in death, Sherlock, whom I was estranged from for over four years after our adventures in Fiesole. Until that moment, I never knew the true meaning of unconditional love. But now, the anguish I felt, the hopelessness of losing my son, and the thought of never seeing him again was indescribable.

Then, my thoughts went to Charlotte. How could I tell our beautiful little girl that the brother she adored and idolised was missing?

Fortunately, Charlotte was holidaying in Rhodes with my dear friend Sophia to help celebrate Sophia's parents, Sergio and Gina Stephanatos' golden wedding anniversary. Charlotte adored the Stephanatos, and they had a real fondness for Charlotte, who was thrilled to be invited to the proceedings and spend time with her best friend, Gabriella.

They wouldn't return for another three weeks, blissfully unaware of the drama unfolding at our home in Milan. I felt relieved Charlotte was away. What if the perpetrators had taken her, too? It didn't bear thinking about. I knew she couldn't cope at the tender age of six. Nicco, however, was quite a different kettle of fish. He was capable of far more than your average eleven-year-old.

At first, I thought the worst, that the underworld in London had discovered Sherlock's secret identity as Lucca Sapori, and they'd kidnapped Nicco out of revenge, although I could tell my husband had his doubts. Upon discovering Nicco's unexplained disappearance, Sherlock responded immediately and precisely. Before venturing out to meet with the Milano polizia, and with scarcely a moment's hesitation, he reached for the telephone and contacted his brother, Mycroft, whose considerable resources and influence could well aid the search. But after exchanging several frantic calls and telegrams, we discovered those doubts were unfounded after Mycroft made extensive enquiries with his scouts and contacts and came up with nothing.

Mycroft said it was not the underworld's style to kidnap children, and had they known about our liaison, they would have instead come after Sherlock and me. Of course, Mycroft was shocked and concerned that someone had taken his nephew and vowed to do all he could to find the perpetrators. In the meantime, he suggested we look closer to home.

"Be vigilant," he yelled. "Expect to hear from the kidnappers imminently, as we suspect it is someone with connections outside the city's underworld community."

Mycroft was convinced, as Sherlock, that a ransom note would swiftly follow — and it did.

I pondered Sherlock's return from his inquiries with the Milano polizia with an air of anticipation. I prayed he had good news to convey and our son was safe. My husband's last words before he left that morning rang in my ears as he held onto me as I collapsed, sobbing into his arms. He took my hand and brought it gently to his lips. The piercing grey astute eyes now dimmed.

"I *am* going to find our son and bring him home, and then I shall bring the perpetrators to justice, and when I do, they will pay the price." He held me by the shoulders and gazed into my eyes. "Until then, Nene, I need you to be strong for Nicco and our family."

I nodded, smiling at him weakly through tear-filled eyes. Like me, my husband had little appetite and had hardly slept the past few nights. He had two days of stubble on his chin, his eyes bloodshot from sleep deprivation, and I suspected from crying, although as a stoic, he was unlikely to admit to that.

Undoubtedly, our son's disappearance had emotionally distanced Sherlock and me, and grief cascaded over us like a shroud. Somehow, despite all of this, my husband managed to carry off the facade of staying positive, hopeful, and optimistic. He did it for my benefit, and I loved him for that. I felt the man I adored slipping away from me. A failure that, to Sherlock, overthrew all of his success. Our love was simple, profound, and passionate, yet rarely spoken of, and as I was about to discover, to be sorely tested.

Chapter Three: Nene Adler
Buffonate Liriche — Operatic Antics

My mind drifted back to that unfortunate night. Sherlock had initially agreed to accompany us to the theatre. Like Nicco, he was keen to meet with my dear friend Enrico Caruso and happily agreed to fit in with our plans. He first raised concerns about whether our son should be allowed to attend the recital due to the late hour. But after explaining how much it meant to Nicco, Sherlock finally agreed.

I arranged with another old friend, Arturo Toscanini, the principal conductor at La Scala, to have supper with him and Enrico at *Lafayette* after the performance. Arturo and I had been friends since our first meeting at La Scala when I joined the theatre chorus many years ago. However, as close as we were, there was never any question of a romantic interlude. Our lifelong friendship had always been platonic, based on admiration, trust, and mutual respect.

Unfortunately, Sherlock awoke with a heavy summer cold on the morning of the recital, complaining of feeling listless and drained of energy. Illness was unusual for my husband, who had a robust constitution and was seldom ill. Despite my protestations offering to stay with him, Sherlock dismissed my concerns, insisting I proceed with our planned trip since he had no wish to disappoint our son.

So later that day, Nicco, coachman Mattia Greco, and I started our journey to La Scala.

When our carriage approached Piazza Della Scala, I remember my son's eyes shining like stars as he gazed up at the splendour of the opera house.

Like me, despite the numerous times we took in the magnificent sight of The Teatro La Scala, highly regarded as one of the most prestigious opera houses in the world, nothing could diminish our sense of wonder. The great Guissepi Verdi was closely associated with the Great Opera House until he died in 1901, while Arturo Toscanini began his tenure in 1898, becoming the company's artistic director and principal conductor, a position he still held to this day, marking one of the finest periods in the theatre's existence.

Nicco looked grown-up in his court suit, white shirt and red tie, making him appear older than his years. He reminded me so much of his father, which brought a lump to my throat.

I took him backstage, and we briefly chatted with friends working behind the scenes, including my old confidante, Madam Emily, head of the wardrobe department. She lived in an elegant houseboat in The Navigli District. A diminutive-looking woman, always remarkably neat in her attire, attractive, yet not outlandishly beautiful, those large, well-shaped dark brown eyes gazed at us fondly behind horn-rimmed glasses. Her once jet-black hair was now bespeckled grey, tied up in a neat chignon. Emily complimented me on my black silk Ponte evening gown while also gently teasing Nicco that he was even more handsome than his father. He'd grown so much since their last encounter two months ago and looked dashing in his evening attire, making my son blush crimson.

But behind Emily's engaging smile was a determined woman. Her elegance was characteristic of her generation where being seen in public was a performance and integral to the job. So she expected every character who took to the stage in one of her fabulous creations to act and dress appropriately.

We staged a production of Rossini's *The Barber of Seville* earlier that year. It was a complicated piece, and our director,

Luigi Ambrosio, a hard taskmaster, was determined to perfect every performance aspect. By the end of each day, the ensemble cast looked worn and weary.

At the dress rehearsal, I remember Alessio Muratori, who played Figaro, having trouble performing the legendary patter song *Largo al Factotum*. He uncharacteristically fluffed his lines as he swayed from side to side on the stage, clearly a little intoxicated from the whiskey it was rumoured he kept hidden in his dressing room.

Like all great tenors over the years, Alessio was often on the receiving end of some waspish reviews and notices, and using alcohol as a crutch helped steady his nerves. He was bawled off the stage by Ambrosio, ordering the intoxicated tenor to sober up and get his act together. Alessio turned on his heels in a chaotic state.

But before he could exit the auditorium, a furious Emily appeared in front of the startled tenor, staring at him over her glasses disparagingly. *"The wardrobe is the last piece of the production. The final step of fleshing out and capturing the essence of the characters. I have spent much time and effort creating magnificent costumes for you and the rest of the ensemble cast to wear for this opera. All I ask in return is that you have a care to look equally magnificent in them."*

This altercation raised a titter from the exhausted cast and me. Mind you, it was at 9 A.M. when Alessio found it hard to look the tea boy in the eye, never mind an enraged Emily. He never got on the wrong side of her again.

After explaining to Emily why Lucca could not accompany us to the theatre, we chatted briefly about Charlotte's holiday with my dear friend Sophia Moon, an accomplished mezzo-soprano with whom I shared rooms as a first-year student at La Scala, and her husband Robert, La Scala's music director, before we said our farewells and slipped back into the auditorium to take our seats, waiting patiently for the performance to begin.

Glancing around the theatre, Nicco drew my attention to the first box on the left-hand side of the stage. My face broke out into a wide beam as we waved excitedly to Ava and the rest of her party. Ava was the principal soprano at La Scala. I'll never forget her heart-stopping debut at the prestigious opera house in 1899. She was seated with her husband, Javier Anka, a talented musician, and Javier's parents, Marco and Isabella.

They smiled and waved back, acknowledging our presence. Ava looked rather fetching in a navy evening dress with silver thread running through, her beautiful light brown hair piled up in an elaborate curl twist cascading over her delicate shoulders. She was a close friend, the daughter of Ludo and Violetta Espirito, who sheltered Sherlock and me all those years ago when Colonel Moriarty was on our trail at their beautiful, isolated farmhouse, La Sole, in Fiesole.

Since then, Sherlock and I had forged a close-knit bond with The Espirito family, including their son Francesco, who was good friends with Nicco and Charlotte.

Arturo introduced Caruso onto the stage to rapturous applause and acknowledgement from the expectant audience. The orchestra played his opening song, *Il fior che avevi a me tu dato*, the famous flower song aria sung by Jose from Act II of Bizet's *Carmen*. The loggione cheered their approval as the acclaimed tenor gave a spectacular performance.

Enrico's presentation was a pleasure to the senses, filled with emotion, rhythm, joy, and hope. Each masterpiece was skillfully delivered, such was his precision. Like all great performers, we saw only the brilliance of each piece, not the prowess behind its creative power. He was undeniably brilliant, remaining in control throughout the performance, at one with the orchestra. He encouraged them to improvise in *ostinato*, knowing they could never diminish him. Our hearts soared, lurched, then soared again. We cried, laughed, and gazed in awe. Although the concert occurred in one of Europe's famous opera houses, it felt profoundly intimate.

The recital and encores finished at 9 P.M. Enrico and Arturo apologised to the appreciative audience for dashing off early, stating they had a pressing appointment.

Lafayette was within walking distance of the opera house, so after briefly chatting with Ava and her entourage, finally bidding them a fond farewell, we set off to the ristorante, arriving around half-past nine. Renowned for its intimate ambience and delectable food, *Lafayette* was busier than usual due to the World Trade Fair and the recital. I was pleased Arturo pre-booked a table in our favourite spot by the window. As we crossed the vestibule, the aroma of freshly baked bread and summer blooms invaded our senses as the head waiter, Dante, greeted us warmly before escorting us to our table.

Fredrik, our *maître 'd*, ensured Enrico wasn't troubled by autograph hunters and well-wishers. He told disappointed admirers that their idol was dining with friends and had no wish to be disturbed. Enrico explained to Nicco that he would consider that rude, which made my son feel incredibly important.

Enrico and Arturo were lovely men. Sitting here in the room with my son and these two legends was a surreal experience even for me, a seasoned performer. Their very presence drew the attention of every soul in the bustling ristorante. Enrico was in his early thirties, with piercing brown eyes, dressed impeccably in a finely tailored suit of deep charcoal, accented by a crisply folded pocket square and a silk cravat of midnight blue. He presented the image of a man who was both regal and approachable. His dark, receding hair that was neatly combed glinted with a hint of pomade, and a slight sheen on his polished leather shoes caught the light with each subtle movement. Arturo was also resplendently attired in a smart, three-piece grey suit with a white carnation in the left lapel.

This living legend, Caruso, received us with an easy smile, a spark of amusement dancing in his dark eyes. There was no impatience in his manner, nor did he exhibit the weariness one might expect of a man so often in the public domain. Instead, he seemed genuinely pleased by our presence, and his voice was rich and warm with the same resonance that captivated audiences worldwide.

His expression to Nicco and myself softened into one of gentle contentment. There was a quiet joy in his countenance, as if he were at peace at this moment, savouring the simplicity of a shared meal and good company amidst the familiar murmur of local voices and the soft chime of the silverware on porcelain. It struck me then that Caruso was not merely a performer but a man whose heart, like his voice, held a profound benevolence for the world around him.

Nicco gazed in wonder at the beautiful, cosy, intimate setting, with its ornate chandeliers illuminating the grandness of the room, crisp white linen tablecloths matching napkins, and cut crystal wine glasses. A male string quartet on a podium in the far corner of the ristorante entertained us with music from Mozart's great works.

Pictures from famous operas adorned the walls, including an oil painting of the great Niccolo Paganini, the celebrated violinist, my husband's personal favourite, for whom I'd named our son, much to Sherlock's delight.

The waiter confirmed our order, which Arturo had sent through earlier. Mindful not to keep Nicco up too late, we didn't bother with a starter or appetiser. The men and Nicco had the Florentine steak with sea bass for me. Arturo ordered a bottle of Giulio Ferrari champagne from the sommelier to be put on ice and homemade lemonade for Nicco, served in a tall, frosted glass. The champagne was delicious, but I only accepted half a flute. When Arturo attempted to top up my glass, I put my hand over my flute to protest, explaining that I had no wish to become tipsy. I knew from experience that champagne tended to go straight to my head.

Fredrik brought the house speciality for dessert. It was the ristorante's renowned homemade classic tiramisu served with a generous portion of Italian ice cream made from a special recipe that went back generations. It was the best I've ever tasted in Tuscany. Observing my son's joyful expression as he savoured each delicious mouthful, it was evident that he felt the same.

The conversation flowed as effortlessly as the champagne. We spoke of music and our mutual love for the vibrant city of Milan and its famous opera house. Over dinner, Nicco sat enthralled as his idol explained how he came from a poor but not destitute background in Naples.

"My mother sadly died in eighteen-eighty-eight," Enrico said, smiling at Nicco before continuing. "I found work as a street singer to raise money for my family. I performed at cafes and soirees before I was eventually discovered. Finally, in December nineteen hundred, I signed a contract at La Scala. It was one of the happiest moments of my career. Then, I debuted as Rodolfo in Giacomo Puccini's *La Boheme,* with Arturo conducting the first of many appearances at the prestigious opera house."

"Yes," Arturo agreed. "And that included performing in the grand concert I organised in February nineteen-oh-one to mark the death of Giuseppe Verdi."

"How could I ever forget that glorious evening?" Enrico beamed at Arturo.

"But you know, my friend, you can never take anything for granted, especially in this business." He laughed, reverting his attention to a wide-eyed Nicco.

"It's only by the grace of God that I'm here with you now," Enrico said, waving his hands theatrically.

"But why?" Nicco asked.

Enrico narrowed his eyes in response. Lighting an Egyptian cigarette, he sat back in his chair and gazed at Nicco intently before his face broke into a wide grin. "In April, after appearing as Don Jose' in *Carmen* at the San Francisco Opera House, I was awakened by a strong jolt. I glanced at the clock showing five-thirteen A.M. in my suite at *The Palace Hotel*. The room suddenly began to shake wildly, my clothes tumbled out of the wardrobe, and for the next minute, I thought my world was about to end when I found myself amid the San Francisco earthquake, culminating in devastating fires that destroyed most of the city. So I feel very fortunate to have survived such an ordeal."

"But what of the rest, the ensemble cast? What happened to them?" Nicco asked, staring at Enrico with newfound admiration.

"Fortunately, the *Met Company* I was touring with were all unharmed, thank God, but we lost all our costumes, musical instruments, and sets. I couldn't get out of San Francisco fast enough. I made a successful effort to leave the city, first by boat and then by train, and I vowed upon the memory of my sainted mother never to return. They say lightning never strikes the same place twice, but I wasn't taking any chances. I felt I had a second chance at life." He laughed. "With all its beautiful memories, I will be sad to leave Milan, but I'm keen to continue my European tour."

"But was it a vocation? Did you always want to sing?"

Enrico smiled, putting down his wine glass and staring at Nicco earnestly. "What can I tell you?" Enrico shrugged. "Music is my passion. As far back as I can remember, I have always sung for the sheer joy of performing." Enrico diverted his gaze to me. "It's no secret that Nene is one of the world's finest contraltos, an outstanding opera ambassador. True artistic talent involves expressing what lies behind the obvious,

The Whistle of Revenge

and your mother has this in abundance. When I began singing, my voice was like Nene's contralto, similar to the range of a countertenor before I eventually developed my rich tenor voice. I sang in a church in Naples from age fourteen to hone my craft." Enrico picked up a brown paper package from the chair beside him. "This is for you, Nicco, a token gift to remember me by. Remember to follow your passion, and never let anyone steal your dreams."

Enrico sat back in his seat, chuckling at Nicco's astonishment.

"Well, don't keep the great man waiting ... open it," Arturo said, pointing towards the package.

Nicco carefully opened the parcel to reveal Enrico's signed 1905 New York recording. One I was familiar with included the Brindisi, with piano accompaniment from Cavalleria Rusticana, one of Nicco and Sherlock's favourite operatic songs. His face was shining with happiness as Nicco thanked Caruso, holding the record as though it were a gift from heaven. He shook hands with the tenor and Arturo, and I embraced the men warmly before we said farewell and retired for the evening.

Our stomachs were sated, and our hearts were warmed by our intimate connection with these two legends. Those ninety minutes after we entered the ristorante's threshold had flown by. We left Arturo and Caruso engrossed in meaningful conversation while enjoying a glass of port and a Canaria d'Oro Cuban cigar.

Chapter Four: Nene Adler
Il Rapimento – The Abduction

Mattia patiently waited as Fredrik escorted us to our carriage, ensuring we were safely ensconced in the brougham.

With a crack of the whip, our journey home to our villa at Via Torino had begun. We were tired from the evening's excitement and the wonderful meal. Nicco soon drifted off to sleep, clutching the brown paper parcel holding Enrico's record. As the carriage rattled over the cobblestones and wound through the tree-laden streets towards the park, the lamps cast slender fingers of light through the darkness, giving the trees a ghostly silhouette. I stared out of the window as our coach driver, Mattia, suddenly pulled up the horses outside the gates to Parco Sempione, a large urban public garden stretching between the Castello and the magnificent Arco della Pace, where Sherlock and I had spent many happy hours with the children. The park had been busy throughout the day, hosting fine art displays as part of *The Milan World Fair International Festival*.

A middle-aged man with dark brown hair and a beard, dressed in a black sack suit and white shirt, frantically waved to flag down our driver as he limped along the road. The man was wildly gesticulating towards a woman lying motionless on the ground beneath a cypress tree.

"Please help my wife," the man implored. "She collapsed a few minutes ago. I twisted my ankle, trying to lift her."

I ordered Mattia to open the carriage door, and as he

The Whistle of Revenge

jumped down, I glanced at Nicco, who was still sleeping soundly like a baby. I looked around anxiously, relieved to find no one else in sight, covering my son with a blanket before stepping down from the carriage to join Mattia. I attended to the lady, a diminutive figure with brown hair tied up in a knot. She was dressed in black, with a red shawl covering her shoulders. She looked pale and drawn but responded to the salts I wafted under her nose.

"She's not drunk," her husband explained. "My wife is expecting, becoming lightheaded as we return from a late-night event in the park."

"Do you live far from here? May we offer you a lift home?" I enquired.

The man nodded. "That would be most kind, thank you. We don't live far," he said, pointing to the opposite side of the park toward an imposing-looking detached house set back from the road, shaded by tall mature trees. It sat next to a row of smart-looking, honey-coloured cottages, offering spectacular views across the park from its elevated position.

The man extended his hand. "My name is Fabrizio Gallo, and this is my wife, Mimi."

I introduced myself to Fabrizio and his wife, who said they recognised me from my photographs at La Scala. Mimi clasped my hands as we helped her into the carriage. She sat on the opposite side of Nicco and me while Fabrizio jumped into the front with Mattia. I handed Mimi a cup of water from a flask, which she sipped from gratefully, the colour eventually returning to her sallow cheeks. Nicco opened his eyes briefly, acknowledging my presence with a smile before falling back into his delightful slumber. I felt a pang of regret for keeping him out so late.

When we finally pulled up before the brooding outline of the darkened house, the night air was still warm and held a mysterious, yet tranquil, atmosphere about it, as if the very shadows whispered secrets amongst themselves, conspiring in the stillness.

Mimi swayed slightly as she slowly disembarked from the carriage. "I still feel a little giddy," she said as her slender fingers clutched mine, her grip tightening and face paling once again beneath the moonlight. "Please won't you come with me to the house?" she murmured, her voice a fragile wisp in the night.

I nodded in agreement and asked Mattia to stay with Nicco while Fabrizio limped ahead, opening the front gate, which I noticed was about five feet high. The house's name, 11Vecchio Cigno, was displayed on a brass plaquette to the left of the mortise door lock.

Fabrizio noticed me staring at the ornamental plaquette. "The previous owner was a bird watcher. He named the house in honour of the swans at Parco Sempione's artificial lake."

A separate entrance to the side led to a good-sized rear garden, an outhouse, and an orchard surrounding the house. Putting my arm around Mimi, I accompanied her through a sizable oak-panelled hallway and into a medium-sized lounge until she was safely nestled into a cosy-looking armchair. The rest of the room was sparsely furnished, absent of the bare necessities of life, save for a vase filled with beautiful purple morning glories, orchids, and a grandfather clock set in the corner.

"God bless you. Few would have stopped." Mimi sighed. "Never mind an acclaimed contralto. May my husband and I offer you some refreshment?"

I shook my head. "No, thank you. It's late, and I need to get my son home," I said, furrowing my brow as my ears were alerted to the sound of a carriage travelling at speed in the lane outside. I figured it must be late revellers from the exhibition.

The Whistle of Revenge

I said farewell to Mimi and her husband. As I stepped outside, I was horrified to discover Mattia lying motionless on the ground, bruised and battered, blood flowing freely from a gaping wound to his head. Our carriage, with my son inside, was galloping away. The driver had their back on us, so I couldn't tell if the perpetrator was a man or a woman. But before disappearing from view, the driver slowed down and turned around for a moment, their shadowy face concealed by a mask. My heart stopped in my mouth. It was as though I'd seen the devil himself as the driver nodded, touching their hat with what looked like a cane, before turning back around and disappearing into the night.

My wails of anguish echoed into the evening stillness as I repeatedly called out my son's name, but there was no answer. The only sign of Nicco was the brown paper parcel discarded on the rough ground, and the record Caruso had so lovingly autographed smashed into pieces was all that was left. I couldn't get that image out of my head, as though seared into my brain.

I ran over to Mattia, who remained unconscious, removing my scarf and binding it tightly around his head in a makeshift tourniquet, attempting to stem the blood flow. Then I ran back to the house, banging frantically on the door. There was no reply. I pushed the door open and rushed inside, calling out to Mimi and her husband. The lounge was deserted save for an empty glass on the side table. Upon entering the kitchen, I found the back door wide open as though someone had hurriedly left. My stomach churned as I ran upstairs to the bedrooms to find them empty and unoccupied. The main bedroom smelled musty, its floorboards bare. The hair pricking on my neck did nothing to diminish my uneasy feeling and the sense that something evil had occurred in that room. My eyes were drawn to a padded cushion lying discarded on the floor. I stared at it, shuddering as the enormity of this discovery flooded over me. Its fabric and size, commonly used in theatres and opera houses, helped create the optical illusion of pregnancy. It was hard to describe the icy terror that descended at that moment.

Chapter Five: Nicco Sapori
La Prigione Ecclesiastica — The Church Prison

I awoke with a jolt as I felt the carriage swaying from side to side. I opened my eyes, wondering what was happening. The carriage blinds were drawn to three sides, with no sign of my mother. Looking down, I was horrified to discover my hands and feet were tightly bound with rope, cutting into my wrists. The gag over my mouth restricted me from protesting. I tried in vain to wriggle free, but the rope only cut into me more deeply. Then I noticed the woman sitting opposite. My blood ran cold, observing her menacing stare.

She wore a black coat and a large green scarf around her neck, reminiscent of a Russian peasant. Her sallow skin and protruding grey eyes continued to stare at me.

"Be still," she hissed. "It will be over soon, you'll see. Nothing will happen to you if you do as I say."

She advanced towards me, a needle glistening in the moonlight shining through the uncovered window. Then, after she rolled up my jacket and shirt sleeves, I felt a stabbing sensation as she pushed the offending needle into my arm. The last thing I remember was floating into darkness.

When I awoke, groggy from my forced slumber, fear etched into every fibre of my being as I was carried by a man of middle age, with grey receding hair and green piercing eyes, that stared at me like a cat. My father instilled in me the importance of remembering details and questioning everything. Questions, he said, lead to knowledge and understanding. *Learning is an ongoing process that always continues.* So I did my best to stay alert and keep my eyes peeled for clues, taking in my surroundings as best I could.

Looking around, I noticed the carriage we'd disembarked from was a hansom pulled by two chestnuts, not my parent's brougham and a pair of greys. We were on the grounds of what appeared to be an old, disused church with overgrown gardens, broken stained glass windows boarded in places, and a spire hovering in the distance. I heard the distinct sound of a whistle as the man carried me through the derelict churchyard.

There, I saw the gravestones pass by me, highlighted by the glow of the evening's full moon. One particular headstone caught my eye, engraved with the name *Turridu Cannio*, who died many years ago. The name struck a chord with me as it had cropped up in conversation earlier that evening. Arturo Toscanini told me that Enrico had given many thrilling performances of the lead singer Turridu in Cavalleria Rusticana.

The man carried me down a flight of crumbling stone steps. He nearly lost his footing twice and was deftly scolded by the woman, who chastised him in a thick European accent. As she flashed a torch light upon us to help the man navigate the steps, I noticed a desecrated religious painting. It was a fresco of a woman, one that was vaguely familiar, hanging on the corridor wall. The mysterious figure wore blue robes and a white habit and looked toward heaven, clutching an olive branch with one hand and what appeared to be a stone in the other. She made an eerie sight in the torchlight.

We finally entered an underground chamber, and the man set me on a single bed before untying the gag. Glancing around the small windowless room in bewilderment, I took in my cold, damp surroundings and the familiar sound of intermittent dripping water from a faucet in the passageway. I realised this was to be my prison cell. In the corner was a commode, a bedside locker with a taper candle, two chairs, and a table holding a pitcher of water, a mug, and a plate of black bread and cheese.

"Don't even think about trying to escape or crying for help. We're underground, and only the dead will hear you." The woman laughed with a defining cackle.

"Where's my mother? Why have you taken me?" I cried.

"Your mother is safe. We're demanding a ransom. When your parents pay, we shall release you," the woman said matter-of-factly. "In the meantime, make yourself comfortable. You'll be our guest for several days." She smiled dryly. "I want you to write a note for your parents, Signor and Signora Sapori." She added with a calm aloofness. "To let them know you are safe and that we're treating you well. If you comply, I'll consider untying your feet."

From the clipped consonants and unmistakable timbre of her voice, reminiscent of a former schoolmistress from Berlin, I discerned a distinctly German accent. As the woman spoke, moving with a disquieting precision, she extracted a worn leather notebook and sleek fountain pen from the inner pocket of her coat. Each motion seemed deliberate and methodical, as if honed through repeated practice. With a casual flick of her wrist, she tapped the pen rhythmically against her gloved finger. It was a gesture both unsettling and assured, like a conductor about to commence a well-rehearsed symphony.

An icy dread seized my heart as a certainty settled over me. This woman had orchestrated such grim undertakings before. The smoothness of her gestures, the detached glint in her eye, revealed a mind steeped in calculated control. Indeed, her manner with her subordinate marked her unmistakably as the one in command, the silent overseer of my abduction, as though each step in this dark affair had been meticulously rehearsed to such a devastating effect, devised to her exacting standards.

At that moment, I detested this woman for making me uncomfortable. I loathed everything about her—her sardonic smile, sallow complexion, and protruding eyes. Still, most of all, I despised her for taking me away from my beloved family.

I returned the woman's gaze, nodding in resignation, thinking she was the stuff of a *Grimm Fairytale*—the witch that hides a deadly poison in an apple with a glib and a sneer. I wondered if she'd ever been kind. Her scowl was enough to sour buttermilk and reduce small children to tears. My thoughts took me back to a line from Grimm's *The Grave Mound*.

At midnight, they are disturbed by a shrill whistle, which heralds the devil's arrival.

The woman placed the notebook and pen on the table, gesturing for the man to untie my hands. "We have pressing matters to attend to but will return within the hour. Make sure the letter is ready," she barked.

The woman's forced smile did nothing to soften her features, and I disliked her even more. Then the man and the woman left the room, locking the door behind them. When the key turned in the latch, it was a grim reminder of my situation. I frantically called into the night, banging on the door and praying that someone would hear me. But it wasn't to be. My voice was just a distant echo inside the thick walls of the chamber. Nobody but my abductors knew that I was imprisoned here.

I stared at the notebook for some time, blinking back tears. I realised it was time to put away childish fears. There was so much I wanted to say, but what could I say without evoking suspicion while trying to alert my father to my whereabouts? I had yet to learn where I was, but what I did have were cold, hard facts. It was my only opportunity to give Father a clue so he could come and rescue me in this lonely and deserted church.

My abductors knew him simply as Signor Sapori, a name as common as it was unremarkable. They appeared to have no clue of the formidable mind concealed behind that guise nor any clue that they were contending with the celebrated Detective Sherlock Holmes. This knowledge sent a quiet thrill through me, a flicker of hope in an otherwise desperate situation. Though I was only eleven, my father had taught me much, sharpening my mind and filling it with the tools of his trade.

I had to find a way to exploit their ignorance. If I could convey a clever, subtle, clue-riddled message, my father would instantly recognise it. His mind leapt to every hidden implication. My enhanced intellect might be my only weapon here and the very thing that could, in the end, ensure my escape.

Then, in a defining moment of clarity, I realised the woman's identity in the picture. We discussed this in scripture lessons. She was Saint Veronica, born in Binasco, 67 miles outside Milan. The problem was that the city was strewn with Catholic churches. We could be anywhere. With some trepidation, I picked up the pen and began to write.

I first discovered my father's real identity when I was nine, during a Christmas vacation at Ash Tree Farm, our second home on the Sussex Downs in England. My father was shocked when I confronted him in his study on Boxing Day. But to give my father credit, he never tried to deny his true identity. On the contrary, he was intrigued by how I knew and even laughed when I explained that it was uncanny how he and my uncle Mycroft shared so many mannerisms and the same grey-penetrating eyes. Then, my father's mood became sombre, and he swore me to secrecy to protect my mother and my little sister, Charlotte.

"No one can ever know, especially Charlotte," Father had implored.

My sister was only four, so I agreed to my father's request. He knew I would do anything to protect our family. Another thing my father taught me was never to give in when facing adversity. *"Never stop fighting,"* he'd said.

The nameless man and woman came back as promised. I held my breath as the women's keen eyes scoured the note.

"You have done well," she said, looking satisfied and flashing a fathomless smile before turning to the man and ordering him to untie my feet.

The woman handed me a book. I glanced at the cover. It was Alexandre Dumas's timeless classic *The Count of Monte Cristo*, and it was one of my favourites.

"It will help pass the time until we release you," she said, placing the note in her pocket before turning on her heels and leaving the room with the man following close behind.

I found solace in the taper candle. Reading the book had momentarily taken me into another world as Dumas's epic narrative told the story with terrific dash and panache. I huddled under the blanket, eating from my bread and cheese platter, which I shared with a baby mouse scurrying in the corner. I longed to be back home with my parents and my sister Charlotte at our villa in Via Torino, safely ensconced in my family's bosom, where my life was complete, happy, content, and everything was as it should be.

As my eyes became heavy, I closed my lids and thought of happier times, like my family seated in the drawing room after dinner. Father curled up by the fire with his pipe and a glass of whiskey or port. Charlotte snuggled on his lap as he begrudgingly read to her, nearly always from her favourite storybook, *Alice's Adventures in Wonderland* by Lewis Carroll. Those stories were as bewildering to my father as they appealed to Charlotte.

Nevertheless, Father would continue reading patiently, to the amusement of our mother, Nene. How I longed to return to those precious family moments. I even missed arguing with my sister, who could be annoying sometimes, but what I would give to hear her voice calling out to me. I missed Charlotte more than I could've ever imagined.

Then the floodgates opened, and I cried like a baby. I was glad my abductors weren't around to see me like this to witness my vulnerability. I had to stay strong for my family. Finally, I drifted off into a fitful sleep.

Chapter Six: Nene Adler
La Realizzazione — The Realisation

After being disturbed by the commotion, a crowd of neighbours descended onto the street. Victor de Soto and his wife, Isabella, from one of the neighbouring cottages, raised the alarm and summoned the polizia and an ambulance.

The ambulance soon arrived to take Mattia to The Policlinico Hospital. I felt guilty for not accompanying him, but he was still unconscious, and my priority was to get home to Sherlock to alert him to the gravity of our situation. The ambulance driver assured me Mattia was in good hands, and after hurriedly scribbling out a note with my details, he promised I would be kept updated on his prognosis.

Isabella de Soto, an engaging young woman in her midtwenties, placed a rug around my shoulders and handed me a cup of hot tea, which I gratefully sipped. She sat with me patiently until the polizia eventually arrived.

I cried out with relief at the reassuring sight of our old friend, Inspector Salvatore Romano. He was of medium height and build, with dark hair that was bespeckled grey, and he had brown and kind, expressive eyes. Sherlock and I had dined with the inspector and his wife, Caterina, just a few weeks earlier.

Salvatore stepped out of the horse-drawn carriage, flanked by two guardie, who surveyed the small group chatting on the grass outside the house.

"Please return to your homes," the first guardia said. Our officers have everything under control. We will come and speak with you soon."

Acknowledging my presence with a nod and a grim smile, Salvatore listened patiently and without interruption as I tried to explain what happened to Nicco.

"This is a dreadful business," Salvatore said. "But mark my words, we shall find the villains responsible and bring them to justice."

While the guardie searched the house for incriminating evidence, Salvatore gently escorted me to the carriage where we sat. He encouraged me to tell him everything that had transpired, including a timeline where possible.

I shook like a leaf, overcome with nausea and fury, as I reviewed the evening's events, which Salvatore recorded in his little black notebook as he quickly wrote up the incident. Finally, Salvatore agreed for one of his guardie to take me home. I knew that by working together, Sherlock and the inspector would have a better chance of finding Nicco and apprehending the culprits.

Salvatore squeezed my hand reassuringly as he helped me into the carriage. The coach driver, attired in a heavy black policeman's cape, briefly nodded, touching his cap before he turned around and cracked his whip, a vaguely familiar gesture. I shrugged, realising the driver reminded me of our carriage and the incident with poor Mattia as we continued to Via Torina.

My mind was in a haze on that journey home. I was desperate to see Sherlock but dreaded telling him that I was responsible for the abduction of our beloved son.

When the carriage pulled up to the gates of our villa, the house was in darkness, save for a taper candle shining in the study. Sherlock was undoubtedly awake, wondering where we were at this late hour.

I put my key in the latch and discovered the door was ajar. Sherlock stood waiting for me in the hallway.

"Where on earth have you been?" he demanded, his voice edged with a sharpness I'd rarely heard from him before. "I was nearly out of my mind with worry until I heard the carriage pull up outside." His keen grey eyes roved over me, narrowing as they took in my messy hair, the dust clinging to my skirt, and the wild look in my eyes. "But where's Nicco?" he asked, a tremor in his voice betraying his rising alarm.

I collapsed into my husband's arms, and my sobs were muffled against his chest as he tightened his hold, his breathing quickening with dread.

"I'm so sorry, but he's been taken, and it's all my fault." I sobbed uncontrollably.

Sherlock took me by the hand and led me into his study. He sat me in a hard-backed chair and handed me a small glass of brandy, his face a mask of concern. "Take a breath, try to calm yourself, and tell me everything. Start from the beginning."

My eyes streamed tears as my husband looked at me with a horrified expression, a long, low moan escaping from his mouth, as for the second time that night, I relayed the events of the evening. I explained that our friend Salvatore Romano and the guardia were waiting outside to take Sherlock to the crime scene.

"Please allow me to come with you," I implored, observing my husband's red-rimmed bleary eyes and pasty complexion.

Sherlock shook his head.

"No, Nene, you've been through quite enough this evening. I will be fine. You should stay here in case Nicco returns or the kidnappers send a ransom demand, which I fear is the likeliest scenario. I must find Romano and see how far he's progressed with the investigation. Please do not blame yourself. By the sound of things, this was not an impromptu kidnapping. On the contrary, somebody played out our son's abduction with military precision."

The Whistle of Revenge

I stared at him, shocked. "You mean Nicco was an intended target?"

"I'm sure of it," Sherlock said, quickly slipping on his cap and ulster.

"But why would they take Nicco?" I cried.

"I don't know, Nene, but I *will* find out. You have my word on that. Please ask Hildegard to come and sit with you. I don't want you left alone. But before I leave, I must contact Mycroft." Sherlock picked up the telephone and called his brother. The conversation was brief and intense as my husband explained what had happened to Nicco. And then, in a moment, Sherlock placed the receiver on its hook and without further ado, deftly left the room.

I watched through the window as my husband's tall, athletic outline jumped into the carriage. The driver whipped up the horses, and the carriage disappeared into the night.

My mind flashed back to happier times with my husband. During our many clandestine midnight conversations, as I lay next to him, my head on his chest, the taste of wine on our lips, I knew I could ask anything from this man who stimulated my intellectual curiosity, who was simultaneously captivated and entranced by it.

I don't know how I would have gotten through the next few hours without our nanny, Hildegard, whose name aptly means The Garden of Wisdom. Hildegard had been with us for the best part of a year. The children adored her kind, no-nonsense attitude, while I appreciated her unwavering support and belief that Nicco would return to us unscathed.

Hildegard was close friends with Sophia's nanny, Emilia Giordano, and came highly recommended. She had an impeccable resume and references of the highest order, each vouching for Hildegard as an excellent person. Her mother was the acclaimed concert pianist Martina Schockomohle, a prestigious talent who retired from the stage in 1902 after the tragic death of her husband, Karl Achen, from lung cancer.

The Schmidt family, from Innenstadt, had previously employed Hildegard as a governess in her hometown of Frankfurt for several years before she met Ilfranco Dachil, a journalist at *The Frankfurter Zeitung*. They fell in love and married before moving to Milan in 1904. Sadly, Hildegard's mother, Martina, disapproved of her only daughter's choice of husband and refused to attend the wedding. She and Hildegard had been estranged ever since.

Ilfranco found employment as an economic journalist at Il Sole, the leading financial newspaper in Milan. The couple rented an apartment in Porta Venezia. Hildegard said they were happy for a while until Ilfranco began to complain of violent headaches, which altered his mood. One moment, Ilfranco was charm personified, and the next, he'd become cruel, abusive and mean, ranting and raving in a ball of rage that only dissipated after he resorted to physical violence, a broken chair, a shattered glass, and eventually Hildegard's hand in a door. Consequently, the relationship became fragmented. Hildegard begged her husband to see a doctor, but he stubbornly refused, putting his affliction down to the pressures of work. Tragically, Ilfranco later collapsed at home with a brain haemorrhage, from which he never recovered, passing away at The Policlinico Hospital in January 1905. His death was a significant loss to Hildegard and the newspaper. Ilfranco was one of their most experienced journalists.

When I interviewed Hildegard for the nanny position, I found her a fascinating subject and felt we had much in common. Seemingly at ease in my company, Hildegard confessed that after her husband's untimely demise, she decided to stay on in Milan rather than return to Germany and face her mother's wrath. Hildegard admitted she had made bad choices since her husband died, briefly embarking on a relationship with a man who was unsuitable until finally, she came to her senses and ended the relationship, subsequently reverting to her maiden name, Achen.

After I quizzed Hildegard further, she explained that having had no children from her marriage, she had no desire to continue wearing her husband's name like an emblem, stating that her late husband had two brothers who could do that. It was an odd thing to say. But above all that, Hildegard was the most modest and unassuming of women, with fantastic charm and an infectious sense of humour. The air of determination on her lovely face, the delicate bone structure, the long blonde hair tied up in a neat knot, and those expressive almond-shaped eyes were genuinely captivating. I decided not to question Hildegard further on the matter. After my past dalliance with Wilhelm Orrmstein and my first husband, Godfrey Norton, who was I to judge anyone? It was none of my business if all had not been well in Hildegard's marriage or subsequent relationship. I had the impression that neither man had been the perfect partner in any shape or form. Having had several of my own, I'd always believed in second chances.

When I asked Hildegard to read a passage from Jane Eyre, her delivery and narrative style were delightfully refreshing. Every word hurtled had tripped off her tongue like poetry. I knew then that Nicco and Charlotte would grow to love this fun, pretty, and vivacious woman.

She adored Nicco and Charlotte, and the children reciprocated those feelings. Initially, I was slightly jealous of Hildegard's burgeoning relationship with Nicco and Charlotte. Jealousy was like a shadow, and it crept up and caught us unaware. Although I considered us fortunate to have found such an agreeable nanny — a far cry from the ones I endured as a child — to my great surprise, my husband, for once, begrudgingly agreed.

To Sherlock and me, our home was a sacred place. It took someone remarkable to be allowed into the Sapori household's inner sanctum.

After Sherlock's departure, I decided not to wake Hildegard. I put my head around her bedroom door to find her sleeping peacefully. In truth, I was in no state to relay the grim news about Nicco for the third time that evening—the anxiety was killing me. I was strained to breaking point. So I decided to wait until morning. I found myself exhausted but restless, tossing and turning, unable to sleep. The grandfather clock in the hall struck out the hours, ticking loudly through the silence. Otherwise, it was a complete absence of sound. Finally, I was disturbed by the familiar and comforting sound of the domestic servants, our cook, Alice, and Ginevra, the housemaid, going about their business in the villa.

Alice and Ginevra Bergamaschi were mother and daughter, and their home was a small apartment in the city centre. Alice's husband, Dario, passed away from tuberculosis two years ago, and she came to work for us shortly after. Alice occasionally brought her daughter to help at the villa during the holidays, working a few hours here and there casually to earn pocket money. My husband had his reservations at first due to her tender age. Still, Ginevra proved to be a hard worker like her mother, a quick learner, a diligent bundle of energy, and an invaluable help with our dog Helen and the children. After much discussion, Sherlock and I finally agreed to offer Ginevra a full-time position. The girl was thrilled to join her mother and Hildegard as a full-time employee at the Sapori residence. I jokingly referred to the ladies as my Three Graces.

When Hildegard finally came to breakfast, I discreetly ushered her into the morning room and gently explained all that had transpired. As we sat, sunlight flooded in through the French window, but the startling beauty of the morning did nothing to distract my mind from the grim reality of the situation.

Hildegard's unassuming manner and obvious concern were genuinely touching. She was a genial and avid listener. However, it was all too much for my fragile state of mind, and everything flooded out with grief and emotion. I said Sherlock wanted to avoid making the domestic servants aware of the situation, at least not until he had a chance to interview them.

Hildegard agreed to my request and nodded through silent tears. "The polizia will find Nicco. They will, Nene, I'm sure. Perhaps it was a misunderstanding or a case of mistaken identity."

I remember hearing Hildegard's words but not fully comprehending what she said. For a moment, I felt suspended in a bubble of incomprehension.

She put her arms around me, holding onto me tightly. "Have you had breakfast?"

I shook my head. "No, I have no appetite, although I could use a Cafe Noir."

Hildegard narrowed her eyes. "You look exhausted. What you need is rest and proper nourishment," she said, guiding me to the sofa in the drawing room. "Lie down here for a moment... take a nap. You need to feel refreshed when your husband returns." Hildegard gently wrapped a shawl around my shoulders as I reluctantly conceded. She closed the blinds before agreeing to my request to slip out discreetly to inquire about any news or gossip in the neighbourhood.

I heard her parting wards as the door closed softly. "*Finchec' e' vita, ce' Speranza.*" They meant *as long as there's life, there is hope. One should never despair, even in difficult circumstances.*

Chapter Seven: Nene Adler
Tradimento — Betrayal

Sister Gina Ronci from The Policlinico Hospital rang at 12:30 to confirm the surgeons had removed a clot from Mattia's brain. The clot was caused by severe head trauma resulting in a coma. She said the surgery had gone well. However, Mattia remained unconscious and in a critical condition. The next forty-eight hours would be crucial. The sister reassured me the polizia had posted a guardia outside Mattia's room as a precautionary measure, for protection, and in the hopes he would be able to identify the culprits should he awaken from his coma. I thanked sister Ronci and said a silent prayer for Mattia's recovery. That poor man did *not* deserve what happened to him.

Ginevra prepared hot water for me to bathe. Then, I quickly changed into a navy silk dress, applying minimal make-up before tying my hair up in a knot. It was 2 P.M. when I heard a coach pull up outside.

Peeping through the blinds, I watched my husband and Salvatore Romano jump down from the hansom and walk up the steps into the villa. I made my way to greet the men in the drawing room. My heart beat wildly in my chest, my breath catching, willing myself not to break down as I tentatively entered the room. I desperately tried to keep my composure, not knowing what might have befallen my darling boy. At that moment, I felt like the earth would open and swallow me. Relaxation was now a luxury, a distant memory from the past. All I had to do now was to keep my composure, not just for

Sherlock's sake, but to convey an air of normality within the household, calming any disturbing thoughts that Alice and Ginevra might harbour once they were made aware of Nicco's abduction.

"Is there any news?" I asked, staring at Sherlock and Salvatore with nervous expectation.

Salvatore assured me the polizia were doing all they could. His men were checking all the ports and railway stations, a task hindered by the large number of visitors thronging the city and its platforms. He said our carriage was discovered toppled over on its side on the outskirts of Milan. The horses were found grazing in a nearby meadow, which seemed unscathed from their exertions. The polizia found wheel marks from another carriage and two sets of footprints. Someone had undoubtedly bundled Nicco into another carriage, probably a hansom, based on the size of the wheel tracks. The brougham was searched and found empty, save for Nicco's scarf and a silver button discovered by a guardia under the driver's seat. Salvatore said he would arrange to return everything to the villa later that day.

He pulled the silver button out of his pocket, placing it in the palm of his hand. Sherlock and I studied it closely. "Could this be from your coach driver?" Salvatore asked.

I shook my head. "No, the buttons on Mattia's uniform are more prominent and metallic black. I never noticed him wearing anything with buttons of that type."

"The button likely belongs to the villain," Sherlock said. "It appears to be a man's and could be from a coat, cloak, or uniform. Can you remember what the driver wore?" Sherlock asked, turning to me.

I shook my head. "No, I'm sorry it was dark, and he was too far away. Did you find anything at the house?" I inquired, looking at Salvatore expectantly.

The inspector grimaced. "Nothing of consequence, I'm

afraid, but my guardie are there as we speak, going through everything with a fine-tooth comb. Your husband and I questioned the neighbours. We discovered the house had been empty since a dreadful incident occurred two years ago. The occupiers, Luis Bandiero and his wife, were found by a relative, brutally murdered. I was holidaying with my family at the time. Still, I remember the case, and despite pursuing several lines of enquiry and a wide-scale investigation, the murderer was never caught.

"The neighbours told us that new tenants, the DeTorres, eventually moved into the property. They lasted a month before handing back the keys, complaining they heard unexplained noises during the night hours. They said there was something ungodly in that house. My men and I followed up on the complaint and interviewed the tenants, who admitted they'd not seen anything, but they'd been disturbed by the sound of a dog howling. Whatever it was, it put the fear of God into them. Once again, my men checked the house and gardens but found nothing. We wondered if the DeTorres had made up the story to get out of the tenancy, as they moved to Pavia shortly after the incident. Since then, the locals shunned the place, claiming it was haunted, so there were no takers. Even after the letting agent drastically reduced the rent by more than half the market value, the property remained vacant."

"The perpetrators knew the property's history and used it to their advantage, breaking in, changing the locks and treating it as their own to carry out their dastardly plan in the knowledge that they were unlikely to be disturbed." Sherlock grimaced.

I shuddered. "Those people are right. There was something ungodly about that place. What about that couple at the house? Do you think they could be actors? They put on quite a show."

"It's possible," Salvatore said. "My guardie are checking with the local theatre companies to see if anyone matches their description, although the culprits were likely in disguise."

"What do we tell Alice and Ginevra?" I asked. "Hildegard already knows about Nicco."

"The inspector and I will interview the domestic servants to see if they can shed light on the situation or report anything suspicious," Sherlock said. "Then we'll wait for the ransom note to arrive. I'm certain our son is still here in Milan."

Sherlock insisted on questioning the servants separately, so I first called Alice into the drawing room. She smiled at us curiously, smoothing her black cotton dress and apron and easing her reassuringly corpulent frame into a comfortable armchair. She wiped her brow with a handkerchief, glancing curiously at Salvatore, who was seated in the far corner of the room, observing the proceedings with his notebook and a watchful eye. Alice looked horrified and visibly upset as Sherlock explained how Nicco had been taken. Her ruddy complexion turned a shade paler as she listened to my husband's narrative.

"That's terrible to hear, sir, that lovely boy. Is there anything I can do to help?" Alice cried, her eyes consumed with emotion.

"This is rather a delicate matter," Sherlock said. "I can't put too much emphasis on the confidentiality of this conversation. I have asked Inspector Romano and the polizia to withhold information that this is a kidnapping inquiry. So there will be no public appeal. The last thing we need is for the press to get wind of our son's abduction. If that happens, this investigation will become a circus. So I need your assurance that our narrative will not exceed these four walls."

Alice nodded in agreement as Sherlock continued. "Did you notice anything suspicious the last few days that seemed out of place? Any strangers coming to the villa?"

Alice shook her head. "No, nothing, sir, except yesterday, when Signora Sapori explained your cold and asked me to send out for laudanum as we ran low. I would typically have asked Ginevra to carry out the errand, but it was my daughter's half-day, so she was visiting her aunt in Gromo. I decided to go myself when Hildegard kindly offered to get the laudanum as she was on her way to meet an old friend."

"What time did she leave, and when did she return?" Sherlock asked sternly, staring at Alice with his astute grey eyes.

"Why, it was just after noon, Signor Sapori. Hildegard told me not to expect her back until later, explaining she had switched her half-day. I asked if you wanted luncheon, remember? You requested something light, soup and bread." Sherlock nodded in agreement as Alice continued. "After I returned to the kitchen and went about my duties, the rest of the afternoon passed in a haze until the clock struck six, and that's when Hildegard returned with the laudanum. The girl appeared pale and deep in thought. But when I questioned her, Hildegard brushed off my concerns, blaming an allergy and a need for a lie-down. But I had the sense that she wasn't telling me everything. I'm not one to gossip, Signor Sapori. I know that Hildegard is liked and well-respected, but if you had observed what I had, you might come to a different conclusion. I could tell you things about that young lady that would curl your hair."

"I don't want idle chit-chat. What I want is facts!" Sherlock snapped, casting the cook a withering glance, his lips pursed in disapproval. "It never ceases to amaze me how keen people are to share irrelevant gossip but never the important news we require."

Alice shifted uncomfortably in her seat, staring firmly at Sherlock with her baby-blue eyes. "Signor Sapori, when I bumped into Hildegard in town two weeks ago, she was

The Whistle of Revenge

dressed in her Sunday best. I saw her talking with an older man. They had a heated altercation. When Hildegard noticed me, she looked mortified. She grabbed the man's arm, and they disappeared into the market. When I confronted Hildegard the next day, I was presented with candies and an apology. She told me the man was an ex-suitor who'd been badgering her. But after pleading with him, the man agreed to Hildegard's request not to trouble her again."

"What did this man look like?"

"I only saw him fleetingly. Still, he was slim-built with lightish brown hair, bespeckled grey, and in his mid-to-late fifties."

"Have you seen this man since?"

"No, sir, nor do I wish to." Alice shook her head. "Something about his face and overall demeanour gave me the shivers. Will there be anything else?" she asked, looking up at my husband nervously.

"That'll be all for now," Sherlock said dismissively. "When you return to the kitchen, please send the housemaid."

A flustered-looking Alice nodded, smiling at me sympathetically before leaving the drawing room. A few minutes later, Ginevra, a fresh-faced sixteen-year-old with expressive brown eyes, entered the room dressed in a black cotton dress and apron. Her long, light brown hair, parted in the middle and drawn back in a tortoiseshell clip, accentuating her prominent cheekbones. She responded to my husband's questions good-naturedly and sobbed when she learned of Nicco's abduction. I handed her a handkerchief as Sherlock continued with his interrogation.

"Have you noticed any strangers loitering around the villa or anything out of place?" he asked.

Ginevra shook her head, blowing into the handkerchief. "No, sir. There was nothing unusual at all. I'm sorry I can't be of more help. I wish I could do something to alleviate your heartache. Your son will continually be in my thoughts and prayers."

Sherlock confidently asked Ginevra not to mention anything to anyone, least of all the press. She immediately agreed to his request. I smiled at her weakly, sensing an inner strength behind the girl's soft-spoken speech and quiet demeanour.

Sherlock dismissed Ginevra, and I asked her to bring coffee, which she swiftly returned with. "Cook said you missed luncheon," Ginevra asked as she poured the coffee. "Might she organise a cold platter?"

"Nothing for me, thank you," Salvatore said, waving his hand.

Sherlock shook his head, protesting he wasn't hungry, before dismissing Ginevra.

"I think we can eliminate the domestic servants from our enquiries. It would be cruel despotism to dismiss them without proof and deprive them of their livelihood. Without further evidence, I'm convinced of their innocence, although I cannot yet speak for Hildegard Achen until I've questioned her. Where is she?" Sherlock asked, staring at me curiously.

"Hildegard went out early this morning to see if there was any news on the street about Nicco. She should be back soon," I explained before turning my attention to Salvatore. "So, Inspector, I must know what fate has befallen my son. What else do you intend to do besides door-to-door enquiries to help find him?"

Salvatore straightened in his chair with his dark brown eyes fixed on me. "This is a testing time for both of you. Let me assure you, Nene, my guardie, are doing everything possible to find the culprits. They're dedicated men who work long, hard hours, often for no extra remuneration. Many have families and young children of their own. Their commitment to the job can never be questioned." Salvatore sighed. "This dreadful business is understandably causing you a great deal of distress and anxiety. We don't want you to be afraid. Your husband and I are convinced your son is still in Milan, and if that is the case, rest assured we *will* find him."

I smiled at Salvatore. "Believe me when I tell you that everything I have ever feared has already happened. So, no, I'm not afraid. I'm angry that someone dared take my son. I don't want any unnecessary trouble. I seek justice, not revenge. I want answers to who, what, where, and why."

"I understand," Salvatore said, smiling at me sympathetically.

"Do you?" I asked, raising a brow.

"On the contrary, I want the head of the snake," Sherlock said, grimacing derisively and turning his attention to Salvatore. "Inspector, you and your team are a beacon of light in this cesspit of despair. Alongside Lestrade from Scotland Yard, you're amongst the finest of the professions. My wife and I will likely need all the assistance we can muster. Even Sherlock Holmes cannot be everywhere."

Salvatore shook his head. "Thank you for the compliment, Mr Holmes. Your reputation precedes you. My guardie and I are acutely aware that you stand alone in such matters, head and shoulders above the rest of us mere mortals. But rest assured, we will leave no stone unturned in the quest to find your son. On that, you have my word. My men and I remain humbly at your disposal."

Despite Sherlock and Salvatore's assurances, I couldn't help but think the unthinkable. Nicco's abduction made me wonder if the devil lived in Milan. Salvatore then excused himself to return to his enquiries, promising to update us on any fresh developments. We agreed to get in touch once the ransom note arrived.

After Salvatore departed, I turned to Sherlock, perplexed. "And what do you suggest we do now?"

"Why, we wait for the ransom note, which I have no doubt will inevitably arrive."

Ginevra entered the room, interrupting our conversation. "I'm sorry to disturb you," she stammered. But there's no easy way to say this. I've just been to Hildegard's room to turn over the bed, and I noticed that her valise, some personal effects, and clothes are missing."

Sherlock and I ran upstairs to search Hildegard's room, which was neat, with a note left on the pillow.

As Sherlock read out the contents, my blood turned to ice.

"I'm sorry, but I had to go. I fear that I'm responsible for Nicco's abduction, but I want you to know that it was not intentional. Your son was taken by a man using several identities. I have yet to learn who he is. All I know is that he has accomplices, and Nicco's abduction was strategically planned. Now, I must find a way to right the wrong and find your son, even at the risk of my own life. Hildegard."

"This cannot be happening," I cried. "But why would she do this? We welcomed her into our home." The pain in my chest felt like a hand gripping my heart. I couldn't move.

Sherlock continued to search the room, opening every cupboard and drawer. Finally, he discovered Hildegard's passport in a bedside locker, holding it up to check that it was still in-date, which it was. Passports were not required for European travel, so few people held them. Discovering Hildegard had an in-date passport begged the question of whether she'd intended to travel outside Europe, and if that was the case, why would she leave the passport behind?

"We're left faced with a fait accompli," Sherlock said, his penetrating grey eyes fixated on me. "Everything about this is wrong. Hildegard Achen can't have gone far. She left under duress, as I doubt it was under her own free will. I shall call Romano and ask him to organise a search." Sherlock sighed, and his face darkened. "This isn't just about money. It's personal," he added with sickening clarity. "Kidnappers rarely work in isolation. There's no time to lose Nene. The clock is ticking."

Chapter Eight: Nene Adler
Liberazione — Deliverance

The inevitable ransom note arrived the following morning, dropping through the letterbox in an unassuming brown envelope bearing a local postmark. It was marked private and confidential and addressed to Signor and Signora Sapori.

Sherlock opened the envelope carefully with a paper knife, examining it closely with his magnifying glass. The envelope contained two notes of the same type on the same paper, one from the perpetrator and the other from Nicco. I gasped as Sherlock read the contents of the first note, which was so dark and harrowing that I could barely contemplate what I was hearing.

Hallo Signor and Signora Sapori,
Your son is well and will remain safe if you follow our instructions. On Friday, you will come to a location to be advised and bring ten thousand lira, in small unmarked notes. Do not alert the polizia, or you will never see your son again. We enclose a letter from the boy and a smaller envelope containing proof of life.

After Sherlock read this singular narrative, I opened the small stuffed envelope with some trepidation to find it contained a sizable chunk of Nicco's newly cut hair and a smattering of fingernail clippings. Angry and distressed, all I could think of as I stared at them was the story of Vincent van Gogh, who in 1888 severed the lower part of his left ear, wrapping it up, before allegedly presenting it to a prostitute in a local brothel. I shuddered, thanking God the kidnappers had not resorted to such extreme measures. The probability of such an event was unimaginable. An overwhelming sense of melancholy washed over me as I held my son's precious note between my shaking hands, digesting Nicco's narrative in his distinctive, neat handwriting. Taking a deep breath, I read the words.

My dearest mother and father,

I am well and don't want you to worry. My abductors treat me kindly. I have ample food and a book to help pass the time. I miss you all so much, and I can't wait for our family to be reunited. In the meantime, please make my excuses and tell my good friend Turridu Cannio and his sister Camoni that I have a cold and cannot attend The World Fair *and church service on Wednesday as planned. It's important you remember, as I fear there may be grave repercussions otherwise, and I have no wish to disappoint my friends, especially Camoni, who, as you know, is like a sister to me.*

Take care until we meet again.

Your loving son,

Nicco

"Thank God, our son is safe. Well, at least for now." I cried, furrowing my brow. "But what does Nicco mean about the church and The World Fair? We already visited The World Fair. Who on earth are Turridu and Camoni?"

A wry smile passed over Sherlock's face, his usual pale cheeks made even more sallow by his heavy cold, now flushed with colour. This message from our beloved son was a tonic for both his system and his soul, so much more than any laudanum could give.

"But don't you see, my darling Nene? Our clever son has given us a clue to his whereabouts."

"Whatever do you mean?"

"These are not random, made-up people. Nene, you, of all people, must surely be aware of Turridu Cannio's identity?"

"Yes, of course." I agreed. "Turridu is the main character in Cavalleria Rusticana, but, Sherlock, Turridu is a fictional character."

"Yes, I know that, but he's important to Nicco."

I furrowed my brow. "Perhaps Nicco saw the name somewhere and recognised it from a discussion with Caruso in the restaurant. I remember Turridu came up in conversation."

"From the clues in Nicco's note, he likely spotted the name on a gravestone. See how he's dramatically underlined the word grave. Camoni is an anagram of Monica, perhaps a shortened version of Veronica or sister Saint Veronica of Milan. The kidnappers likely hold our son in some religious order, a convent, a church, perhaps. We just need to find the resting place of any deceased bearing the name Turridu Cannio."

"And how do we do that?"

"The Public record office should indicate any such burial sites, while the church record office may give us the identity of any local churches depicting shrines to Saint Veronica."

"So let me get this straight. You believe Veronica represents the name of a church where Nicco is possibly being kept hostage?"

Sherlock nodded. "It's more than possible. On the contrary, it's highly probable, but there are many churches named after Saint Veronica in Milan. It's just a question of knowing where to start. At least now we have something to work with."

"What about the kidnapper's note? Were there any further clues?"

Sherlock pointed to the note. "The kidnappers posted the letter locally. It's written in a woman's hand . . . nothing remarkable about the notepaper, readily available from your commonplace local post office. The thin sheets of paper make the writing appear mean and untidy. It's also unrefined. Whoever wrote this is uneducated and certainly no lady."

"But how can you know?" I questioned, staring at my husband incredulously.

"Observe the heavy, exaggerated, high-pointed strokes,"

Sherlock said, pointing to the letter. "This woman writes with authority and egotism, yet she's no mastermind. She's an operative working for someone else, so the question is, for whom and why? See how the full capitals slant to the left. I suspect she's of European origin, with a limited English vocabulary. Observing the spelling of hallo instead of hello, she's most likely German. Today is Tuesday, so we have three days before the ransom is due. In the meantime, we must gather as much information as possible. But we must be vigilant. We have no idea what these people are capable of. But I promise you this, Nene. If the perpetrators harm our boy in any way, then they will not leave Milan alive."

"What about when we must pay the ransom? Do we need to go to the bank and risk attracting suspicion?"

"No need," Sherlock said, shaking his head. "I can cover the ransom from our money in the safe."

During our conversation, I noticed Sherlock's jaw tensing slightly. Like me, he felt lost, angry, and confused. This profound feeling of fear and anxiety was equally unsettling and disturbing to him because, for the first time, it made him doubt himself, not only as a consulting detective but as a father and a husband, leaving him to question his extraordinary abilities.

We found ourselves at a crossroads, struggling to handle the emotional ramifications of Nicco's abduction. Undoubtedly, Sherlock would be prepared to go through a burning building and lay down his life a thousand times over for our family. But now, at least, there was a glimmer of hope, and we were one step closer to finding our son.

My husband gazed at me pensively.

"I know that look, Sherlock. Do you have a lingering question you need to ask?"

He nodded, and his expression turned sombre. "I know of your dalliances with Ornstein and Norton, but were there any previous suitors I should know about? It's unlike you to be coy, Nene."

I hesitated momentarily, taking in the implications of my husband's words, and then I reacted almost aggressively from a position of defence. I glared furiously at my husband, responding in a slightly raised voice. "Sherlock, I'm too tired to argue with you. But, yes, I saw someone for a while before I married Godfrey."

"Define your relationship. Did this man declare himself?" he replied matter-of-factly, his voice devoid of emotion.

"Sherlock, it was years ago. Why should it matter?"

"In the scheme of things, it shouldn't matter at all, but somehow it does, and I need to know so I can exclude any such person from my inquiries. Was it a physical relationship?"

I shook my head, the words sticking in my throat as I attempted to convey them. "No, nothing like that."

"Then pray, tell, what was it like?"

I sighed deeply. "It was a spiritual alliance. His name was Henry Hodgson, a stockbroker from Southampton. We met at a concert in London, after being introduced by friends. Our liaison ended after Henry discovered I had no romantic feelings, so nothing untoward happened, and we parted amicably. We stayed in touch until Henry married the artist Marissa Hoffman the following year. So no, Sherlock, I don't have a string of ex-lovers hiding in the wings, hell-bent on revenge if that's what you're implying," I replied sardonically, casting my husband a withering look. My posture stiffened as I took a small, sharp breath. "Sherlock, how could you?" My voice trembled with anger and hurt. "Do you genuinely believe I would hide such secrets from you, a man who sees through everyone's mask?"

I was about to question him on his youth and bohemian cavalier approach to women and relationships. Still, something in the way he looked at me, those grey eyes filled with sorrow, made my heart lurch as I fought back tears, reminding me of how Sherlock had paid the ultimate price for his supercilious behaviour with the loss of his firstborn son, who sadly died in the womb when Sherlock's fiancée Victoria Bennett suffered a catastrophic postpartum haemorrhage and tragically died herself.

An agonising silence between us seemed to last forever. Sherlock met my gaze. A haunted expression hung over his usual stoic features, a glimmer of vulnerability and desperation that I rarely saw in him.

"Forgive me, Nene," he murmured, his voice low and steady, though a trace of pain edged in his words. "It distresses me to suggest any impropriety. We're clutching at straws, and I must explore every possibility, however distasteful the questions may appear, to bring our son back to us." His face, usually carved in the hard lines of a man who'd faced countless dangers and secrets, now bore the unmistakable strain of a father's anguish. The sight softened my anger, replacing it with a deep and sincere understanding. I fell silent, watching him, and then rose from my chair and put my arms around my husband, gazing into his eyes.

"Sherlock." My voice was a gentle whisper. "My past holds no shadows that could harm us now, only the one cast by this unspeakable loss. I stand before you, a broken woman, a shell of the person I used to be. But this grief is not just mine to bear. So feeling sad, scared, uncomfortable, or whatever you feel is all right. Our son needs you to be his father, not just a detective. With the help of our good friend Salvatore and the polizia, together, we *will* find Nicco and bring him home."

He nodded, his steel-grey eyes holding mine in mutual grief and determination.

"Then we shall face this together, my dearest Nene, and see justice done." His gaze had an iron resolve, resulting in a promise that nothing in Heaven or on Earth would deter him.

"Very well," I said, my voice barely above a whisper. "Then let us proceed ... whatever it takes."

Sherlock held my face in his hands. "Forgive me, Nene, but you are missing the point. We will likely make illogical choices when swept away by emotion. So if I want to have any hope of finding our son and the monsters who took him, then I'll have to distance myself from you at times and become Holmes, the detective, the calculating machine. I won't lose another son. And I promise you this ... I'll do everything I can to save Nicco."

"I know you will. I understand," I said through tears that I thought I'd used up over the last few days.

I realised that Sherlock was right. He must become Holmes, an independent entity devoid of emotion, not Sherlock, the loving husband. By trying to do both, he put himself in an impossible position. Solace and seclusion were imperative to him, enabling his remarkable brain to weigh up every piece of evidence.

I kissed him tenderly on the cheek. "We have some serious business to attend to."

"Yes, indeed," Sherlock said, agreeing. "A moment of courage against a lifetime of regret. When we hit back, the miscreants won't see us coming, and they'll rue to the day they took on the Saporis."

"So you have no objection to me assisting with your enquiries?"

"You have an unfathomable voice, Nene, which makes you invaluable as a wife and an accomplice. We chose each other for a reason, all those years ago."

Sherlock opened the safe and pulled out a pistol, carefully checking the barrel that contained four bullets before handing it to me. "Keep this with you, day and night, and if you're approached or feel threatened in any way, then remember what I told you in Fiesole. *Never reveal your body to the enemy."* Sherlock held out his hand. "Come, we're close, Nene, to finding our son. It's time to assemble the missing pieces of the jigsaw and hunt the villains down like the dogs they are."

Chapter Nine: Robert Barrett
Giano — Janus

Checking into The Majestic Hotel in Milan and signing the register as Robert Barrett was another stopgap before taking up my temporary position as manager of a prestigious racing stable in Lombardy. Until then, I was hotel hopping, using several pseudonyms and disguises, which was nothing new. It was the life I'd chosen. However, I was always careful not to draw attention to myself at the concierge desk and arouse suspicion. My overall demeanour and general benignity, invariably complimented by a well-tailored suit aided by various facial cover-ups and wigs, gave me the appearance of an honourable professional man. Like The Scarlet Pimpernel, I was the master of the three D's — disguise, deception, and duality.

I'd lost count of the endless false identities I'd used over the years, all because of the man who had cost me everything — the celebrated Detective Sherlock Holmes.

Although it was seventeen years since our paths last crossed, I had to maintain the facade of a false identity, even though most people believed me to have died in the Great Grimpen Mire on Dartmoor. The following events did nothing to diminish my habitual prejudice against the authorities. Even after the Metropolitan Police dragged the bog and discovered no sign of my body, they were satisfied that Jack Stapleton had perished there. Everyone wrote me off, but I rose from the dust like Lazarus. Indeed, it was by sheer bloody-mindedness and pure instinct that I managed to claw my way to that island of refuge as I struggled through the thick fog. Since that fateful night, my life and freedom have been constantly scrutinised. I saw it as some kind of Devil's Island from which there was no chance of escape.

Despite everything in Dartmoor and with Sir Henry Baskerville, I still considered myself a good man. I'd assumed that what happened on the moor would alter me, that I'd be devastated by my actions. But nothing changed. I'd been robbed of my inheritance and denied my birthright. Those people deserved what happened to them. There was a wave of anger in those memories that couldn't be diminished. Your first kill, in many ways, was like your first kiss or sexual encounter. You're startled by its potency and look forward to it happening again.

To those few confidants closest to me, including my wife Beryl, I was nick-named Janus after the Roman God of beginnings, transitions, time, and endings. He was often depicted with two faces looking in opposite directions, most appropriate for someone like me leading a double life. When I discovered Holmes was on my trail all those years ago, I devised an elaborate alibi for my wife so the police would exonerate her from any further investigation and wrongdoing. I owed her that at least, as admittedly, I had mistreated her, even if it was for the greater good.

But as a dutiful wife, Beryl refused to give me up to the police, although I suspect it was more out of fear than love. It was true she'd been appalled by my actions and refused my request to participate in the Baskerville murders, leaving me no other option but to turn to the beautiful Laura Lyons, an impetuous young woman. Her husband, Frank, soon tired of domestic bliss and abandoned his wife after she miscarried, leaving Laura to fend for herself. She eventually found employment as a typist in the nearby town of Coombe Tracey. Still, besides her meagre income, she depended upon the generosity of others, including Sir Charles Baskerville, who helped her in the past and with whom she struck up a close friendship. It was apparent Sir Charles was smitten with Laura. She was jaw-droppingly beautiful, a brunette with hazel eyes that appeared to look right through you. Tall, statuesque with a peaches-and-cream complexion reminiscent of a sulphur rose. She would turn the head of any man.

I'm ashamed to say that to enable my murderous intentions towards Sir Charles, I pursued Laura relentlessly, preying on her precarious position in society, when out of desperation, she turned to me for help. Like Sir Charles, I, too, struck up a friendship, although, admittedly, my motives were anything but honourable. I could tell Laura was flattered by my attention, so I seduced her with the promise of marriage on the proviso that she raised enough money to divorce the man responsible for abandoning her. Laura was terrified that Frank would come back and force her to live with him, something he was legally entitled to do if he thought fit. New legislation was passed in the late 1800s, assisting women to divorce their husbands, but because of the costs involved, the procedure remained exceedingly rare.

I continued my courtship of Laura, spending hours discussing ways we could raise money for the divorce, freeing us to marry and start a new life together. I showered her with gifts and flowers, wined and dined her at the top restaurants, and spent many enjoyable weekends away at the best hotels until she was completely under my spell. Laura finally agreed to my suggestion to lure that old fool, Sir Charles Baskerville, onto the moor for what he believed would be a romantic rendezvous and for what Laura assumed would be a plea to Sir Charles for financial help until I gently explained what I needed her to do.

At first, Laura was shocked by my suggestion, but when I explained that our future happiness was at stake, she

The Whistle of Revenge

reluctantly agreed to go along with my plan to seduce Sir Charles and secure the money in any way she could. Laura was used to a life of misogynistic men taking advantage of her, expecting sexual favours. She agreed to write the letter asking Sir Charles to meet her on the moors. The poor girl had no clue that Beryl, posing as my sister, was my wife.

After writing the letter, Laura called to see me in great anxiety, and she explained she'd managed to procure the money from another source, an unexpected inheritance. I begged her not to cancel the meeting, saying I would handle everything, but instead, I sent my bloodthirsty hound Carlos in her place. When Laura heard of Sir Charles's death by heart attack the following day, she confronted me at our favourite beauty spot on the moors. When Dr Watson interviewed her, Laura said she rebuffed his questions and denied asking Sir Charles to meet her. But when Watson explained he knew about the letter, Laura changed her mind. At first, she was upset that Sir Charles had not destroyed the letter, but she calmed down when Watson told her that the elder Baskerville had attempted to do so. When Watson told her he was trying to protect Sir Charles' reputation, she agreed to cooperate without giving away our relationship.

I somehow managed to convince a distraught Laura that what happened to Sir Charles had been a tragic accident, but at least she now had the money for her divorce, while I had Sir Henry, the new heir to Baskerville Hall, to contend with. Now, with means and money to support herself, I felt relieved when Laura's ardour suddenly cooled towards me. However, after the attempted murder of Sir Henry, Laura showed an invincible spirit rather than the weak, unassertive woman people assumed her to be. When Holmes revealed my plans, she turned devil's advocate, telling the detective everything she knew and agreeing to testify against me in court. As for Holmes and Watson, as I later discovered, they never thought

Laura had anything to do with the crime, assuming she was a tool of the real criminal—me.

Beryl was of Latin American heritage and had an unforgiving nature. When she learned of my affair with Laura, she described it as the ultimate betrayal. The dynamics of our relationship changed, and all hell broke loose. Beryl found it hard to conceal her contempt for my actions, and her passive unwillingness to assist in what she described as my wrongdoings and her active sabotage when she tried to warn Sir Henry from stepping out onto the moor almost scuppered my plans. But I loved Beryl so much that I forgave her. She told me I was beyond change, and she was right. Consequently, I never bothered to try. I realised long ago that redemption was not for the likes of me.

Beryl never responded to any of my letters sent incognito, but then neither did she alert the police to the fact I was still alive. I purposely kept my actual address from her. If she'd been questioned further by the Metropolitan Police, it would have been safer if she had no clue about my whereabouts. Even a little knowledge had drawbacks, multiplying the margin for error and, therefore, the risk of being caught. I knew that I'd hurt my wife very deeply and that the risk of being discovered was ever-present.

Still, I was hopeful that after a discreet passage of time, she would join me in Ireland once I'd established my business, taking on the role of an assistant trainer in County Kildare, a position found for me through the influence of my second cousin, Jim Sweeney.

During the transition, I connected closely with my Masonic contacts in London and the Peaky Blinders, a criminal organisation from The West Midlands that operated in Birmingham. This kept me updated on events in and around the capital.

My job as a bloodstock agent and assistant trainer to Jim at his Maddenstown, County Kildare stables, which also acted as a cover for a small protection racket, was a calculated decision. Jim suggested I cut all ties with my previous occupations and interests to keep Holmes off the scent. He said I shouldn't underestimate the celebrated detective's remarkable powers of deduction. So I transitioned to a hard-headed countryman with considerable aplomb, becoming a man of mystery, a master of disguise and deception.

Jim was a controversial figure in the horse racing fraternity. After being refused by the Jockey Club to set up in Newmarket, he based his racing and breeding operations on his home turf in Ireland. He briefly trained with Atty Parkinson at Sandyford, near Dublin, where he was promoted to head lad, before becoming assistant trainer to Fergal McCabe at Maddenstown. When Fergal retired in 1890, Jim took over the licence, and it was there in Maddenstown that I came to take up my position as assistant trainer.

My wife was a delicate, sensitive soul, and all those months without me by her side, having to carry on the pretence that I was dead began to take its toll. Beryl sadly succumbed to tuberculosis, which was rife in 1890s England. At a low ebb and in a weak state of health, Beryl quickly deteriorated and sadly passed away before she had a chance to join me.

The autopsy report revealed that she was six months pregnant. As I was directly unable to involve myself in the proceedings, Beryl and the child she was carrying, my son, were buried in a marked grave with an engraved headstone at Bovey Tracey cemetery in the market town of Newton Abbot. This was all thanks to the kindness and intervention of my friends at the Masons.

I was heartbroken and overcome with grief and remorse when I learned of Beryl's demise from John Gregson. He advised me not to attend the funeral, and I reluctantly agreed, acknowledging that it would be far too risky—a decision I bitterly regretted. Losing Beryl had cut through my soul. She was the only woman I ever loved. I'd lost the most important person in my life, and I vowed never to marry again. Although I couldn't be at the internment, John agreed to my request to have the priest recite a few words at the graveside by the English writer and poet Christina Rossetti. I chose *Remember Me*, a heart-rendering poem that personified the hope and grief of death and remembrance.

Remember me, when I am gone away,
Gone far away into the silent land:
When you can no longer hold me by the hand,
Nor do I half turn to go, yet turn to stay.
Remember me, when no more day by day,
You tell me of our future that you planned:
Only remember me: you understand,
It will be too late to counsel or pray.

Those lines had remained indelibly on my mind for the past seventeen years and would remain so until I shuffled off this mortal coil.

Wracked with grief and remorse for what could have been, Jim could see how much I was suffering and took pity on me. He told me to take some time out and travel. From the money he gave me and my savings, I soon had enough to try to make my mark on the world. I'd read about the vast discoveries of gold worldwide. So I put a pin on the map and decided on South Africa, setting sail in the spring of 1890 for Durban. Jim thought I was mad but promised there would always be a place for me in Kildare if things didn't work out. I found work as an individual miner, then joined a company in 1895 before returning to Ireland four years later.

While in South Africa, I became heavily involved with various criminal organisations. In 1886, the Witwatersrand Gold Rush in the Transvaal resulted in the formation of Johannesburg. By 1896, it boasted a population of 100,000. The young, vibrant city nurtured every species of vice, and criminal syndicates with roots in New York and London flourished in the new city.

By the mid-1890s, control of the entire Witwatersrand gold industry was in the hands of half a dozen massive mining houses, with capital raised mainly from London and New York. Corruption was rife. It was in this environment that I cut my teeth—abduction, embezzlement, extortion, and protection were the order of the day. Officials in London wanted the gold field to be brought within the orbit of the British Empire. The denial of foreign, primarily British, miners having the right to vote in Johannesburg resulted in the Boer War in October 1899, signalling that it was time for me to put down my tools and return home to Ireland.

Jim welcomed me back to the fold, greeting me with open arms. I could see the glint in his eye at the considerable funds I'd acquired through dubious means in South Africa. I repaid all the money I borrowed, and to show goodwill towards Jim and the business, I added a considerable amount of investment, thus increasing my shareholding in the stables and bloodstock agency. I was no longer just an assistant trainer but a true partner with a fifty per cent stake in a thriving business. I was determined to work hard to see the enterprise flourish and become a respected challenger to other leading equine establishments.

Yet, despite this newfound purpose, there were still moments when melancholy weighed upon me. Thoughts of Beryl cast a dark shadow over my spirit. During my bleakest hours in South Africa, despair had pressed upon me so heavily that I even contemplated ending my life. But during those bleak times, I had a few good friends who helped and encouraged me to see the positive things in life. I was determined to move forward and clung to a single, unwavering resolve to honour my wife's memory and to persevere and make right what had been lost. It was an interlude I would not like to relive nor wish on anyone else, with one exception—my sworn enemy, Sherlock Holmes.

Even after all those years, my heart was still bursting with malignancy towards the detective, like an itch I couldn't scratch. He'd taken everything from me. The love of my life, my inheritance, and my child. I was determined to exact my revenge no matter how long it took. I wanted him to know what it felt like to have one's world end. Consequently, I was cautious about whom I kept company, continuing my protection racket at arm's length. It was by chance that I discovered Holmes's double life.

The irony was never lost on me that I found out about his secret marriage to the enchanting Irene Adler just as he'd found out about mine. How fitting that, after discovering my wife's identity, I came to discover his.

Chapter Ten: Robert Barrett
Una Cosa di Bellezza — A Thing of Beauty

Jim Sweeney and I travelled to Milan in the summer of 1905 at the invitation of one of our owners, Paddy and Niamh O'Doherty, who insisted on paying our travelling expenses.

The O'Doherty's had a runner in the Gran Premio di Milano, a prestigious annual flat horse race held at the San Siro Milan Racecourse for three-year-olds and upwards. Initially, Paddy and Niamh had reservations about their colt, Olmo. He wasn't much of a looker, a plain, sparely made bay, notoriously hot-headed and highly strung.

I remember the cold February day Paddy and Niamh came to inspect the horse at the stables to see how he'd fared over the winter. I heard them debating with Jim whether to enter the colt in a valuable Stakes Race at *Ballydoyle* on St. Patrick's Day.

The O'Doherty's shook their heads in disbelief. They doubted the colt was up to the task. A racing journalist had unkindly described Olmo as slow as an old boat, but Jim brushed off their concerns.

"Ah, he'll be grand," he said in his thick Irish brogue as he puffed away on his cigar over a mug of coffee in the stable's kitchen.

Jim explained to the bemused O'Doherty's that the colt had flourished over the past few months thanks to my unconventional training methods. Each morning at dawn, I took Olmo to the gallops before the rest of the string appeared, working him hard and feeding him a mash of oats grown in the richest soil. Moreover, I insisted he had one of our grey Connemara ponies, Pumpkin, in his box for company, a comfort that seemed to settle his spirit. Through these unorthodox methods, the colt's behaviour and general deportment had improved significantly, having grown strong, with plenty of natural vigour. Jim was highly complementary in explaining this marked improvement was a fine testament to my continued efforts.

The O'Doherty's followed Jim and me to the stables, watching as Jim opened the loose box and removed the rug before leading the colt into the yard, where his groom, Tom O'Connor, quickly mounted him. Paddy and Niamh released a collective gasp of delight, staggered by how their rangy bay colt with a large white star had filled out and developed into a sleek, capricious, well-made specimen, rippling with well-defined muscles. The colt had grown into himself over the winter months, standing at 16 hands high. He was the double of his sire, Orme.

Paddy and Niamh were even more impressed when Tom rode the colt onto the gallops, joining two of Jim's best milers, Speculator and Rosallion. Paddy gazed at his stopwatch in astonishment as Olmo streaked past, tearing up the ground in a blistering display of speed and stamina. Despite being eased down before the finish line, the colt finished five lengths in front of the other horses. This was an impressive performance and a massive step from Olmo's juvenile form. Of course, the O'Dohertys readily agreed to Jim's advice to enter their horse for the Stakes Race, which he went on to win emphatically by ten lengths.

The bookmakers and punters were equally impressed, promoting Olmo as the third favourite of the Gran Premio di Milano. What a day that was, racing at its most exquisite, nothing more, nothing less. The race attracted an audience from far and wide from around the globe.

We joined the men in top hats and tails, shouting words of encouragement as they cheered their riders from the rails. Well-suited to the strong gallop, Olmo responded to his jockey's urging, cutting up the ground as he rallied from mid-field in the final furlong. Carrying the O'Doherty's distinctive purple and gold silks, he finished a commendable second to the remarkable Keepsake, who crossed the line half a length ahead, greeted by the crowd's thunderous reaction, as he reclaimed his crown, first won in 1903. Securing second place in such a prestigious event was a triumph for a bloodstock agency, acknowledging our noble endeavours and building on the colt's remarkable heritage. As an entire, Olmo's value would later be proven at stud.

The O'Doherty's, having backed their horse to win at 10-1 for the Stakes Race in Ireland, took each-way ante-post at 8-1 for the Gran Premio di Milano, winning a substantial amount of money, as those odds were quickly slashed to 7-2 after the colt's impressive run at Ballydoyle.

We celebrated our good fortune with drinks in the hospitality tent. That's where I first spotted Miss Adler and her husband, Lucca Sapori, congratulating Keepsake's owners and chatting freely at the bar, along with the braying toffs and a gaggle of champagne socialites dressed in satins and bows, raising an elegant glass of bubbly, while smiling and clinking glasses. But it wasn't just Miss Adler's charm and outstanding beauty that drew my attention. Something in the way the man next to her looked at her, those strangely familiar mannerisms. "May I introduce my wife, Nene?"

Recognising those dulcet tones, I spun around as if I'd seen a ghost. At first, I couldn't believe my eyes, but there was no mistake. It was undoubtedly Holmes. Despite the disguise, I would have recognised Sherlock Holmes anywhere—those astute grey eyes, the slim, raw-boned athletic figure.

Admittedly, he was older and spoke in an Italian accent

when he introduced Adler to the guests in the hospitality tent celebrating the jubilant owners.

My instinct was to confront my nemesis, alias Lucca Sapori, but then I realised that security would likely bar me from the course, and the polizia would arrest me if I made a scene. I couldn't risk the detective recognising me and discovering my secret identity, so I made my excuses to Jim and the O'Doherty's, faking a headache, blaming my affliction on too much champagne. I headed to the exit of the course with a wry smile on my face and a happy heart in need of intoxicating refreshment to toast my good fortune.

I was about to hail a hansom when I bumped into the renowned horse trainer, Ernest Angelino, who, after shaking hands and greeting me warmly, invited me to his house for drinks with a handful of friends, mainly fellow trainers and owners, for what he described as an intimate gathering.

Being congenial, I gladly accepted the invitation and the ride in Angelino's chauffeur-driven, lavish, *A five Limited Edition*, upper-class tourer. It was an astonishing piece of work—a car that would turn heads wherever it went. I sank back into the comfortable, plush leather seats, admiring the scenery as Angelino and I chatted on our journey.

Ten minutes later, we arrived at Angelino's magnificent residence, the prestigious Innanzitutto Racing Stables, di Milano. The car pulled up at the end of a sweeping driveway, overlooking landscaped gardens with peacocks strutting along the lawn. The gardens boasted a beautiful ornate water fountain with a bronze statue of the black stallion Bucephalus, Alexander the Great's favoured steed.

We entered a vast hallway with parquet design marble flooring, its ceilings adorned with cut glass crystal chandeliers. Angelino ushered me into a grand drawing room, where I was introduced to the rest of the gathering. We sipped wine and entered a genial conversation for some time before the guests made their excuses one by one and retired for the evening. While Angelino was bidding farewell to the last of the revellers, I took a sip from my glass, glancing around the room. My eyes were drawn to an exquisite painting on the wall that had caught my attention earlier. I had a little knowledge of Renaissance art, which I studied as part of my school's curriculum. I was also familiar with the many Renaissance paintings of my ancestors that decked the walls at Baskerville Manor.

Apart from that, my appreciation of fine art would have been considered shallow. Since childhood, I'd always found it hard to divorce appreciation from possession. But I had never felt such a sensation of utter and complete rapture as I did sitting in front of that canvas. Everything else paled into insignificance. I tried to turn away but couldn't divert my gaze. The impetus to gaze up at the portrait, hung in all its glory, over the fireplace proved irresistible. I quivered with excitement as the figure of Saint Veronica met my imperious attention, mesmerised by its stunning beauty. I felt a burning desire to walk out with the portrait under my arm.

When Angelino re-entered the room, he noticed me admiring the artwork, appearing amused by my interest. He then became animated, laughing when I asked if he'd ever considered selling the painting. Angelino explained that it would never be sold. He had previously turned down three highly competitive offers from dealers and a Renaissance collector. The portrait had been in his family for almost 200 years and would be handed down to his eldest son, Leandro. Angelino pointed to the picture, saying he had four passions, which were his family, horses, his fledgling company, Liguria Cars, and this little masterpiece.

When I inquired about the artist, Angelino told me the painting was said to be by Giorgione, who was born in Venice in 1477. It was apparent that Angelino was smitten and highly knowledgeable about his precious little treasure. He continued to explain that after the artist's apprenticeship under Giovanni Bellini, his talents were duly recognised amongst his peers. He soon rose to prominence, becoming a master of his craft. Despite a rapidly successful career, Giorgione's life was tragically cut short in his early thirties after contracting bubonic plague. His body became covered with pustules, finally succumbing to the deadly disease.

Unfortunately, only six pieces of Giorgione's artwork remained, leaving much of his work to idle speculation and rumours. One precious and characteristic piece painted in his innovative style was a small to medium-sized portrait of *The Blessed Veronica of Milan*, painted in extraordinary detail and now hanging on Angelino's wall. The painting was dated around 1500 and, despite considerable research, could not categorically be attributed to Giorgione, one of the most enigmatic Renaissance artists, a master of poetic mood created through idealised form, colour and light. Although, as Angelino was keen to point out, despite the painting being unsigned, all the leading experts on Giorgione and his contemporaries who had the privilege of inspecting the painting harboured no doubt that the master had created it. All of this, the fascinating background of the artist, and this exquisite work of art instilled in me a desire to own this beguiling piece one day.

I suddenly felt jealous of Angelino's influence, money, and appreciation of fine art. I realised relieving him of one of his great passions in life would be no simple or easy task. His elaborate alarm system was wired meticulously to the painting, secured to the wall by heavy-duty combination bolts, with a frame shielded by reinforced unbreakable glass. For now, I was prepared to let it be. After all, I already had Holmes to contend with. Eventually, I bid farewell to Angelino, offering him a smile and a firm handshake, mindful that

I needed to remain in favour for now. I realised I was in a unique position being privy to this information about the painting.

We would return to Ireland by boat in ten days, so the following morning, I hired the services of Emilio Rodriguez, who was said to be the finest undercover agent in Milan. He came highly recommended by the Camorra, one of the oldest and largest Italian criminal organisations originating from the Campania region of Southern Italy.

I was careful not to disclose Lucca Sapori's true identity. I decided to keep that knowledge to myself in case anyone with a grudge had the same idea. I knew I wasn't the only person whose feathers had been ruffled by the world-famous detective. My contacts in London told me his list of enemies was as long as my arm.

It took nearly a year to gather all the information needed, including the Saporis' address, where their children went to school, and how frequently Lucca Sapori went away to work in London. My agent ascertained that Sapori would return to Milan in June for the summer holiday to spend time with his family and accompany his wife to the races, as was his custom. Emilio sent me photographs of the children, Nicco and Charlotte, their pet dog, a chocolate-coloured labrador, and the family villa in Via Torina.

Before putting my plan into action, I decided rather than inflict physical harm on Holmes or his family, as part of my abduction plot, I intended to hit the celebrated detective where it hurt in his pocket, in addition to causing mental anguish. Consequently, I spent days meticulously preparing, going through everything, continually writing and rewriting possible outcomes, and biding my time until the right moment for my plan to have the most significant impact on the Sapori family. Holmes may have been celebrated for his powers of deduction, but I, under my alter ego, Janus, who perceived with precision, would take the upper hand and wound him most deeply. Nothing afforded me greater satisfaction than witnessing my nemesis crumble beneath my design and come out the ultimate victor.

It was a risky strategy. If anyone recognised my position, it would be untenable. Still, with my eyes on the prize, I was willing to take risks, knowing I would secure sufficient funding to finance my operation following my meeting with Emilio.

I had no personal axe to grind against Irene Adler, having met her once at a wedding in London many years ago. It was before she married the lawyer Godfrey Norton. It turned out that she was a friend of the groom, my cousin's half-brother Henry Hodgson. My wife and I were introduced to Miss Adler at the reception as Mr and Mrs Valderlour, our assumed names at the time. We found Irene Adler charming, witty and intelligent, but she only stayed briefly, stating that she had a pressing engagement later that day.

It wasn't long after she met Godfrey Norton. I knew this because Jim's sister Attracta delivered Miss Adler's daughter at their home in Kensington. The child, Rosemary, was born prematurely and tragically died shortly after birth.

The fact that Irene Adler had already lost one child under tragic circumstances played on my conscience for a while. Still, she was married to my hated enemy and had to be prepared for the consequences of that liaison. As my mother used to say, *"If you lie down with dogs, you'll get up with fleas."*

I considered abducting Miss Adler instead of the boy, but then I decided my first choice would have a much more significant impact. Holmes was going to suffer all right, like I had. It was hard to imagine the great detective with a wife and children, and I wouldn't have believed it if I hadn't seen it with my own eyes. Although, as a man of the world, I could understand it. When Irene Adler locked those violet eyes on you, there was nowhere to hide. They were mesmerising, although she seemed impervious to the spell she cast.

Chapter Eleven: Robert Barrett
Intenzioni Mortali — Deadly Intentions

Jim and I arrived back in Maddenstown to cheers and whistles from the stable staff and an abundance of congratulatory notes from numerous owners and trainers.

Then, two weeks later, Ernest Angelino wrote to Jim to say the connections of the equine heroines, Princess of Lombardy and Duchess of Tuscany, were impressed with how my controversial training methods had transformed Olmo, initially an unconsidered horse, a humble selling plater with dubious form, now risen to the giddy heights of group two status, and a potential future champion. The owners, John and Christina Upton, whom I was introduced to at Angelino's drinks reception, insisted on sending the fillies to Kildare for the winter months to receive specialised training before their upcoming group races the following spring. Angelino's passion for horses was unprecedented. He told me in Milan that he'd used a huge chunk of his director's income from Liguria Cars to invest in breeding high-quality thoroughbreds, snapping up the best broodmares at Tattersalls Sales, ensuring the leading stallions covered them. Angelino had an almost obsessive ambition to win the Triple Crown in England. But, of course, he needed money, and lots of it, to realise that dream.

Based in Genoa, near the docks, Liguria Cars was a recent addition to the car market. The company was formed three years before by Angelino, the director and principal shareholder. The company's future looked assured, but Angelino needed further investment to expand and compete with the leading manufacturers. He was confident that creating a share issue would attract the right investors, giving him the funds necessary to ensure his company's long-term future.

With Liguria Cars' much-anticipated success, Angelino was confident he could take on the big boys and boasted he would build a world-beating racing car that would make him rich beyond his wildest dreams and fund his grand passion.

I must admit I had my reservations. Angelino was keen for us to accept the fillies. Still, they were high-flyers with formidable reputations, and I was concerned about how they would adapt to the arduous boat journey and the transition to Irish soil. Unfortunately, my concerns were justified. After arriving at the receiving centre in Dublin, both horses contracted epizootic lymphangitis, which remained dormant during transportation to our stables.

The fillies became listless after a few days of training and being turned out in the paddocks with the other horses. When their feed of oats and grass hay remained untouched the following morning, it became apparent that they were unwell. Jim immediately called our equine vet, Oisin O'Flaherty, who confirmed our worst fears after taking routine blood tests. It could be seen from the tell-tale modules swelling along their legs and necks that the fillies had tragically succumbed to the deadly contagious virus with little chance of recovery.

The only humane thing to do was to shoot the infected horses. This was a wretched and painful affliction that rendered them lame and feverish as the infection spread insidiously through the lymphatic vessels. An air of hopelessness descended, profoundly affecting every staff member. This epidemic was a disaster for our stables. Between the winter of 1905 and the spring of 1906, Jim and I lost many of our fine thoroughbreds.

The few horses we managed to save were quarantined for six months. Jim and I lost valuable prize money and training fees, massively diminishing our stock. Future potential owners, once keen for us to train their horses, turned away, ignoring our calls and letters. Consequently, I had to dig deep and borrow money from unscrupulous people to keep my share of the business going. It was all too much for Jim, who, after watching his life's work destroyed along with his reputation, hit the bottle hard and smoked opium copiously, propelling himself into a prolonged drug-induced breakdown. He knew I blamed him for accepting the fillies in the first place, and relations between the two of us became strained.

Apart from what occurred with my wife, Beryl, I'd never been an exceptionally forgiving man, never one for turning the other cheek. I was more of an eye-for-an-eye type of man. That was my nature. My hatred for Holmes and the man I'd once looked up to, Ernest Angelino, after the loss of so many prize-winning horses, dug deep into my soul. "Revenge will be mine."

In my darkest hour, I wracked my brain until I eventually thought of a way to settle the score with Angelino while simultaneously exacting revenge on Holmes. It would require careful planning and an influx of money. The plan was to relieve Angelino of some of his substantial income by disrupting the manufacture of Liguria Cars, destroying his dreams if he refused to comply in giving me what I wanted—his beloved Giorgione painting.

It was an elaborate, detailed project, but I'd secured the backing of Rodriguez and his cronies. When I laid out my proposal before them, pointing out the substantial financial gains, they agreed to bankroll and assist me. They queried how I intended to remove the picture from Angelino's sight and override the comprehensive security system connected to his mansion. After I explained there was no risk involved to Rodriguez or his men as they wouldn't steal the painting, they agreed to fit in with my plans.

Rodriguez demanded heavy interest, of course, but I was prepared for that. I didn't expect anything less from the man known as Il Resolver. I was confident the consulting detective and Irene Adler would pay handsomely for the return of their son, paving the way for the implementation of Operation Whistle. This would be my final hurrah before disappearing again — this time outside the continent.

Initially, the first part of my plan was to target certain horses at The Ernest Angelino Racing Stables di Milano. Connie would be responsible for organising the team to administer the same deadly fungus that infected the fillies, carrying out the deed late at night when the stables were closed to the public. That would ensure Angelino's prize-winning horses would infect the rest of the thoroughbreds, thereby jeopardising the future of the stables. But, of course, that was only the beginning of my act of vengeance.

Chapter Twelve: Sherlock Holmes
Gl Cincinnati – The Beguiled

Some would call it ironic that the most significant blow that had ever befallen me professionally was the abduction of my beloved boy.

I couldn't shake off a sense of hopelessness and impending danger. Of course, I couldn't reveal my feelings to Nene, who blamed herself for Nicco's disappearance and for allowing Hildegard Achen into our home. My wife could barely look me in the eye. But I didn't blame Nene. No, she was an innocent victim in this charade. She had always been an excellent role model to our children—resolute, tenacious, timeless in relevance and resilience, doggedly determined, incredibly kind, and compassionate towards others.

Life was seldom fair, and we rarely get what we want or think we deserve. I did things early in life that I wasn't proud of, but then there were other things I found later in life. Things like my affection for Nene and our precious children. I was never particularly adept at expressing my feelings regarding matters of the heart and the softer passions. Still, I cared for my family with a deep, abiding intensity, so it was elementary that I love them in the way I've come to understand love.

My son's abduction was a poignant reminder that no life was without regret, and sooner or later, everything turned into work.

I called Romano for an update on the investigation and to inform him about the contents of the ransom note and why those burial sites were significant and of the utmost importance. He assured me he had his best men on the job, and they would check out the churches and burial sites and report back urgently. I considered carrying out the task myself but realised it would be far too time-consuming, and I wanted to return to that house and speak to the rental agent. I couldn't put my finger on it, but something was not quite right about that property.

I called ahead and asked to meet Rodolfo Abbati at 1 P.M., keen to check the area during daylight hours. He seemed hesitant at first but finally agreed to my request after I explained the urgency of the matter. However, after hearing a brief history of the property from the neighbours, I could understand why.

Nene was naturally reluctant to return to the scene of Nicco's abduction, so I dropped her off in a cab at The Policlinico Hospital to check on the progress of our coach driver before continuing my journey to 11 Vecchio Cigno. When I arrived at the house at 1 P.M., the agent was already in attendance with a locksmith, busy securing the property after the external doors were boarded up the night before by the polizia after several days of searching the home.

Abbati was a tall, slim fellow. His keen blue eyes sparkled brightly from behind a pair of gold-rimmed glasses, and his broad face and prominent jaw were bronzed and glistened from the heat of the Tuscany sun. He was impeccably dressed in a three-piece, pinstripe suit with a cravat and a gold watch chain burrowed into his waistcoat. He shot me a look of resignation, offering a firm handshake, brushing my fingers with a selection of striking dress rings that adorned his index and ring fingers on both hands. Abbati pulled a silk handkerchief from his breast pocket, wiping both cheeks, before introducing himself and removing his hat to reveal a dark, receding hairline.

He then ushered me into the property. Abbati gave me free

rein to search the house, showing me around the ground-floor accommodation but refusing to go upstairs to the bedrooms, the alleged scene of the murders. Despite meticulously searching the property, I found little fresh evidence save for the cushion discarded on the bedroom floor. The room that had claimed the lives of two people struck me as odd. It reeked of mould and death, and on a hot, humid afternoon, it felt icy cold. Picking up the cushion, I inspected it closely, but there was nothing remarkable. A few loose strands of black silk were stuck to it, presumably from the perpetrator's dress.

Next, I searched the gardens and large outhouse, but apart from garden tools, a stapler, and chain, and a couple of broken chairs, the place was empty save for a cupboard filled with tins of ham, corned beef, and peaches — enough provisions for days on end. After discovering scratch marks on the inside of the shed door, Abbati explained that the previous tenants kept a dog and must have left the food behind when they hurriedly left the property. My inspection continued to the garden area, where I discovered four fresh footprints embedded in the soil. One set was much smaller than the others, most likely made by a woman or a child.

Finally, I turned my attention to Abbati, who appeared on edge and eager to leave. "I understand the house has been empty for quite some time?"

"Yes, Signor Sapori, ever since the murders, we have struggled to find tenants. People say 11Vecchio Cigno is cursed."

"Can you tell me about the history of the place? Who owns the deeds to this property?"

"Why, it was left to the brother of the deceased, Leonardo Bandiero. He moved to Ireland shortly after the funeral. He became frustrated when we failed to find a suitable tenant and recently sold the property at a knockdown price to an Irish holding company in Naas."

"Do you know the name of this holding company?"

"Yes, indeed, it's Shire and Allen. We deal with the company secretary, a fellow called Denis Rafferty. He recently instructed us to withdraw the property from the rental market, as the company intends to undertake some renovations and sell 11Vecchio Cigno by public auction." Abbati shook his head. "But despite my company providing estimates to the new vendors, nothing has been done since my last visit. I won't come here if I can help it." He shivered. "They never caught the murderer. Some say it was Rosetta's lover, Dominzia Santora, who was determined to exact his revenge after Rosetta Bandiero threw him over and decided to stay with her husband. When Luis confronted his wife about the affair, Rosetta confessed and blamed her lover, claiming Dominzia seduced her."

"What was Santora's occupation?"

The agent sighed deeply before continuing his narrative. "Dominzia was a carpenter, and my company employed him to replace two upstairs windows. Rumour has it that with her husband at work, Rosetta and Dominzia began a torrid affair. When Luis discovered the deception after being tipped off by a neighbour, he confronted Dominzia at his workplace. According to witnesses, Dominzia vehemently protested his innocence, resulting in a scuffle and a fistfight. Luis retreated with wounded pride, a bloody nose, and a cut lip. That's the last anyone saw of Rosetta and her husband. Three days later, their bodies were found by Rosetta's father in the bedroom."

"How did they die?"

"Luis died from a blow to the head, while Rosetta was strangled."

"And Santora?" I asked.

"Why, he simply disappeared. The polizia discovered Dominzia's affair with Rosetta and his altercation with Luis, and despite issuing a warrant for his arrest, the polizia never found Dominzia." Abbati sighed. "It never ceased to amaze me the extremes people will go to for love, Signor Sapori."

I nodded in agreement, flashing Abbati a wry smile as he continued his narrative. "People who knew Dominzia were shocked and appalled by his behaviour. He always struck them as a decent man who would do anything for his neighbours. The murder was entirely out of character, although the polizia took a different view. They saw cold-blooded, calculated homicide, as they called it. Although now a cold case, Dominzia is still the prime suspect."

"Did you know the couple well? How did you evaluate them as tenants?"

"They were nice enough. I didn't know Luis well, but I remember Rosetta from school. A year below me, she was a wilful girl, headstrong, beautiful, and bright as a button. Half the boys were infatuated with her. We lost touch when I left for college. Then, when I returned and started work at the agency, I was delighted to hear that she'd settled down and married, and she and her husband became our tenants."

"Was there ever a romantic interlude between the two of you?"

Abbati shook his head. "Good God, nothing like that! You appear to be a man of the world, Signor Sapori. I never married and have no plans to do so. Let's just say Rosetta, as lovely as she was, simply wasn't my type." Abbati smiled at me knowingly.

I raised an eyebrow, observing his well-turned-out appearance—the immaculate fingernails, neatly trimmed waxed moustache, and the way he strutted his hips as he walked were all tell-tale signs of *the love that dare not speak its name* as so famously quoted by Lord Alfred Douglas, in the first and only publication of the Chameleon magazine, in 1894.

"So, Rosetta Bandiero was a friend?" I probed, staring at Abbati intently.

"That's right, Signora Sapori. Although admittedly, she

was more of an acquaintance, I was fond of her, so I was concerned when Rosetta told me she and Luis had problems. She explained that Luis had lost many customers at his barber shop since a rival establishment opened across the road, undercutting Luis's prices. In impoverished times, clients departed in droves, leaving the couple in a near-constant state of financial worry. More often than not, they found themselves short of funds when I called each Friday to collect the rent. One day, things came to a head when Rosetta was forced to apologise yet again for the lateness of the rent. She broke down in tears and confided she had taken a lover and intended to leave Luis to start a new life."

"Did Signora Bandierro reveal the identity of her newfound love?"

Abbati shook his head. "No, Signor Sapori. She didn't need to. The gossip was widespread in the neighbourhood that Rosetta was carrying on with Dominzia. I felt sad that my friend was garnering quite a reputation, but she refused to listen to reason. Despite my protestations that her husband was a good man whose only crime was to have fallen on hard times, Rosetta dismissed my objections. She said she'd made up her mind, which was the end of the matter. She swore me to secrecy, and I begrudgingly agreed due to our past allegiance." Abbati sighed. "Rosetta placed me in an impossible position because, although I had a duty of care to my employers, I also liked and respected Luis, as I explained to the polizia when they interviewed me at the time of the incident."

"Did you see Signor and Signora Bandiero on the day of the murders?"

Abbati shook his head. "I had an appointment with Luis and Rosetta to discuss the arrears and conduct an inspection of the property. The new landlords were losing patience with the tenant's rent arrears and instructed our company to serve an eviction notice. But when I arrived at the property, there was no answer. I knocked for a while before posting the notice through the letterbox. I couldn't wait any longer as I had a pressing appointment across town."

"These noises reported to the polizia and heard by the neighbours and tenants... what do you make of them?"

"Who knows?" Abbati shrugged. "People described it as a chilling bone-deep howl, a chain rattling, then an eerie silence, followed by animal-like footsteps. Some describe it as the night beast. Others swear it's a poltergeist or the haunted spirits of Rosetta and Luis, walking within 11Vecchio Cigno's walls at night, attempting to escape."

"We have more to fear from the living than the dead," I said, scoffing. "Thank you, Signor Abbati. I've taken up enough of your time. You have been of material assistance with my enquiries."

Abbati flashed a melancholy smile. "I hope you find what you are looking for, Signor Sapori."

Upon returning to the villa, I found Nene anxiously waiting in the drawing room, alerting me that a telegram had just arrived from Mycroft. I opened it, reading my brother's narrative, which said Charlotte was safely ensconced in Sophia Moon's parents' secluded villa in Rhodes. My brother said all was well, assuring us he arranged for an additional security man to put a watch on the door. Reading those words, we cried out, "Thank God", in unison, both giddy with relief that at least our beloved daughter Charlotte was safe.

"How did you get on at the hospital?" I enquired.

Nene offered me a weak smile, her face flushed with emotion. "Sherlock, Mattia has regained consciousness, although understandably, he's confused by his ordeal. I wasn't allowed to see him, but he told the guardia and the consultant that he was attacked from behind. The doctors confirmed he'd been hit with a single blow to the back of the head with a blunt instrument. Mattia said he didn't see the person who attacked him, but the last thing he remembers was hearing a whistle before being rendered unconscious."

Chapter Thirteen: Nicco Sapori
Alta Ansia — High Anxiety

The man came back alone the following morning with breakfast, consisting of a slice of panettone and an apple, which he placed beside me on the bedside locker.

"Forgive my meagre offerings, but it's the chef's day off," he said, chuckling at his joke.

My eyes followed him around the room, taking in every detail. He was of average build, and I guessed in his mid to late forties, although it was hard to tell. His lengthy grey hair fell lankly over his collar and shoulders, which were bowed and stooped, making him appear older than his years. The top two buttons of his white shirt were unfastened, showing a gold chain and crucifix. He'd tucked his shirt into a pair of black trousers half an inch too short, held up by a pair of red braces.

Sitting on a chair beside the bed, the man stared at me intently. His dazzling green eyes sparkled with a dry shimmer as he spoke softly in a thick Italian accent. "Don't worry, Giovanni. This business will all be over soon, you'll see."

"My name is Nicco," I replied indignantly. "Although I have yet to learn yours. When will I be released?"

The man stared at me before his face broke into a lop-sided grin. I could smell whiskey on his breath. "Nice try, Nicco. I cannot divulge my identity, but you may call me Gino." His smile deepened, observing my perplexed expression.

"When my father arrives, this will not end well for you or your accomplice, but if you let me go, I'll ask my father to go easy on you."

Gino's face soured, and his expression turned grim. "Enough of that talk, for goodness sake. Don't let my boss hear you." He gestured towards the door, shaking his head. "You'll make her angry. Believe me, it's best not to do that." He appeared to consider saying something else for a moment but then let it go.

Gino sat back in his chair, removing a packet of English cigarettes from his pocket, lighting one with a match of vestas, and blowing circles of smoke into the damp air. His gaze travelled up towards the smoke, remaining there for some time as he shifted in his seat. His fingers twitched on the cigarette packet in a rhythmic tapping motion.

"There are so many questions, young Nicco, but you must know I can't answer them." He paused momentarily. "Look, I shouldn't be telling you this, but the powers that be intend to move you somewhere more comfortable." He glanced around the room. "As alluring as this place is, I'm confident you'll be happier with the new arrangement."

I sensed Gino wasn't telling me the whole story. His lack of eye contact and constant fidgeting, as my father said, were all classic signs. "When will you move me?" I asked.

"Maybe tomorrow." He shrugged. "Or the day after. Best not to mention our little tete de tete, eh?" He gestured towards the door, placing a finger on his lip.

"What am I supposed to do in the meantime?"

"Why, we sit tight, Nicco, until the money arrives, which should take no more than a few days. Trust me, and I promise you will be home soon, safe in the bosom of your family. In the meantime, I suggest you enjoy your breakfast. I'll return shortly with buttermilk and bread. Sit tight, little soldier."

Surprised by my hunger, I ravenously devoured my breakfast and read another two chapters from the book. Then, I lay on the bed on top of the blanket, drifting into a nap, until an altercation in the passageway outside raised me from my slumber. The man, named Gino, and the unnamed woman had words. Her sharp voice rang out from the corridor, talking disparagingly.

"I want out," Gino protested. "This is above and beyond my regular duties and far more onerous a task than I have ever been asked to do. I have children, for goodness sake, and I wouldn't house a dog in this God-forsaken place."

"You will do as I say," the woman said. "You're either with us or not. It's your choice. But it will be the worst for you if Bob gets wind of this. You know how much Operation Whistle means to him. The man is remorseless. If you rat out, then there are consequences, simple as that. Pull yourself together, and remember you're doing this for your wife and children. Never forget that Lucca Sapori brought all this on himself."

"I just want it to be over and for that boy to be returned to his family like we agreed," Gino said.

The woman cackled, speaking in a lighter tone. "Of course, Bob and I gave you our word, didn't we? And have we ever let you down or lied to you?"

"No," Gino asserted, his voice low and intense.

"Come then, let me take you for breakfast and a cold beer. We have a full day ahead."

My mind raced as I listened to their narrative. Two questions lingered — who was Bob, and what was Operation Whistle?

I sat back on the bed, holding my breath until the footsteps disappeared from the passageway and became a distant echo. Whoever this Bob was, he appeared to have a personal vendetta against my father, although it still wasn't clear if they knew my father's true identity. These thoughts bewildered and scared me simultaneously. I missed my mother holding me close, singing softly in her beautiful contralto voice, reassuring me everything would work out fine.

The Whistle of Revenge

I prayed that my father would recognise the clues in my letter and come soon to rescue me. God help Gino, Bob, and that woman when he did. I opened the book and removed the pen hidden in my shoe. Not to be too obvious and raise attention, I wrote the words shilling and Hewli St on the sleeve, knowing that my brilliant father would pick up on the fact these were code names, before closing the book and placing it under the pillow.

Chapter Fourteen: Robert Barrett
Alleanza Difficile — Uneasy Alliance

A knock at the door disturbed me from my thoughts. The bellboy ushered Connie into the room before swiftly leaving with a tip. Connie looked at me with disdain, her eyebrows raised, lips parted, revealing two gold teeth. She struck her hand against the table in an impatient gesture.

"Our situation is becoming increasingly difficult. The nets are closing in," Connie said, speaking in a thick German dialect. "My contact informed me Romano and the English detective are on the case. The polizia will discover our hiding place soon. We have no choice. We must move the boy."

I nodded in agreement, gesturing towards a hardback chair in the corner of the room. Connie sat down, accepting the tumbler of whiskey I pushed towards her. She took a swig from the glass, downing the amber nectar in one, wiping her mouth with the back of her hand. I refilled the glass from the decanter and sat back in my chair.

"You never told me the whole story about Sherlock Holmes and why this mission is so important to you," Connie said, taking another sip from her glass and staring intensely into my eyes.

"What happened between me and the detective is personal."

Connie raised an eyebrow. "Sure, I'm curious, that's all. Don't worry, Bob, nothing will go wrong as long as we keep Peppo in the dark. The less that man knows, the better. He's already getting itchy feet."

"Agreed," I said. "You and Peppo will move the boy tonight. Put a sedative in the lad's milk. That should make the transition easier. Tell Peppo not to divulge the boy's identity to the driver. This is most important."

Connie glanced up at me, pushing the empty glass to the edge of the table. There were hollows beneath those watery grey eyes that moved furtively around the room, dark circles, no doubt caused by lack of sleep. I knew she couldn't rest until she'd seen the job through to the bitter end. Whatever anyone said about Connie, she was a consummate professional through and through. She was utterly unimpressed by social standing and wealth despite the fact she had always craved a healthy dose of the latter.

"Why the cloak and dagger? Don't you trust us?" Connie asked slyly, tilting her head to one side as she stared at me curiously. Her slightly crooked lips curled into a sardonic smile, revealing a hint of hostility that made me wonder what she might be thinking or, indeed, have to hide.

I shifted my gaze to meet those watery eyes. "Peppo won't let us down. He has too much to lose," I added emphatically. "Of course I trust you. I trust you both." It was on my tongue to tell Connie that she, Peppo, Emilio, and the driver, Eduardo, were the only ones privy to my secret location in Lombardy, where the boy would soon be safely ensconced. "Let's have another drink," I said, filling the tumblers again from the decanter and raising my glass to Connie. "To Operation Whistle," I said.

Connie slowly raised her glass, flashing me a sardonic smile before repeating the sentiment.

I sat back in my seat as my thoughts returned to the task. Moving the boy was inconvenient. I didn't want to bring him to the stables in Lombardy, where there were many prying eyes, but Connie was right. If Romano and Holmes were onto us, then we had little choice.

Our designated driver, Eduardo Balducci, was already known to me. He'd been carefully selected for the job by the man who had become one of my most trusted confidants, the mafia agent, Emilio Rodriguez, widely known and feared in Italy as *Il Resolver*, the man who gets things done.

As our friendship grew over a sumptuous meal and a bottle of the finest claret at his villa in Lombardy, Emilio told me a little of his earlier life, which was disturbing and incredulous in equal measure, given his bleak upbringing.

Emilio was an imposing, six-foot-tall, dark-haired man with a handlebar moustache and a distinct scar under his left eye. Born in Salerno in 1856, his Italian mother, Cecelia, died in childbirth, which had a devastating effect on Alejandro, his Spanish father, who became a broke man, culminating in mental health issues. It all became too much, and one day, after putting a hessian bag over his head, Alejandro shot himself through the head, leaving his son an orphan to be placed in various unsuitable foster homes.

Neglected and ill-treated, Emilio faced a grim future until one day, he was thrown a lifeline by the local Catholic Church's priest, Father Joseph Mancini, an academic who noticed a spark in the boy.

Thanks to Father Joseph, Emilio received a decent education. He left school at 15 and took up a clerical position at the local library. By the time he was 18, Father Joseph secured a full bursary for Emilio, enabling him to study for a degree in business studies and law at the University of Naples.

After graduating with honours at 21, Emilio was exempted from National Service and conscription due to the savage blows to his left eye and ear inflicted by one of his foster parents, resulting in total deafness in his left ear.

He undertook various menial jobs before securing a position teaching economics and business studies at a local school in 1895. Two years his junior, Emilio met the love of his life, Virna Lamaro, the daughter of Ugo Lamaro, a local mafia leader based in the Campania region of Italy. The couple married the following year. Emilio became Ugo's business manager, and under his father-in-law's guidance, he progressed well within the organisation.

After a while, Emilio decided to branch out and, with Ugo's approval, formed an independent operation, using the many contacts he'd made during his time with the mafia.

In the spring of 1904, disaster struck when Virna and their daughter Matilda were ruthlessly gunned down by a rival gang on their way home from a wedding in Bomio. Emilio had crossed the gang on several occasions. He told me the day he lost his wife and child was the darkest day of his life. Seeking vengeance, a week later, he executed Franco Mizzia, the notorious gang leader responsible for the killings, at the Focolare Ristorante in Bergamo, Lombardy.

The polizia confirmed Mizzia was killed instantly by a hail of high-impact bullets fired from a *Hotchkiss Machine Gun*. Emilio ensured he had a cast-iron alibi, of course, but the execution caused unrest and disharmony amongst the rival gangs. Emilio, fearful for his life, headed north, setting up his operations and the private detective agency he used as a front to cover up his shady dealings, enhancing his dubious reputation as the man who gets things done.

Sitting here in quiet reflection, sipping from my glass, I realised that I couldn't afford to trust anyone, not even the loyal subordinate Peppo Barbieri, who came highly recommended by Emilio, who told me that while Peppo was no Einstein, he was nevertheless savvy, cunning and reliable.

As for Connie, observing her trademark raised eyebrow and mocking smile as she drained her glass, I wouldn't put it past her to stab me in the back. An intimidating woman,

Connie Gallagher-nee Rosenbaum, was not a person to be trifled with. Her parents, Otto and Helga Rosenbaum, migrated to Ireland from Germany twenty years ago. They succumbed to typhoid on the boat journey, leaving Connie, an only child aged sixteen, to fend for herself. She was a beauty in her youth until alcohol, drugs, and tobacco later ravaged her looks.

When Connie's husband and my right-hand man, Seamus Gallagher, died unexpectedly in mysterious circumstances, she took over my protection racket, running operations with an iron rod, never one to suffer fools gladly. No one crossed Connie. Our operatives were terrified of that icy and acid persona, unkindly referring to her as *The Black Widow*. They complained she was an unwelcoming, joyless husk, almost impossible to please. I'd witnessed the most brutal men reduced to tears after a dressing down from Connie. Admittedly, she had proved a valuable ally over the years, a perfect partner for the task.

After Connie left, I showered and dressed in readiness for my assignment across town at The Excelsior Hotel, where I'd booked a reservation under the name Guippea Bianchi, and it was there that I had arranged to meet the enchanting Miss Achen later that evening.

Chapter Fifteen: Nicco Sapori
Indizi Velati — Veiled Clues

I woke to the rattle of clogs along the corridor, and the woman came in with a cup of buttermilk, placing it beside me on the locker.

"Drink this," she snapped. "Gino will return shortly to collect the empty cup."

She glanced around the room with suspicious eyes as my heart thumped widely in my chest, praying her attention would not be drawn to my book of notes. She muttered something under her breath before turning around and leaving the room. I picked up the cup, wondering if the woman was trying to poison or sedate me. It was out of character for her to come to the room. She typically left all the daily menial tasks to Gino. The milk smelt funny, so I had no intention of drinking it, but what would I do with the liquid to avoid suspicion?

Hearing footsteps approaching in the corridor, I ran over to the commode and emptied the milk into it, firmly closing the lid and replacing the cup on the bedside locker before Gino entered the room.

"I'll return within the hour, be ready," Gino said, picking up the empty cup.

"Where are we going?" I asked.

Gino laughed. "I can't tell you, Nicco, so please don't test my patience. However, I will say that the journey will be short. We'll arrive at our destination soon, where you'll be accommodated in more amenable surroundings."

Later, when Gino returned, I feigned drowsiness as he

helped me put on my shoes and jacket. We took one last look around the room that had been my prison for the past few days before Gino gently put his arm around me and guided me towards the open door. As we reached the passageway, Gino stopped for a moment.

"What about your book, young Nicco? Should we return for The Count of Monte Cristo?"

"No," I muttered sleepily. "I already finished the story, thank you."

Gino nodded. Appearing satisfied with my answer, he guided me up the treacherous steps, once again passing the fresco of Saint Monica in the passageway until we were finally out into the fresh Tuscan air and the full moon's glare. I heard muffled conversations as Gino carried me to a waiting carriage, placing a blanket on my knees and slamming the door shut before sitting beside me. I pretended to sleep as Gino and the driver, a male voice, spoke to each other in Italian.

"Is the boy all right?" the voice asked.

"Yes, he's fine. Giovanni is sleeping soundly like a bambino." Gino laughed. "How soon before we reach our port of call, my friend."

"Twenty minutes or so," the voice said.

"Good," Gino replied. "I'm glad to get out of this place. It has an ominous atmosphere, and I, for one, will be glad to see the back of Saint Monica Church."

The voice laughed. "Why is Palmiro not with you?"

"Connie has gone ahead. She'll meet with us later."

Many thoughts were whirling around in my brain as we began our journey to my unknown destination. From the sound of it, I was destined to meet the woman named Connie again. I wondered if the mysterious Bob would finally appear and if my father would find the clues and crack the whistle code. I had no idea what it meant, although I sensed it was something far more significant than my abduction.

Chapter Sixteen: Sherlock Holmes
il Nascondiglio – The Hiding Place

Nene and I were about to venture out when the telephone rang. I answered it to discover Romano on the line. The inspector explained his men found three burial sites for Turridu Cannio in separate churchyards throughout the city. The First Turridu was discovered interned at Basilica di Sant Ambrogio, the patron saint of Milan. At the same time, the other two were buried at Basilica di San Lorenzo and Basilica di Santa Monica, an abandoned church five miles from the city centre.

After Romano gave directions and further details, I immediately discounted the first two sites. I arranged to meet the inspector and his men on the old, disused San Monica Church grounds after reassuring me two of his men would check out the remaining sites as a precautionary measure.

"What is it? Have they found Nicco?" Nene asked, staring at me anxiously.

"No, but we think we know where our son may be held hostage. I must go now to meet Romano."

"Then I'm coming with you," Nene said, staring at me defiantly.

I nodded resignedly, realising there was little point in refusing my wife's request. It was an argument that I was never going to win.

Nene remained silent for much of the journey, reflecting what we would find at the end of our trip. I was immensely relieved by my wife's calm reaction. She offered me a half-hearted smile as I patted her hand reassuringly.

"It'll be all right," I said. "Trust me, we'll see this through together."

The carriage proceeded at a steady trot until we were out of the busy city onto the quieter country roads. In happier times, we marvelled at the unexpected wonder of this scenic city and its historical sites. But, sadly, not today. All I could think of was the task ahead and finding our son. I whipped up the horses until they broke into an extended trot and finally a gallop. The coach lurched from side to side as I navigated it and horses through the narrow Tuscan country lanes, finally reaching our destination thirty minutes later.

When we arrived, Romano and three guardie stood patiently waiting. Their meticulously varnished carriage was tethered outside the church, the horses sweating copiously, their coats gleaming in the glare of the Tuscan sun.

A guardie searching the small private graveyard shouted out, waving his arms and alerting us that he'd discovered the raised headstone of Turridu Cannio, who, according to the inscription, died fifty years ago. He pulled up a clump of weeds to reveal the outline of the grave. As I glanced around the graveyard, it appeared the church had been abandoned some time ago. Observing its derelict state, the boarded-up windows, the overgrown gravestones, and the moss-covered flagstones, it was a bleak place, considering it had once been a place of worship.

I shuddered at the thought of strangers bringing my son here and what fate had befallen him. The only signs of life were carriage marks and several fresh footprints in the soil. We followed the prints. Two were masculine, and the third a woman's, made by some type of heel, likely from a pair of clogs. The prints ended abruptly at a large oaken door adjacent to the church's side door. There were no signs of Nicco's footprints, suggesting he may have been carried by one of the

The Whistle of Revenge

assailants.

A fresh-faced guardia pushed open the door, which made an unearthly sound as it creaked slowly back on its hinges. We found ourselves staring down steep stone steps, crumbling in places. I gestured for Nene to stay with one of the guardie, explaining it wasn't safe. She nodded in agreement, looking as though she was about to faint. The guardia guided her toward a bench before I descended the steps with Romano and the other two guardie. They shone their torches to help navigate our passage down the treacherous steps, each thickly coated with moss and outlining fresh footprints.

As we made our way downwards towards a passageway, I saw the Fresco of Saint Veronica, and I knew then without a shadow of a doubt that we were in the right place, although judging by those footprints, I was very much afraid we were already too late.

We entered an inner chamber and discovered another opened door with a padlock on the outside. Like the first one, it had been left unlocked. Whoever had been here had gone quickly. I took a breath as we entered the chamber. My eyes flashed around the room, taking in the windowless damp space where Nicco's abductors had kept him against his will.

In the corner of the room was a single bed and blanket. On the bedside locker next to a plate of half-eaten black bread and cheese lay a copy of *The Count of Monte Cristo*, presumably the book Nicco told us about in his letter. I opened the book with some trepidation. On the inside sleeve, written in my son's unmistakable handwriting and dramatically underlined, were the words *shilling* and *Hewli St.*

I turned my attention to Romano. "This is an inside job, Inspector. The perpetrators were tipped off after someone raised the alarm."

Romano nodded in agreement, and his expression changed quickly in response to my narrative, instantly becoming sombre.

"My worst fears have been founded. There's something I need to discuss with you. Today, events have crystallised something weighing on my mind." He hesitated for a moment, glancing around the room, a grave expression on his face. "But not here where walls have ears. I implore you to return to the station with me. I have something to tell you of the utmost importance."

Chapter Seventeen: Salvatore Romano
Amici e Nemici — Friends and Foes

Outside the gloomy confines of the church, the world seemed brighter. White clouds floated across the Tuscany sky, the afternoon sun beating as my men and I returned to the station.

Holmes and Nene Adler followed in their brougham, pulled by a smart pair of greys. I sat puffing away on a cigarette, reflecting on the magnitude of the past few days' events, thinking if only those horses could talk. Feeling an all too familiar discomfort in my chest, I pulled out a small bottle of nitro-glycerine from my coat pocket, stubbing out my cigarette before taking a swig of the dense, colourless liquid.

We arrived at the Commissariato di Polizia Station around 2:30 P.M. I ushered Sherlock Holmes and Nene into my office and invited them to sit across from the mahogany desk. I had to keep reminding myself that I had a job to do. As law enforcers and officers, my team and I were trained from an early stage not to allow our emotions to interfere with the task at hand.

Still, it pained me to see my friends suffering like this, victims of this cold, premeditated crime. Even though my wife and I were blessed with two children, it was hard to imagine what Holmes and Nene must be going through. Can there be any grief greater than a parent losing their child, no matter the circumstances? Who can comprehend the raw emotion and say anything to soften the visceral blow? So let no man take it lightly because my men and I certainly did not. Like me, the great detective was keenly aware that in most abduction cases, the longer it took to find the victim, the odds of discovering them alive were greatly diminished. But by the look of things, Nicco Sapori's abduction was not your typical kidnapping.

I first met Irene Adler in 1895. It was the year that shaped my life and one I shall never forget for several reasons. I was promoted to inspector shortly after becoming engaged to the love of my life, the beautiful raven-haired Caterina Di Botti, a teacher at the Via Galvani school in Lombardy. I was introduced to Caterina at a dinner party the previous year, and there was an immediate attraction. I found her a delightful, witty woman with a magnetic personality and mesmerising hazel eyes. Caterina was five years younger than me at 33 and still single.

At the grand old age of 38, Salvatore Alberto Romano had given up on women and affairs of the heart. After a disastrous relationship in my youth, I decided to concentrate on my career, which left little time for romance. But then I met Caterina and fell deeply in love. We married in 1896 after a whirlwind, three-month courtship. Of course, this was just after Holmes and Adler's adventures in Fiesole with the late Colonel Moriarty, who was subsequently shot dead by my colleague from the Fiesole polizia, Inspector Carlos Montalabo, an old acquaintance now retired from the force. Montalabo was instrumental in developing my career. I worked alongside him as a rookie detective in my hometown of Parma, where I was born and raised, honing my craft until I was eventually promoted to chief inspector. Now, aged fifty, with a loving wife, two exceptional children, and ten officers working under me, I realised I had much to be thankful for.

The Whistle of Revenge

Fate destined me to cross paths once again with the Saporis. In 1905, when I investigated the attempted murder of Luigi Amato in Milan, Amato's wife Renatta was wrongly suspected of the attempted poisoning of her husband. Thanks to Holmes's remarkable abilities as a detective and with the assistance of Nene, who was confident of her friend's innocence, we brought the malevolent persons to justice. Holmes and I remained friends ever since. He wasn't a particularly social man, but we met up for the odd beer or glass of whiskey and recently had dinner together, hosted by my wife Caterina, at our villa in Duomo. Caterina and Nene shared a love of horses, and we would occasionally meet up at the San Siro Racetrack for an afternoon of racing and hospitality.

Our children, Carlo, aged nine, and Andrea, seven, adored Irene Adler, affectionately known as Nene to those closest to her. The children were captivated by her kindness, wit, and engaging personality. Generous to a fault, she remembered their birthdays and always sent cards and gifts at Christmas. She couldn't have been kinder.

As I came to know Holmes, I discovered some of his eccentricities. Most notably, his complete lack of interest in astronomy and astrology, or whether the world was round or flat, his wanton untidiness, and almost obsessive love of personal cleanliness, which Nene said drove her to distraction at times. While best known for his brilliant detective reasoning and crime-solving abilities, he was fascinated by how, throughout history, people could read the same thing yet have different perspectives. Towering over six feet, with a formidable presence and an unorthodox manner, the celebrated detective possessed an effortless confidence that commanded admiration. Were it in my power to grant eternal life, none would be more deserving than this peerless legend. He was a true Man of The Millennium and the finest detective of his age.

There had been others before him who were no match for

the man's genius, and indeed, others would follow in years to come, attempting to emulate his remarkable powers of observation. That's the thing about Holmes... he had a reserve that you never really penetrated, and as a consequence, you never knew what he was thinking or what was coming next.

Consequently, I came to have high regard and the utmost respect for the man I was proud to call my friend, even if he could only be acknowledged as Lucca Sapori. I felt privileged to be one of the few, along with my most trusted officers, who knew his undercover identity. How ironic that the celebrated detective was the first to discover my dark secret.

Contrary to my Catholic faith, I was ordained as a Freemason, even though Catholics were forbidden to join Masonic lodges since 1738. I was admitted as an apprentice by the Grand Master in 1901 at the request of my late father, Alberto. My mother, Georgiana, a staunch Catholic, raised me firmly in the orthodox church. My father's allegiance to the Masons did not fit in with her beliefs, causing many arguments. Mother sadly passed away from scarlet fever when I was ten, and my grief-stricken father never got over her demise. On his deathbed, Father made me promise on the Bible to carry on the doctrine.

He admired the ideals and ethics of the famous Italian general, Patron, and revolutionary Garibaldi. He was initiated in the lodge in Montevideo, where he retained the honorary title of Past Grand Master and remained active until he died in 1882.

My father, God bless his soul, was desperate for me, his only son, to continue the family tradition, so I reluctantly agreed. Even though my induction often blurred the lines between my public and private lives, as a dutiful son, I was determined to see it through and fulfil my father's dying wish. My involvement with the Masons had remained secret until six months ago when Holmes and I met for supper in the

Baronia Bar in the old town. Holmes was uncharacteristically late for our appointment, citing work pressure as an excuse for his tardiness.

I thanked him for coming and hoped I'd not kept him from anything pressing.

"Nothing that won't keep," Holmes replied, his eyes dancing in amusement. "I simply can't allow you to drink alone, old chap. Why, it's the first step to perdition."

We were enjoying our second whiskey when a fellow Mason entered the bar. I recognised him at once from the Masonic meetings. The man was Enzo Guiliano, a doctor from Legnano, a tall, slim fellow with black wavy hair and an English-style moustache. Enzo removed his hat and acknowledged my presence with a nod and a smile. I beckoned him over so as not to arouse suspicion. We chatted briefly, and I introduced him to Lucca Sapori. Enzo refused our invitation to sit and join us for supper, explaining he was just passing through, visiting relatives, and had only stopped at the inn for a glass of port.

When Enzo finished his drink, we said our farewells and shook hands. But the world-famous detective's eagle eyes hadn't missed a thing. After Enzo left the public house, the waiter finally served our food. Holmes remarked that he recognised *The Shibboleth Grip*, a handshake commonly used amongst fellow Masons. The shibboleth is similar to a regular handshake, except the Mason presses the top of his thumb against the space between his fellow Mason's first and second knuckle joints.

The secret to the Masonic handshake was not how it was given but what it represented—friendship, morality, and brotherly love. Holmes, of course, was aware of this, having had dealings in London with a fellow Mason, Jabez Wilson, in 1890. So, until then, Holmes joked he'd always associated the Masons with equestrian men. Far from being shocked, he appeared highly amused by my induction. Utterly unlike any person I had come across. I considered Holmes a sympathetic voice to reveal my secret. After I explained the link with my late father and how my allegiance to the Masons had come about, Holmes gave me what I imagined to be a smile and, to my great relief, promised never to speak of it again. When he slapped me on the back as we raised a toast to my late father, I knew I was in the shadow of a giant.

I'd seen it all in my career, fraudsters, rapists, paedophiles, drug gangs and murderers, but investigating Nicco Sapori's abduction as a law enforcer, father, and friend proved to be a traumatic experience. In its banality, this evil act reminded us that the most disturbing heinous crimes were often carried out not by monsters but by ordinary people driven by typical human traits, such as ambition, greed, or, in Stapleton's case, a misguided sense of worth and jejune self-entitlement. Caterina was devastated by what happened. She begged me to find the perpetrators, and I reassured her that my men were doing everything possible to bring the culprits to justice. Consequently, my wife and I hugged our children tighter at the end of each day.

Chapter Eighteen: Salvatore Romano
Giuda — Judas

I'd promised the Saporis that my men were beyond reproach, but as I had now discovered, there was at least one rotten apple in the barrel. Glancing downwards, a mountain of paperwork cast a long shadow over my desk. I pushed it to one side, then scooped it up, stuffing the papers into one of the filing cabinets before emptying the overflowing ashtray into a wastepaper bin.

"Forgive me," I said. "It appears my paperwork and tobacco ash have superiority over me."

I opened the drawer of my mahogany desk, pulling out a profile of Guardia Luigi Giarcosca dressed in full uniform. His black curly hair, dark penetrating eyes, and severe expression stared at me from his identity picture. I slid the profile over the desk towards Holmes.

"This is Guardia Luigi Giarcosca. My colleagues tell me he's been behaving erratically lately, spending money freely. Yet, he's a divorced man with gambling debts and the responsibility for the upkeep of two properties. While his ex-wife has custody of their child, he's expected to pay support for them both ... all this on a guardia's wage." I shook my head. "Giarcosca let slip to a colleague that he'd been doing a job on the side that pays well. My men have had him under surveillance for the past few days."

Our conversation was interrupted by Nene Adler. "Then why are we waiting, Salvatore? When will you stop speculating and interrogate this Giarcosca?" she asked, looking at me searchingly.

Despite our friendship, I sensed a strained formality, a distance between us. Behind that grace and indomitable spirit, Nene struggled to control her emotions. I hesitated momentarily, taking in her appearance. She looked desperately tired. White kid gloves covered her hands, which were continually fiddling with the blue silk scarf draped around her neck. Her eyes were red-rimmed from crying, yet a fearlessness about her was alluring. She remained heart-stoppingly beautiful.

I smiled at her reassuringly before continuing my narrative. "Giarcosca finished his shift half an hour ago. I asked him to come to the interview room because I needed his help." I turned my attention to Holmes. "I presume you would like to sit in on the interview?"

"Yes, Inspector, thank you. I take it this man was aware of our visit to the church this morning?"

I nodded. Holmes glanced over to Nene, speaking to her softly. "You look exhausted. I think it best you return home and rest. If you come with us, it will only evoke suspicion."

He leaned forward to take her hand, brushing a finger over her knuckles in a soothing motion. She took his hand in hers and squeezed, staring up at her husband with an expression of the utmost tenderness. Nene's unwavering belief in Holmes, sense of unity, and dogged determination to find their son were heart-wrenching. To me, a humble onlooker, this was a testament to the couple's incredible bond.

Nene agreed to her husband's request that she return home after promising to keep her updated on any fresh developments. I summoned one of my guardie to drive Signora Sapori back to her villa, ensuring she was safely ensconced in the carriage before Holmes and I made our way to interview room number two at the far end of the station, taking our seats in anticipation of Giarcosca's arrival.

Chapter Nineteen: Salvatore Romano
Doppio Gioco — Double Crossing

Giarcosca gazed at me questioningly, removing his helmet as he entered the room. I gestured for him to sit before introducing him to Lucca Sapori. "Signor Sapori is the father of the missing boy Nicco. We have reason to believe that you may have information as to the identity of the kidnappers?"

Giarcosca looked at me appalled, shaking his head. "I have no idea what you're talking about, Inspector. I swore to uphold the law, not break it. I can assure you that the poor child's disappearance has nothing to do with me."

"This extra job you've been bragging about, who are you working for?" I demanded, staring at Giarcosca suspiciously.

"You have it all wrong, Inspector. I'm not working for anyone. I have nothing to hide."

"Then, in that case, you won't object to me, Guardia Russo, and Signor Sapori, accompanying you to your house to search the premises?"

"No, why would I?" Giarcosca answered, flashing us an enigmatic smile. "We can go now if you wish. As I have just said, I have nothing to conceal."

Throughout our conversation, Holmes had uncharacteristically barely spoken. He sat on his chair, his fingers pressed together as though in deep concentration, no doubt digesting every word.

We arrived at Giarcosca's place in Centro Storico twenty-five minutes later. He lived on the first floor of a converted house, a rambling affair, which consisted of a lounge, kitchen, bathroom, and two bedrooms. The apartment was basically furnished save for an elegant chaise lounge littered with racing papers, which looked oddly out of place next to two battered armchairs and a long, low, occasional table cluttered with dirty glasses and several empty whiskey and beer bottles, standing next to a well-used pack of cards. A cheap blue woollen rug covered the tiled floor.

We entered the kitchen, which was messy and cluttered. It consisted of a sink, stove, and a small card table with four chairs. The potent aroma of stale smoke hung thickly in the air. The bedrooms were each adorned with wardrobes, chests of drawers, and matching bedsteads made from the finest African Blackwood. These items are out of reach for many, never mind someone surviving on a guardia's wage.

Russo searched the lounge and kitchen while Holmes and I concentrated on the bedrooms and bathroom, pulling out every drawer and inspecting all the cupboards and wardrobes. We found nothing sinister in the bathroom, only toiletries, towels, and a wet razor. It looked like we had a fruitless task until Holmes opened the wardrobe in the second bedroom to find four work shirts on hangers, an assortment of jackets and trousers, three pairs of shoes and boots, and a selection of ties hanging on a hook.

Holmes' darting glances alerted me to his sudden interest as he asked to borrow my torch. Then, tapping the bottom of the wardrobe with his cane, we heard a hollow sound coming from a loose, misaligned panel. Holmes prised open the seam with a jackknife to reveal a secret compartment, concealing a shoe box.

He scrutinised it, finally removing the lid and taking out the pair of Italian leather shoes inside to reveal both were stuffed with notes and coins amounting to around a thousand lira. The box was nestled directly beneath a guardia's blue uniform, which was damp, dusty, and heavily stained. Holmes's shocking discovery immediately eradicated the self-assured smile on Giarcosca's face.

During briefings at the station, I instilled into my men that to get to the truth, one had to ask the right questions. And no one did this better than the celebrated detective.

As the atmosphere in the room became increasingly tense, Holmes only asked one question regarding Giarcosca with a sceptical eye. "When did you last wear this?" he asked, frowning as he pointed to the uniform.

Giarcosca took a nervous gulp of air and shifted uncomfortably as the detective's penetrating eyes burned through him. "A few days ago, I put my spare uniform in here to remind me that it needs valeting and a trip to the tailors, as I carelessly lost a button," Giarcosca spluttered, giving me a perplexed stare. His face flushed crimson as Holmes reached into the pocket of the uniform jacket and pulled out a black mask.

"Ah, Inspector, we would appear to have found the driver who was instrumental in abducting my son."

"I'm sorry," Giarcosca said, with bowed head and lowered eyes. "But I was a desperate man," his voice trailed off, observing Holmes's baleful stare.

"What about the money," I asked. "Who gave it to you? Don't insult my intelligence by telling me you won it playing poker or backed a winner at the races."

Giarcosca stood before us, his hands nervously gripping the dressing table, and a slight shudder became apparent throughout his body. He uttered two words, "Emilio Rodriguez."

There was a knowing glance of recognition as Holmes and I turned to face each other. Reaching into my pocket, I pulled out the silver button retrieved from the coach, holding the navy serge material toward the light streaming through the window. It was a perfect match.

Chapter Twenty: Nicco Sapori
in Movimento – On the Move

I stared out of the carriage window as we continued our journey, and the horses broke into a steady trot, trying not to alert Gino's attention. From the position of the night sky, I figured we were heading in a north-easterly direction and roughly estimating the speed of the coach and time travel, we would be around six miles from Saint Monica, and that being the case, this meant we would be approximately three miles from Milan city centre.

Due to the lack of any outside noise, with the hustle and bustle of the city and The World Fair now in the background, we were on our way to somewhere quiet and unassuming in the northeastern region of Lombardy.

I must have dozed off for a few minutes. When I opened my eyes, the coach travelled along a quiet country road. The only sound was from the horse's hooves and an owl hooting in the distance. The coach veered off to the left until we were on a long, winding lane. Before us stood an imposing white stone-detached farmhouse surrounded by various outbuildings, sheds, and open fields, with silhouettes of several horses grazing in the meadow.

The coach pulled up in front of two wrought iron gates that closed the driveway entrance. They were bronze casts of two Neapolitan horses welded to them.

A mysterious figure dressed in black suddenly appeared to open the gates. He waited until the coach eased further into the driveway before closing the gates behind us and disappearing into the stables next to the house. A large hound resembling a Neapolitan mastiff sat at the edge of the drive with its loose skin and distinctive wrinkles. It barked as our carriage drove past, culminating in a deep-chested growl. I felt relieved that its master had chained the beast to the wall.

Gino helped me out of the carriage, and that's when I noticed the establishment's sign swinging in the gentle night breeze above the flickering gas lights. Unfortunately, tarpaulin covered the sign, hiding its name and location, yet despite this, the place seemed vaguely familiar. I felt a sense of deja vu, as if I'd been here before.

Gino ushered me towards a side door, and within moments, we were met by a man I didn't recognise, a tall fellow with dark, shoulder-length hair. He gestured to Gino to follow him, not uttering a word to either of us. We walked through a large kitchen until we found ourselves in an imposing wood-panelled hallway, its highly polished walls covered with ornate multi-coloured rugs, holding console tables with vases of summer flowers, and a red couch with gold trimmings set in the corner.

We continued off to the right to a sweeping staircase leading to the first floor of the building. We passed what appeared to be a trophy room, its door ajar, displaying a vast array of glittering trophies in glass cabinets. They glittered in the glare of the moonlight shining in from the window. Gino and I followed the man into a large, well-appointed room on the right. I glanced around, realising that this was my second prison, although the surroundings were much more amenable than the vaults of Saint Monica Church, as Gino predicted.

A large double bed was in the centre of the room, with a mahogany bedstead covered with a green counterpane and matching curtains that hung from the two windows, their views blocked by thick wooden shutters. Both windows bolted to the inside with bars running across, no doubt to stop me from escaping. In the middle of the room sat a large mahogany wardrobe and a matching chest of drawers, a marble wash hand basin with soap, a toothbrush, and a toilet closet set in the corner with white hand towels hanging from a hook on the wall. The silent man handed the key to Gino before turning around and leaving the room.

"Don't mind him, Nicco, he's a deaf-mute," Gino explained. "Why, young Giovanni, I can't believe your good fortune. You have landed at the Ritz." He laughed, slapping me on the shoulder.

Gino opened the wardrobes and the chest of drawers to reveal an assortment of clothes, and although not new, they were all in pristine condition. Amongst the collection were underwear, nightwear, a pair of slippers, and a dressing gown, all more or less my size. Whoever had organised this appeared to have gone to a lot of trouble. Two shelves within the wardrobe contained various books, including a *Game of Goose* board. On the bedside table sat two taper candles, a jug of fresh lemonade, a mug, a plate of biscotti, and panettone.

I shifted slightly on the embroidered chair, glancing towards the window. However, it revealed only darkness, turning my attention back to Gino, who lingered awkwardly by the bedside table, casting me a furtive glance.

"I wonder where the bell is for room service," Gino said, picking up a slice of panettone and devouring it hungrily.

"Tell me, Gino, I'd wager you're a family man who understands the importance of loyalty. One does not betray family, does one?"

Gino shifted uncomfortably, his eyes darting around the room. "We do what we must," he muttered. "It's a harsh world we live in. Much more challenging for some than others." He paused, glancing at the door as if in fear someone might overhear. "I have a wife and children. Of course, my family is important to me. I would do anything to protect them."

"True," I nodded, studying Gino furtively. I leaned forward, my eyes narrowing shrewdly. "Well, it will be the same for my parents. They will be worrying, wouldn't you agree? Surely, you could give me a clue as to where we are so I know I may be close to them. It's not as thorough I can escape."

Gino's face tightened, and he stepped back, regarding me with a look that conveyed sympathy and fear. "Not now, Giovanni," he stammered. "I wouldn't want to give you the wrong idea of me, but it would be more than my life's worth to divulge our whereabouts. You're safe and comfortable enough here, aren't you?"

"Indeed," I replied, leaning back thoughtfully. "But I suspect there are others here who question the wisdom of my enforced incarceration." Looking directly into Gino's eyes, I uttered, "Perhaps I'm not the only one who would feel relieved if my parents took me off your hands?"

Gino hesitated. "Listen, Giovanni," he whispered. "I'm not heartless. I don't like seeing you here, if truth be told. But Connie is of a callous, unforgiving nature. I'd sooner cross the devil than get on the wrong side of her. I wish it were different." He sighed. "But sadly, there's no way out of here until the ransom is paid. That's all I will say on the matter, so please, no more questions. One word to the wrong person, and even I won't be able to protect you. It's best to keep quiet about such things, little soldier."

I studied Gino for a moment, his gaze sharp and not missing a beat. With a nod of acknowledgement, he gave me a wry smile.

"I shall take your caution to heart," I replied.

"I must go now, but I'll return in the morning, hopefully with news of your release. I'm confident we're much closer to receiving the ransom, which will resolve the situation for everyone. In the meantime, get some rest. It's not too tricky in that comfortable-looking bed, eh?"

After Gino left the room, locking the door behind him. I sat on the bed, comforted by his words and new surroundings. I wondered if my father had reached my first hiding place and found the book containing the clues.

In the meantime, I vowed to make the best of my situation. After getting back up, I splashed my face in the sink's water, removed my dirty clothes, and washed myself as best I could. Opening the chest of drawers to retrieve the pyjamas, I furrowed my brow as I heard something rattle. I pushed my hand into the back of the drawer and discovered a hand-held electric torch surrounded by a sturdy metal casing similar to the type used by law enforcement officers. I examined it closely, and the battery was in place. I prayed it wasn't a dud before flicking the switch.

To my great relief, the torch worked perfectly, shining a bright amber glow across the room. Afraid my find would be discovered, I switched off the torch, concealing it under the back of the wardrobe, before pulling on the pyjamas and crawling into bed. I burrowed my head into the comforting softness of the plush pillow, falling into a deep slumber within moments, totally exhausted from the night's events.

Chapter Twenty-One: Nicco Sapori
Scacco Matto — Checkmate

Gino returned the following morning with breakfast, carrying a leather satchel over his left shoulder. I stared at him curiously as he opened the bag to reveal an old wooden chess set.

The subject of chess came up during yesterday's conversation. Gino boasted that his father taught him to play and asked if I would be interested in a game. I accepted, saying I would do anything to pass the time and alleviate the monotony. Gino said he'd spoken to the boss, who I presumed was Connie, and after a little subtle persuasion, she finally permitted him to bring in the set.

We laid the pieces on the table before sitting down to play. I couldn't believe my luck when Gino pulled out a small commemorative religious medal from his pocket, turning it over in his hand. The medal bore a Pope Pius X head on one side and a church on the reverse. Gino flipped the coin to determine who would play white and have the advantage of starting first. Gino tossed the coin into the air, calling heads. It spun around before falling to the floor, landing head downwards at my feet.

Picking up the coin, I quickly examined it, noticing an engraving of San Giuliano Church on the reverse before returning it to its proud owner. I wondered if the church on the medal could help identify the location where I was being held. Gino appeared to be religious. He wore a gold chain and a crucifix around his neck and would likely attend mass and

The Whistle of Revenge

confession at one of the local churches, if my suspicions were correct. As the game got underway, we heard the musical ringing of a church clock chiming eleven times. The sound was reminiscent of a church near my home.

I diverted my gaze to Gino, staring at him curiously. "The bells sound like a clock I'm familiar with, the sound of Chiesa di San Giovanni striking the hour," I said, my heart in my mouth, hoping that Gino would take the bait.

Gino looked up at me, a wry smile on his face. "No, Nicco, you are wrong. It's the San Guiliano," he replied, fixing his gaze back towards the chessboard, appearing eager to make his next move.

San Guiliano was close to a livery stable where my mother used to take me and my sister Charlotte. However, I couldn't remember the stable's name for my life. I pondered how I could get this information to my parents.

Gino played far better than I expected for a simple man. Still, sadly, he was no match for the intellectual reasoning and deductive prowess I'd inherited from my father and uncle.

Nevertheless, aware that I needed to stay in Gino's good books and gain his trust, I played strategically, giving him a good game and finally allowing him to checkmate my king. Gino chuckled in amusement and thanked me, wishing me better luck next time before venturing outside for a cigarette break, leaving the chess set behind for me to amuse myself.

I was engrossed in a solitairy game of chess when I heard the key turn in the lock. I looked up, expecting to see Gino. Instead, the woman, identified as Connie, entered the room, followed by a man of middle age, slim build, and medium height. He wore a tweed suit, a white shirt with a starched collar, and a blue tie. His salt and pepper hair was brushed back from his face, revealing two dazzling blue eyes that smiled at me in amusement from behind a pair of horn-rimmed glasses.

"Good morning, Nicco. I trust you slept well? Allow me to introduce myself. My name is Bob."

I stared at him defiantly. "You need to let me go before the polizia find you. What did my family do to make you want to punish them this way?"

Bob threw back his head and laughed. "I have no argument with your mother, Nicco, but as for your father, let's just say he and I have unfinished business. Our paths crossed before you were even born. I have waited a long time . . . since eighteen-eighty-nine, nearly seventeen years, to punish him for what he did."

I shook my head, staring at Bob, perplexed. "I don't understand. My father is a good man. He would never hurt anyone intentionally. Why are you lying?"

Bob sighed. "Sadly, I speak the truth, Nicco. The story is far too tangled to go into now. All you need to know is that your father was instrumental in ruining my life. But please don't worry. I have no intention of hurting you. Your abduction is purely a business transaction, nothing more, nothing less. When your parents pay the ransom, you can return home. On that, you have my word."

"Your word," I retorted. "How on earth can you expect me to trust you?"

Bob gave a tight-lipped smile that didn't quite reach his eyes. "Ah, there's the rub, Nicco. You seem like an intelligent kid. You see, I don't expect anything other than the ransom, and to be frank, I don't care. If I have caused your father a fraction of the angst he caused me all those years ago, then my job is done." Bob's eyes narrowed. "I'm responsible for some terrible misdeeds, Nicco, and have experienced some unimaginable horrors, but as God is my witness, I have never hurt a child. Pedicide is not my thing. Although, if your father were here right now, that would be different. He's responsible for everything, you see, the death of my wife and child,

The Whistle of Revenge

everything lost because of him. The irony is your father believes I'm dead. However, as you can see, son, I'm not so easy to kill."

"I'm not your son," I cried, flashing Bob a hateful stare. "And if I were, I would be ashamed to call you father. Real men don't lay their hands on women or children." A shiver went down my spine as those dazzling blue eyes that twinkled a few moments ago now looked upon me with a glare as cold as ice.

His tone measured and calculating, now turned dark and sinister. "I hope not to inconvenience you for too long, Nicco. On the contrary, we hope to restore your liberty soon. The irony is you would be free now if your father hadn't interfered and involved Inspector Romano and the polizia, so I'm afraid you have him to thank for your prolonged incarceration."

I stared at Bob hard, trying to take in every detail. "When do you expect the ransom?" I asked with a faux bravado.

"Within the week. However, I shall be in touch with your father before then to remind him that this isn't a game. In the meantime, is there anything you would like me to relay to your parents on your behalf? Something only they and you would know, Nicco?"

I nodded, trying to think of something that would give a further clue to my father without arousing suspicion. "Yes, thank you. Please tell my parents that I love them and wish I could be with them this weekend. We were due to walk Uncle Toby's nature trail, an event we were very much looking forward to as a family. Will that suffice?" I asked, staring at Bob anxiously, although the thought of my father following a nature trail made me smile inwardly.

"Perfect, Nicco, that's a good choice. Your father will realise we would have no way of being privy to that information. I suggest you make the most of your new surroundings.

You'll continue to be treated well during your stay, just as long as you don't try any funny business. Gino may come across as an amenable fool, but you don't want to get on the wrong side of him." Bob nodded to Connie before turning around and leaving my prison.

Connie's grey eyes glanced around the room. She wore a brown dress and jacket. Her hair was tied up in a knot beneath a straw hat with a green velvet ribbon, and a pair of brown leather boots complemented the outfit. My heart was in my mouth as Connie walked over to the wardrobe and drawers. She thoroughly inspected the contents with a bemused expression, checking under the bed and pillows until she finally appeared satisfied.

"Do as Bob asked, and all will be well," she hissed. "But if you don't, and you try to cross us . . ." She added menacingly, making a throat-slashing gesture as she stared straight into my eyes with a bone-chilling gaze. "Then never mind underestimating Gino. You will have me to answer to. Test me at your peril."

Then, without another word, Connie turned on her heels and flounced out of the room, locking the door behind her. I heaved a sigh of relief that at least the torch remained undiscovered.

Connie and Bob's presence had created so many unanswered questions. I had a hunch that Bob wasn't the man's real name, but he was giving nothing away. How did Bob know my father, and what happened all those years ago to make him hate him so much? If the events had occurred as he said, then Bob must surely know my father as Sherlock Holmes. Father told me in confidence that he only took over the identity of Lucca Sapori seven years ago, in 1899, after he reunited with my mother when they subsequently re-married in Milan.

My father often recounted a few of his most famous cases

when we were alone together, others I read about in Doctor John Watson's chronicles in *The Strand Magazine*. I couldn't think of anyone at liberty or still alive capable of such extremities unless it was the unthinkable or the unbelievable. Jack Stapleton, the deadly antagonist from *The Hound of The Baskervilles*, was regarded as one of my father's most exciting and intriguing cases.

Still, Stapleton was supposed to have perished all those years ago in the Great Grimpen Mire. I shook my head. No, it couldn't be him unless he returned as a ghost. Like my father, I didn't believe in such entities. There had to be another logical explanation. Then I remembered the date Bob mentioned, 1889, almost seventeen years ago, the year John Mortimer asked my father to investigate the suspicious death of his dear friend Sir Charles Baskerville, who died from a heart attack in the Yew Valley of his estate, Baskerville Hall on Dartmoor.

My blood turned cold at the thought Bob could be Jack Stapleton — this wolf in sheep's clothing. From what Father told me and what I read, Stapleton and Bob would be around the same age. But what would he be doing here in Milan if that were the case? It wasn't just illogical, and it seemed highly improbable.

My thoughts were interrupted by Gino entering the room, flashing an enigmatic smile. "I feel bad for beating you, little soldier. How about a rematch?" he asked, his eyes brimming with confidence as they diverted to the chessboard.

"Why not?" I shrugged, smiling resignedly, as I helped Gino set up the board for the second time.

Chapter Twenty-Two: Nene Adler
il Ritorno del Prodigo – The Prodigal Returns

The guardia dropped me off at the villa, which I was surprised to find empty, except for Helen, our foundling dog. She bounded over to greet me, wagging her tail and looking up at me expectantly as I stroked her silky head. Then I remembered it was Ginevra's half-day, and Alice had gone to the market to order our fruit, vegetables, and meat supplies for the coming week. I was still desperately tired but determined to stay awake in case there was any news from Sherlock and Salvatore after they interrogated Guardia Giarcosca.

I felt melancholy as I entered the kitchen, pouring a cup of Cafe Noir and re-filling Helen's water bowl before unlocking the kitchen door to let her run out into the garden. I inhaled the fresh Tuscan breeze cutting through the olive trees, taking in the delicate scents of the beautiful summer flowers. The almond tree that Nicco loved so much now burst into a cloud of white blossoms, its branches filled with the incessant buzz of the honeybees as they pollinated the tree. Since Nicco's abduction, I found it hard to breathe at times because the pain was so intense.

I'd overheard Ginevra and Alice deep in conversation about what had happened to Nicco only yesterday morning. Inevitably, they whispered words such as shock and disapproval of his abduction. The kindness and empathy in their voices reduced me to tears. I splashed cold water on my face from the kitchen tap, gazing at my woeful image in the overhead mirror. The woman reflected there was unrecognisable, a shadow of her former self. Dark circles under my eyes had been dimmed by grief. My usual healthy glowing skin, tinged grey.

Later, as I sat in the drawing room, sipping from my coffee cup, I contemplated taking Helen for a walk. The poor creature had hardly eaten these past few days. She was pining for the children, and I, of all people, could relate to that.

A knock at the front door disturbed my thoughts. I furrowed my brow since I wasn't expecting anyone. The servants and Sherlock had their keys unless Salvatore sent one of his guardie with news to convey. I answered the door with some trepidation.

My hammering heart almost burst when I saw Hildegard standing on the doorstep before me. I stared at her in disbelief, mixed with a surge of anger and outrage that she had the audacity to come here, this woman I had trusted implicitly and who was complicit in abducting our son. Her demeanour had an expression of the utmost sadness and regret etched upon her face, which was drawn and had a deathly pallor. Her once sparkling eyes had lost their lustre. She sighed, glancing down at her trembling hand, which clutched an envelope.

Hildegard, visibly disturbed, took a deep breath. "We urgently need to talk," she said quietly.

As she spoke, anger and loathing consumed me as I considered her utmost disrespect for my feelings and the betrayal of our friendship. But behind those words she spoke came a ray of hope. Was she here to confess and beg for forgiveness? For an awkward and uneasy moment, time stood still, waiting for a break in the contrasting tension between us.

Swallowing the bile that rose in the back of my throat and forcing my voice to remain calm, I uttered, "You dare show yourself here after all that's transpired?" My voice trembled despite my effort to keep calm. "Tell me, Hildegard, what message would you convey that might begin to explain yourself?"

She flinched, her gaze flitting from my face to the crumpled envelope she was clinging to before reverting to my face. She held the note as though it could shield her from my wrath. I held her with my unyielding gaze, demanding that she answer and confirm what I already thought I knew.

Chapter Twenty-Three: Nene Adler
Penitenza — Pentenence

As if in a trance, I ushered Hildegard inside. After I agreed to her request for a glass of water, she followed me into the kitchen and inner hallway until we were finally seated in the drawing room.

Hildegard was dressed simply in a powder blue dress, matching jacket, and hat, with broderie anglaise edging her hair, which was tied up in a neat knot. She placed the envelope down on the coffee table. I noticed the writer had addressed the envelope to Signor Lucca Sapori. It was typewritten, and from the looks of it, from an old *Remmington* machine, as the print was similar to one Nicco and Charlotte used to correspond with their friend, Francesco, in Fiesole.

"Where is Nicco?" I demanded, looking Hildegard straight in the eyes.

She returned my gaze, placing her hand on mine, flinching as I pushed it away. "Your son is safe, Nene. I promise he was taken by a man calling himself Robert Barrett, although I doubt that's his real name," she said with a resentful tone. "Please believe me when I tell you that I'm so sorry for the heartache and worry I was instrumental in causing you and your husband. But you must heed what I tell you, for we are dealing with an extremely dangerous individual. A man with a treacherous heart."

"But why would he do such a wicked thing? And what hold does this man have over you? Why are you protecting him?"

Our conversation was interrupted by the sound of Helen barking. I turned and gasped as I saw my husband's tall, astute, familiar figure standing motionless in the doorway. His eyes fixated on us as he digested every word—an expression of the utmost gravity on his face. Sherlock walked purposefully towards us, sitting on the couch across from Hildegard, pursing his lips in contemplation, his gaze stilted in suspicion.

"Do you know where my son is?" Sherlock asked in a sharp but concise tone. I could see he was having trouble keeping his composure.

Hildegard shook her head. "No, sir, I'm sorry, I don't, although Robert promised Nicco was safe and that no harm would come to him. He will return your son to you as soon as the ransom is paid."

"And you believed him," I scoffed.

"My patience is exhausted," Sherlock said. "You must tell me everything about this man, where you met, and how. I need every detail, no matter how trivial."

"All right," Hildegard agreed. "Then I will do as you ask and start from the beginning." She took a breath, wiping a tear from her eye, taking a sip of water before continuing her narrative. "I first met the man known as Robert Barrett around a year ago, just before I started working for you, Signor and Signora Sapori. With my husband gone, I sometimes felt lonely. I even contemplated going home to Germany and begging for my mother's forgiveness.

"Then, I saw the governess position advertised in the local paper, and I decided to apply after discovering that my friend Emilia worked for Signor and Signora Moon. Emilia promised to vouch for me and put in a good word, although there was no need due to the impeccable references forwarded from my previous employers. I was elated after a successful interview and meeting with Charlotte and Nicco. The following day, I ventured out to the post office to post the formal acceptance of your kind offer of employment and a letter to my mother informing her of my new position, hoping she would look upon me more favourably. On the way back to my apartment, I called into the library to return two books.

"I remember asking the librarian if she could recommend a suitable title on botany, as it's a subject I've always been fascinated by, along with wildlife and birds. Still, before she could respond, our conversation was cut short by a man of middle age, introducing himself as Robert Barrett. I noticed him staring at me earlier with a puzzled expression. He apologised for interrupting but said he couldn't help but overhear our conversation and felt compelled to speak to me, a fledgling botanist. Before I knew what he was about, he beckoned me to a nearby section on botany and plants, pulling out a book entitled *The Poetical Language of Flowers* by Thomas Miller. He told me it was the best in the library and one he would highly recommend.

"We ended up having a lengthy conversation about books and nature. I found him to have great charisma. One thing led to another, and he invited me to afternoon tea. Later, we walked together in the park. Robert paid scant interest in my life story. I remember his curiosity piqued when I mentioned my mother was a retired concert pianist and told him of my new position with Irene Adler, the acclaimed contralto.

"Admittedly, thinking back, it was rather odd. Still, despite the age gap, I admired Robert so much that I brushed my concerns aside."

"Did this man attempt to make love to you?" Sherlock asked, stretching out his long legs and leaning forward in his seat, staring at Hildegard with a curious expression.

I arched an eyebrow and gasped, thinking it was an impertinent question, even for my husband. However, I shuddered at the thought of Hildegard being intimate with Nicco's abductor. I felt sick at the prospect.

Hildegard shook her head, seemingly unflustered by Sherlock's question. "No, Signor Sapori, apart from an occasional chaste kiss, nothing physical developed between us. Robert made it clear that he was a widower who had not yet come to terms with the tragic death of his wife."

"Did he say how his wife died?"

"No, and I never asked. Robert didn't discuss it. However, I was hopeful Robert's feelings would deepen as time evolved and we could continue our relationship more intimately. I remember being disappointed when he told me he was due to leave Milan within a few days to continue working at his bloodstock agency in Ireland. He said he had much to do before returning to Milan the following year. Robert promised to keep in touch by letter, and true to his word, he wrote to me every month, asking me how I was getting on with my new position, what the Sapori family and children were up to, etc. I assumed he expressed a friendly interest, so I thought nothing of it until he returned." She smiled bitterly.

"Do you still have the letters?" Sherlock asked.

Hildegard shook her head. "I'm afraid not. Robert asked me to burn all correspondence immediately after I read them. I was not to show them to anyone else without exception. When I questioned this, he said he had enemies, people who wished him dead. He had no wish for any harm to come to me. Reluctantly, I agreed to his request. I burned all the letters, just as he asked." She paused momentarily, reaching into her bag and pulled out an envelope with an Irish postmark and a folded drawing paper. "Except for this one. This is the first letter Robert sent to me. I couldn't bear to destroy it, so I kept it hidden in my bedroom all this time. When I left the other day, I put the letter in my bag with this sketch drawing I made of Robert last year, thinking I could use them as leverage or hand them to the polizia if needed."

"May I see?" Sherlock said, gesturing to the letter and the

drawing.

"Yes, of course," Hildegard reached over, placing the letter and sketch into Sherlock's palm.

My husband's eyes widened as he glanced at the contents. "Tell me when this man arrived back in Milan? When did you first see him?"

"I heard from Robert four weeks ago. He sent a note, and we arranged our first rendezvous in the park. At the start, he was his usual charming, affable self. But then, after some time, Robert's demeanour suddenly changed, like he carried the world upon his shoulders. He became distant and aloof, his behaviour bordering on obsessive at times. I noticed that he'd developed a manipulative nature and became ill-tempered, demanding to know Nicco's every move. I knew then that something wasn't right.

"When I tried to end our friendship, telling him I wasn't prepared to divulge any further personal information about the Sapori family, that was when Robert's mood became acrimonious. In my letters, I had foolishly told him about my estrangement from my mother and her underlying health issues. I'd even given away her address. Robert used that to his advantage. You see, he had contacts in Germany, and Robert threatened they would hurt my mother if I didn't do as he asked. He said one word from him, and his agents would ensure my mother never played the piano again. So, you see, I had no choice. I felt trapped by his manipulation."

"Tell me, why did Barret pick the night of the recital at La Scala to abduct our son? It could only have been you who alerted him," Sherlock said, his manner brusque.

I felt a sliver of sympathy for Hildegard as her face paled and then crumpled at Sherlock's words. She buried her head in her hands and wept, her entire body shaking.

An uncomfortable minute passed before she continued. "Yes, it was me," she admitted through tears, her voice hoarse and intense.

"I realise this will be challenging and difficult for you, but pray tell me exactly what happened," Sherlock said.

Hildegard wiped her eyes with a handkerchief before continuing. "On the day of the abduction, I called into the pharmacy to pick up the laudanum. Then, I met Robert in the park after receiving his note that morning. He apologised for his behaviour and threats, begging me for forgiveness, explaining he was under pressure from evil people and had no intention of hurting anyone. He appeared genuinely remorseful, so I agreed to his request to join him for luncheon at the Albany Hotel, where we spent an engaging afternoon. Robert admitted he'd developed feelings for me and suggested we become engaged once he sorted out his affairs and business arrangements."

"And did you accept him?"

Hildegard shot Sherlock a tense smile, appearing hesitant to meet his eyes. "Must I answer that question.? This is all rather embarrassing."

Sherlock closed his eyes and said, "A simple yes or no will suffice."

Hildegard shook her head. "No, sir, I may have been infatuated, perhaps a little tipsy, but I hadn't taken leave of my senses. I gently turned down Robert's half-hearted proposal."

"You must know this man has no intention of honouring his promise," Sherlock said.

Hildegard nodded. "My mother once told me *you have to like the person you become when you give your heart to someone.*"

"Your mother gave you good advice. So what happened next?" Sherlock asked.

"Robert took the news remarkably well when I explained how I needed more time to consider him as a suitor and potential husband. He plied me with wine, and our afternoon continued with coffee and brandy. Then, intoxicated by the wine, I'm afraid I foolishly gave away how excited Nicco was at the prospect of visiting La Scala and seeing his idol Caruso later that evening, but, unfortunately, due to illness, his father, Signor Sapori, was unable to accompany his wife and son as planned. Robert appeared thrilled with the news. There was a gleam in those dazzling blue eyes, but I swear to God that I would never have said anything if I'd known for one second of his dastardly plan.

"The next day, when I suspected Robert had abducted Nicco, I was mortified and realised that I alone was responsible for your son's disappearance. I had to find a way to find Nicco and bring him home. I'm ashamed to say that I couldn't face you, so I slipped back into the villa while you were interviewing Alice and Ginevra in the drawing room with Inspector Romano. I quickly ran upstairs, threw a few things in my valise, and made a reservation at a small hotel under an assumed name.

"Then, I returned to the park the following day to meet Robert again as planned. But there was no sign of him. I was about to make my way to the police station to give myself up when a boy approached, handing over an envelope with a note inside. It was from Robert instructing me to meet him at eight that night at The Excelsior Hotel, where he'd made a reservation under the name of Guippea Bianchi." Hildegard rolled her eyes. "Which I suspect is one of his many pseudonyms. When I got to the room, there was no sign of any luggage or personal effects that one would expect from a hotel guest. Instead, I found Robert sitting alone on a chair in the dark, the room illuminated by a single taper candle set in the corner, and a cigarette that he held in one hand, a glass of whiskey in the other. A chill ran down my spine observing his thunderous glare, and the evil glint in those cold staring eyes."

"And then what happened?" I asked impatiently.

Hildegard furrowed her brow and gave another slight nod. "What followed was a heated altercation. I told Robert about the letter and threatened to alert the authorities. He laughed aloud and told me the polizia would never find him or Nicco if I did that. He said the machinations of what he'd set in motion would outwit everyone, even the polizia. I calmed down a little after Robert gave me a glass of water and promised Nicco was safe and would be back with his family as soon as the Saporis paid the ransom. He even showed me a photo of Nicco reading a book.

"Robert explained he was no murderer of infants. He was only going to such extremities because the businesses were failing, and his partner at the bloodstock agency wasn't exactly renowned for his business acumen. Robert owed money to despicable people who threatened his life. He said he would leave Milan when he had the money, and no one would be any the wiser. Although I didn't believe him, I suspected there was much more to it than his narrative." Hildegard picked up the envelope on the coffee table, handing it to my husband. "This is for you, Signor Sapori."

Sherlock stared at the envelope curiously. "Ah, a message from the enemy. I suspect these are the details of the pick-up. The abductors said they would send word, or a note, telling us where to drop off the ransom." He stared questioningly at Hildegard.

"Yes, sir." She smiled dryly. "I fear I have been used as Robert's courier. I can only apologise for that."

Grasping the envelope in both hands, Sherlock tentatively lifted the sealed edge and pulled out a piece of thick white embossed writing paper. Perfectly formed typewritten words filled the page. I waited with bated breath as my husband paused momentarily before reading the letter out loud.

"Signor Sapori, thanks to you and Inspector Romano's meddling, ten thousand lira is no longer enough. If you want to see your son again, the worth of his life is now twelve thousand lira. This money compensates for out-of-pocket expenses and the inconvenience of moving the boy. I'm so disappointed that your cavalier actions have led to this. Of course, this could have been avoided if you had stuck to the original plan and not involved the polizia as instructed. I will contact you again shortly with further details on how and when you can pay the ransom. You can see how easy it was to get to your family. I'm not part of Signor Sapori's story. On the contrary, you are part of mine. To prove we are not entirely heartless, here is a message from your son."

"*My dearest father and mother, I want you to know I love you very much. I remain well and look forward to seeing you soon. In the meantime, please wish Uncle Toby all the best at the nature trail this weekend. I wish I could be there with you all to celebrate as a family.*

"*Your loving son,*

"*Nicco.*"

I digested my son's words with a furrowed brow. We had no such relative named Toby. My head was swirling with a thousand images, wondering why Nicco had singled out Toby. Who was he? I couldn't recall any of Nicco's friends with that name. My thoughts were interrupted by Sherlock as he continued narrating the letter.

"Remember to keep looking over your shoulder, Signor Sapori. Although you will never find me, I will be there watching. I don't care if you do involve polizia again. I'm a lot smarter than they'll ever be, but be warned, if you do necessitate a third party, then expect the hell's wrath of Janus."

The bottom of the page was peppered with quotes. The first was from *The Count of Monte Cristo*. "For all the evils, there are two remedies-time and silence." Followed by, "Shylock says, If you prick us, do we not bleed? And if you wrong us, shall we not revenge?"

Sherlock looked at me with an ashen face as the blood

drained from his face.

"Sherlock, I think Nicco is trying to give us a clue as to where he's being kept, but I have no idea what he means by Toby. What about the abductor? Do you know the identity of this man?"

"Yes." Sherlock sighed deeply. "I know with absolute certainty who this man is."

Chapter Twenty-Four: Nene Adler
La Rivelazione — The Revelation

After what seemed like an eternity, Sherlock finally regained his composure, ordering Hildegard to rest upstairs so we could speak more freely. First, he explained it would be unsafe for her to return to the hotel, promising to contact the concierge and arrange for any luggage to be dropped off at the villa later that day. Hildegard stared at Sherlock as though about to protest. Then, a look of deep gratitude infused her face. My husband's overall demeanour and divisive tone must have made her think twice, and she agreed to his request, thanking us both for keeping her safe before retiring to her room.

Once Hildegard was safely upstairs, Sherlock called Salvatore, filling him in on the chain of events.

I stared at my husband as he carefully replaced the receiver on its hook. "Well, are you now ready to reveal the identity of this man, this monster who took our son?"

Sherlock nodded, looking at me grim-faced. "His real name is Jack Stapleton. You may remember me telling you about him, the man I revealed as a cunning adversary in my investigations for Sir Henry Baskerville at Dartmoor many years ago."

"You mean the same man Doctor Watson describes in his chronicles as the Keeper of The Hound of The Baskervilles?" I gasped, looking at my husband in disbelief. "Sherlock, this cannot be. Stapleton's dead. You told me so yourself."

"He was presumed dead by the police. However, the body

was never found. Stapleton recognised every inch of that moor. He knew it like the back of his hand. During all my years as a detective, I have rarely encountered a more dangerous adversary. At the time of the Baskerville case, Watson and I agreed that we seldom met an antagonist more deserving of our steel."

"So Jack Stapleton, a known felon and man of dubious character, vanishes into thin air on the Great Grimpen Mire, Dartmoor, presumed dead, and somehow emerges years later as a bloodstock agent in Ireland. Why, it beggars belief that this could be the same man as Hildegard's admirer and our son's kidnapper," I said.

"But if we look closely, the facts are all there, Nene. Stapleton is a master of disguise and not averse to using various pseudonyms, making him a formidable adversary."

"But, what of his wife? Wasn't she alive when you last encountered her?"

"Yes, indeed, she was very much so. I remember Beryl Stapleton well. She was a slim, elegant lady with a curious lisp, but, of course, that was years ago, seventeen if my memory serves me well. But we will find out if she's still alive. I'll wire Mycroft and make enquiries. With the help of Lestrade, they will get to the bottom of what became of Beryl Stapleton." Sherlock took my hand in his, staring intensely into my eyes. "You have been blaming yourself all this time for our son's abduction, and all the while, it was because of me that Nicco was taken. If anything happens to him, I will never be able to forgive myself."

I put my arms around my husband. "Sherlock, this is no more your fault than mine. As you said, we're dealing with a dangerous man who kidnapped Nicco out of revenge." I furrowed my brow. "I don't understand why Stapleton took seventeen years to make his move?"

"Who knows?" Sherlock shrugged. "Stapleton has the

means and motive for revenge, and he must have somehow discovered our secret identity, which also gave him opportunity. He does not refer to me as Holmes in the letter, which leads me to believe he's not yet divulged my real identity to anyone else, which we must use to our advantage. He's a ruthless individual who needs to be caught and pay for his outrageous crimes."

"Yes," I agreed. "But what happened at the police station with the guardia? Anything that could help with our inquiries?"

Sherlock nodded. "After you left, we questioned Giarcosca further in what proved to be a disquieting interview. Romano promised to go easier on him if he revealed who he'd been working for. Giarcosca agreed and broke down in tears, giving us everything we wanted. When Romano finished interrogating him, the man was singing like a canary. He signed a full witness statement and told us of his gambling habits, how his life had spiralled out of control until he met a man at the Milano Racetrack, Emilio Rodriguez."

"Who is this Rodriguez?"

"An unsavoury character, otherwise known as Il Resolver, of dubious disposition, and according to Romano, a loan shark, money launderer, and private law enforcer with connections to the Italian mafia."

"He sounds like a terrible man." I shuddered. "But what's his connection to Nicco?"

"Rodriguez is one of Stapleton's agents. They bribed Giarcosca to attack Mattia Greco and render him unconscious. A woman of European origin, identified as Connie, lay in wait in the rear garden at the house. She jumped into the carriage and sedated our sleeping son with a chloroform rag before tying Nicco up and gagging him. This Connie is undoubtedly the same woman who sent the first ransom note. The couple in the house were Romany gypsies and part of the deception.

After having been paid handsomely by Rodrigeuz, they fled, joining their group of travellers, leaving Milan by train the following day."

"Where did Giarcosca take Nicco?"

"He said Rodriguez instructed him to drive two miles outside the city, where he was met by a man waiting with another carriage. The driver was middle-aged, with grey shoulder-length hair, and spoke Italian. Although he only uttered a handful of words, the woman did most of the talking. Giarcosca cycled back to the city using the bicycle he'd strategically hidden in the long grass the previous day. He arrived back at the police station in ample time to start his shift, attired in full uniform, which he concealed under the cloak used during the kidnapping, which Giarcosca later hid in his work bag, along with the mask." Sherlock sighed. "He didn't realise he'd lost a button in the transition. Giarcosca is the same man who drove you home that fateful night and took me back to the crime scene, giving him a perfect alibi. It was timed like the movements of a *Swiss Army* watch."

"So what do we do now?" I asked.

"Rodriguez owns a villa on the outskirts of Milan. Romano and his men asked the courts to issue a warrant as they plan to search the property, although I fear Rodriguez will be long gone, no doubt hidden in a safe house by Stapleton or the Italian mafia. I planned to go with them until I realised you would be home alone in the villa. I'd forgotten the domestic servants would be out on errands in all the madness. So, concerned for your safety, I headed home. Romano promised to call if there was any news, but it would appear that the boot is now on the other foot, and we have news. And what news do we convey, Nene? With the help of Romano and the Milan polizia, we can finally make our move and go find our son."

"Are you sure it's wise for Hildegard to stay with us?"

"Yes." Sherlock nodded. "Although I need to question her

further."

I turned to Sherlock with a puzzled expression. "Why? What makes you say that?"

"Something she said about Jack Stapleton-slash-Robert Barrett, or whatever he's calling himself. You see, the man I knew had no qualms about cheating on his wife while she was alive, so why would he bother now if she was dead? Either Robert Barrett is not the man I think he is, or Hildegard Achen is not telling us the whole story unless she wasn't the only woman privy to his affections."

"Perhaps Hildegard slept with him under duress and then felt embarrassed after everything that transpired."

"It's a possibility," Sherlock said, agreeing. "But I think it best we keep our powder dry until we have exhausted all possibilities. Although, I fear our governess was used as a pawn in Stapleton's wicked game. There was no malice aforethought on her part. She was as much of a victim as Nicco."

"Yes," I nodded. "I agree that Hildegard spoke the truth when she bared her soul to us earlier. She's not the only woman to have been duped by a man. I would hate for anything untoward to happen to her."

"That's settled then," Sherlock said. "Miss Achen must stay with us until Stapleton is found."

"What did you make of those clues left by Nicco in the book?"

"I believe the words *Hewli St* to be an anagram of *whistle*. And *shilling* is *Bob* in monetary slang terms. Indicating Bob Barrett. However, *whistle* is not a code for our son's kidnapping nor those responsible for his abduction. This is something much bigger. Knowing Stapleton, the code will mean something personal, or symbolic even, and which, with the help of Romano, I'm determined to solve."

Sherlock put on his ulster and hat. "Nene, I need you to stay here while I go to the telegraph office to wire Mycroft and

Lestrade. The servants are expected to return soon. I know this is difficult, but please try to rest. I shan't be long. I need you to listen for the phone in case Romano calls with further news to convey."

The house was eerily cloaked in an uneasy silence, thick with the fear that had settled over us for days.

Sherlock stood by the doorway, ready to leave, his tall, lean figure silhouetted against the dim light, a pillar of strength and resolve. He stepped toward me and tenderly wrapped his comforting arms around my shoulders with a gentleness that belied his fierce determination, allowing me to sink in his warm embrace. With my head against his chest, I heard the steady, reassuring beat of his heart, gradually calming the unsteady beat of mine. Oh, why couldn't this moment last forever? Looking up into this face, those steel-grey eyes that had solved countless mysteries, slightly blurred from silent tears, still sparkled. His thumb grazed my cheek, a small gesture but enough to push back the shadows that the sleepless nights had carved into my face.

"Sherlock," I whispered, my voice betraying my raw fear. "Promise you'll bring Nicco safely home. I can't rest or think straight until I know he's back where he belongs."

His gaze softening, but his voice as steady as steel, he said, "Do not despair, Nene. You have my word that I will not rest until our boy is again back in your arms."

A tear slipped down my chin, but I nodded, still holding onto the warmth of his loving embrace, not wanting to let go. For a brief eternal moment, we stood together like that, my heart clinging to the silent vow I saw in his eyes.

Then, with a final squeeze of my hand, he moved away from me, stepped through the large oak door of the villa, and closed it gently, leaving me alone to wallow in the silence. My mind was a storm of hope and fear, mingled and inseparable, as I awaited my son's return.

The Whistle of Revenge

I poured myself another cup of Cafe Noir and pondered what happened between us. I felt as though my entire world had been turned upside down. My heart broke at the thought of my beloved son, unable to defend himself, being overpowered with chloroform by some deranged woman. It made my blood boil. I traced my fingers over the outline of the gun in my pocket, wondering how I would react if Connie and Stapleton, leading contenders for the low moral ground, stood right before me. I had one bullet for each and two spares should I miss.

But the question lingered—would I be capable of pulling the trigger?

Chapter Twenty-Five: Sherlock Holmes
1Morti ci Dicono Tutto — The Dead Tell Us All

I returned from the telegram office after having messaged Mycroft and Lestrade. Later that afternoon, I had barely removed my hat and coat when Nene appeared in the hallway to tell me Guardia Colombo from the Milano polizia was in the drawing room with vital information to relay from Salvatore Romano. Colombo, a tall, gangly, amenable fellow, explained that the polizia had thoroughly searched Rodrigeuz's home, but there was no sign of him or our son.

The guardia sighed. "There has, however, been a further development that may be pertinent to the investigation."

"What development?" I asked, staring at Colombo keenly.

"Dominzia Santora was arrested this morning after a guard on the train travelling from Parma to Milan recognised him. The authorities were alerted, and the polizia arrested Santora when he disembarked from the Milano Centrale Railway Station train. The man is now in custody, and Inspector Romano asked that you come to the police station to assist with his inquiries. We have a carriage outside for your convenience."

I agreed to Colombo's request, asking him to give me five minutes to ascertain all was well with Nene. My wife assured me she would be fine, explaining that the domestic servants had returned to the villa while Hildegard Achen slept soundly upstairs.

"Do you think Santora's disappearance has anything to do

with Nicco's abduction?" Nene asked, staring up at me anxiously.

"It's possible," I agreed. "But Romano and I will know more when we interview him." I reassured Nene that I would be in touch as soon as there was any news before leaving the villa and joining the guardia in the carriage.

Romano greeted me with a firm handshake and a sombre expression before ushering me into his office, pushing a sizable buff-coloured file within my reach.

"These are the cold case files pertaining to the unsolved homicides of Luis and Rosetta Bandiero. I would like you to study them before we interview Santora so you know all the facts from the outset."

After agreeing to Romano's request, the inspector kindly organised a pot of coffee as I scrutinised the file for some time, puffing away on a pipe full of tobacco, painstakingly reviewing every detail. According to the autopsy report, Luis Bandiero suffered a blow to the back of his head, causing internal bleeding and a haemorrhage to the brain. The cause of death was head trauma. The pathological report revealed traces of alcohol were found in his blood.

Furthermore, it was impossible to ascertain from the trajectory of the fall if someone had pushed him or whether his death had been premeditated in any way. Subsequently, the coroner at the inquest recorded an open verdict, ruling in favour of suspected homicide. Romano and I were aware that it naturally encourages speculation since the openness of the verdict refers to the technical possibility that the case could be brought back to court and re-examined later.

As for Rosetta Bandiero, her death was an entirely different matter. I sat upright in my seat as Romano drew my attention to a photograph of Rosetta Bandiero showing distinct marks to her face and neck, consistent with having been inflicted by a sharp object. I aired my observations to the inspector.

"Yes," Romano said, agreeing. "The autopsy report revealed that following the physical examination, the findings into Rosetta's death were caused by an obstruction of airflow and direct trauma. The cuts on the neck, although significant, did not contribute to her death. They are likely defence wounds inflicted by the sharp edge of a ring or something similar. I believe the murderer attacked Rosetta and squeezed her neck. She put up her hands to defend herself, and the marks were likely made by either her wedding or engagement rings when she attempted to push the assailant away. The autopsy report revealed the little finger on her right hand was dislocated in the struggle. It was likely that Luis Bandiero strangled Rosetta. Then, in a drunken stupor, fell backwards, hitting his head on the fireguard. The blow to the back of the head caused internal bleeding and trauma to the brain, resulting in his death."

I shook my head, glancing over to Romano. "If the perpetrator grabbed Rosetta Bandiero by the neck, then I agree that she would naturally put up her hands to defend herself. However, if her injuries were self-inflicted by the shank of those rings, the marks would only be visible on one side of the face and neck. The assailant wore rings on both hands, and it could only be they who either intentionally or accidentally inflicted the wounds. Observing the report and these photographs, Rosetta Bandiero wore only wedding and engagement rings at the time her body was found. Do you know if her husband or Santora were known to wear jewellery?"

Romano shook his head. "There was no jewellery found on Luis Bandiero's body, not even a wedding band. As for Santora, I have no idea." He grimaced. "But I think we're about to find out. Shall we?" he asked, gesturing to the door.

I rose, shrugging resignedly as we returned to interview room number two.

Chapter Twenty-Six: Salvatore Romano

L'Imputato – The Accused

Holmes and I entered the interview room to find Santora sitting on a chair, his head in his hands, dressed in black trousers and an open-necked white shirt.

Santora glanced upwards, acknowledging our presence with a resigned nod and a deep sigh. His long, angular face looked world-weary and haggard. Dark matted hair hung loosely over his shoulders as his suspicious brown eyes, dimmed and bloodshot, followed us around the room. Barely recognisable from his mug-shot photographs and the wanted posters, this once remarkably handsome young man had aged considerably during the past two years.

I pushed a cup of water towards him, offering a cigarette, which he accepted gratefully. I noticed that his fingers bore no rings, tell-tale indents, or discolourations on his skin. Lighting the cigarette with a vestas match, Holmes and I sat across the table.

I nodded to Santora, waving my identity badge. "My name is Chief Inspector Salvatore Romano, and this is my friend and colleague, Signor Lucca Sapori. May I remind you that we are questioning you under caution about the suspected homicides of Luis and Rosetta Bandiero."

Santora wrung his hands nervously, drawing on his cigarette, as I continued. "Dominzia, we want you to talk us through the events of Wednesday, the 1st of June 1904, the day Luis and Rosetta Bandiero were discovered murdered in their home. We need to know your every move."

The room was silent for a moment, and then Santora spoke in an acute Italian accent, his voice raspy and hoarse. "I didn't go to work that morning, Inspector. I had been out the night before celebrating a friend's birthday. I was a little hungover when I awoke. My head was banging. I felt much better by mid-morning, so I went to Rosetta's house as arranged."

"Ah, so, Rosetta was expecting you?" I interrupted.

Santora nodded. "No, but it's not what you think, Inspector. It's true what they say . . . Rosetta and I were having an affair. At first, it was just a meaningless fling, but then we developed feelings for each other and fell deeply in love. Rosetta confided she wasn't happy in her marriage. She agreed to leave Luis and come away with me to start a new life in Florence."

"So you decided to kill Luis Bandiero?"

Santora looked at me, horrified. "No, of course not, Inspector. You don't understand. When I got to 11Vecchio Cigno, I knocked on the door, but after receiving no answer, I went around the back and discovered the kitchen door ajar. So I entered the house, calling out to Rosetta, but there was still no response. I knew she wouldn't go out and leave the door unlocked, so I crept upstairs and entered the bedroom, slowly pushing the door open, and that's when I discovered a horrifying scene I shall never forget until my dying day. The bodies of Luis and Rosetta lying on the floor. I ran over to check for pulses, but it was too late. They were already dead. Their lifeless bodies sprawled grotesquely on the floor, eyes wide open in a horrible fixed stare. There was blood everywhere from Luis's head wound that trickled down his shirt and onto the floor. I slipped on the blood as I tried to move Luis and Rosetta. I remember closing my eyes for a moment, trying to block out the image of that dreadful scene. Then I turned around in a blind panic, intending to raise the alarm and alert the polizia. The next thing I remember, someone hit me from behind, and then everything went black."

"What happened next?"

"I awoke sometime later with a lump on my head, thinking it had all been a terrible dream. Then I looked around. The bodies were still there, my hands and clothes bloodied from where I had touched Luis and slipped on the floor. I realised then what it would look like if I alerted the polizia. Who would believe me? A humble tradesman, due to our previous history and the bad blood between us, the polizia would think it was me who killed Luis out of a jealous vendetta. I'm ashamed that I ran home, hurriedly packed a bag, and fled the city."

"And where have you been for the past two years?"

"I travelled to Florence by train, changing my name to Bruno Conte. I worked on a farm as a labourer near Calvary Hill, renting a caravan from the farm manager. I kept my own company and read the Milan papers daily in the local library. I was horrified to find my name and picture splashed all over the front pages, and discovering the Milano homicide detectives wanted me for murder and were offering a reward for my arrest made me feel sick to my stomach. Then, after a few weeks, the news was reduced to a few lines until, eventually, the murders were never mentioned again. I was mortified when the polizia took no further action. They believed that it was me who committed the crimes, leaving the real murderer free to walk the streets."

I looked at Santora, exasperated. "But don't you see, Dominzia, that by running away, you gave people the wrong impression and every reason to believe you were guilty?"

Santora nodded. "I can see that now, but I could not risk being arrested by the polizia for a crime I did not commit. I knew it looked bad for me. I loved Rosetta so much. I could never hurt her. You and the polizia need to explore other lines of inquiry, Inspector."

Holmes, who'd not spoken a word until that moment, smiled at Santora, sitting back in his chair and staring at him with those piercing grey eyes. "What was the real reason you went to Rosetta Bandiero's house? Surely it was a risky strategy, knowing her husband would be there?"

Santora shook his head but remained silent, appearing deep in thought. Holmes shifted in his seat, stretching out his long legs. The celebrated detective wasn't used to being kept waiting, especially when asking a primary question. Finally, Santora took one last puff of his cigarette, stubbing it in the ashtray, shooting Holmes a sideways glance as he began his narrative.

"I had a business appointment with the rental agent on the day of the murders. We arranged to meet at the property so he could check the work I had recently undertaken, the installation of new bedroom windows."

Holmes raised an eyebrow, leaning forward in his seat. "But if you made this appointment through the agency, surely they would have kept a record of any such meeting? Yet, according to the crime file, when the polizia questioned the staff, there was no mention of their agent meeting you."

"No," Santora agreed. "There wouldn't have been. You see, I bumped into the agent the night before the murders. He came into the bar where I was celebrating with friends. He said he recognised me. We'd met briefly, having completed previous work for the company. Then, three men entered the bar and came to join us, introducing themselves as friends.

"We chatted together, laughing and joking. The men were a friendly bunch who insisted on buying the drinks. We engaged in friendly banter for some time, the beer flowing freely. While we were talking, the agent told me about the pup he adopted from the pound. He showed me a picture of a bull mastiff named Caesar. Then, our chat reverted to work matters. He was due to inspect Rosetta's property the following day to check on the windows. He suggested we meet at 11 Vecchio Cigno, so he could sign off the job and pay my invoice simultaneously. I was delighted, as I needed the money and realised it would be a perfect opportunity to see Rosetta again.

"Sadly, our furtive meetings had become more sporadic after a recent and very public altercation with Luis, resulting in a brawl. I was forced to deny romantic involvement with his wife to protect Rosetta's reputation. Luis was naturally suspicious, and after that, he watched his wife like a hawk. He had no clue she was about to leave him."

Santora sighed, brushing his hair back from his eyes. "Do what you will with me, Inspector, for you see, I don't care. Without Rosetta by my side, I am a shadow of the man I used to be. But I swear before God and on my father's grave that I am not responsible for the deaths of Rosetta and Luis. That is why I returned to Milan, in great distress of mind. I couldn't keep up the pretence any longer. The polizia must hunt down those responsible to ensure they receive the ultimate punishment. That's the least Rosetta and Luis deserve."

"Did you see this agent on the day of the murders?"

"No, sir. When I arrived at the property, there was no sign of anyone, so I figured he was running late. Looking back, I wondered if someone had laced my drink that night, and the whole episode had been a nightmare."

"What was the name of this man you met in the bar? Can you describe him?" I asked.

Santora looked at me curiously. "He was tall, slim, astute in appearance, dressed in a well-cut three-piece suit, not what you would expect from your typical office worker. Like a fop, he dazzled us in an array of glittering fashion accessories, including a handsome cravat pin with matching cufflinks, a gold watch and chain, and several ornate dress rings. My friends joked that he looked like a dandy."

"His name?" I demanded sharply.

"I can't recall his surname, Inspector. He introduced himself to me at the bar, but it was so long ago, and I was pretty intoxicated. But I remember his friends called him Rolf."

Holmes looked at me, arching an eyebrow.

"Yes. My men interviewed a man from the agency who had dealings with the tenants at the time of the incident. His name is Rodolfo Abbati."

Chapter Twenty-Seven: Robert Barrett
L'opportuniste — The Opportunist

After I met with Connie and the boy, I entered the kitchen and poured a glass of water from the pitcher. I would have preferred a drop of something more substantial, but I needed a clear head to keep my wits about me. There was too much at stake to falter now. Seeing the boy had unnerved me slightly. He was a few years younger than my son would have been had he lived.

Nicco was a replica of his father all right, with the same piercing eyes, although the boy's were blue, tall, dark-haired, handsome, and smart as a whip, just like his famous father. I was impressed by how he stood up to me during our meeting and at such a tender age. I wondered if Nicco Sapori knew his father's real identity. So I decided not to broach the subject because it would likely all come out in the wash, and I figured the boy had suffered enough already. I wouldn't be the one to shatter his dreams.

Sipping from my glass, I gazed out of the kitchen window, perusing the acres of open fields dotted with thoroughbred horses, all bred and descended from the finest lineage. Thanks to my friend Ludovico Galli, who was more of an acquaintance, I was appointed temporary manager of his prestigious racing stables for two months. This new position fitted my plans perfectly. It helped me get closer to achieving the funds and backing needed for my new business venture while simultaneously bringing down my enemies, Sherlock Holmes and Angelino.

Ludovico Galli, 56, was a widower with an only child. When his wife of 25 years, Alicia, died in a riding accident four years ago, Ludovico was inconsolable. Alicia had been a wealthy woman in her own right, and the money Ludovico inherited and the life insurance payment ensured he would have no financial worries for the rest of his life.

Ludovico, understandably sinking into a deep depression after Alicia's demise, lost interest in the day-to-day running of his business. Then, one day, he read in one of the horse racing journals about a forthcoming auction of the ailing Milano Prestige Stables in Lombardy.

Deciding that a project and a new direction in life were needed to pull him out of his melancholy, Ludovico submitted a cheeky bid for the premises and subsequently took over the stables, changing the name to San Sior Scuderia di Cavalli da Corsa. Ludovico gradually built it up, first as a livery stable and later taking out a trainer licence. The business flourished until it became the successful stable it was today.

Ludovico, a fellow Mason, frequented the same Italian lodge as his friend Alberto Patrese, who recently returned from a business trip to Maryland, USA. Over dinner at his club, Alberto heard Sam Perkins, the original arranger of the inaugural Walden Stakes, would be unable to fulfil his duties in starting and completing the preparation of the prestigious race, which was to be held at the Pimlico Race Course in Baltimore, Maryland. The event was named in honour of Maryland-based trainer and owner Wyndham Walden, affectionately known as Wink.

Three weeks before the race, Perkins suffered a heavy fall from a ladder and was admitted to the hospital with a slipped disc. The doctors diagnosed treatment would take around a month before Perkins was back on his feet, meaning he would be temporarily out of action and unable to resume his duties in Baltimore.

Alberto immediately thought of Ludovico Galli, realising he would be the perfect candidate to replace him. Upon returning to Milan, Alberto contacted Ludovico to outline the situation and his proposal. He said that if Ludovico wanted the short-term position, then the job was as good as his. Realising the job would only enhance his already successful career, Ludovico jumped at the chance, telling Alberto he considered the offer an honour. He knew if he could pull this off, it would only boost his reputation in the USA. Subsequently, Ludovico signed a contract accepting the two-month post, with an option to extend if required. He was expected to start work at the beginning of June. In the meantime, Ludovico needed someone to take over his Milan stables for the interim period. I was surprised but delighted to discover Alberto recommended me as an ideal candidate.

Apart from overseeing the horses on the morning gallops, I kept a low-profile at the stables, using Peppo as a go-between, odd job man, and stable hand so I could stay in contact with Connie. I continued to use hotels throughout the city, adopting various names and disguises for my meetings with Rodriguez, Connie, and Hildegard Achen so as not to draw suspicion. I raised my glass, toasting my good fortune in gleeful anticipation and the knowledge that everything was at last falling into place.

Chapter Twenty-Eight: Sherlock Holmes
La Confessione — The Confession

A wet, drizzly morning descended, with rumbles of Tuscan thunder, as I pulled back the blinds, reminding me of a line from Tennyson's *In Memoriam A.H.H* that my son often recited.

He is not here but far away.
The noise of life begins again,
and ghastly thro the drizzling rain,
on the bald street breaks the blank day.

I wiped a tear from my eye as I donned my hat and coat. I couldn't allow such thoughts to bring me down. I must put sorrow and grief aside and concentrate on the task ahead. Alerted to the sound of horses approaching, I saluted Romano and his men, steadfast and punctual as ever, as they pulled up in a carriage at precisely 10.30 A.M.

The Tuscan skies had predictably swept to a clear Mediterranean blue as I made my way outside and jumped into the hansom. With a crack of the coachman's whip, we embarked on our journey to the cursed house to meet the unsuspecting agent. The inspector confirmed he had messaged the rental company ahead, insisting that Abbati meet us at 11 A.M., although not revealing two undercover polizia already had 11Vecchio Cigno under surveillance.

When our carriage pulled outside the property, Abbati stood waiting for us, pacing up and down in agitation like a caged lion, wiping sweat from his brow as he saw us approach.

Romano waved his badge and explained we'd come to search the house after someone came forward to help with our enquiries. Abbati hesitated before opening the door, standing motionless in the hallway like a statue, as the guardie went upstairs to check the bedrooms and bathroom. At the same time, Romano and I concentrated on the ground-floor accommodation, searching every room. Finding no clues in the house, we went outside to the shed, which was no different from my last inspection, except for a stack of boxes, brown paper, and gummed paper tape lying on a shelf. Opening the panel in the wall, I pulled out the large brass box, which had been empty at my last inspection but now contained two sizable brown paper parcels.

"Whatever is in the parcels doesn't look like drugs," Romano said in an exasperated tone.

Romano and his men were used to discovering drugs and contraband concealed in hollowed books, bottomed containers, and secret compartments in furniture, not parcelled up in neat packages ready to post.

"No, indeed," I replied, carefully opening one of the packages. "But if my deduction is correct, Inspector, then what we have here is just as valuable, perhaps even more so if you're a Russian citizen terrified of contracting a deadly disease."

Romano shrugged, looking on bemusedly as I opened the box beneath the brown paper to reveal several vials of liquid and syringes. For some people, the word *cholera* signified the highest kind of fear. It was a disease that did not discriminate. Symptoms included diarrhoea, nausea and vomiting, leading to a quick and agonising death, but to Rodriguez and his gang of reprobates, it meant a sack full of Russian roubles.

The last cholera epidemic in Russia occurred in 1904. However, fears of further outbreaks of this dreadful disease were rife due to poverty, poor sanitation, turmoil, and the influx of immigrants flooding into the country, which was constant, with current sporadic cases building up in southern Russia. Although a vaccine was available to prevent contracting the disease, such mass vaccination programmes were not commonplace. The available ones were generally taken up by the unscrupulous and the prosperous.

As I explained to Romano, following the creation of a new political order in April 1906, with the Tsar confirmed as an absolute leader, Rodriguez and his cronies, using Abbati as a foil, saw a potential market for supplies of the vaccine to the privileged few who were able to pay.

The world-famous composer Tchaikovsky, whose works included the ballet *Swan Lake* and the famous *1812 Overture*, succumbed to the disease on November 2, 1893, after drinking a glass of unboiled water.

A young guardia entered the shed to speak to Romano. He explained that after being tipped off by the surveillance team, he and his colleague searched Abbati's brougham and found twenty more parcels the agent concealed in the back of the carriage, covered by a dust sheet. Having arrived at the property just after 10 A.M., Abbati hoped to remove the evidence before we arrived, unaware that the Milano polizia were monitoring his every move.

Romano and I stepped back into the house to confront Abbati, who looked shaken and close to tears after we informed him of our findings. Romano told the traumatised agent he would be looking at a lengthy sentence if he wasn't prepared to assist with our enquiries. Furthermore, he would face a tough time in prison once other inmates became aware of his sexuality.

"Why should we keep your secret if you don't tell us what you know?" Romano said.

The agent, visibly shaking, agreed to comply with the inspector's request and told us everything. Abbati's eyes fixed on the inspector's sombre face, acutely aware that his future lay in Romano's hands.

Abbati told us he was singled out as a potential target after his clandestine encounters in the park were spotted by one of Emilio's henchmen, who wasted no time in alerting his boss to Abbati's sexual tendencies. Knowing the agent's activities would bring shame and embarrassment to his friends, family, and employer. Emilio targeted the hapless Abbati, confronting him at a club and threatening to expose him if he didn't do as he asked. Backed into a corner, Abbati had no choice but to comply.

At first, he was given a few drugs to hide, primarily cocaine and heroin. Not wanting them about his person, Abbati decided to store them at the haunted house, confident that his hiding place would be secure. He returned to the house several times at night with the dog he bought for protection, training it to howl on demand. Abbati rattled the chains, making ungodly noises to unnerve the neighbours and stopping people from becoming curious about the premises. The house became the perfect hiding place, often used as a bolt-hole by Rodriguez's agents.

Then Abbati told us Rodriguez's stipulations became more demanding. He was ordered to store several boxes at the house. His job was to wrap and label them securely until a courier, usually one of Rodriguez's henchmen, came to collect them.

"Did you ever wonder what was in the packages?" Romano enquired.

Abbati shook his head. "At first, Inspector, I had no idea, and that's by design. You see, I didn't want to know. It was more than my life's worth to cross Rodriguez and his gang. I was also fearful for my job, my livelihood, and my reputation, and I couldn't handle jail. I've heard what happens to the likes of me in such places. But then, Emilio couldn't help but brag over a drink one night. He revealed what the packages contained, dragging me further into his web of deceit. I heard the devil whispering in my ear." Abbati stared at us wide-eyed. "What will happen to me now?" he asked, removing a silk handkerchief from his jacket pocket and wiping his nose.

"You'll likely receive a jail sentence," Romano said. "There is nothing I can do about that. However, if you continue to tell us everything, your cooperation will be considered at your trial and looked upon more favourably by the judge. I will personally sign an affidavit confirming you were complicit in helping us with our enquiries. There will be no mention of your sexual orientation."

"And if I don't, what then?"

Romano shook his head. "Then you must enlist in the ranks of deviancy and take your chances. I can only imagine the consequences."

Abbati nodded resignedly. "All right, Inspector, I'll tell you everything, but can we do it somewhere else, away from here, as I fear we are being watched?"

Romano agreed to Abbati's request and read him his rights before instructing the guardie to return the contraband packages to the station. Instead of following the guardie, Romano agreed to my suggestion.

We took a little detour off the beaten track to a small, secluded cafe, which served the best coffee in Milan and where I often took Nene and the children. Agata, the slim, dark-haired proprietor, acknowledged our presence with a smile and a nod, showed us to our table, took our order, and returned promptly with coffee, brandies, and a plate of biscotti.

Finding himself in a more pleasant atmosphere away from prying eyes, Abbati appeared to relax. Puffing away on a cigarette and taking a liberal swig of brandy, his anxiety seemed to dissipate even more. He responded to Romano's probing questions, telling us all he knew about Rodriguez, including his address.

"But we already know this man's address," I said. "When we got to the house, Rodriguez had disappeared. Do you have any idea who may be hiding him?"

Abbati shook his head. "Emilio Rodriguez is a dangerous man, with powerful friends and contacts all over Italy, although I guess few would be prepared to hide him. Emilio has quite a reputation. He destroys the lives of enemies and anyone who dares to cross him. He spoke of someone called Bob or Robert on more than one occasion. I believe he has connections with Lombardy and has something to do with horses. But, other than that, Emilio could be holed up anywhere."

My ears pricked up at the mention of Bob. "When Rodriguez spoke of this Bob or Robert, did he ever mention the kidnapping of a boy or a ransom demand?"

"No, sir, nothing like that. Although he loved to boast, I wasn't privy to the man's darkest secrets, and while he mingles with some cut-throat characters, I've never known Emilio to become involved in child abduction. I think that would be a step too far even for him."

"What makes you say that?"

"Because he lost his only child in a gangland shooting two years ago after, the carriage Emilio and his family travelled in was ambushed by a rival gang. Emilio escaped with his life, just a few cuts and bruises and a flesh wound, but tragically, his wife, Virna, and their daughter, Matilda, were killed instantly in the spray of bullets and carnage. The girl was barely eight years old. So if you're looking for a kidnapper, I doubt Emilio is your man."

I leaned forward in my seat, staring at Abbati curiously. "But that's not the only reason you think that? What else are you withholding from me and the inspector?"

"One of Emilio's cronies confided in me that Rodriguez had experienced a great deal of trauma in his childhood years.

During his time at the orphanage, he was shunted from one foster home to another. The people who took him in were only interested in the money. He was repeatedly beaten, violated, and mistreated by the people entrusted to take care of him. Sadly, while Emilio's story is not uncommon, it's yet another reason why I'm convinced he would never intentionally set out to hurt a child."

"Thank you for sharing that. Do you think it possible Rodriguez and his cronies are assisting the kidnappers in any way?"

Abbati shrugged. "I don't know what to say, Signor Sapori."

"Yes or no would be helpful."

"I suppose it depends if they're being paid enough. There would have to be something in it for them. How much is the ransom?"

"Twelve thousand lira."

Abbati whistled. "So no small change, then. If I were you, I would check in the Lombardy region for someone who owns land and keeps horses. It's possible that Bob or Robert could be hiding Emilio and have a connection to the kidnapping. I'm sorry I can't be of further help."

"Did Rodriguez ever speak of anyone called Jack or Stapleton? Did those names ever crop up in conversation?"

"No, sir, I don't recall either of those names being mentioned."

"When did you last see Rodriguez?"

"Two nights ago, at the Black Cat Inn. Emilio told me the courier would call to collect the packages at eight P.M. this evening. He said they had better be ready, or it would be the worst for me. I panicked when my secretary told me that Inspector Romano demanded I meet with him that morning. My first thought was to remove the packages before the polizia arrived. I had no idea the house was already under surveillance." Abbati averted his gaze to Romano. "What will happen this evening when the courier arrives and discovers I'm not at the house to meet him as arranged?"

"My men will be there to greet the courier and subsequently arrest him, but quite frankly, that's the least of your concerns right now," Romano said.

Abbati stared at the inspector questioningly.

"You promised to tell us everything," I said, leaning forward in my seat, staring the agent straight in the eye.

"But, like I already said, I'm happy to tell you everything, Signor Sapori."

"Then, in that case, you must tell the inspector and me what happened on the day Rosetta and her husband, Luis Bandiero, were discovered dead. I believe you're ultimately responsible for their demise, even unintentionally."

Chapter Twenty-Nine: Sherlock Holmes
Un Peso Rimosso — A Weight Removed

Abbati removed his glasses and laid one hand over his eyes. He began to cry a tsunami of shoulder-shaking sobs.

"You must believe when I tell you, Signor Sapori, that it was all a terrible accident."

"Tell us what happened."

"I got to the house early that morning to explain to Rosetta and Luis why the agency was serving them notice. Luis let me in, and while Rosetta was in the kitchen making coffee, I followed Luis upstairs to inspect the windows. Luis was intoxicated. I could smell liquor on his breath, and he ranted and raved in a drunken rage, saying he suspected Rosetta was about to leave him, but he couldn't understand why. Then he boasted about his sexual prowess, joking that a man like me would never be able to satisfy a vigorous, beautiful woman like Rosetta, taunting me about my sexuality.

"So, I pulled out the eviction notice, thinking that would wipe the smirk off his face. Luis saw red. He said everyone was against him and slung out his arm to hit me. I grabbed him and pushed him, accidentally knocking Luis to the floor. He fell backwards, hitting his head hard on the fireplace iron guard with such force that he was rendered unconscious. There was blood everywhere. I tried to stop the flow, but the bleeding just wouldn't stop. Luis died very quickly."

The Whistle of Revenge

"And then?"

"Hearing the altercation, Rosetta ran up the stairs. When she entered the room, she looked horrified at seeing her dead husband lying on the floor and my hands dripping blood. She let out a terrifying scream and flew at me like a mad woman. She started beating at my chest with her bare hands. I tried to explain what had happened and that it had been a terrible accident. But Rosetta was distraught and unbelieving of my story. Then she began laughing hysterically, saying I had done her a favour. She was now free to be with her lover, but she would see me arrested first. She said she knew about my shady operations with Rodriguez and was going to neighbours to summon the polizia. She turned on her heels and headed towards the door."

Abbati hesitated momentarily, taking a sip from his cup, tears streaming down his face.

"I know this must be difficult, but you must tell us what happened next."

Abbati nodded, taking a breath and then sipping brandy before continuing his narrative. "I ran after Rosetta, cutting her off at the door and blocking the entrance. Looking around desperately, Rosetta grabbed the poker from the hearth and ran forward, aiming to strike me."

"And did she?"

"No, Signor Sapori, somehow I managed to evade Rosetta's clumsy blow, and I'm ashamed to say that I grabbed her by the throat. The more Rosetta struggled, the tighter I squeezed. I had to stop her somehow. I knew I'd be finished if the polizia were alerted."

"So with your large, powerful hands around the throat of this defenceless woman, what happened next?"

"Rosetta began to choke. She tried to push my hands away. For a petite woman, she was powerful, but finally, her body became limp. I realised then that I'd gone too far. I was horrified by my actions. I attempted to wake Rosetta. I tried everything, slapping and pouring cold water over her face. Then I realised it was too late, and because of my actions, that beautiful, vibrant girl was dead."

"You strangled her, restricting airflow to the trachea, resulting in cerebral ischemia. Death was caused by impaired blood flow to the brain."

"I'm so sorry, but why did you suspect it was me?"

"The rings you wear on both hands give you away. The marks found on Rosetta Bandiero's face and neck were consistent with a sharp object, likely made by the shank of a ring. Signora Bandiero's husband and lover were not known to wear rings, so it could only have been you with the means and opportunity to carry out the crime. And then, of course, you decided to frame Santora to cover your tracks. I have a fair idea of what transpired next, but please, for my curiosity and the polizia record, tell us what happened in your own words."

Abbati shot me a woeful gaze, shaking his head. "Yes, I'm ashamed to say you are correct, Signor Sapori. I expected Dominzia to arrive for the inspection, so I waited for him. I prepared myself and hid in the second bedroom. I left the back door on the latch when Dominzia finally arrived and banged on the door. I knew it was only a matter of time before he would enter the house and come upstairs. When I heard footsteps approaching the landing, I waited until Dominzia opened the bedroom door. Then, I hit him with the poker on the back of the head, and he fell to the floor. I went over, praying I hadn't killed him. Mercifully, he was still breathing but down for the count. I realised it was only a matter of time before he regained consciousness."

"So you decided to set him up as a scapegoat?"

"Everyone in the village was aware of Dominzia and Rosetta's affair, so I saw it as an ideal opportunity to set the deaths up as a love triangle gone wrong."

"Ah, how convenient! Triangle amour qui a mal tourne." *It's been a while since I investigated one of those.*

"I must say, Abbati, for an accident gone wrong, you went to a lot of trouble in covering your tracks. Pray to tell what occurred next."

"Using the poker, I smeared Dominzia's hands and clothes with Luis's still-warm blood, spreading it over Rosetta's face and neck, before cleaning myself and wiping away fingerprints from the areas I touched. Then I washed the blood-smeared poker, replacing it on the fireplace stand before leaving the house. I remembered the eviction notice, so I returned and posted it through the letterbox." Abbati glanced up at me with tear-filled eyes. "I bitterly regret the heartache I caused the families of the deceased and my framing of Dominzia. All that sorrow and devastation, the result of a tragic accident."

"What happened to Luis Bandiero may have been a tragic accident, but one that could have been avoided if you had only walked away from the altercation, although we only have your word for that, Abbati. However, what you did to Rosetta Bandiero was murder. I accept that you probably didn't mean to kill either of the Bandieros. So, with a good lawyer, you may get off with the lesser manslaughter charge, citing mitigating circumstances. As for the framing of Santora, that will be entirely up to the judge to decide. But let me tell you that your actions, attempting to frame an innocent man, are likely to have serious consequences. Inspector Romano assures me that you will have access to the best defence lawyer available should you continue to assist with our inquiries. But there is one more thing. Where did you go after you left the house?"

"I let myself out of the back door, and then, using the back roads, I made my way to one of my local hostelries, where I spent the rest of the afternoon and evening with two of my gentleman friends who owed me a favour, and who I was sure would provide me with an alibi, which was, of course, not needed in the end. The polizia issued a warrant for Dominzia's arrest. When I heard he'd fled the scene, I was elated."

"Well, why wouldn't you be?" Romano asked." You were well and truly off the hook with Santora in the frame. It was fortunate for you that when polizia finally caught up with him, he had no recollection of who hit him. What he did reveal, however, is that he was meant to meet you at the property but that you failed to show."

Abbati sighed. "Inspector, Signor Sapori, I knew in my heart that this day would eventually arrive. Still, you have been very clever, drawing me into your confidence to reveal everything I know while at the same time concealing that you already held me responsible for the deaths of Rosetta and Luis. But now you have caught me red-handed, so rest assured I will continue to assist with your enquiries, especially if it means a lesser sentence." Abbati banged his cup on the table, shooting us a sideways glance. "Then so be it. To hell with Emilio and his cronies. I will tell you everything I know."

"I must say, Abbati, that I'm staggered by how you managed to maintain the deception, fooling your employers and the owners of the property for such a long time, by fabricating the howling dog you named Caesar, who you trained to respond to a distinct whistle — rattling chains, fabricating ghosts, creating discord and gossip amongst the neighbours. You knew that by instilling the fear of God into those people, everyone would steer well clear of the place. You did all this to stop people from becoming curious about the house. But, of course, you had a vested interest in doing so, not only as a cover for your illegal profanities, your den of reprobates, but also to conceal the fact that you had committed the murders."

Abbati sat quietly, his chin on his hand, his other arm folded. Throughout the conversation, I stared at Abbati intently, observing his every move. Based on his overall demeanour and body language, I was satisfied that he spoke the truth about the murders and Nicco's kidnapping.

"Thank you. The inspector and I appreciate your honesty. Tell us how your friend Rodriguez got hold of the vaccine?"

Abbati blinked hard, shifting in his seat. "Emilio spoke of a contact in Berlin, a chemist named Gustav Bauman, who owed him a favour. He boasted that the chemist agreed to supply him with a vast amount of the vaccine in return for Emilio releasing the hold he had on Bauman and his family, along with a cash sum for each batch supplied."

"And who are the buyers, the recipients of the vaccine?"

"Emilio told me he could offload the entire batch to an organisation of medical professionals in Moscow to sell to selected clients at a greatly inflated price. Such was the need and desperation to garner protection against the deadly disease."

"These are despicable people, responsible for trading in people's fear, misery, and desperation."

Romano nodded in agreement. "Yes, indeed, their intent is crystal-clear, and they must be stopped at all costs."

After we finished our drinks, Romano and his driver dropped me off at the villa before proceeding with Abbati on their journey to the station. There, he would be charged, processed, and offered legal representation. He would remain in custody until the preliminary court hearing, at which point he would be entitled to apply for conditional bail. However, as I had advised the man earlier, at least until Rodriguez was apprehended, he would likely be far safer in jail than walking the streets of Milan.

I arranged to meet Romano the following morning at the villa to discuss our findings, aware that we were one step closer to cracking the code my clever son revealed in the book.

CHAPTER THIRTY: NENE ADLER
Tobia di Lombardia—Tobias of Lombardy

When the postman arrived the following morning, I was disappointed to find no word from the abductors. There were only two bills—a telegram for Sherlock and a letter from Violetta, who, at my husband's insistence, remained blissfully unaware of the turmoil threatening our family.

I entered the morning room door to find my husband sitting at the breakfast table with a cup of coffee, making notes in a commonplace book with a fountain pen, seemingly engrossed in his work. However, I could sense the rumblings of vexation and discontent, a far cry from my husband's congenial demeanour the day before. He looked up, frowning at my approach.

"Good morning, Sherlock. Did you hear that sound?"

"What sound?" he asked, staring at me perplexed. "I didn't hear anything."

"Ah, now I've got your attention. Why, my love, that's you executing the silent treatment. Over the years, I have become used to its startling sound."

"Very droll, Nene, but as you can see, I'm in no mood for banter."

"I know you expect Salvatore later this morning, but have you had breakfast?"

"I'm not hungry. I have no time for food," he returned in a somewhat peevish tone, his sallow face very much agitated and now masked in anger.

"But, darling, you should have something to keep up your

strength. How about some toast?"

"I've just told you that I don't want anything," my husband snapped irritably, staring at me with disdain. "Let that be the end of the matter."

"All right," I conceded, making my way towards the door. "I'll let you know when Salvatore arrives. Will you receive him in the study?"

Sherlock nodded. "Please remind the domestic servants that we are not to be disturbed."

"I will, although Alice might be keeping a wide berth. I heard her confiding to Hildegard that you were rude to her this morning. She was discovered crying in the kitchen earlier."

Sherlock looked at me aghast. "Rude!" he exclaimed. "Our son is missing, and you accuse me of being rude? Anyway, the woman dared to talk back to me after I challenged her over a trivial matter."

"Well, your demeanour is not helping Sherlock. I don't think you realise how disparaging your caustic remarks can be at times. You know Alice is a sensitive soul who wouldn't say boo to a goose, yet you made her feel uncomfortable."

Sherlock threw down the commonplace book on the table, exasperated. "It's not my job to make people feel comfortable," he answered, his eyes narrowed, and his lips thinned. "I'm sorry that my present mood isn't suiting everyone in this household, and breakfast isn't my priority right now. But I, for one, have far more pressing things to deal with than pandering to the whims of the hired help. What about you, Nene? Who would you have me be today? Sherlock, the loving husband and father, or Holmes, the calculating machine? Please let me know when you have decided, and if you have any better ideas on finding our son, I'm all ears."

I felt a tight knot in the pit of my stomach as I glared at my husband in disbelief. "Could you be any more obnoxious?" I expounded.

Sherlock shook his head in exasperation, giving me a withering look that was swiftly returned. Then, without uttering another word, he rose from his chair and picked up the book before quickly leaving the room to retire to his study.

I heaved a sigh as he slammed the door behind him. Sherlock's petulant words cut like a dagger. It gave me an ache in my heart to be on the receiving end of my husband's acerbic tongue, but I could sense his frustration. The hours and days were ticking by, and Nicco's abductors were still alluding us, albeit we were hopefully one step closer to finding them.

It had been a while since I'd witnessed Sherlock in such a contentious mood, and I knew he would never dream of speaking to me in such a manner under normal circumstances. Still, our circumstances were anything but ordinary. So I decided to put my frustrations aside and find Alice in the kitchen to apologise for my husband's unpleasant behaviour.

Salvatore arrived at 11 A.M. I kissed him on the cheek as he hugged me, holding me in a warm, friendly embrace. For a brief moment, our faces were so close that our lips would inadvertently brush if any sudden movement was made. Sherlock and I hadn't shared a bed since Nicco was abducted. Salvatore's simple gesture was a physical connection I had been starved of recently, and it was overwhelming. It reminded me of how I missed my husband's embrace. I missed everything—the way he held me, his athletic body pressed close to mine, and I even missed the brutal wit I had experienced earlier.

I had to wipe a tear from my eye as I escorted Salvatore, who favoured me with a kindly but quizzical smile, to Sherlock's study. "I shall organise some coffee. Good luck," I said, furrowing my brow as Salvatore knocked on the door.

"Come," Sherlock's dulcet tones echoed.

The Whistle of Revenge

When I returned a few minutes later with a tray of coffee, milk, sugar, and biscotti, Sherlock took the tray from me and set it on the occasional table in the corner of the room. I dutifully poured the coffee, adding milk and sugar, before handing the cups to the men.

Sherlock smiled at me, pointing to the whiteboards on the study walls. "I would like you to stay, Nene. Romano and I would value your input. Please excuse my rudeness earlier. It was just a few words between husband and wife in the heat of the moment. There is no need to apologise."

"Good," I retorted, shooting him a killing glance incensed by his haughty arrogance. "Because I'm not offering one. Our petty altercation does not change the fact that our son is still missing, and we're no nearer to finding a solution."

Still bristling from our earlier disagreement, I refrained from further discourse with Sherlock, who looked at me stony-faced. It was on the tip of my tongue to call him a pompous ass, but I had no wish to cause an argument or embarrass my husband in front of Salvatore. Instead, I helped myself to a cup of black coffee. I sat back in my chair, staring at the whiteboards on the wall in utter amazement. Each was covered with maps of Milan and the surrounding areas, primarily regions of Lombardy marked off in red.

At the top of each map, the word *whistle*, again highlighted in red, was written in large bold letters.

"What we are hoping to achieve is to establish the route to where Nicco is likely being held captive," Sherlock said, observing my bemused expression.

"But, Sherlock, there must be hundreds of possible routes?"

"Indeed, Nene. But I hope to reduce the possibilities during the afternoon until the odds become more favourable."

"Why are you concentrating on the word whistle?"

"Because it's the only anagram of the *Hewli St* clue given

by Nicco. Our son considered it a worthy clue, one not obvious to others. Whistle is a specific word pointing to someone or something highly significant." Sherlock turned his attention to Salvatore. "What about you? Anything good, Inspector?"

Salvatore nodded. "My men and I have strategically studied all the road maps in Milan and the surrounding areas, and we can categorically confirm that there is no such address containing *Hewli St* or *whistle*."

"Exactly," Sherlock said. "So, at least we can discount them from our calculations."

By observing the street map and his policeman's knowledge of the city, Salvatore suggested several possible locations of interest. After carefully considering each one and further in-depth consultations with Salvatore, my husband decided to concentrate on four potential route options in the Lombardy area.

"As we have already established," Sherlock said, pointing towards the boards. "Romano and I believe Operation Whistle is far more notable than the abduction of Nicco. Location is the key. If we can only pinpoint where Nicco is being held, we can rescue him and flush out the ring leaders of this so-called operation."

"Sherlock," I protested. "I'm sorry, but I don't care what else these people are up to. I just want Nicco home. Why don't the abductors simply give us the ransom exchange destination so we can pay the money and get our son back? If only we could speak to them and make them see reason."

"One cannot negotiate with the enemy, Nene, when they have their hands around your throat." Sherlock paused momentarily. "I'm sorry, I'm getting a little ahead of myself, but don't you see one thing links to the other? Of course, our main priority is the safe return of our son. As for the ransom demand, the perpetrators appear to be toying with us and playing for time. There seems to be no line these people won't cross."

"But why?" I asked.

"I don't know, Nene, but we will find out."

I nodded, smiling at my husband as he continued his narrative.

"First, we must look at the facts we have so far."

"Which are?" I asked, raising an eyebrow.

"We now have compelling evidence that Jack Stapleton is behind Nicco's kidnapping. Somehow, he escaped from his watery grave at the Great Grimpen Mire, and over the years, undoubtedly, using a series of aliases, came back to inflict his wrath on the world, first posing as a bloodstock agent in Ireland, using the pseudonym Robert Barrett, otherwise known as Bob. He's known to check into various hotels, using different disguises, yet carries no luggage and rarely stays overnight. He lives elsewhere in Milan. Someone in this city, who could be anyone from a complex list of associates, is harbouring him.

"Abbati confirmed that Bob is a horseman, who he suspects is living in the Lombardy area, so the person hiding him has a connection with the land and the horse fraternity. Bob regularly corresponded with Hildegard Achen while he lived in Ireland. However, the address he wrote to her was traced to a cottage in Timolin County, Kildare.

"Mycroft enquired with his agents in Eire, and the registered owner of the property is Mrs Constance Gallagher, a widow whose husband died a few years ago under mysterious circumstances, and her occupation and current location remain unknown."

"What else did your brother discover?"

Sherlock unravelled the lengthy telegram from Mycroft that had arrived earlier. "My brother said that after making various enquiries with the assistance of Inspector Lestrade, he discovered Beryl Stapleton passed away several years ago. She's buried at Bovey Tracey Cemetery in Newton Abbot.

"Mycroft also identified five racing stables in the Kildare area. Four have been established for over forty years, while the fifth in Maddenstown is run by Jim Sweeney, who took over the licence nearly two decades ago. He's a man of dubious reputation. After chatting amongst the stable hands on the gallops, the agents discovered that Sweeney employed an assistant trainer, Bob Barrett. The grooms appeared to hold this Bob in high regard, championing his impressive skills as the trainer of Olmo, the horse who finished second in the Gran Premio di Milano last year to that remarkable example of equine talent Keepsake."

"But, Sherlock, we were there when Keepsake won. Surely, you remember we had drinks with the owners in the champagne bar?"

Sherlock nodded in agreement. "Indeed, that's where Stapleton undoubtedly recognised me and formulated his dastardly plan. He had revenge in mind, all right. He had means, motivation, and opportunity. From the footprints at the house and the testimony of Giarcosca, Stapleton had at least three accomplices . . . the German woman named Connie, who we now know has roots in Ireland. The man with silver hair who drove the second carriage, and Rodriguez, of course. Which begs the question, are these people aware that they're dealing with a dangerously manipulative narcissistic psychopath?"

I gasped as my husband's narrative unfurled. "Forgive me, but I need to lay the facts before you precisely as they are. Doing otherwise would be a cruel deception," Sherlock said.

"It's all right, I understand. You don't have to pussyfoot around me."

"Indeed, Nene. There is double play here. Behind Stapleton's wicked actions is the concealment of a second act that is even more despicable than the first. The grooms also revealed that Bob and Sweeney had a falling out last year after a deadly virus swept through their stables. Some of Sweeney's best thoroughbreds were sent to the kill pens or destroyed after being infected by two fillies sent over from Milan by Ernest Angelino.

"Overwhelmed with the catastrophic loss and desire for vengeance, I have no doubt Barrett would do what he could to settle the score with Angelino. He also blamed Sweeney for ruining the business after accepting the fillies into the stables. The men are no longer on speaking terms. Barrett has not been seen at the stables for some time." Sherlock paused, shifting in his seat. "And this is where it gets interesting. When the Garda, accompanied by Mycroft's agents, interviewed Sweeney's veterinary surgeon, Oisin O'Flaherty, they made a shocking discovery. O'Flaherty told them that Barrett blackmailed him into supplying two vials of the same deadly toxin that infected Sweeney's horses.

"Furthermore, Barrett intends to inject two of Ernest Angelino's top thoroughbreds with the toxin in a wicked act of malice and revenge before the Gran Premio di Milano Race meeting on Sunday, where Angelino saddles two fancied runners. The Italian colt, Massena, is the likely favourite for the big race. At the same time, Angelino trains the second favourite, Sandura, who I understand is strongly fancied. In addition, he also saddles the hot favourite, Rubicon, for the Champagne Stakes. Angelino and the owners have been openly bullish about their horse's chances and have placed a considerable wager to win at three-to-one. Such is their confidence in their horse and jockey."

"Those poor horses. But why would a veterinary surgeon do that?" I gasped. "They swear an oath to protect animals, not destroy them."

"Barrett threatened O'Flaherty's father, Thomas O'Flaherty, a retired doctor, who was weak from the ravages of cancer and convalescing in a private nursing home in Kildare. Barrett sent his henchmen around to O'Flaherty's surgery. They gave him a severe thrashing as a warning that they meant business. Under duress, Oisin O'Flaherty finally agreed to Barrett's demands but insisted he only did this to protect his father after Barrett and his henchmen's threats. The man had little choice in the matter."

Sherlock leaned forward in his chair, his eyes shining like stars. "O'Flaherty told the agents that the night before Barrett was due to board the boat to Milan, his father passed away peacefully in his sleep. The doctors confirmed he died of natural causes. He was devastated by his father's death, enraged by the way Barrett and his cronies treated him and his father, blatant disrespect shown to a well-regarded pillar of society. Bitter and resentful, O'Flaherty decided to teach Barrett a lesson he would never forget."

"So what did he do?" I asked, staring at my husband with a burning curiosity.

"He switched the vials, so instead of being filled with the deadly toxin, he replaced them with a vitamin solution. Genius! The race is on Sunday. Murphy told Barrett the toxin should be injected three days beforehand to have maximum impact, which would simultaneously infect the rest of the horses in the stables."

Sherlock shook his head. "I cannot imagine Barrett carrying out the task himself. He'll have minions doing his dirty work for him, carrying out his deadly intentions." Sherlock diverted his gaze to Salvatore. "I suggest we visit Angelino today. Please arrange for one of your men to put a watch on the stables, for I fear the culprits will make their move by nightfall. In the meantime, what else do you have, Inspector? Is there anything of interest?"

Salvatore nodded, opening a file on the table in front of him. "Your husband paints a compelling picture, Nene. Here is a list of all the livery and racing stables in Lombardy."

I looked at Salvatore's list. I hadn't realised there were so many establishments in Lombardy, ranging from riding schools, showjumping, three-day event consortiums, and several racing and livery stables.

I turned my attention to Sherlock. "But why would Stapleton go to all this trouble?"

Sherlock sighed deeply. "In the fog of war, the desire for revenge is powerful, Nene. Stapleton is a narcissist who simply cannot help himself. He's displaying his power and arrogance. After literally getting away with murder in Dartmoor, the brute believes he's invincible. He blames me, of course, holding me accountable for becoming marginalised and outcast from society. But, more than that, Stapleton cannot handle the fact that he's become nothing more than a fading legend. His incomplete life has been reduced to a few columns of sensational newsprint, so he's fighting back the only way he knows how. Revenge is his raison d'etre, his reason for living."

Salvator interrupted, "From my experience, those who seek vengeance invariably risk swallowing a bitter pill. Everything about this man screams sociopath. People like Stapleton can never be reformed."

"If revenge is the only reason to live, then God have mercy on us all." I scoffed. "This monster is a vindictive parasite, feeding off people's misery and pain."

Sherlock nodded in agreement. "I agree wholeheartedly. The man is a meticulous and calculating despicable character, but one we're closer to finding."

I glanced again at Salvatore's list and the map of Lombardy. And then suddenly, like a bolt from the blue, the true meaning of Nicco's cryptic message came to me. I took a breath. "Sherlock, I think our son may be closer than we think."

My husband smiled at me curiously. "Whatever do you mean?"

"I've been wracking my brains about Nicco's second clue. I couldn't understand why he mentioned this person called Toby, and that's because Toby isn't a person."

"Please clarify?"

"Do you remember me telling you in my letters about my friend Claudia Furmagalli?"

"Yes, vaguely, but you told me your friend moved away."

"Yes," I agreed. "Neither I nor the children have seen Claudia for over two years. Still, we spent some wonderful afternoons together. We often took the children horse riding to a livery stable in Lombardy, where Claudia kept two horses, including an Andalusian dapple grey pony. The children could ride at the establishment if an instructor supervised them. Fortunately, amongst her other fine skills, Claudia is a qualified equestrian riding coach."

Sherlock stared at me with a puzzled expression and shrugged. "Nene, I fail to understand the point you are making."

"I just remembered the dapple grey pony Charlotte often rode and took such a shine. It was named Tobias."

Sherlock's penetrating eyes fixated on me, staring at me keenly. "Can you remember the name of the establishment?"

I shook my head. "No, I'm sorry, I simply can't remember, and unfortunately, I can't ask Claudia. She's away holidaying in Budapest until the end of the month. She told me she would be staying with friends but didn't reveal the address."

"How did you and your friend get to the stables?"

"Claudia would collect me and the children in a brougham, appearing like clockwork every second Sunday, just after luncheon. We chatted along the way, catching up with our news, so I'm afraid I didn't pay much attention to our direction. It was over two years ago, but I kept a photograph

Claudia took of the children. If my memory serves me right, the picture is in a drawer in the morning room. If you give me a few minutes, I can find the photograph."

I fixed my eyes on my husband. "While searching for the picture, I shall ask Ginevra and Alice to organise a cold platter. And I'm not taking no for an answer, Sherlock." I gestured to Salvatore. "We cannot allow our guest to starve. Caterina would never forgive us if we allowed that to happen."

Sherlock smiled pensively, nodding in resignation.

I slipped out of the study, leaving my bemused husband and Salvatore to talk among themselves.

I called into the kitchen to ask Alice to organise a luncheon before entering the morning room, rummaging through the chest of drawers until I found the photograph album containing numerous pictures of the children. Disappointment washed over me as I turned the pages, desperately searching for the image. And then I found the *Kodak* snapshot I was looking for at the back of the album, stuck between two pages. I stared at it for a moment, my heart beating wildly in my chest before I placed the photo in my dress pocket and returned to the study.

Salvatore was devouring a platter of cold meats, antipasti, olives, cheese, and bread. Sherlock reluctantly nibbled on a piece of bread and cheese to keep the peace.

"Look, I could be speaking out of turn, but I think I might have discovered the location where Nicco's being kept hostage," I said excitedly.

I carefully placed the photo of Nicco and Charlotte, celebrating a precious moment in their lives, on the desk before Sherlock and Salvatore. The photograph showed the children sitting astride two horses, Nicco on a black mare named Beauty, while Charlotte sat beaming from ear to ear on her favourite dapple grey pony. I pointed to the picture.

"Gentlemen, let me introduce you to this cheeky little

chappie. His official title is Tobias di Lombardia, although he was always affectionately known to Charlotte as Toby." I smiled at Sherlock.

"Ah, so this is the infamous Uncle Toby," he said, picking up the photograph and studying it closely before turning it over. On the reverse, Claudia had written the date and place the picture was taken in black ink.

1st June 1904, San Siro Scuderia di Cavalli Livery Stables.

"Right," Salvatore said, picking up his pen. "Then we shall give that establishment priority and add it to the list. It's located in one of our designated areas."

"I pray it's not a red herring, but I have a good feeling about Nicco and the photograph," I said, staring expectantly at the men.

"Anything at this stage is worth checking," Salvatore said. "This could be the smoking gun we've been looking for. I will order my men to put the stables under surveillance, discreetly, of course, so as not to alert undue suspicion. The welfare of your son is our main priority."

My husband looked at me with a wry smile. "If our son is not being kept at those stables, then Nicco must have recognised something familiar, such as scenery, a building, or a landmark. Perhaps some childhood memory was triggered when the abductors moved him. It would appear that our remarkable son has done it again."

I smiled appreciatively at my husband. "So, what happens now?"

"Why, my darling, first Salvatore and I will visit Angelino while Romano's men discreetly check out the stables near San Sior. But we must be careful. We don't want to go in all willy-nilly to alert undue suspicion and do anything that may put our son at risk."

"And when will you do this?"

Sherlock rose to his feet before diverting his gaze to Salvatore. "There's no time like the present. Are you, game,

Inspector?"

Salvatore nodded, putting on his hat and coat.

I stared at Sherlock anxiously. "Please be careful. God knows what the two of you could face."

Sherlock took me by the shoulders, staring intensely into my eyes. "Try not to worry. We will both be armed. In the meantime, I need you to stay here where it's safe, and in case there's any word from Mycroft or the kidnappers. Romano and I will bring Nicco home, where he belongs."

"Do you promise?" I asked, staring wide-eyed at my husband.

"How could I not?" he whispered.

"We will get this animal," Salvatore said, doffing his cap and squeezing my arm reassuringly before leaving the villa with Sherlock.

Chapter Thirty-One: Robert Barrett
Inganno e Devastazione – Deceit and Devastation

Connie and Peppo found me in a sociable mood on Thursday morning when they arrived at my suite on the second floor of the Athena Hotel. Food and drink had already been delivered to the room, ensuring our little gathering could be conducted privately.

Peppo tucked into his steak dinner with relish as I poured liberal amounts of *Brunello di Montalcino* red wine into crystal glasses before reverting my gaze to Connie.

"An update, please, on the horse doping. I trust everything is going to plan?"

"Of course," Connie said. "Our agents are now familiar with the layout of the premises and have identified the stalls where Angelino's two fancied runners are housed. They intend to break in through a side gate when the staff leave later this evening."

I pushed a white envelope towards Connie.

"What is this?" she asked, frowning suspiciously.

"Why, it's your passport to freedom, Connie. You can go anywhere you want when all this business is over."

Connie opened the envelope to reveal a fake passport in the name of Beatrice Shaw. She smiled sardonically. "I take it this is courtesy of your friend, Il Resolver."

I nodded as Connie continued her narrative. "It's of remarkable quality, what you would expect from the man who gets things done." She laughed. "What about you and Peppo?"

"I already have my passport but have yet to decide my next destination." I shrugged. "I can only tell you that it will be outside of Europe. As for Peppo, he intends to head south to be with his wife and children." I glanced over towards Peppo, who was enjoying the remains of his delightful meal, appearing oblivious to our conversation.

"I hear you, boss," Peppo said, wiping his mouth with a napkin before taking a large swig from his wine glass. "What of the boy and the ransom demand?"

"You don't need to worry about that. The Saporis will receive their instructions later this afternoon. The pick-up point will be Parco Sempione at seven A.M. on Monday when fewer people are around."

"But that's the day after the races when I travel to Genoa," Peppo said.

"Indeed, it is, my friend, but don't you see, by then, we'll have collected our winnings from the track and secured the ransom money."

"What about the commission from the painting?" Connie asked.

"Rodriguez promised to pay us as soon as we hand it over."

"But what about the boy? How will he be rescued?" Peppo asked, staring at me suspiciously.

"After securing the ransom money, we will drop him off at a location close to his home, leaving Connie and me free to embark on our journey out of Milan."

Peppo nodded. "All right, boss, that sounds good. I'm glad Nicco will finally be reunited with his family. It's a pity I won't be here to witness that happy moment."

Connie shot Peppo a look of disdain as she drained her glass. "Careful, some might say you are going soft in your old age."

"On a more serious note, we still must secure the painting to achieve our goals and satisfy Rodriguez. So I'm counting on both of you to be up to the task and prepared for the next part of the operation on Monday, especially you, Peppo."

"You'd better believe it. Neither of us will let you down," Connie said, filling her glass before raising it toward Peppo and me. "To Operation Whistle," she declared.

Peppo and I raised our glasses in unison, repeating the toast.

On Friday evening, Angelino's Liguria car factory was set to close for their annual one-week summer holiday. This was when the crucial cog in the whistle machinery would be set in motion. Operation Whistle was an intricate plan involving Angelino handing over his most prized possession, the valuable Giorgione painting of *The Blessed Veronica of Milan* in exchange for the non-destruction of his precious car assembly line.

Rather than risk attracting the attention of the Italian authorities, I decided to contact the dynamite manufacturer, DeBeers, using a private mailbox in Milan. Using a false identity, I requested a quote for the explosives to be delivered to an address to be determined in Busella, just outside Genoa. My eyes watered when I opened the envelope containing the quote in the privacy of my study. I knew Emilio would never bankroll such a sum. I replied immediately, rejecting the quotation, and arranged an urgent meeting with Emilio to discuss an alternative way forward.

By the end of the afternoon, we had come up with a solution that satisfied us both, one that would incur minimal cost yet be fully effective. Emilio agreed to fund the operation and recover the costs, which would be repaid with interest once the painting had changed hands to the buyer Il Resolver had already secured but only referred to as Mr X.

On Sunday evening, during the second week in May, Connie and Peppo took the train to Genoa, then the connection to Bogliasco, located a few miles outside the city. There, they stole an empty, unmarked covered wagon parked within the grounds of the Bogliasco Flour Company. Discovering the keys concealed under the right front tyre, they drove to a property demolition company, breaking into its warehouse and helping themselves to two tons of dynamite, a detonator, and a large reel of cabling. After loading their haul into the wagon, they drove the short distance to the storage facility in Basulla provided by Emilio.

They returned to the storage facility a week later, driving to the Manzoni Tyre Company in Turin, where they purchased a small quantity of new tyres. The following week, Peppo and Connie took the wagon to the local used tyre dump in Genoa and, for a nominal sum, bought a hundred used tyres, paying in cash again, explaining when questioned by the bemused proprietor that the tyres were to be used as safety buffers to be secured at the end of one of the docks in Genoa. The proprietor bought their story and gladly took the money. Once completed, the explosives were loaded onto the wagon before being covered and concealed with the tyres, ready to await the next phase of the operation.

If he failed to comply, the devastating destruction of the Liguria car factory in Genoa would hit Angelino hard. The damage would be caused by detonating the two tons of stolen dynamite concealed in the truck, which would be driven to the store's warehouse adjoining the assembly facility. Emilio and I estimated that if we went ahead, the explosion would destroy both buildings, putting back production by at least a year.

We knew security was not a concern, as Connie recently visited the site, managing to enter the building and walk around the entire factory unchallenged. A delivery note for the tyres had been forged on official headed paper, and wearing a stolen *Manzoni* uniform, Peppo was to drive the lorry to Liguria Cars security entrance, arriving at 10 P.M. on Monday, the day after the races.

The method for delivering the dynamite had been meticulously planned and recognised as the most crucial element of the operation. The factory layout had been well researched from previous visits and detailed building and survey plans. Several dry runs had taken place to ensure everything would run like clockwork. There could be no room for error.

I sipped from my glass, closing my eyes momentarily, reflecting that the stage was set. I was only a few days away from realising my goal. We would generate income three ways with several bites of the cherry. First, we would relieve the bookmakers of their bulging satchels at the Milano Racetrack on Sunday, secure in the knowledge that Angelino's horses would fail to show after being injected with the virus. Then, we'd placed a substantial wager on Break the Bank in the Stakes Race. As far as the punters were concerned, there were only two runners with a realistic chance. After nobbling Angelino's much-fancied entry and barring mishaps, the odds were stacked considerably in our favour. The ransom would be collected on Monday morning at Sempione Park by one of Rodriguez's agents before finally, the piece de resistance, receiving a handsome commission for the stolen painting, thus ensuring maximum humiliation for Angelino and a bumper payout for Rodriguez and me.

For the first time in a long time, life felt good. It would have felt even better if I'd been able to keep hold of that painting. Still, thanks to Angelino, that dream was now well and truly shattered. I needed every penny to pay off my expenses before disappearing to start my new life.

Chapter Thirty-Two: Salvatore Romano

Non Cambiare I Cavallo a Metà Flusso — Don't Change Horses in Midstream

Holmes and I arrived at Ernest Angelino's stables at 2 P.M., having messaged ahead. The double-fronted detached villa with its impressive sweeping in and out driveway was a handsome example of its period. A private wrought iron fence surrounded the property.

We were duly greeted by Angelino's private secretary, Gina Boccaccio. This petite, dark-haired woman patiently waited, smiled, and gave us a firm handshake as we stepped down from the hansom.

We were escorted into a grand vestibule, dominated by a sweeping oak staircase to the left, lined with glass railing and a mosaic floor covered with Aubusson rugs. Pictures of prize-winning thoroughbreds adorned the walls, and several glass cabinets containing a wide selection of glittering trophies, medals and bronze busts lined the interior. We followed Gina into an impressive drawing room. Its heavy oak door with brass fittings included a series of metal locks to the outside, connecting several bolts to the door's interior.

She laughed, observing Holmes' sudden interest as he closely examined the door. Gina pointed to a picture on the wall, explaining that her employer had used an elaborate security system to protect one of his most prized possessions, an image of *Saint Veronica of Milan* and said to have been

The Whistle of Revenge

painted by Giorgione.

"Ah, yes, of course," Holmes said, completely ignoring the painting, diverting his gaze back to the door. "I'm familiar with this type of security system. It's an ingenious little invention. The pins only open using the correct key, while an incorrect one ensures the door remains securely in place, making it almost impossible to gain entry."

Casting my eyes around the room, I noticed a modified system had secured the toughened glass frame, protecting the painting.

Holmes and I sat together on a Chesterfield settee as Gina excused herself to inform Angelino we had arrived.

A few minutes later, Ernest Angelino appeared, an imposing figure dressed in a tweed suit, flat cap, and a pair of plus-fours. He was a tall, stoutly built, middle-aged man with sandy hair, his body worn, slack, and past its best, no doubt from an indulgent lifestyle. He gazed at us with astute brown eyes, flashing an engaging smile, before shaking hands with us warmly. As we stood, I introduced myself and Lucca Sapori, waving my badge towards him. Angelino insisted we remain seated. He was followed into the room by a smiling Gina carrying a silver tray with three crystal glasses filled with claret, which she handed us before deftly leaving. Angelino sat opposite us in a delicately upholstered wing-back chair, smiling in bemusement as he took a sip from his glass.

"Well, gentleman, pray tell why Ernest Angelino, a humble horse trainer and motor trader, should attract the interest of the Milano polizia."

"I don't think there's anything humble about your racing stables, nor indeed your car manufacturing company in Genoa," I said.

Angelino threw back his head and laughed out loud. "Indeed, I am a fortunate man, but you still haven't answered my question, Inspector."

"Are you familiar with a fellow in the horse racing fraternity, Robert or Bob Barrett, whom we understand has connections in Ireland?"

Angelino furrowed his brow. "Why, yes, of course, Bob visited me here last year. On the day of the Milano Race meeting, we had drinks in this room afterwards. He had an agreeable disposition, and we got on well. One of my owners was so enamoured with Bob's training skills in the Gran Premio di Milano with Olmo they insisted on sending two of their top fillies to Bob and Jim Sweeney's stables in Kildare."

"We understand this did not end well for the fillies?"

Angelino shook his head. "No, Inspector, and if I had known what was about to happen, I would never have sent them. Such a tragic end to two equine superstars, the thought of it still brings a tear to my eye, after they contracted a deadly disease and had to be destroyed, sadly, along with several other of Bob and Jim's finest thoroughbreds."

"Have you heard from Sweeney and Barrett since?"

"No, Inspector. I wrote to them, expressing my deep regret, and asked if I could do anything. But I received no reply. I believe Jim Sweeney suffered some kind of breakdown after that dreadful tragedy, and as for Bob, I understand he tried to carry on for a while, but with most of their best horses gone, it proved an arduous task. I was told he and Jim parted ways. The last I heard, Bob had gone abroad."

"This man is nearer than you think," Holmes said in a grave tone. "And I'm afraid he has revenge on his mind. You, Senor Angelino, are his intended victim."

We proceeded to update Angelino about the events in Ireland, including the veterinary surgeon Oisin O'Flaherty and the horse doping scandal.

Angelino fell back in his chair, stunned. He pulled a handkerchief from his jacket pocket, wiping away beads of sweat from his brow. "I simply cannot believe that Bob Barrett

The Whistle of Revenge

would exact his revenge in such a way. But if what you say is true, then there's not a moment to lose, Inspector, Signor Sapori, I must alert my staff, without delay, and order them to put a watch on the stables."

Holmes held his hand as Angelino jumped from his chair, heading towards a bell pull in the room's far corner. "Please hear me out," Holmes said, gesturing for Angelino to sit back in his seat. "Oisin O'Flaherty told our contacts in Ireland that before Barrett embarked on his journey to Milan, he replaced the contents of the vials with vitamin solution. Barrett has no clue about this deception and will undoubtedly send agents to inject your two entries, which are scheduled to run on Sunday. Would you mind showing us the stalls occupied by these horses?"

"All right," Angelino begrudgingly agreed. "But only if you can guarantee that it is safe."

Holmes nodded. "You have my word, but I would implore you not to mention a word to the stable staff, just in case any of them are involved in this deception and the mercantile activities of Barrett's gang. We can't afford to trust anyone. We must keep this deception to ourselves for now."

"Don't worry," Holmes said, observing Angelino's forlorn expression. "If you follow my instructions, I guarantee nothing will happen to your horses."

Holmes glanced around the stables, his eyes focused on two empty stalls at the far end of the block. Angelino pointed to two magnificent-looking beasts housed at the other end of the stable block—a handsome bay and a striking chestnut with a white blaze. Their names were proudly displayed on brass plaques hung to the side of each stall.

Angelino beamed. "Allow me to introduce you to our stable stars, Sandura and Rubicon," he said while affectionately stroking the horses underneath their forelocks, feeding each a carrot. "Gentlemen, I'm in your hands," Angelino continued. "These handsome boys are both strongly fancied on Sunday. The chestnut, Sandura here, has a tough task in beating Messana, the firm favourite for the Gran Premio. The owners are confident he will give a good account of himself on the day. They have backed him each-way to win substantially, while our entry for the Champagne Stakes, Rubicon, has been tearing up the home gallops. He's expected to win and win well. If anything happens to these fine animals, there will be hell to pay. I have a reputation to withhold."

"Don't worry. If you follow my instructions to the letter, I guarantee nothing will happen to your horses," Holmes said. Then he pointed to the two empty stalls. "Where are the horses who normally occupy those stalls?"

"They house Rathrea and his brother, Riptide, two fine sprinters," Angelino explained. "They both incurred recent injuries on the gallops and were turned out in the fields to graze and recuperate. Would you like to see them?" he asked, staring at the celebrated detective curiously.

Holmes nodded, and we made our way out of the stables to a gated meadow, where we found two geldings grazing nearby next to an orchard covered in the last droppings of apple blossom. Angelino whistled, calling out to the horses, who turned around and slowly walked towards us, softly whinnying.

Holmes smiled, and they both observed the colours of the horses, bay and chestnut, the same as the two fancied runners. "What time do your stable staff usually leave for the evening?"

"Between six-thirty and seven P.M., just after the evening feed," Angelino said. "Why? What do you have in mind?" he asked, looking at us suspiciously.

"As soon as the staff have gone, I want you to move Sandura and Rubicon to the stalls occupied by the injured horses.

Then bring Rathrea and Riptide in from the fields and into the stalls usually occupied by your two runners. When the horse dopers attack, which I suspect will be later this evening, they will syringe the wrong horses, but you have my word that no harm will come to either beast."

"But I don't understand how they will gain entry. I have a night watchman and two dogs patrolling the premises."

"Give your nightwatchman the evening off, and ensure you tether the dogs after the staff leave."

"But why make it easier for these thugs?" Angelino sounded exasperated.

"Because we're going to beat Barrett at his own game. Inspector Romano's guardie will be keeping a careful watch incognito. They will follow the villain's home and make a note of their address, but there will be no arrest so as not to alleviate suspicion. But rest assured, after the races, the miscreants and thugs will be rounded up and duly arrested for their audacious crime."

Angelino put his hands up in protest. "Gentleman, are you sure we're dealing with this matter correctly? There is so much at stake for me, my owners and the livelihood of my stable staff."

"It's the only way to guarantee the safety of your horses and garner a positive outcome for you and the owners of these splendid horses at the Milano Races on Sunday," Holmes said. "Barrett will appear there. I'm sure the temptation will prove irresistible, although I presume he'll be heavily disguised. This way, we catch him red-handed and kill two birds with one stone."

Angelino nodded in agreement. "But what do I tell the stable hands in the morning? I will do anything to protect the reputation of this establishment, so just give me the word, gentlemen, and I promise I will comply."

Holmes paused for a moment, then nodded. "Your

challenge if you wish to accept it, Signor Angelino, is this . . . you must tell your staff that the vet was called in overnight after finding the two fancied horses unwell in their stalls. After a thorough examination, Sandura and Rubicon were discovered to have a temperature and, therefore, deemed unlikely to run on Sunday. You will be amazed how quickly rumours spread. Once this news hits the racetrack and the bookmakers get wind of the situation, the price of your horses will drift considerably. You can tell your owners to have another wager at greatly enhanced odds before your runners arrive at the track. But, in the meantime, you must keep this conversation to yourself. No one, not even your most trusted employees, can know."

"What about the stewards at the racetrack? What do I say when they challenge me about my horse's participation?"

"Then you tell him that the vet made a mistake, the horses were placed in the wrong stalls overnight, and misdiagnosed. You won't officially withdraw the horses, so technically, no crime will be committed. Just explain the rumours were idle conjecture fuelled by malicious gossip. The bookmakers will probably take a dim view of the proceedings."

"What if Bob Barrett's agents try to sabotage the horses?" Angelino asked, protesting.

"They won't, I assure you," Holmes said. "Inspector Romano's men will be surrounding the route. Other agents will be at the racetrack, posing as punters, keeping their eyes peeled for anything or anyone suspicious."

"Will you and the inspector be in attendance? I would feel more secure if you were."

Holmes sighed. "Sadly, as much as we would like to, I cannot guarantee that will happen. We're looking into another pressing matter involving the welfare of a young boy. But rest assured, the inspector and I will be there if possible. Let's just say I, for one, have a vested interest in apprehending Bob

The Whistle of Revenge

Barrett."

We shook hands with Angelino, bidding him farewell, and turned to leave. As we reached the grand hallway, Holmes turned on his heels, focusing on Angelino with those penetrating eyes and said, "The picture in your drawing room of Saint Veronica of Milan, pray tell me, how long has it been there?"

Angelino laughed. "Why Signor Sapori? That painting has been in my family for generations. It has hung on that wall for the past twenty years, ever since my father died, and the picture was passed down to me, his eldest son."

Holmes nodded, appearing satisfied. We shook hands with Angelino before returning to Via Torino.

When we arrived at the villa, Nene was sitting in the drawing room, tears rolling down her beautiful face.

"Whatever is the matter?" Holmes asked as our eyes diverted to a letter Nene held in her shaking hands.

She looked up at her husband, woefully holding up the letter, which I noticed was printed on thick, rough-edged paper. "Sherlock, it's arrived, the ransom demand."

"Let me see," he said, his voice low but commanding.

Nene held the letter towards him, appearing reluctant to release her grip. "They . . . they said Monday. Seven in the morning. Parco Sempione. They want the money brought there." Her voice broke as fresh tears spilled down her cheeks. "What if we don't make it on time? What if they —"

"Enough," Holmes interrupted, gently removing the note from Nene's hand. His fingers brushing against hers lingered for a moment. "We will make it on time. Nicco will return home."

Holmes' jaw tightened as he read out the demands.

"It's him, isn't it?" Nene said, her voice wavering but edged with a desperate kind of certainty. We had both witnessed the shift of Holme's expression, the flash of grim recognition that no amount of icy detachment could conceal.

"Yes," Holmes replied, his voice a cold whisper. "It is indeed Jack Stapleton."

The name fell between them like a stone rippling in calm, deep water. Nene let out a strangled sob, her hand covering her mouth as her body started to tremble. Holmes moved to her side, lowering himself onto the chaise lounge. He hesitated before placing a hand lightly on her shoulder. It was an awkward gesture — tentative — but it steadied her.

"Nene," he said, his voice softer now. "You must trust me. This note is a piece of the puzzle, another link in the chain that will bring Nicco back to us."

She looked at him, eyes wide with grief and a child-like expectancy. "Do you truly believe that? You speak so calmly but haven't slept in days. You never stop chasing shadows. What if . . . what if we're too late?"

"We won't be," he said, his grey eyes meeting her with an intensity that appeared to silence all doubt. "I've faced Stapleton and his like before. The man is cunning, but he underestimates me and the law. He always has, and that ultimately will be his downfall."

Nene let out a shuddering breath. "What if it's a trap?"

"That is a possibility," Holmes admitted, folding the letter and placing it into his pocket. "I wouldn't expect anything less from Stapleton. But a trap works both ways. He's shown his hand, which immediately makes him vulnerable. If Stapleton or Bob Barrett wants to play cat and mouse, so be it. The game is afoot."

For a moment, a complete absence of sound reigned over the room. Standing in silence, hardly daring to breathe, I felt a tinge of regret eavesdropping on this profoundly private moment between husband and wife, two remarkable people born of great courage. It was an overwhelming reminder of

The Whistle of Revenge

the strength and resilience of the human spirit. Their words resonated deeply, highlighting the acute intensity and sensitivity of the situation. This languid spell continued for a moment. The only sound was Nene's laboured breathing and the faint creak of the old building settling into the early evening following the day's heat.

Then, with a surprising air of empathy, Holmes spoke again. "You must rest, Nene. Your strength, both in body and mind, will be needed in the coming days."

She shook her head, clutching his arm, as though he might vanish. "I can't. Not while Nicco is still out there, while those monsters—"

"Nene," he said, interrupting her, his voice still firm but warmer. "I promise you, we will bring him home. You have my word."

Her grip loosened, and she nodded, though her tears continued to fall. Holmes rose with a visibly renewed determination and turned towards the window. He gazed out at the evening sky over Milan, where the flickering gas lamps would soon be reflected off the granite paved street of this great city. The celebrated detective's calculating mind no doubt measured the steps needed to outwit Stapleton and rescue his son.

Nene whispered a single plea. "Whatever happens, don't let them hurt him."

Holmes did not turn. Instead, he maintained his steady gaze out the window, but his answer was sharp and precise. "They won't, not while Sherlock Holmes draws breath."

Chapter Thirty-Three: Salvatore Romano
Verso la Luca—Into the Light

I sat in my office amidst a mountain of paperwork, relaxing with a cup of coffee and a cigarette as rain pelted down the windowpanes on a cool, wet Sunday morning.

Officer Cipriano Esposito, who operated the front desk, entered my office to tell me Sergente Maggiore Ferraro had arrived back at the station and needed to speak to me urgently.

I furrowed my brow and asked Esposito to send for the sergente, wondering what had brought him back so early from his surveillance duties in Lombardy. Ferraro was one of the best officers in my ranks. He joined the Milano polizia two months earlier and was recently promoted to sergente. A decision that raised a few eyebrows amongst my men. He was considered a solitary individual, rumoured to have a penchant for liquor and a pretty woman. Still, as a clever, insightful law enforcer with a bright, enquiring mind, he was an undeniable asset to the Milano polizia.

Ferraro entered the room. I nodded, urging him to sit. "What have you got?" I quizzed, staring at him curiously.

Deep-set brown eyes stared at me from Ferraro's sharp features, which were taut and serious-looking, aided by his raw-boned frame. His response was sharp and concise. "Guardia Egidio Capo reported suspicious activity at The San Siro Scuderia Stables just before dawn. He was on the lookout near the rear of the main house when he noticed a flashing light coming from an upstairs window, which was closed and covered by blinds. Whoever was flashing was clearly in trouble from the slats of the window shutters. They continually messaged *S.O.S.* in Morse Code, followed by the name Nicco.

"Capo came to find me at a neighbouring stable, and we returned to San Siro together. By the time we arrived, the yard was deadly quiet. Then, a man appeared with a dog on a leash. He seemed nervous and kept looking toward the window, refusing to answer our questions. I was about to ask Capo to cuff him and read him his rights when a young lad appeared out of the stable block, pushing a wheelbarrow. He looked surprised to see us and asked if he could help. When questioned, the lad identified himself as Orlando Fontano and said he'd only worked at the stables for a few weeks. He'd been left behind to oversee the horses and prepare the evening feed. He expected the staff to return later this afternoon.

"When I questioned him about the man with the dog, asking why he didn't respond to questioning, the boy explained the man was a deaf-mute employed on a casual basis as security to guard the house and stables. I asked him if he'd seen a boy or noticed any suspicious activity at the premises. He shook his head and said no, explaining how his work with the horses kept him busy. His boss, the temporary racing manager Bob Barrett, was a stern taskmaster who expected hard graft and one-hundred per cent commitment from his staff. He seemed like a decent lad, and I believed him."

"Did you make any progress with this deaf-mute?"

Ferraro smiled. "Yes sir, my youngest brother, Ello, was born afflicted with impaired hearing, so I used lingua dei Segni, Italian sign language, to establish a dialogue with the mute. He told me the owner of the stables, Ludovico Galli, was away working in America. He'd left the temporary running of the establishment in the hands of a trainer from Ireland, a man named Robert Barrett, otherwise known as Bob.

When questioned further, the mute admitted that Barrett kept a boy in the house against his will. His description matches Nicco Sapori."

"So, by the looks of things, Nicco Sapori is imprisoned at The San Siro Stables?" I asked, staring at Ferraro in what was a real seminal moment as a surge of adrenaline suddenly overpowered my fatigue.

Ferraro nodded. "It would appear so, Inspector."

"Was there any other activity from the house?"

"No, sir, we knocked but received no answer. Then, when we tried to enter the property's rear, we found all the doors and windows locked. The mute explained that he was not entrusted with a key. He was instructed to patrol outside with the dog and not allow anyone to enter the grounds. No one was allowed access except the staff and the keyholders to the house, Robert Barrett and his assistant, a man named Peppo Barbieri. He's the one who gave the orders and is primarily responsible for looking after the boy."

"Did he say where this Bob and Peppo were now?" I asked.

Ferraro shook his head. "No, sir, that's what we're trying to establish. Barrett has not been seen at the stables for the past two nights. However, the mute told us, by lip-reading banter in the stables, he learned Barrett was expected to attend the race meeting later this afternoon to oversee Viscusi, the stable's runner in the first race."

"And Peppo Barbieri?"

Ferraro shrugged. "When questioned, the mute said he didn't know. He presumed Barbieri would attend the race meeting with Barrett and return with him later."

"Where's the mute now? Do we know his name?"

Ferraro nodded. "His name is Mario Renaldi, from Bergamo. He's in custody and being processed as we speak. I'll interview him again, although I doubt he can tell us anything else. He's not privy to Barrett's inner circle. He's merely a domestic servant."

"Right," I replied. "We'll apply for an immediate warrant to search the premises. Gather your men, Ferraro, and summon the locksmith. I will join you shortly, but first, there's something I must do."

I waited for Ferraro to leave my office before picking up the telephone. My hands shook as I took a deep breath and dialled Sherlock Holmes' number. The phone was answered after three rings.

The connection was poor due to the inclement weather and terrible crackling on the line, but there was no mistaking that clipped, well-modulated voice that said, "Hello?"

"We finally have the breakthrough we've been looking for, my friend. We have found your son."

Holmes took a sharp intake of breath, responding with one word. "Where?"

"The San Siro Scuderia Stables, we've asked for a warrant, which is being fast-tracked. My men and I will collect you in twenty minutes."

"Right." Holmes paused for a moment. I could hear the anxiety in his voice — that cool, calm composure had slipped like a mask. "Is my boy alive?"

"We have every reason to believe so."

Holmes released the breath he held, replying. "Thank you, Salvatore. I will see you directly."

I smiled, taken aback by the detective's narrative, replacing the receiver on the hook. That was the only time Holmes called me by my Christian name. It was touching coming from him.

Our carriage arrived at Via Torina at 10 A.M. It was still raining, but the clouds were starting to lift, with the promise of the sun attempting to break through. I prayed this was a good omen. Holmes jumped into the hansom, and we set off to the stables. The celebrated detective was pensive and barely spoke during the journey, his expression stern and self-possessed.

The coachman, aware of the urgency of our trip, whipped the horses, and the carriage moved along at a reasonable speed. Thirty minutes later, the coachman reigned in the horses to an extended trot as the road ahead narrowed. We found ourselves on a country lane, surrounded by fields and outbuildings. After a sharp turn to the right, we discovered The San Siro Stables right before us, its signpost blowing gently in the cool Tuscan breeze. The coachman expertly guided the carriage through two stone gate posts before pulling up the horses and bringing the brougham to a halt.

We jumped down from the carriage to find a group of guardie patrolling the main house. Having arrived minutes ahead of us, the locksmith gained entry through the kitchen door, which he explained was the least robust of the property's formidable locks. Within minutes, we were inside the house, finding ourselves in a vast hallway that veered off in two directions.

Pushing open the door to the left, we found ourselves looking into a room that served as a changing room. The interior smelt of saddle soap and earthy leather, with hats, riding jackets, and horse rugs hanging off rails.

Holmes pointed with his revolver to the door to the right. "This way, gentlemen," he said, his long legs striding purposefully ahead as we entered what was a tack room for the stables. There was a collection of snaffle bits, saddles, bridles and blankets, with a further door at the end. Through the portal were steps leading to the first floor of the building. We ascended to the top of the landing to be faced by two heavy-panelled doors.

Holmes pushed the left one open. We tentatively stepped over the threshold and looked around the dim interior of the long, narrow room with a mullioned window set low in the wall. This had all the appearance of a trophy room, newspaper, and photographic gallery. Turning on the light revealed a shrine to equestrian glory. Gleaming trophies stood in neat rows within glass cabinets. Photographs of proud horses and their victorious riders adorned the dark wood-panelled walls. A Persian rug stretched across the polished floor, its intricate pattern dull under the shadows of the dimly lit room, but there was no sign of Nicco.

The second door to the right was set in the thickness of the wall. Holmes put his shoulder to the door in an attempt to open it, but it was locked from the outside. With a nod from the detective, the locksmith skilfully removed the lock at impressive speed. He stepped back as Holmes slowly pushed the door open. There was a deadly quiet as he put his finger to his lips, warning us to be quiet and explaining that he did not want his son to be placed in unnecessary danger. My heart missed a beat, wondering what we would find. I was excited, nervous, and terrified simultaneously.

We slowly entered a long room, which was bright, airy, and beautifully decorated with green willow-patterned wallpaper. Holmes' keen eyes darted across the room, dissecting every corner. At the front of the room, his gaze fell upon a small chair next to a mahogany writing desk. A plate of half-eaten food sat beside it, with its edges crusted.

In the middle of the room was a double bed with an oaken frame, matching bedroom furniture, and two chairs. On one of them sat Nicco, shoeless and dressed in pyjamas. The boy turned around at our approach. The expression on his face was one I shall never forget, one of pure, unadulterated joy. My heart leapt in my chest at the realisation that we'd found him safe and well.

Standing, he ran towards Holmes, flinging his arms around him. "I was never afraid, Father. I knew you would come and rescue me," Nicco said through tear-filled eyes.

Holmes gathered the boy in his arms, tenderly placing a hand on his son's cheek. "Thank God. I'm sorry it took so long to find you. Did they hurt you?" he cried, holding his son gently by the shoulders and staring into his eyes with an expression of the utmost tenderness.

Nicco shook his head. "No, father, I'm well. The abductors treated me kindly, well, most of them." He smiled ruefully.

Holmes held out his hand, beaming at his son. "Then come, my brave boy, on with your clothes. Mother is waiting."

I instructed Ferraro and two guardie to remain at the property. I asked them to make their way through the rooms of the house, searching for any incriminating evidence and signs of foul play. They would remain until the staff returned to the stables, where they would be cautioned, questioned, and interviewed.

As we made our way out to the carriage, our senses were infused by the aromatic, pungent aroma of jasmine, honeysuckle, and lavender wafting through the air. The sun shone brightly as a rainbow appeared on the horizon. The guardie stood in line applauding Nicco's rescue with cheers and several bravos. I felt inordinately proud of my men. They had worked so hard in the past few days, and now, at last, our combined efforts had been duly rewarded.

Holmes glanced up at the coach driver. "Take good care," he said. "You have precious cargo."

I agreed with Holmes's request not to take Nicco to the station for questioning. The boy had endured enough trauma for one of such tender years. He was also eager to be reunited with his mother.

On the journey back to the villa at Via Torina, Nicco told us all he knew of his captors. Gino, who on the surface came across as uncouth and a little rough around the edges, had shown great kindness towards him. The sinister woman

The Whistle of Revenge

named Connie and his meeting with Bob a few days earlier. That thought sent a shiver down my spine. It was a memory I immediately wanted to erase from my mind.

Nicco looked at his father curiously. "Is Bob who I think he is?"

Holmes furrowed his brow. "Yes. It would appear so, but I don't want you to worry. Inspector Romano and I will find Stapleton. He and his cronies will be arrested by the day's end." Holmes smiled at his son. "But how on earth could you know? Did Barrett reveal his identity to you?"

Nicco shook his head, staring at his father with a solemn expression. "No, sir, I figured it out from what Bob said. He's a bitter man who holds you wholly responsible for the death of his wife. The timing, what you told me of the Hound of the Baskerville case, what I read in Doctor Watson's chronicles, of the events that occurred seventeen years ago, finally gave him away. But you and the inspector must go find him before he hurts anyone else."

"Ah, so you don't object to me leaving you so soon after your rescue?"

"No, sir, but please be careful. I don't want anything to happen to you or Inspector Romano."

"I promise we will be on guard," Holmes said, appearing humbled and touched by his son's narrative.

"Are you sure Mother will be home? I can hardly wait to see her," Nicco said, staring anxiously at his father.

Holmes nodded. "Yes, indeed."

"If not, then Nene is in for a wonderful surprise," I added, smiling warmly at the boy.

The brougham had barely stopped outside the villa when the front door swung open, and Nene raced down the steps towards us. Oh, the ecstasy, but perhaps even more endearing, was the relief on her face as she ran towards her beloved son. Helped by his father, Nicco jumped from the carriage straight into his mother's arms. Nene held him tightly, sweeping him in a loving embrace as she rained tender kisses onto his face.

"Forgive me, I'm sorry, I'm so sorry," she said.

For the first time in days, there was laughter and tears. But there were tears of happiness and joy. Nicco slipped his hand into his mother's, his face breaking into a wide grin, and then, with her arm wrapped protectively around her son, they entered the villa with us following behind.

Nene looked up at Holmes and me, beaming. "Thank you for bringing Nicco home, Sherlock. You and our cherished friend Salvatore have been fundamental to finding our son. The cost of losing him was almost my soul," she mused. "I will be eternally grateful to you both."

Nene turned her attention to me, arching her eyebrow in mock humour. "As for you, Salvatore. I want to thank you and your men for top-notch police work and showing humility, compassion, and true leadership throughout this horrendous ordeal while under the most intense pressure. Some of it, I know, was instigated by me. I can only apologise for that."

I shook my head. "There's no need to apologise. You did what any mother would do under the circumstances."

I had always considered Nene to be a handsome woman, but she never looked as beautiful as she did then. I flushed crimson as she leaned over to kiss me gently.

"What about your husband?" I teased. "Is Signor Sapori not worthy of a kiss?"

Nene flashed a smile as she led Nicco through into the hallway. "Ah, Salvatore, I'm sure I will think of a way to thank my husband later."

There was a commotion in the villa as Helen, the Saporis' dog, bounded towards us like a puppy, barking, twirling around, jumping up, and wagging her tail. The domestic servants, Alice, Ginevra, and the Saporis' nanny, Hildegard, now aware of Nicco's return, fussed around him. The bevvy of women shrieked with breathless excitement, their laughter and incessant chatter echoing throughout the villa.

Ginevra brought Nicco a cool glass of lemonade, a slice of Alice's freshly baked lemon ricotta cake, and a large bowl of Italian ice cream, which he wolfed down before the ladies were eventually ushered out of the room by Nene, who was desperate to spend quality time with her son.

Holmes poured three glasses of brandy into crystal glasses, handing one to each of us as we raised a dutiful toast to Nicco Sapori's safe return. After finishing our drinks, Nene ensured Nicco was settled comfortably in his room. The boy was understandably tired and said he needed rest.

Nene rejoined us in the drawing room and topped up our glasses. "Helen is at the bottom of his bed, keeping watch. He's drifted off to sleep. What now?"

"It's not over. On the contrary, this is far from over," Holmes said, nodding grimly. "Romano and I must find the perpetrators and bring them to justice. I can't allow Stapleton to slip through my fingers again."

"And where will the perpetrators be found?" Nene asked, arching an eyebrow.

"The Milano Race Track. The meeting is due to commence at two this afternoon. But first, the inspector and I must take a detour to the stables of Senor Angelino. If our little ruse has worked, we're about to relieve Stapleton and his cronies of a great deal of money, first at the Milano Racetrack, then when he discovers Nicco's escape and the loss of the ransom money. Stapleton will be left on a very sticky wicket. I don't want you to worry," Holmes said, acknowledging his wife's perplexed expression. "The inspector and his men will have agents covering the racecourse. There will be nowhere for Stapleton and his cronies to hide."

He took Nene's hands in his. "I need you to stay here and

look after our son. I will ask Doctor Pease to call around to check on Nicco. Two guardie will keep watch outside, but, on the face of it, Nicco thankfully appears largely unscathed from his ordeal."

Holmes and I finished our drinks, and while the detective went upstairs to change, I asked Nene if I could use the telephone to check on things at the station. The officer on duty told me Ferraro and the guardie were continuing their search at the stables.

Then I called Caterina to let her know that Nicco was safe and well, handing the receiver to Nene before heading off to Angelino's stables with Holmes, who looked rather dapper, dressed in disguise of a typical racegoer, donning a trilby, dark glasses, and a fake moustache. He was attired in a white dress shirt with a stiff collar and blue silk bow tie beneath a well-fitted, three-piece navy suit, and a pair of brown, well-polished ankle boots completed the outfit. With a pair of brass *Carl Zeiss Jena* field glasses draped over his shoulder, Holmes looked every inch a member of the horse racing set.

CHAPTER THIRTY-FOUR: SALVATORE ROMANO
Una Giornata alle Corse dei Cavalli — A Day at the Races

In perhaps the most extraordinary twist of the story, Holmes and I arrived at Angelino's stables at noon to find him in the stable yard, pacing up and down in a state of nervous excitement. He explained he had been feeling unnerved and apprehensive since Friday morning after one of the stable hands discovered two empty syringes discarded on the stable floor, close to the boxes of the switched horses.

The perpetrators had struck the night before, as Holmes predicted.

Angelino escorted us to the stables, pointing out puncture marks on the necks of the switched horses, Rathrea and Riptide. It was clear where needles had been administered into the neck muscles. Rathrea's neck had swelling and slight bruising, indicating that he had likely moved during the procedure.

"He's highly strung and hates needles." Angelino sighed, pointing in disdain to the loose scab forming on Rathrea's neck, admitting that other than the puncture marks, the horses appeared none the worse from their ordeal.

I assured Angelino that my guardie got a clear view of the perpetrators, following them back to their homes on Friday evening. The culprits, petty felons who were known to the polizia, would be rounded up and arrested later that day.

Next, we inspected Angelino's two runners, the stable

stars, Sandura and Rubicon, now safely ensconced back in their original stalls, knee-deep in fresh straw, looking content and as fit as a butcher's dog. They whinnied at our approach, looking out over the stable doors, with dark brown intelligent eyes, their ears pricked forward, a clear sign of their well-being and engagement with the environment. We all agreed they looked magnificent, robust pictures of health, their sleek coats gleaming like burnished copper. Angelino said they were more than ready to give a good account of themselves.

Before leaving, Holmes instructed Angelino to arrive at the racetrack with the horses and grooms no earlier than 2:30 P.M. Angelino stared at him oddly before nodding and finally agreeing to the request.

When we arrived at the San Siro Racetrack on a pleasant sunny afternoon, bustling crowds were already forming at the multiple entrances for spectators of different social classes. Members of the general public accessed the main grandstand, already filled with excited revellers. At the same time, the nobility and Milanese bourgeoisie arrived directly with carriages and coachmen, looking a picture of elegance dressed in all their finery. But once everyone entered the inner sanctum of the Milano Racetrack, it was one of the few places where nobility, the hierarchy, and the lower classes mingled together around the betting ring and paddocks in perfect harmony.

The San Siro Racetrack was a significant venue for horse racing in Italy, celebrated for its grand design and the excitement it brought to the city of Milan. The track was extremely well maintained and part of a broader horse racing tradition, focusing on gallop and trot races. This meeting had all the hallmarks of a classic event. It was Italy's largest and most prestigious race meeting in the year's calendar. Here, small fortunes could be lost or made, following a good tip or the study of the horse's form, but to those less fortunate, it would mean a trip to the local money lender the following day.

The gates opened before us, revealing a sprawling scene of organised chaos. We joined the queue, waiting until we were finally ushered through the clicking turnstile by a steward after paying our modest entrance fee. The crowd before us surged and swayed, a thousand voices blending into a restless sea of chatter, laughter and the occasional cheer.

Holmes adjusted his trilby, tilting it lower over his brow, and cast a sharp glance at me, "Stay close," he murmured, his voice barely audible above the din. "The fox hides best when the hunt is loudest."

As we stepped further into the grounds, the air thickened with a heavy mix of aromas–freshly mown grass, the earthy tang of horseflesh, and the tempting scent of roasted chestnuts mingled with cigar smoke. Vendors called out their wares in musical cadences, offering a variety of cold and warm pastries and cups of strong, spiced wine, coffee, and cold lemonade to eager passer-byes, catering to the tastes of the upper-class and general public alike, providing a mix of convenience, sophistication, and satisfaction.

The smell of freshly baked bread, scones, and other culinary delights lingered in the air, invading our senses. On one of the warmest days of the year, it was no surprise that the ice cream parlour was the centre of attraction. Newsies, selling racing form papers and cards, stood beside the other hawkers, barking over the sound of the bustling racetrack.

We strolled down to the betting ring between the grandstand and the racetrack, keeping our eyes peeled for any unusual activity. I recognised a couple of my men in plain clothes strategically placed around the course.

My hand rested lightly on the revolver concealed beneath my jacket, eyes scanning the throng for the elusive Stapleton.

I could see Holmes gazing towards the grandstands, his

penetrating eyes lingering briefly on the private boxes where the city's elite perched like birds of prey. Their laughter and clinking champagne glasses were a world apart from the rowdy, working-class enthusiasts crowding the railings below.

A brass band in the common area struck up a jaunty tune, its brassy notes rising above the chatter and cries of the bookmakers.

Our eyes caught every detail — the banners announcing the day's races and the rhythmic bobbing of hats and parasols among the throng.

"There," I muttered, gesturing subtly towards a cluster of men standing near the paddock alongside four members of the clergy and three nuns. "The one in the dark grey jacket."

Holme's eyes followed, narrowing as they fixed on a figure I remarked seemed too still, too detached from the frenetic energy around him. The man stood by a vendor's cart, his hands clasped behind his back, his eyes scanning the crowd with a predator's calm.

"That's not Stapleton," Holmes replied quietly, his tone tinged with intrigue. "Observe his stance. Too deliberate, too exposed. Stapleton would not risk himself so openly. No, he's likely watching from a vantage point or safely nestled within a group of people, close enough to feel secure but far enough away to appear unremarkable."

The bugle's call interrupted our exchange. A ripple of excitement passed through the crowd as the stewards announced the runners and riders for the first race.

Holmes adjusted his stance, his keen gaze shifting from the racetrack to the grandstand again. "He's here somewhere," he said, his voice carrying the quiet certainty of a man unravelling a puzzle. "And when the race begins, so shall ours, but we will first be past the winning post to claim the spoils."

We studied the runners and riders as outlined on the race

card. The first race was due to start at 2, including Barrett's runner, Viscusi. The second race, scheduled at 2:30, was for two-year-olds to run over seven furlongs. The anticipated main event at 3 was rumoured to be a match between the hot favourite, Messana, and Angelino's runner, Sandura. Next came the Champagne Stakes at 3:30, featuring Break the Bank and Rubicon. The last two races at 4 and 4:30 were sprint handicaps, to be run over six furlongs.

Although the first race was yet to start, the betting market was buoyant, with a flurry of activity in the ring, especially for the Gran Premio di Milano and the following Stakes Race. We heard a few rumblings of discontent around the betting ring that something was amiss with Angelino's horses.

Men in trilbies and dark glasses ran from pitch to pitch, placing hefty wagers on Break the Bank, owned by Ric Ricardo, a member of the Italian mob. Ricardo's horse was now the short-priced favourite for the Stakes Race.

The opening show 3-1 was quickly taken, and the horse was now the 4-5 favourite, while at the same time, Angelino's entry Rubicon, previously the firm favourite, had drifted like a barge to 4-1.

The bookmakers scratched their heads in confusion. They were no doubt wondering what was happening. Their bewilderment was not helped by the antics of Break the Bank's owner—a dark-haired, thick-set man in his forties--who'd been spotted earlier downing his hip flask as though it were water. Now visibly inebriated, he was shamelessly goading the bookmakers, boasting that his horse was ready to live up to its name by breaking the bank before he and his cronies opened their satchels and grabbed the winnings. It was far from a congenial atmosphere.

We strolled to the parade ring to look at the runners in the first race, keen to inspect Barrett's runner, Viscusi, while trying not to draw attention to ourselves. Holmes scoured the course with the binoculars, hoping to get a glimpse of the trainer, Bob Barrett, approaching the paddock. "There was no sign of him. Only Viscusi's owners, a middle-aged Italian couple, and the horse's groom appear to represent The San Siro Scuderia di Cavalli Stable."

After a few minutes, the bell rang, and the jockeys in coloured silks came in to mount their steeds. Each was a picture of focused determination.

We watched closely as the owners chatted briefly with Viscusi's jockey, Francesco De Sousa, before he received a leg up into the saddle, deftly mounting the horse. As the groom led horse and jockey out onto the course, De Sousa put his feet into the stirrups then, leaning forward in the saddle, cantered down to the start with the other runners, each horse looking sleek and powerful, their hooves pounding on the firm Tuscan turf.

Nothing was remarkable about the race. Barrett's horse finished a distant third to the winner and second favourite, Lorenzo, with the favourite Touch and Go a close second.

We watched at the unsaddling enclosure as buckets of water were thrown over the steaming bodies of the horses, the stable hands attempting to cool their charges before returning to the racecourse stables. There was still no sign of Barrett, which came as no surprise to me or Holmes, although we were both convinced that he was on the track somewhere, most likely in disguise.

There was a collective gasp of astonishment from the crowd when Angelino's horse box arrived at the track with his entourage and the two runners at precisely 2:30, just as the second race was about to start.

We observed Angelino's horses walking down the ramp, led by their grooms, looking every inch like true champions, adding further spice to the proceedings. Holmes's eyes shone excitedly as we returned to the betting ring, as punters who

The Whistle of Revenge

---

watched the scene scrambled to get their bets on for the Champagne Stakes.

The starting odds for Rubicon, previously 4-1 and seemingly friendless in the market, was now chalked up on the betting boards as 15-8 favourite. Break the Bank was then relegated to second favourite and easy to back at 5-2. By now, the runners were coming out onto the course for the event the crowds had all been waiting for — the race to top all races, the highly esteemed Gran Premio di Milano, a group two flat race run over a distance of 1.9 miles.

The crowds roared with excitement as the starter stood on his podium. At the fall of the flag, The Gran Premio di Milano Race began.

The favourite, Messana, put in an impressive display of equine speed and stamina, winning the race of would-be champions by two lengths, claiming the valuable purse to roars of delight by the excited crowd and groans of despair by the bookmakers. The gallant favourite fought off the late challenge of Sandura, who was a noble second and magnificent in defeat. He finished in the frame as his trainer expected, earning his connections a nice payout on a promising start to their each-way doubles.

Sandura, previously thought unlikely to trouble the judge, had been heavily backed each-way at 8-1, dramatically reducing the odds. He was returned as a 2-1 second favourite.

Amidst all the excitement, Holmes grabbed my attention, and his penetrating stare was momentarily diverted to three men standing close to the rails chatting to Ricardo, swigging brandy together from silver hip flasks retrieved from their jacket pockets. They were dressed in dark suits, trilby hats, and dark glasses covering their eyes. One of the men, the shortest of the three, was instantly recognisable from his earlier almost manic betting activities, running up and down the line of bookmakers in the ring, nearly knocking over the tic-tac man, lumping on Break the Bank and Messana, taking the best prices available before the odds were dramatically reduced. The amount of money changing hands was eye-watering. Connections were set to win a handsome sum if Break the Bank duly obliged, which was a scenario that looked less likely by the minute if the reformed betting market was anything to go by.

Having backed Messana, the men congratulated each other with pats on the back, handshakes, and punches in the air. The third man was sent into the betting ring to collect the winnings. They seemed more shocked than surprised that Sandura had given the winner a run for his money. There were several raised eyebrows and clandestine mutterings, although we were too far away to hear what the men were saying.

We followed them, keeping a discreet distance down to the paddock as the horses entered the parade ring for the next event, the Champagne Stakes. Such races were famous at the San Siro Track, in which the prize money offered was made up, at least, in part with entry fees, paid by the owners of the entered horses, hence, the title Stakes Race.

Break the Bank and Rubicon admittedly looked magnificent as they paraded to whistles and shouts of appreciation from the enthusiastic crowd.

As the horses made their way down to the start, striding out with purpose, there was yet another flurry of betting activity. Rubicon was now the short-priced favourite at even money. There was a frisson of excitement and anticipation, as many savvy punters had combined both Angelino's horses in each-way to stake about doubles.

We continued to scrutinise the men from a distance. Where earlier they'd been laughing and joking together while quaffing champagne and liberal amounts of brandy, their once bullish mood had now suddenly turned sombre. The men's body language spoke volumes as they stared at the bookmakers' boards in astonishment. Their subdued expressions had an air of death in life. A lot was riding on the outcome of the race.

Holmes and I found a place on the rails. From our position, we had a good view of the pavilions, the betting ring and the winning post—the scent of sweat mingled with the odour of leather, creating an intoxicating atmosphere. The tension was palpable as the horses lined up, jostling for position at the starting gate. Other sports required either discipline, tenacity, or resilience, but racing required it all. The Stakes event was more than just a race to the bookmakers, Bob, and his cronies. It was about money and power. But for Angelino and his connections, it was a test of skill, equine courage, and heart.

Within minutes, the starter raised his arm, and at the fall of the flag, the much-anticipated Champagne Stakes Race began.

Break the Bank sailed into an early lead with the outsider of the field, Leeroy, matching him stride for stride as their hooves pounded over the turf, snorting and straining every sinew. Rubicon, a hold-up horse whom Angelino told us tended to travel off the pace and finish his races with a late surge, was in mid-field, finding much-needed cover on the rail behind the free running. Willo the Wisp, who was giving his jockey an uncomfortable ride. He was tugging at the snaffle bit, eager to have his head as the field approached a sharp bend, facing a steep uphill incline into the home straight.

The crowd, from the well-dressed elite in the VIP boxes, the enthusiastic fans in the stands, and the bettors standing on the rails, were roaring and cheering, enthralled by the beauty and power of the horses. Looking every inch the likely winner, Break the Bank had now pulled clear of Leeroy, who, after running his race, was floundering and running on at one pace.

Over the noise of the crowd, we heard Angelino's distinct cry as his horse Rubicon, who his jockey had restrained, emerged from the pack with his surging run, literally eating up the ground as he drew level with Break the Bank—the jockeys glancing at each other, with a shake of the reigns, with no whip required. Angelino's horse thundered up the home straight, the jubilant jockey punching the air as his mount crossed the finishing line in first place, winning by an impressive three lengths, to ecstatic shouts, whistles, and applause from the crowd of punters watching from the rails.

There was an agonising wait before the stewards announced the winner as number 7 on the board located next to the grandstand. That resulted in more cheers from the crowd.

The result garnered mixed reactions from the bookmakers after paying out the delighted punters queuing around the betting ring, all eager to collect their winnings. The tic-tac man and bookmakers spokesman, Aldo Cardinale, admitted they were still up on the race after laying Break the Bank for a substantial amount.

Back at the winner's enclosure, Angelino was congratulated by Rubicon's thrilled owners, who were smiling and grinning from ear to ear before the horse was led away by his groom to be attended to at the stables. When I turned around to speak to Holmes, I found him on the rails, standing behind the men in suits, who were in a heated altercation. Their faces were grim and unsmiling, and one lowered his head, shaking it in frustration and anger.

I furrowed my brow as Holmes leaned forward, appearing to whisper something in one of the men's ears before returning to join me on the rails, a wry smile on his face. The man turned on his heels and looked at us, taking off his glasses. I shall never forget the expression on his face—it was one of a condemned person. The corners of his lips curled, and then, in a moment, the three of them suddenly disappeared into the crowd.

Holmes and I gave chase, but it proved an impossible task, trying to wade through the masses of punters, mindful it would be too dangerous to use our guns with so many people around and cause a mass panic. Nevertheless, we ploughed on until, agonisingly, the three men disappeared.

With a wave of my hand, while simultaneously blowing my police whistle, I signalled to my men. They appeared, running in every direction, blocking each entrance to the course, and only allowing people to enter or leave after first showing proof of identity or agreeing to be searched.

An hour passed, the day's final race concluded, and the jockeys weighed in, but no one matching the descriptions of the three men had been identified. Finally, when the course was emptied and every racegoer had gone home, my guardie discovered three sets of trilbies and dark glasses in the cloakroom of the pavilion concealed in a valise. When questioned, my officers confirmed that three Catholic priests and a nun had left the racecourse minutes after The Champagne Stakes Race. They were given special dispensation after confirming their identities, which, in hindsight, were forged. When questioned by the polizia, the priests explained they had a special mass to officiate later that evening at the Ducomo di Milano Cathedral Church in honour of Andrea Carlo Ferrari, the Archbishop of Milan.

Chapter Thirty-Five: Robert Barrett
L'Ultima Cena — The Last Supper

Safely ensconced in Emilio Rodriguez's *Mercedes-Simplex*, Connie took the wheel and drove us on the ten-mile journey to a safe house just outside the city. Other than asking directions, Connie was unusually quiet. Having discarded the nuns' habit she wore earlier, she was now attired in a black felt hat, pink silk scarf, and *Rodenstock* sunglasses covering her eyes.

Emilio took his place in the passenger seat beside Connie while Peppo and I sat in the back. The atmosphere was unbelievably tense. Il Resolver and I had already exchanged strong words earlier on the racetrack. Angelino's dramatic entrance and his horses' spectacular performances were not expected by Emilio, me, or the Italian mafia.

We now had the polizia to contend with. Ricardo and his mob had lost a packet on the Stakes Race and were undoubtedly on our trail, baying for blood by now. With that in mind and fear for our safety, we decided to head to the safe house to stay overnight. We couldn't risk being caught together by the polizia, so we agreed to disband and go separate ways by morning.

I had to resign myself that returning to the stables was impossible now that Holmes and Romano had discovered my ruse and secret identity. The polizia would be combing the area. With the boy gone and the ransom exchange aborted, we had lost all bargaining power, which Emilio quickly pointed out. We would have been left with nothing if not for our winnings from the Gran Premio.

It was only after I was able to convince Emilio over a dram of whiskey that all was not lost and that the best was yet to come. The acquisition of Angelino's precious painting, I argued, would tip the balance and solve all our problems. Although begrudgingly agreeing to give me the benefit of the doubt, Emilio raised his glass, and with a sombre stare, warned me I was a dead man walking should I fail to deliver the painting. I brushed off his concerns with a smile and a toast, confident we would soon lay our hands on Angelino's masterpiece. I wasn't too concerned about Ricardo. I knew Il Resolver and his mob could handle Ric and his cronies. They would get over their loss, given time.

I couldn't get the thought of Holmes and the inspector's discovery of the boy out of my head. How, where, and why were the questions flooding my brain. Could someone who knew about Nicco and the horse doping scam have betrayed me?

When I heard that narrative whispered to me on the racetrack earlier, my blood ran cold at the realisation that Sherlock Holmes had gotten one over on me. The words the detective so eloquently spoke with his clipped, well-modulated voice played over and over in my mind.

"The game's up. We have the boy. Your dastardly plan was thwarted." After saying the words, he suddenly stepped backwards, and his penetrating eyes couldn't fail to notice my hand slipping into my coat, my fingers tracing the outline of the gun concealed in my pocket.

I stood there for a moment in shock and disbelief before slowly turning around to face my nemesis, removing my glasses to glimpse that imposing statuesque physique. Although dressed heavily in disguise, there was no mistaking it was the detective standing next to Romano, who raised an eyebrow, flashing a sardonic smile as I alerted Emilio and Peppo to our situation before we quickly disappeared into the crowd.

Dinner that night at the safe house was a strange affair. Peppo found it hard to conceal his delight that the boy was now home safe and sound, where he belonged, with his family. His remorselessness rankled me. Emilio took me aside, advising me not to read too much into things. Peppo, he explained, is a family man who adores his children. It was clear he'd taken a real shine to Nicco Sapori. Emilio had made no secret of how strongly he disapproved of the kidnapping.

Although Emilio's words had a good meaning and were sincere, they did nothing to stop me from pondering. Could it be that Peppo was the Judas amongst us? He seemed to have developed a close relationship with the boy and told Connie he wanted out. On the other hand, Connie took a more diplomatic view, stating she was keen to proceed with the task at hand and secure the painting. She had grown tired of being an unpaid childminder and wanted to get on with her life, one she declared did not include present company.

When I questioned her about this, she replied, "No offence, Bob." Then she laughed at my perplexed expression.

"None was taken," I respectfully replied, sitting up straight and giving her an assuring smile, although I was seething inside, wondering if this loose cannon with a glint in her eye was the rat who'd betrayed me.

I stared at both her and Peppo for a moment. Our once cosy working relationship was now, in my mind, fragmented by disloyalty, suspicion, and treachery. Loyalty to me was a treasure beyond measure—a currency to be held above all else. However, betrayal was a debt that demanded repayment in blood. There was no deviation from this. I tried to weigh each detail carefully. The path forward must be treated with absolute certainty, for only those steadfast in their allegiance to me could remain at my side.

My instinct was to act, to confront them both. I would then know if they lied to me. But then I decided I couldn't risk it, not yet. I had to withhold my wrath. Otherwise, my anger may compel me to act with a severity that leaves no room for hesitation but a decision I would regret. I really had no choice. I needed Connie and Peppo's combined skills since they were crucial for the next part of Operation Whistle. If they got an inkling that I suspected them, the game would be well and truly over. We had worked together planning and rehearsing every move of the heist, leaving nothing to chance. So I decided to carry on as planned, knowing that trusting them might come at a price. One I was not prepared to pay should we fail.

I was reminded of an Italian phrase often quoted by Emilio. *Fidarsi e bene, ma non fidarsi e meglio* — trusting is good, but *not* trusting is better.

After dinner, Connie dropped Peppo off at Milano Centrale Station for his journey to Genoa. From there, he would collect the truck, arriving at the car factory at 10 P.M. on Monday. Then, checking into a hotel close to the factory, he would remain there until the following morning, taking instructions by telephone from me and Rodriguez.

Emilio and I played cards until Connie returned to confirm that Peppo was safely on the evening train. Filling our glasses, we enjoyed a nightcap before I excused myself, saying I was exhausted from the day's events and needed an early night.

The following morning, after a hearty breakfast, Connie and Emilio dropped me off at Milano Centrale, where I embarked on the train to Genoa in disguise. Connie and Emilio headed north to another safe house, where I would keep in touch with them later by telephone, and from where Connie would travel on Tuesday with a trusted art expert, a contact of Emilio's, to collect the painting from Angelino. Emilio would stay with Connie at the safe house until Tuesday morning, where he would be collected by an unmarked car to travel to the Trattori in the town of Tortona, the halfway point between Milan and Genoa.

Arriving at my destination, the Genoa Place Colombo Railway Station, later that afternoon, I decided to walk the short distance to The Grand Hotel Savoia, where I had booked a reservation under the pseudonym of Gormo Sanju.

Chapter Thirty-Six: Salvatore Romano
La Congiura delle Polveri – The Gunpowder Plot

Following the rescue of Nicco Sapori and a thorough search of the house and The San Sior Scuderia Stables, an envelope from De Beers was discovered tucked in the breast pocket of Bob Barrett's hacking jacket. The envelope contained a quotation addressed to a private mailbox in Milan and marked for the attention of Samuel Delori, who Holmes and I agreed was yet another nom de plume used by Barrett, this time passing himself off as a mining engineer.

The quotation was for two tons of dynamite, detonator boxes, cables, and fuses, all to be delivered to a lock-up in Busalla. The address and delivery date were to be determined, and the customer was to onward transmit the items via boat to a mine at the French gold seam at Chatelet in Creuse.

Holmes and I were stunned by the findings. We couldn't rule out the possibility that Barrett had plans to use the dynamite closer to home. The French mine was, in all probability, a ruse to avoid drawing attention to the purchase of such deadly materials.

We decided to investigate further and called De Beers. Upon checking the records, a clerk told us the customer had cancelled the order, and the enquiry was routinely filed. Next, I called the Busalla constabulary and spoke to my old acquaintance, Inspector Sal Claudio. After explaining the importance and delicacy of the situation, I asked if Sal and his men could conduct a low-profile search of the many lockups in the area to ascertain if anyone had been acting suspiciously or if any unusual activity had been reported.

We continued to monitor the Sapori residence, with round-the-clock protection discreetly posted close to the villa. Holmes agreed that his family should remain at home until Stapleton was apprehended.

In the meantime, the search for Stapleton and his accomplices continued with officers on patrol at each port and railway station, but so far, there was no sign of him, the woman called Connie, Emilio Rodriguez, or the man Nicco described as Gino. Although, as Holmes pointed out, that name was likely a false identity.

I called Sal Claudio at his home Monday morning at 6. After five rings, he answered the phone.

"Ciao," he said in his distinct Genoese accent. "Why are you bothering me at this unearthly hour?"

After I explained the nature of my call, the inspector told me in a curt tone that he and his family had celebrated his son Alexio's eighteenth birthday only the night before at Bruxa Boschi. Consequently, he felt rather delicate this morning and did not appreciate his sleep being disturbed. But after I apologised profusely for bothering him, Sal's tone mellowed, and he agreed to fill me in on Genoa polizia's findings so far.

A recent development was reported after Sal returned from the ristorante, and it was likely pertinent to our investigation. He said that due to the late hour, he had planned to call me later in the morning. I waited with bated breath as Sal continued with the update.

"Late-night activity was reported in Busalla, twelve miles north of Genoa. A subsequent search of the building found a lock-up. Upon opening the door, the polizia discovered several Bogliasco Flour Company sacks, its forecourt, and its floor splattered with fresh paint. There were tins of paint, a few used tyres, and more notably, a dozen or so empty dynamite boxes. An alert on a stolen flour company lorry has been distributed to constabularies in the local region."

Sal assured me he would contact me if there were any further developments. I felt annoyed he hadn't bothered calling sooner, but I was grateful for the information. Before replacing the receiver on the hook, I wished the inspector good morning and Alexio a happy belated birthday.

I realised I needed to contact Holmes, wondering if the great detective would be awake. But before I had a chance to do anything, the phone rang. I answered it, thinking it was Caterina, but I was surprised to hear Holmes' dulcet tones on the line. There was no welcome greeting or hello . . . the celebrated detective got straight to the point.

"The dynamite was never meant for the Saporis. If Stapleton wanted to kill us, he could have done it at any time." He paused for a moment. "Think about it, Romano. Who's the only person we know Stapleton had a grudge against, apart from me?"

"Why, Angelino, of course," I replied briefly before updating Holmes on my earlier conversation with Inspector Claudio.

"Right, that's interesting. With the horse doping scam gone wrong and Stapleton and his cronies losing a vast amount of money, it can mean only one thing."

"Yes, Angelino's car manufacturing company is in Genoa. But why would Stapleton and his gang want to blow up the factory, and from whom did they procure the dynamite?"

"They probably obtained the dynamite unscrupulously and intended to blackmail Angelino. He has something they want. He's a wealthy, self-made man, so it could be money the perpetrators are after or something else. Either way, we need to visit Angelino and find out what's going on, as I fear he's the intended target of Operation Whistle. But first, there's some business I need to attend to. Can you pick me up at eleven?"

"Perfecto, that will give me time to complete the paperwork for my superiors. If I don't make the deadline, my head will be on the block. The station has a new acquisition due to arrive shortly, so I shall collect you at ten-fifty, leaving us ten minutes to arrive at our destination."

"Ten minutes? Pray tell, what exactly is this new acquisition? Winged Pegasus?" Holmes asked, airing a somewhat sceptical tone.

I laughed out loud. "Better than that, my friend, the Milano polizia are taking delivery of the new unmarked nineteen-oh-five *Fiat Supercar*, which will not only cut down our travelling time, it's rumoured to outclass any other car in a chase."

"Hmm, I'll see you directly," Holmes said.

Chapter Thirty-Seven: Robert Barrett
L' Allestimento — The Set Up

I had barely settled into my suite at the hotel when Peppo called in a bullish mood to confirm that, so far, everything was going according to plan. Wearing the stolen Manzoni uniform, Peppo told me he drove the lorry to Liguria Cars security entrance as planned on Monday evening, arriving as instructed at precisely 10 P.M., finding little activity around the site other than a cleaner and two tired-looking security guards drinking coffee and playing cards.

Peppo feigned a surprised expression and told the security guards he had not been informed that the factory was closed for a week's summer holiday. He explained he'd just driven 135 miles from the Manzoni Tyre Factory in Turin. He entered into friendly banter with the guards for some time. They took pity on him and even offered coffee. Gaining their trust, Peppo eventually received clearance and strategically parked the lorry in front of a maintenance hole cover, identified from the sewerage system plans, just outside the factory loading bay, next to the assembly line. As the dynamite in the lorry was covered by a motley assortment of car tyres, it quickly passed inspection by the guards, who barely glanced at the interior.

After further discussion, the guards granted Peppo permission to leave the lorry outside the factory until the following afternoon, when a skeleton staff member would come on duty from noon to five. They would then unload the tyres into the stock room. Peppo returned to the lorry, grabbed his valise before securely locking the vehicle with a unique key, and armed the booby trap, which would trigger the explosives, should an attempt be made to open the doors without the correct key.

Peppo bid goodnight to the guards and went to the hotel across from the factory gates, where he'd pre-booked a room under an assumed name. He later met with one of Emilio's special agents, Roaul Benigni, who arrived by car just before midnight.

Benigni was an ex-army officer who served with the Alpini, Italy's elite mountain troops, which protected the northern borders from France to Austria. He saw plenty of active service as an explosives expert in The Chinese Boxer Rebellion in 1900 and received several commendations for bravery. The slim, diminutive, wiry Bengini was mainly known as The Eel.

In the early hours of Tuesday morning, Benigni would leave the hotel using the sewerage and water flow system as outlined on the factory building plan. Then, using his wiry frame to his advantage, he would access the spacious underground channels covering the distance from the maintenance cover near the gates to the second where the lorry was parked. Then, using the stolen reel of cable, he would take it through the sewer system, attaching one end to detonators, placing them in the lorry, having opened it with the special key Peppo gave him, with the other end connected to the detonator box hidden in bushes outside the factory gates.

Wearing field glasses, he would lay patiently in wait, scanning the hotel's roof for Peppo's signal, red for abort and green for go, so there was no confusion. Or in the unlikely event that the weather might obscure vision, it was agreed that the sound of a whistle would be added, one blow for abort and two for go, to determine if The Eel depressed the plunger or not.

I sat back in my chair, took a sip from my whiskey tumbler, and then lit a cigar, blowing rings of smoke up into the air.

The next part of the operation was down to me. I could hardly wait.

Chapter Thirty-Eight: Sherlock Holmes
L'attacco Artistico di Angelino — Angelino's Art Attack

Romano pulled up in the new *Fiat 60 HP Supercar* at precisely 10:50 A.M. The car was an expensive improvement on the *Fiat 3 HP* the polizia sometimes used. Painted red and black, it looked as grand as its name suggested, admirably fitting Romano's astute description of an elite luxury machine, a far cry from the humble hansom or brougham carriages we were used to.

The inspector proudly explained this extravagant automobile had been sent to the Milano polizia for a month's road testing trial and to compete with the high-speed *Mercedes-Simplex 40/45 HP* models, capable of speeds of up to 50 miles an hour and a popular choice of transport amongst the local mafia.

Although the car spun along at an impressive speed, Romano's driving standard left a lot to be desired. His lack of clutch control was quite alarming. Nevertheless, we arrived at Angelino's stables ten minutes later, just after 11 A.M.

Romano had to quickly slam his foot on the brakes as a sporty *Laurin and Klement* motorcycle roared out of the drive and onto the road, missing hitting our car by inches. The driver and a pillion passenger were dressed in black, their faces concealed by goggles. We watched them for a moment until the motorcycle and its passenger disappeared from view, heading south into the distance. Judging by the purity

The Whistle of Revenge

of the exhaust emissions, they weren't hanging about. I couldn't shake off the feeling that something untoward had just occurred.

We approached the house with some trepidation to find Angelino alone in the drawing room in floods of tears. His head bowed, shoulders slumped, he looked every inch like a broken man. He looked up as we approached, pointing towards the fireplace. The painting of Saint Veronica was missing.

"You're too late," Angelino said, slowly shaking his head, his eyes red-rimmed.

Romano went to the drinks cabinet and poured Angelino a stiff brandy. Once he'd calmed down, the inspector assured him his men would do everything humanly possible to retrieve the painting.

Angelino sat back in his chair. Pulling a handkerchief from his jacket pocket, he wiped his eyes and began sharing his tale of woe.

The day had started ominously after Angelino, breakfasting alone, received an unexpected call from a security guard at his car factory. The guard, who began his shift earlier that morning, became suspicious when he noticed an unexpected delivery of tyres. Out of curiosity and concern, the guard rang Manzoni Tyres, who confirmed the order was not scheduled for delivery until the following week due to the summer holiday. Angelino thanked the guard and said he intended to report the matter to the appropriate authorities. Still, within moments of replacing the telephone on the receiver, he received an incoming call as the clock struck 10:15 A.M. He was astounded to discover the caller was Bob Barrett.

Holmes and I looked at each other in amazement as Angelino continued his story. Barrett demanded Angelino release *The Blessed Veronica of Milan* painting to two associates, who were on their way and would be with him within minutes.

If Angelino failed to comply, his beloved car assembly plant would be blown to kingdom come by his gang. If the polizia were alerted or there was any sign of the Genoa Constabulary at the site, the car assembly plant would be destroyed. Angelino explained he didn't know what to do. There were only a few maintenance workers on duty at the plant, so he knew casualties would be minimal, but then one life taken was one too many. Angelino argued that he needed more time to make such an earth-shattering decision. Barrett reluctantly agreed to extend the deadline to 11 A.M.

Angelino then rang the Milano polizia station, asking to speak to Romano, and was told the inspector was away from the office. Still, the duty sergente would pass on the message upon his return. Having no clue we were on our way to see him, Angelino explained what had happened. The sergente agreed to alert the Genoa Constabulary and the carabiniere, asking them to search the factory with a bomb disposal team as a matter of urgency. Angelino begged them to be cautious, explaining Barrett told him his accomplice booby-trapped the truck holding the explosives, which was only accessible by use of a special key held by one of the perpetrators. The sergente explained the only alternative was for the carabiniere to tow the truck away to an open space and blow it up if they weren't already too late.

At 10:30 A.M., Angelino realised he was running out of time. Aware of Barrett's history, the horse doping scam, and his past criminal activities, he didn't want to risk losing his beloved car factory, which he'd worked so hard to establish. He only had one choice. With a heavy heart, he removed the painting from the wall, dismantling the lock bolts.

When Barrett finally called back, Angelino agreed to his terms and handed the painting over to a woman who, along with an accomplice, had broken into the rear of the house. Both were seated on Angelino's chaise lounge, where the woman flashed him a menacing stare as she scratched the coffee table with tapering red-painted fingernails.

She was sitting next to a tall man who remained silent. Both were dressed in black, with scarves and goggles concealing their identities. The woman showed the painting to the accomplice, who inspected it carefully, using a torch and a magnifying glass before giving a nod of approval. The woman then picked up the earpiece and spoke to Barrett, the conversation tense, as she spoke in a thick European accent, confirming she was now in possession of the painting, which had been authenticated by her partner in crime.

"Ja," she said in a guttural German voice before placing the receiver back on its hook.

Angelino could only watch out of the window as the perpetrators left the house, carefully placing his beloved painting into a red leather pannier bag mounted on the rear frame of a motorcycle before driving away.

Romano picked up the telephone, alerting his team to the description of the people on the motorcycle. We could only hope and pray the Genoa authorities and carabiniere wouldn't be too late to deactivate the bomb. I wouldn't put it past Barrett to detonate it anyway out of spite, although looking at the anguish on Angelino's face, I decided to keep those thoughts to myself for the moment.

Chapter Thirty-Nine: Robert Barrett
Il Bottino di Guerra — The Spoils of War

After speaking to Connie, she confirmed she'd taken possession of the painting, validated by Emilio's art expert, Roberto Santini. The two of them were now heading to Tortona to meet Rodriguez.

As strategically planned earlier, down to the finest detail, the following was an outline of how events were expected to pan out.

Connie would find Emilio waiting in the front garden of Trattoria del Cicco in Tortona, innocently enjoying a cup of freshly brewed coffee. On seeing Connie as the motorcycle approached, he would stand, acknowledging her with a doff of his hat, indicating that it was safe for her to steer the motorcycle into a bicycle shed at the rear of the trattoria before she and Santini joined Emilio for coffee, posing as husband and wife. There, at the trattoria, the exchange would take place. The painting was safely enclosed in the red pannier bag. A large envelope containing unmarked lira, the commission for the painting, would be checked by Connie's eagle eyes in the trattoria's restroom.

While Emilio, draining his cup, would strike up a conversation, entering into social chit-chat with the cameriere, slipping him a handsome tip, ensuring Connie could make use of the phone, using the excuse of checking on her daughter, who had taken poorly, and whom she and her husband were on the way to see in Recco, a small commune in Genoa. From there, Connie would call me, but there would be no conversation for fear the line might be overheard by prying ears, other than uttering the code word. Whistle, to confirm all was well, she had the money and was continuing the fifty-mile journey to Genoa.

On arrival, Connie would park the motorcycle in a lock-up at the docks, covering it with a dust sheet, before hailing a hansom to take her on the last leg of the journey to meet me at the hotel. At the same time, Emilio and Santini would travel by car from the trattoria to join friends in Campagna, a small town set in the hills of the Campania region, where Santini lived and worked. He would introduce Emilio to the new owner of the painting, assisting with the transition and ensuring everything went smoothly.

I shook with excitement as I called Peppo at his hotel at 11:10 A.M.

"Good morning, boss. Do we have the painting?" he quizzed, speaking rapidly.

"Yes, Connie secured the artwork, mission accomplished comrade."

"Good, then I shall signal Raoul to abort, and we can get out of here."

"Not so fast, my friend." I took a deep intake of breath. "I've changed my mind. Tell Raoul to go ahead and blow up the factory."

There was a deathly silence on the line, followed by Peppo's gasp of astonishment. "But, Bob, you have what you want. There are people in that building. I'll not go down for murder! It isn't necessary now that you have the painting. The place could be swarming with polizia at any moment. Why, this is madness!"

I laughed out loud, highly amused by Peppo's startled reaction. It felt good to get a rise out of him. "It's nice to know where your allegiances lie, but don't worry, amico mio, I was joking. Go signal Raoul, and then the two of you can travel to Traso." I paused for a moment. "Oh, and Peppo, be sure to thank The Eel for me."

"Yes, boss, I shall." I could hear the relief in Peppo's voice. "I'd better go now. I will speak to you soon," he said, quickly terminating the call.

I looked around my hotel room towards the whiskey decanter on the sideboard. I desperately needed a drink but decided to shower and venture out for fresh air. Instead, I could celebrate later. Traso was only a twelve-mile journey from Genoa, and I would return from my walk in plenty of time before Peppo got in touch. I pondered if he and Raoul would escape like heroes or instead slip down my rabbit hole into the arms of the polizia, whom I'd alerted five minutes earlier by way of an anonymous call.

When I returned to the hotel thirty minutes later, the maid was just leaving. I made myself comfortable on the freshly made bed and lit a cigarette, planning what to do with my newfound wealth. The penetrating ring of the telephone interrupted my thoughts. I picked up the receiver, surprised and disappointed to hear Peppo's animated voice on the line.

He gave me a quick briefing on the events that occurred since our earlier conversation.

Peppo said he made his way onto the hotel roof as instructed. A wave of the red flag and one blow from the whistle was enough to alert Raoul that I had aborted the mission. At this point, The Eel dismantled the cables in the detonator box. Having just completed the task. He was startled by two security guards who quickly gave chase, but they were no match for the athletic Raoul, who sprinted clear like a whippet, having lost the guards by jumping over a six-foot wall.

The Whistle of Revenge

Raoul went to the hotel, where Peppo waited in an unmarked car, its engine running.

Then, with the route already mapped out, Peppo and Raoul made their dramatic escape through the narrow back streets, finally arriving at their destination in Traso at an address organised by the Camorra.

After cutting short our conversation, wishing Peppo and Raoul all the best in their future endeavours, I uncorked the decanter, pouring the whiskey into a crystal tumbler. Then, standing by the window, I closed my eyes as the single malt hit the back of my throat, savouring its heavy oak flavour. I was about to top up my glass when I heard a hansom cab pull up outside to the entrance to the hotel. Pulling back the curtains, I watched just as Connie jumped from the cab and entered the foyer.

Filling my glass with whiskey, I set aside another tumbler in preparation for her arrival, alerted to the sound of footsteps on the stairs.

"Come, it's open!" I shouted, responding to a knock at the door.

I had my heart in my mouth as the bellboy escorted Connie into the room. She was dressed in black, holding a pair of goggles in one hand and a leather hand-crafted bag in the other, containing our ill-gotten gains. I tipped the bellboy, who quietly left the room, closing the door behind him.

Connie eyed the decanter wistfully as I poured the amber nectar into a glass. "Keep going," she said. "After the day I've had, I need a few glasses of something strong to calm me down, so keep pouring until I say stop."

"You deserve the bottle. Well done." I beamed, sinking into the dark blue cushions of a high-backed chair. I watched as Connie removed the pair of black leather gloves, jacket, and a green silk scarf and threw them over the back of a chair.

Connie expertly cradled the glass in her right hand. She

drained the whiskey in one spectacular gulp while emptying the contents of a large envelope onto the bedspread with the other. I sat staring in wonder and awe as bundles of lira flew through the air, landing on the bed. I traced my fingers lovingly over the notes like a lover's embrace before Connie interrupted the languid spell.

"Where do you propose I sleep tonight? Have you booked me a room?" she asked as she kicked off her leather boots and looked suspiciously at the king-sized bed.

"Don't worry, you can have the bed," I said. "I'll take the couch. Let's face it, I've slept in worse places. As you're already aware, we're booked as a married couple so as not to arouse suspicion. For the next three nights, you will continue to be known as Signora Eliana Sanju, the wife of Gorma Sanju, an accountant from Portofino." I chuckled, observing Connie's bemused expression. "It's too late to change it now," I explained. "And, anyway, the hotel is full."

Connie opened her mouth to protest but gave a resigned nod, yawning as she stretched out her long arms. "I'm too tired to argue with you. I could sleep on a clothesline." She raised an eyebrow as those grey eyes, for once, uncharacteristically twinkling, took on a mischievous gleam.

"But no funny business, mind you, Bob, or should I call you Gormo?"

"Your honour is safe with me, young lady." I laughed. "How about room service? You must be hungry unless you prefer to go down for dinner. Although I wouldn't recommend it, it's not as though you're dressed for the occasion. I'll let you know that royalty often frequent this establishment." I sneered, staring in disdain at her well-worn, dusty attire.

Connie nodded. "I brought a change of clothes, something more befitting a married woman. But for tonight, room service is fine. Please make it snappy, Bob, I'm famished."

"Steak, medium rare, only the best for Signora Sanju," I

said sardonically.

"Perfect," she replied, appearing not to notice my flippant tone. "And a nice bottle of claret would not go amiss, and whatever you're having, of course," Connie said as she bounced onto the bed, and from the smile on her face, appeared more than satisfied with the well-sprung mattress. "I'm going for a shower before I spark out," she said, grabbing a towel and a complimentary robe from the console table.

"Go ahead. I'll order the food, and it should arrive by the time you finish pampering yourself."

After placing our order with the bellboy, I sat back on the couch, reflecting on how I could easily have booked Connie into another room. But I needed to keep a close eye on her, acutely aware from the revolver concealed at the bottom of the leather bag, that I couldn't entirely trust her.

The plan was that on Saturday, we would travel incognito to the docks and board the boat to Dover. From there, we would go our separate ways, Connie returning to her homeland in Germany, while I would make my way to Birmingham, to a safe bolt-hole organised by John from the Peaky Blinders. With Connie attending to her ablutions, I counted the notes and slipped some into an envelope, which I placed on the pillow.

Whatever my thoughts about Connie were, she'd done well and fully deserved the generous commission. It was a pity that she would only have a short time to enjoy the fruits of her labour. I removed the fixed-blade hunting knife from the leather sheath in my valise that I'd sharpened with a whetstone earlier. Sticky tape securely wrapped around the shaft, ensuring a non-slip grip, running my fingers lightly over the blade's edge, feeling for that familiar sharpness, carefully placing the knife back in its sheath before returning it, safely concealed at the bottom of my valise.

I had considered finishing Connie with my revolver but

decided it would be too noisy. I couldn't afford to risk alerting the attention of the hotel staff before I made my escape. Emilio had agreed to settle up with Peppo and Santini. The rest of the money would be mine.

When Connie finally emerged from the bathroom wrapped in an oversized bathrobe, the pungent aroma of castile soap and lavender oil lingered heavily in the air.

I stared at her curiously. "Tell me, Connie, did you enjoy the heist and the chase to Genoa?"

Connie nodded, quirking a brow as she flashed me a wicked smile. "You know me, Bob, I've always enjoyed inflicting suffering on others, especially those who deserve to be punished."

The waiter had already delivered the food and wine, so we sat at the dark oak table in the middle of the high-ceilinged room. Two taper candles flickered in the corner. Our celebratory dinner, a veritable feast of antipasto, olive bread, and steak, was soon an alcoholic affair.

Connie attacked the food with gusto, washing it down with copious amounts of red wine and whiskey before we started on dessert—two generous slices of olive cake infused with orange juice and fresh rosemary, all served with a dusting of sugar. It was delicious, although Connie's nefarious smile was slightly unnerving.

She stared at me across the table with the air of a tiger inspecting its prey, her head tilted to one side and said, "When we get to Dover, it doesn't have to be the end of our collaboration. Come with me to Berlin?" she asked with a contrived smile and arched brow, although her suggestion sounded more like a demand than a request. "We could be good together, the perfect business partners." She spoke slowly, staring at me with expectant eyes as a thin wisp of smoke rose from her cigarette.

I gazed at her in baffled confusion, spluttering my drink as

I struggled to stay focused, perplexed by the propriety of the question. By now, my head was spinning from the alcohol. I glanced around the table bleary-eyed, shocked to discover we'd consumed two bottles of claret and a bottle of single malt.

When I reacted to Connie's suggestion, I casually told her that, regretfully, that could never be. We were better off alone . . . it was safer. Somehow, I managed to say all this while feigning a calm composure and flashing a polite smile. The last thing I wanted was to get on the wrong side of her.

There was a wicked glint in those grey eyes as she nodded in agreement, her expression a mix of curiosity and condemnation. "You're right, of course, Bob. One should never allow sentiment to get in the way of business. Perhaps in another time and place, we may meet again one day."

"I'll drink that. I'm certain there will be more commissions to come in the future," I said, raising my glass while breathing an inward sigh of relief that she'd graciously accepted my rebuff.

Connie paused momentarily, wiping her mouth with a napkin, that warm smile now replaced by a frosty stare. "I hope for your sake you're not still hankering after the Achen whore. You should have let me finish her while we had the chance."

I gave a weak smile. "Connie, you, of all people, must realise that the mere idea of a liaison of a sexual nature with that young lady is abhorrent to me."

Connie paused, offering a thin smile, then nodded in resignation. I exhaled as that forced smile was replaced by a frown. Connie stood pushing the chair to one side, then climbing on the bed. She opened the envelope, counting out the money. I stared at her for a moment as she sat facing me. Although not the most eloquent of women, her slender frame was toned and in perfect proportion.

To some, Connie would have been considered still young at thirty-six, yet her weathered skin, frosty disposition, and overall deportment made people believe she was much older than her years. But on the rare occasion that she smiled, her face had a notable prettiness. We chatted for a while about the heist and our impending departure to Dover until inebriated by the alcohol, and in a drunken stupor, we drifted off into unconsciousness.

I awoke the following morning from a deep, dreamless sleep to find Connie still lying on top of the floral bedspread, her usual sallow cheeks still slightly flushed from the alcohol she'd consumed the night before. Although I had no interest in her sexually, or any other woman for that matter, the intimacy of our close but tenacious encounter had stirred feelings within me I had not experienced since I was with Beryl. Not even with the beautiful Miss Achen, despite all her endearing qualities. Hildegard would be considered a catch for any red-blooded man, yet . . .

Glancing around the room, which was in a state of disarray — several cigarette and cigar butts rested in the once-smouldering ashtrays set next to two half-finished glasses of wine. I almost retched at the sight. My head spun, and my back ached from sleeping on the hard couch.

I suddenly felt nauseous from dehydration. Pouring a glass of water from the pitcher, I walked over to the window and opened the curtains. The day that was just starting was overcast, with a chilly north wind prevailing.

Chapter Forty: Salvatore Romao
L'Anguilla è un Pesce Scivoloso — The Eel is a Slippery Fish

The developments of the next few days occurred at a breathtaking pace.

I was in my office at 9 A.M. with Holmes and Angelino, who looked tired and drawn. I took a breath as I contemplated narrating the startling chain of events that had taken place over a glass of whiskey. Angelino stared at me, his face deeply etched in crevices of anxiety. He wrung his hands in an edgy manner.

"I have been a bundle of nerves since our last encounter, gentlemen. But I'm curious to learn why you had me summoned here?" he asked, staring at us hopefully, his usual ruddy cheeks now drained of all colour. "Have you heard anything about my factory and the painting?"

"I'm afraid the painting hasn't been seen ... not yet. But I'm pleased to tell you that your factory and all who work there remain safe," I said.

"Thank God for that," Angelino said, making a sign of the cross. "Then, for the sake of my sanity, I implore you, gentlemen, to tell me all that has transpired."

I glanced down at my notes. "Very well. The following is an account of everything we know about your car factory, Liguria Cars." Angelino half closed his eyes and nodded as I continued my narrative, periodically referring to the pages from the polizia report. "Alerted to an anonymous tip-off and following a statement from a security guard at the Liguria car Factory, the guard was able to identify Raoul Benigni, who served in the carabiniere's bomb disposal unit, where he was widely known as The Eel."

"I have never before heard of this man," Angelino said.

"The Eel is an associate of Emilio Rodriguez, who is in cahoots with Barrett and the ringleader of the gang," Holmes explained, furrowing his brow and giving Angelino a disparaging look. "Pray allow the inspector to continue."

Clearing my throat, I continued with the story. "Armed with this information, I wasted no time calling my counterpart in Genoa, Captain Marco Lipati, and quickly explaining the situation and how the door key to the lorry needed to be recovered without any delay. Although a controlled explosion was feasible, according to the bomb disposal team, who had cordoned off the area and evacuated the adjoining building, the recovery of the key would be the safest solution for all concerned. When I further explained to Lipati that one of the perpetrators involved with the dynamite was The Eel, the captain said he was shocked and saddened to hear that Benigni, who was known to him, could be involved in something so evil and outrageous."

"I, too, am shocked and deeply saddened that this man had the nerve to target my factory," Angelino expounded. "It's hard to believe he's ex-military. Someone who promised to uphold the law and respect human life."

"Quite," Holmes said, taking a sip from his glass. "It goes to show that any man, or woman for that matter, is capable of turning to the dark side given the right circumstances."

"The Eel was considered a legend in past times," I continued. "But had spectacularly fallen from grace after being headhunted by the Camorra. The temptation of entering a life of crime with the Italian mafia offering quick and lucrative rewards proved impossible to resist. When I told Lipati that an anonymous informant had come forward, revealing the two men would be hiding somewhere in Traso, while an exact address wasn't forthcoming, the anonymous tipster suggested they would likely be found holed up in a safe house in Bargagli. Signor Sapori and I agreed that the informant was most likely Barrett, although we have no way of proving that at the moment."

Angelino rolled his eyes, letting out a sigh of exasperation, but remained silent, observing Holmes's cold stare.

"Checking with his staff, Lipati got back to me to say Raoul had been spotted only a few days ago, enjoying a beer at a local hostilery named Toit. Acting on this information, Lipati immediately sent a small armed unit of his best men to scour the area, tracking the escapees and quickly finding their hiding place. After being discovered making merry in a local osteria, Raoul, distracted while sweet-talking a woman of dubious reputation and oblivious to the siege, soon found himself surrounded by Lipati's men. The Eel, overpowered by four burly officers, was subsequently arrested and patted down before being taken away in handcuffs. In his pockets, the polizia discovered a silver key. Alerted to the commotion, the kerfuffle allowed the second man to escape through a restroom window. The polizia gave chase on foot, but the fugitive, flagging down a passing motorist, overpowered the unfortunate man, stealing his car and escaping deep into the countryside. The polizia were unaware of the man's identity, but from the witness description in the hostilery, they suspect it was Rodriguez's henchman, Peppo Barbieri.

"Realising the game was up, The Eel agreed to cooperate and confirmed the key found about his person was the one required to immobilise the bomb, stating that, although a willing accomplice, he had no wish to endanger innocent lives. Raoul was taken back to Genoa for questioning but stubbornly refused to give the polizia any further information, answering *no comment* to their numerous enquiries and demanding an attorney. Meanwhile, two bomb disposal officers collected the special key from Lipati and then travelled the short distance to the car factory. They secured the bomb, ensuring your factory's future, Signor Angelino."

"And, of course, the many people employed by Liguria Cars," Holmes added.

Angelino shook his head in disbelief. "So my factory is safe, thank God!" he cried, raising his glass to me and the detective. "I want to thank you both from the bottom of my heart. I don't want to appear ungrateful. I know I have much to be thankful for, but what about the painting? I presume it's lost forever."

Holmes shook his head. "On the face of things, it would appear so, Signor Angelino, despite Romano and his men's best efforts, it's fair to say we were no nearer to finding Rodriguez, Barrett, and his cronies, who are no doubt hidden deep within the bowels of the criminal fraternity, aided and abetted by the mob. Indeed, all seemed lost until an unexpected development occurred only yesterday."

"And what is this development?" Angelino implored. "Please, sir, don't keep me in suspense one moment longer. My poor heart can't take the strain."

Holmes laughed, observing Angelino's pitiful expression. "At last, we may have found the breakthrough we've been looking for. A man fitting Rodriguez's description was seen at a church in Salemo, holding forth with a group of parishioners. He was one of many mourners attending the funeral of a local Catholic priest known as Father Joseph Mancini. A man held in high regard amongst his peers and people whose lives he touched."

"I'm sorry to learn that the man is dead. God bless his soul," Angelino said. "But what has Father Joseph's demise got to do with this sorry state of affairs, and why would Rodriguez be mourning a man of the cloth?"

"The late Father Joseph was a mentor to Rodriguez in his formative years before he got involved with the Italian mafia.

It would appear that the man known as Il Resolver wasn't always a villain. He was once a promising student with a glittering career ahead of him. Rodriguez's appearance at that church tells me he must have held this priest in very high esteem to risk being seen at such a public event and in broad daylight."

"So what happened? Did the polizia arrest this man?" a wide-eyed Angelino asked.

"Sadly, no." Holmes sighed. "Rodriguez spotted the polizia as he was coming out of the church. He ran around the back of the building, pushing his way through the crowd, making his escape in a waiting car. The polizia gave chase, but their black *Maria* was no match for Rodriguez's high-powered car."

"How far can he run?" Angelino said, his soulful eyes shifting from Holmes to me.

"It's more a question of where *can* he run," I said. "The polizia will be covering all the stations and ports. It's possible he's heading west to join the rest of the gang. You know what they say. *Gli uccelli di una piuma si radunano insieme*, birds of a feather flock together."

Holmes patted Angelino reassuringly on the shoulder, offering him a sympathetic smile. "Rest assured, Signor Angelino, the inspector and I plan to travel to Genoa by train later this morning and hopefully resolve the final pieces of the puzzle together. We have a reservation on the eleven A.M. train. We believe Barrett and the rest of his cronies are likely hiding in the area. I promise we will do everything possible to procure the painting and bring these people to justice. The inspector and I are confident of an imminent arrest."

Angelino smiled appreciatively. "Thank you, but I plan to travel to Genoa myself tomorrow to check over the factory and reassure my security staff." Angelino handed over a card. "This is the address and phone number of Liguria Cars and my apartment in Busalla. I would be obliged if you could keep me updated on any fresh developments. As an act of appreciation, I intend to donate to a charity of your choice should the painting be returned." Angelino rose. "I shan't keep you any longer, gentlemen. I hope to hear from you soon with good news." He held out his hand towards Holmes and me. We both stood to shake hands and then in a moment, Angelino left the room.

Holmes sat back in his chair, lighting a cigarette, blowing circles of smoke into the air, and staring at me amusedly. "Romano, you have excelled yourselves during this investigation. You and your men should be commended. The irony is not lost on me that Genoa's name is thought to derive from The God Janus."

"Ah, yes," I agreed. "Stapleton's pseudonym. How very clever of you to point that out, Holmes. Historically, Genoa, like Janus, has two faces. One that looks towards the sea and the other that turns into the mountains. It's true what you say that the most obvious explanation is often the simplest and correct one."

"Yes, indeed," Holmes said, drawing on his cigarette. "It's no coincidence Stapleton chose to hide out in Genoa. I hope you're prepared for the journey ahead, my friend. I'm confident it will be an interesting one. Barrett and Rodriguez are men both known to bear a grudge. Their relationship is not destined to last. The net is closing in fast, and our fish is well and truly on the hook."

Chapter Forty-One: Salvatore Romano
La Fine e Vicina—The End is Nigh

Holmes and I arrived at The Hotel Chopin in the bustling port city of Genoa later that afternoon, having already secured reservations in separate rooms on the first floor. The hotel was three and a half miles from the Genoa Place Colomb Railway Station, with easy access to the city's heart.

After an early dinner, we took a cab to the central polizia headquarters, Questura di Genova, at Via Armando Diaz. We soon found ourselves sitting across from my old friend, Captain Marco Lipati, a tall, thick-set man with large, expressive brown eyes and a waxed moustache. He reassured us the railway stations and ports were being rigorously monitored. Roadblocks and foot patrols had been set up by his officers, ensuring there would be no escape from the city for Barrett and his cronies.

In the meantime, the guardie were in the process of checking hotels in the vicinity, each concierge given a detailed description of Barrett, Gallagher, and Rodriguez, with instructions to immediately alert the polizia if they spotted anyone fitting their descriptions.

We agreed the fugitive Peppo Barbieri would likely have left the city by now, and he could be anywhere. As for the woman known as Connie, it was only thanks to Nicco Sapori that we had a detailed description after he drew a picture of her and Barrett. Curiously, the man Nicco referred to as Gino, whose identity we now knew as Peppo Barbieri, was not included in the drawing. When Holmes questioned his son about that, Nicco shrugged his shoulders, saying he couldn't remember.

The following day, with still no reported sightings of the gang, things took another unexpected turn. Lipati arrived at the hotel where Holmes and I were at breakfast, joining us for coffee in the hotel's restaurant. Removing his hat, the captain smiled, clearly amused by our curious expressions as we gazed at him intently.

"Well, gentlemen," Lipati said, now feigning a solemn expression. "I have news to convey to your enquiries. The Campagna constabulary asked me to personally alert you to the fact that Emilio Rodriguez's body was discovered earlier this morning at the wheel of his car. He was gunned down outside The Banca di Italia, Salerno. He'd been shot in the head in what eyewitnesses described as a cold-blooded execution. A passenger travelling in the opposite direction opened the window as they approached Rodriguez's car and fired at point-blank range with what looked like a revolver before speeding off into the hills. The first officer arrived at the incident with the medico legale, who pronounced Rodriguez dead at the scene. The execution has all the hallmarks of a mafia hit. It was rumoured Rodriguez had recently taken out the leader of a rival gang responsible for the murder of his wife and child."

"Was Rodriguez alone in the car?" Holmes asked.

Lipati shook his head. "There was one passenger, Roberto Santini, an art dealer. He was unharmed and attended to by medics. Santini was later taken to the hospital, suffering from shock, where he is currently being kept under surveillance."

"And what of the painting?" Holmes asked, raising a brow.

"It was in the back seat of Rodriguez's car, wrapped in brown paper, at the bottom of a valise. Luckily, the painting did not appear to suffer any material damage when the car crashed into a lampost outside the bank . . . only a small chip to the frame. The precious masterpiece is now safely under lock and key back at the station. When we questioned Santini, finding himself surrounded by such compelling evidence, he immediately came clean and admitted to his part in removing the picture of Saint Monica from Angelino's home. He said his job was merely to authenticate the artwork and assist with the transfer due to take place later this afternoon at his house in Folcata. My officers will wait for the unsuspecting art dealer. Santini identified Gerard Francescone, also known as Mr X, as the man prepared to pay a tidy sum for something as rare as the Saint Veronica painting. Francescone will be arrested for frode di arte . . . attempting to acquire a piece of precious art illegally."

"Your men have done well, Captain," I said, smiling broadly as Holmes and I stood and shook his hand.

"Indeed," Holmes said, sitting down to finish his rashers and eggs as the waiter deftly topped up our coffee cups. "Signor Angelino is going to be one very happy man," he remarked as he buttered a piece of toast, adding a sugar lump to his cup. "Now, we must find Barrett and his accomplice, Connie Gallagher. I fear they will prove far more elusive, like slippery fish evading the net."

The captain smiled, looking like the cat that got the cream. "I recognise that look, Marco. There's something else, isn't there?" I quizzed.

"Of course there is. The man is practically bursting with excitement," Holmes said. "Pray, do tell us, Captain."

Lipati nodded. "There are two more fresh developments to report, gentlemen. After being interrogated, Santini revealed that Barrett and Gallagher were staying somewhere in Genoa in disguise as a married couple, but, unfortunately, their address was unknown to him."

"And the second development," Holmes quizzed, leaning

forward in his seat and staring at the inspector keenly.

"One of my men, searching the docks and surrounding area, discovered a leak of fresh engine oil seeping from a lock-up. After further investigation, he discovered a *Laurin and Klement* motorcycle covered by a dust sheet, which matches the description used by the couple in the art painting heist. Upon quizzing the hansom cab companies that operate in the area, a driver remembered picking up a woman dressed in black only two days ago. He remembered her because she carried a pair of goggles under her arm and spoke with a thick German accent."

"And where did the cab driver take this woman?" I asked.

"The Grand Hotel Savoia."

"Why, that's not far from here," I exclaimed. "It's merely a stone's throw from the Genoa Place Colomb Railway Station."

Holmes stood, quickly putting on his hat and jacket. "Then what are we waiting for, gentlemen? Onwards, my friends, to The Grand Savoia!"

Chapter Forty-Two: Robert Barrett
Uccidi Bob — Kill Bob

Connie was in a buoyant mood during dinner this evening. When questioned, she admitted she felt a frisson of excitement about her future and couldn't wait to board the boat the following morning. We'd ordered champagne and a bowl of my favourite salted almonds to celebrate our last night at the hotel on a pleasant evening with the last movement of Brahms' *Second Piano Concerto* playing in the background.

"Prost mein Freund!" Connie said, raising a glass. I joined her in the toast, sipping slowly from my glass.

It was a disingenuous ruse on my part, but at least this way, Connie would experience some fleeting happiness before I sent her to a watery grave.

I'd suffered from a fever the past two days. First, a terrible headache, then constantly drifting in and out of fitful sleep, dreaming of people from my past, like Laura and my late wife, Beryl. But this morning, I was feeling somewhat better after showering and enjoying a hearty breakfast.

Connie and I had already packed in preparation for our journey to the port. I'd aborted my plan to finish her with the knife, reasoning it would be far too messy, deciding instead to wait until we were on the boat, where I would invite her to my cabin and then get her intoxicated with whiskey and a sleeping draught before plunging her overboard. I figured it would take a while with the tide before the body was discovered. The pathologist would find traces of alcohol in Connie's system and presume she'd fallen into a drunken stupor.

I didn't care either way. By then, I would be in England, hidden by the Peaky Blinders, with ample money to start a new life. So, for now, I was making the best of our situation, even engaging in some light-hearted banter with Connie while consuming our nuts and the delicious champagne.

A knock at the door disturbed us from our indulgence. I rose from my chair and opened the door, ushering the waiter into the room. He was carrying a second bottle of the finest champagne from The Sangiovese Vineyards on a silver tray, which he placed on the table. He acknowledged the silver coins I placed in his hand with a smile and a courteous nod before leaving the room.

I uncorked the bottle, topping up our flutes before sitting back in my chair. "Here's to us, Connie! A world of endless possibilities awaits." I suddenly felt tired, and exhaustion wrapped around me like a devil's shroud.

Connie took a sip from her glass, lit a cigarette, and turned her attention to me. That warm smile had now faded, replaced by a frosty stare. "For me, perhaps, Bob, but sadly not for you."

"Whatever do you mean, don't you expect me to be happy?" I scoffed.

Connie shook her head. "No, Bob, I expect you to perish like you should have done all those years ago at the Great Grimpen Mire."

I stared at her in horrified astonishment. "But why would you want me dead, Connie? I thought we were friends, not merely work colleagues."

"Friends?" Connie gave a throaty laugh. "With friends like you, who needs enemies?" She sighed. "I discovered the knife when I searched through your belongings as you were taking a shower. And I have to say, I'm impressed. You made an excellent choice. It's a pity you didn't slit my throat sooner, then you wouldn't have found yourself caught up in your present predicament."

"What predicament? What have you done, Connie?" I shouted, exasperated, as my eyes darted around the room, my heart beating wildly in my chest as the grim realisation of my earlier symptoms and fate hit me like a sledgehammer. "You poisoned me with what? Cyanide? Arsenic?"

"Indeed," Connie said. "I've been sprinkling drops of arsenic in your tooth powder for the past few days, and I'm curious to see what effect it would have. This is the reason you've been feeling out of sorts. Sorry about that."

I sat back in my chair, my stomach churning, horrified, her maniacal laughter echoing through the room. "And now?" I asked, dreading the answer that was inevitably coming.

Removing the cigarette from her mouth, Connie stubbed it out in the overflowing ashtray beside me and bent down to kiss me on the cheek. "Something to remember me by." She sighed. "You know, I thought I would feel vindicated about your demise. But I just feel sad that you rejected my business proposal. Together, we could have conquered the world if only I had been able to trust you."

Connie rose from her chair, putting on her jacket, before collecting her valise from the bedroom.

"You treacherous hag, I never expected to be double-crossed by a woman." I tried to stand, but my legs gave way beneath me. "How long have I got?"

"Twenty to thirty minutes at most." She shrugged. "Ample time to collect your thoughts and think what might have been." Connie gently removed the champagne glass from my hand, her heavy perfume lingering in the air. "See you on the other side, Bob," she whispered. Then, in seconds, my ruthless, unsmiling assassin was gone from the room, taking with her my money and all my hopes and dreams.

I tried to call out, but no words were forthcoming. I struggled to swallow and catch my breath. I picked up a notebook from the table in front of me. My hands were unsteady as I scribbled a few notes with a fountain pen. With a bleak irony, I could hear the porter outside cleaning the corridor, whistling out of tune as he did his work. The song was *Oh, Whistle and I'll Come to You My Lad* by Robbie Burns, one of Beryl's favourites, which she often sang when we first walked out together. Apart from the pen and notepad, my gallows humour was the only flimsy tool at my disposal.

I closed my eyes, releasing my grip on the pen and the breath I had been holding. Laying back in the chair, resigned to my fate, grateful at least that I hadn't faced the indignity of the London gallows or, worse, caught red-handed by Holmes or Romano. My death, when it came, would be peaceful. Someone told me once that the absence of one's misdeeds is abolished by death, although I'm unsure if that will happen in my case. I can only hope for the sake of the child I leave behind that it does.

As I took my last gasps and floated away into oblivion, reflecting that The Whistle of Revenge had finally come to be, but tragically, not in my favour. I could hear my wife's voice whispering in the darkness.

"Beryl." I sighed. "I'm coming, my darling. Didn't I tell you I'd love you to the end?"

Chapter Forty-Three: Sherlock Holmes
Come Vive l'Altra Metà — How the Other Half Lives

We arrived at The Grand Hotel Savoia in Lipati's horse-drawn police vehicle. We entered the foyer, stepping into an elaborate, vast lobby with a spectacular ground-floor bar, an impressive array of marble chandeliers, and floors adorned with antique furniture.

The captain introduced us to the concierge, a short, wiry chap who spoke with an air of authority not quite matching his overall deportment. He stared at us behind a pair of horn-rimmed glasses, regarding us with suspicious eyes. After Romano briefly explained the urgency of the situation, that the hotel was likely harbouring two dangerous criminals who were wanted for questioning by the polizia, the concierge's manner became more congenial. He opened the black leather visitors' ledger, allowing us to read the entries. We flicked through the list of names to discover eighty couples had booked reservations at the hotel earlier that week. According to the register, fifty-five remained in residence.

I quickly scanned the list, and one name made me stop in my tracks. "What room was assigned to this couple?" I inquired, pointing to the entry.

"Ah, Signor and Signora Sanju are checked into the Aphrodite Suite on the second floor."

"Are they in residence at the moment?" Romano asked.

The concierge nodded. "Yes, Inspector. As far as I'm aware,

there was no sign of them at breakfast. Signor and Signora Sanju tend to keep to themselves and seldom make an appearance in the dining room, preferring instead to take all meals in their room."

Romano turned his attention to me. "Are you sure?" he asked.

I smiled derisively at the inspector. "I would stake my life on it. It's no coincidence that Sanju is an anagram of Janus."

After a brief animated conversation with the hotel manager, who'd come out of his office to find out what all the fuss was about, the inspector signed for the spare key, secure in the knowledge that four of Lipati's plain-clothed guardie were on watch outside the building. In the meantime, the three of us made our way up the sweeping staircase to the second floor. Each of us was armed, and I suspected a little apprehensive about what we might face.

The Aphrodite Suite was at the end of a long winding corridor to the rear of the second floor. Lipati rapped on the door but received no answer. He rapped again, this time more urgently, nothing but a deadly silence. Romano pulled the key from his pocket and turned the lock. The door opened slowly, and we tentatively stepped inside. The suite appeared empty and was elegantly furnished with a chaise lounge and two hard-backed chairs, which sat next to an oak coffee table. A marble fireplace was the room's centrepiece, with two urns filled with flowers.

To the side was a dining table with an ice bucket, hosting a half-empty bottle of champagne, a half-eaten bowl of salted almonds, and two half-filled flutes. I inspected both with a magnifying glass. One flute was smeared around the rim with red lipstick, while the other held the faintest residue of white powder, which would be undetectable to the human eye. Next to the dining table was an easy chair, and on that lay the body of a man of middle years, his lips blue, his eyes wide open in a haunting fixed stare.

He was dressed casually in black trousers and a white shirt. One arm trailed on the floor next to a notebook and a fountain pen. I checked the man's pulse, shaking my head. I was flooded with a sense of recognition. There was something familiar about Jack Stapleton's full lips and high cheekbones. He looked much older than I remembered. His blond hair, once described by Laura Lyons as spun gold, was now streaked grey, and his face was lined and covered with liver spots from too much drink. I stared at him. I had often pondered how I would react if I ever came face-to-face with the antagonist instrumental in kidnapping my son. This man who relentlessly pursued me, driven forward by hatred and revenge. But looking at him now, his deathly pallor, the pathetic circumstances of his demise, I felt almost sorry for Jack Stapleton.

I turned my attention to Romano and the captain. "This man has been dead for several hours. And from the looks of it, he's been poisoned, most likely by arsenic."

"What do you think happened? A lovers' quarrel? A love affair gone wrong?" Romano asked.

"Possibly, but more likely, Stapleton met his end by treachery and double-dealing," I said as my attention was drawn to a valise in the corner of the room.

I opened it, pulling out a knife from its sheath. Amongst the other possessions we found in the suite was a cache of private papers, including a diary. Rifling through the contents, I had no doubt who they belonged to.

"What of the accomplice?" Lipati asked.

"We shall check the rest of the suite, Captain, but my theory is that the perpetrator of this heinous crime, Connie Gallagher, has long gone. The deceased man is Jack Stapleton, otherwise known as Robert Barrett. Of that, I am certain."

Romano and I continued with our inspection of the suite,

checking every nook and cranny, while Lipati went downstairs to summon an ambulance and the medical examiner. Romano drew my attention to a tin of tooth powder found in the bathroom. My magnifying glass revealed parts of the powder differed slightly in colour and size and would be almost indistinguishable to a layman untrained in the history of poisons. Still, to Romano and me, there was no double that it was there, and it was most likely arsenic.

Securing the lid, Romano placed the tin in his pocket to be checked out by the medical team and later used as evidence. The inspector and I exchanged glances before I left him to continue his search of the bathroom and stepped back into the lounge.

My eyes darted around the room and noticed something glittering on the floor. I bent down to retrieve the notepad and a woman's silver earring from under a chair. There was a page in the notepad addressed to the attention of Lucca Sapori, the handwriting barely legible, reminiscent of a spider having crawled over the page.

"That note looks like it's been written by an illiterate child," Romano said while peeking over my shoulder, his eagle eyes missing nothing.

"No child," I said. "It's not what we see, Inspector, it's what we don't observe. This note was penned by a man who knew he hadn't long for this world."

I read the note's contents, trying to decipher the writing as best I could. "These are the last words of a dying man. *I was done for by Connie Gallagher, who intends to flee by boat to Germany using the pseudonym Beatrice Shaw. I've wronged you. It's true, Sapori. I shouldn't have taken the boy, I know.*

"*But, as a father, I implore you to help protect my only child, who I swear is innocent in all of this. I beg you to shield them from their father's true identity.*"

What looked like the start of another sentence was dramatically cut off into a faint squiggle. I folded the note, tearing off the second section and placing it into my pocket, leaving the narrative about Gallagher on the table beside the body.

"Holmes, you can't do that. You're withholding evidence," Romano said, his steely gaze fixed on me.

"This is a private note from one man to another. It has no bearing on the case or Stapleton's demise. Please trust me on this, Inspector."

Romano nodded. "They are clearly the rambling words of a man who'd lost all sense of reasoning. Were you aware Stapleton had a child?"

I shook my head. "No, it's alleged that his late wife Beryl was pregnant when she passed away. There are no other children that I'm aware of."

"All right, I'll let it go for now. The man was undoubtedly hallucinating when he scribbled out that note." Romano cocked his head to one side, staring at me with a curious expression. "But if I didn't know better, Holmes, I would swear you have a grudging respect for the woman who outwitted Jack Stapleton. Ring any bells, my friend?" The inspector punctuated his statement with a slap on my back.

I stared at him incredulously. "There is no comparison to what happened with Nene. This woman, Connie Gallagher, is an extremely dangerous individual who will have no qualms about killing again if anyone dares get in her way. She's a game player, and this game is far from over."

Romano looked about to say something else when the captain returned, striding purposefully into the room. "Gentlemen, the ambulanza has been summoned, along with the medical examiner. We will know more after the autopsy, of course. Although I think it's pretty obvious how this man died. And now Connie Gallagher has a murder to add to her list of offences. We have additional men covering the port. If this woman is still in Genoa, I promise we will find her. Come, gentlemen, it could be a while before the medical examiner and the ambulanza get here, and I think we could all make use of a drink."

When we arrived back at the hotel, the medical examiner confirmed what we already suspected. Stapleton's death had all the hallmarks of being caused by arsenic poisoning. Although it would take a few days for official clarification, pending the autopsy report.

I immediately called Nene to let her know that Stapleton and Rodriguez were both dead, with Gallagher and the other fugitive on the run. It was unlikely the now depleted gang would dare threaten our family again.

Exhilarated by the news, Nene said she was looking forward to my return home the following day. She laughed when I told her of Angelino's expression of faint disbelief when Romano and I returned his beloved painting.

They say a picture paints a thousand words, and this was certainly true, having observed Angelino's delighted expression when he was reunited with his treasured family heirloom. True to his word, the car mogul wrote a substantial cheque there and then in favour of Doctor Barnardo's, a charity close to Nene's heart, of which she was a proud patron. She gasped when I revealed the amount, humbled and stunned by Angelino's kindness and generosity.

In my absence after the holiday, Charlotte had returned home earlier than expected and was her usual buoyant self. Her antics had lifted Nicco's mood somewhat. Nene said our son was overjoyed to see his little sister again. To celebrate and as a special treat, she planned to take the children to Parco Sempione, along with Sophia Moon and her family, later that afternoon. I agreed it would do Nicco good to get out of the villa, dragging him away from his studies to take in some invigorating fresh air and return to a normal routine.

Our son had understandably been quiet for the first few days after his release from captivity. At our request, Doctor Pease, a renowned child psychiatrist and medical practitioner, called to see Nicco the day after his rescue. At Nene's insistence, they spent over an hour chatting in the familiarity and comfort of our son's bedroom. When Pease eventually came downstairs, my stomach lurched in anticipation of what the good doctor would have to say. What damage had those brutes inflicted on our beloved son?

However, thankfully, my fears were unfounded, and all doubts vanished after observing the medic's broadly smiling face. Ushering him into the drawing room, with a glass of whiskey in one hand and a Cuban cigar in the other, he sat back on the chaise lounge to report his findings to me and an anxious Nene.

"Your son is a remarkable boy and, ultimately, an astonishing example of the resilience of the human spirit. You must be very proud," Pease said. Nene and I nodded in agreement as the doctor continued. "Children, for the most part, have no fear. They are born naturally curious and remain so until taught otherwise."

"But the poor boy must have been terrified," Nene said.

The doctor nodded. "Yes, it's true, he was at first. But Nicco told me he always believed you would come through for him. In the end, Signor Sapori," The doctor paused momentarily, sipping from his glass. "Your son appears to have struck up a close bond with one of the abductors, a fellow named Gino." Pease laughed, observing Nene's shocked expression. "I assure you, Signora Sapori, this is not unusual in such cases, especially for someone so young. There is no need for alarm. Your son will likely never see or hear from this man again. He will forget him soon enough."

"Nicco hasn't spoken much about his ordeal, and we had no wish to traumatise him any further. I know he's had nightmares about that woman and her rage-twisted face, but please tell me, did you find any signs of physical abuse?" Nene asked, speaking in a hushed tone.

Pease shook his head. "No, nothing like that. I examined your son, and there doesn't appear to be any signs of physical trauma. On the contrary, from what Nicco told me, the perpetrators treated him well, even that woman you mentioned earlier named Connie . . . apart from giving Nicco the injection, I don't believe she mistreated him." The doctor handed Nene a prescription. "This is for your son. It's a little something to help him sleep. The nightmares will lessen as he occupies his mind with other things. Nicco told me he has been studying hard to pass the Harvard exam. If your son focuses on that, he should be fine."

Relieved by the doctor's narrative, we bid him farewell, thankful that our son appeared to have survived his ordeal, displaying tenacity and bravery that took my breath away.

I hadn't mentioned Stapleton's note during the telephone conversation with my wife, so I decided to wait until I returned to Milan to speak to her confidentially. If my theory was correct, then we had much to discuss. According to Nene, our governess, Hildegard Achen, was set to leave our employment imminently after receiving a letter from her mother pleading for a reconciliation.

With a reputation as a formidable woman, Martina Schockomohle was unlikely to take no for an answer. The celebrated concert pianist was due to arrive in Milan the day after tomorrow, having booked a reservation at one of the city's oldest and most prestigious hotels, The Regency. She would travel to the Sapori residence later that evening, having accepted a dinner invitation from Nene. This revelation came as quite a surprise and was a welcome distraction from the contents of Stapleton's cryptic message that kept playing over and over again in my mind. When I closed my eyes, the image of him lying there in that room, the stench of death, felt oddly detached from reality. Even when rotting in hell, Stapleton was manipulating me. I could scarcely believe how foolish I'd been.

Chapter Forty-Four: Nene Adler
Ricongiung Imento tra Madree Figlio — Mother and Child Reunion

Ever since our beloved son was returned to us, I'd been walking on air, thanking God every day in my prayers that no harm had come to him. But, of course, I was aware that the true heroes behind Nicco's rescue, like a cavalry galloping to the rescue, were Milano polizia, Salvatore, and my brilliant husband. And now, with Charlotte home, the villa was once again filled with laughter and the incessant chatter of our beloved children. I even disregarded Charlotte's exuberant antics, which she took full advantage of. Even Nicco, who announced he wished to study in peace, allowed his sister into the inner sanctum of his bedroom, where he chatted to her at length, reading her stories with a patience that touched and humbled me simultaneously.

Sherlock and I decided not to tell our daughter about her brother's kidnapping. Nicco said he had no wish to see his little sister upset. We all agreed that our funny, precocious, curious six-year-old would struggle to cope if she discovered what had happened. The last thing we desired was for her to feel any measure of fear or to become the subject of ridicule or ill-treatment, should she, by some misstep, let slip a word of the abduction and allow the matter to reach the ears of the general public.

The thought of having the press congregate outside the villa, firing off questions every time we opened the front door, was not conducive to a stable family environment. I knew from personal experience that journalists were not always receptive to children. Therefore, Nicco's capture became a secret we agreed to keep within our tight-knit family unit.

The evening after Charlotte returned home, I entertained my close friend, Sophia, after she accepted my dinner invitation. The invite was also extended to Hildegard, who politely declined the suggestion, explaining she had much to do before her mother arrived, preferring instead to take her evening meal earlier in the kitchen with Alice and Ginevra. I didn't attempt to argue with her. I knew our governess had mixed feelings about meeting her mother again. On the other hand, she was understandably excited about being invited back into the bosom of her family.

After a delicious dinner of roast chicken and seasonal vegetables, expertly prepared by Alice, Sophia and I relaxed in the garden, partaking in wine while catching the last of the Tuscan rays as the sun slowly began to set. Sophia seemed to sense my sombre mood. I was admittedly quieter than usual during our conversation, not yet fully restored to my usual self after everything that had transpired.

"Where's Sherlock, and what are you keeping from me?" Sophia asked, staring at me with a burning curiosity over the rim of her glass. "I've known you too long, my dear, not to know when something is amiss."

I stared at Sophia, perplexed. "Sophia Moon, you never could resist meddling in people's personal lives in a way that some would describe as snooping."

"Well, you may call it snooping, but I call it natural curiosity. I'm looking out for my dear friend. Anyway, it's only snooping if one has something to hide. Do you?" she asked, raising an eyebrow in mock humour.

I sighed deeply. "I have never been able to keep anything from you, Sophia. But what I'm about to tell you cannot be repeated to a living soul, not even Robert. I hope you understand?"

"All right," she agreed. "You have my word."

I sat back in my chair, taking several sips from my glass of Barolo before I calmly explained to Sophia all that had transpired with Nicco. As tricky as recounting the sorry tale was, I had to smile as my story unfolded. Sophia raised a brow, staring at me in jaw-dropping incredulity, her beautiful brown eyes flashing like molten chocolate in the moonlight.

"Why, it's unimaginable," Sophia said. "I'm so sorry that you and Sherlock were left to face all this. I wish Robert and I had been here to help."

Sophia rose from her seat, tears coming to both our eyes as she threw her arms around my shoulders, wrapping me in a loving embrace, reminiscent of Salvatore's innocent welcome hug only a few days earlier and a stark reminder that Sherlock and I had barely exchanged a peck on the cheek since all this saga began. I longed to be enfolded in his loving arms again and back on that pedestal he proudly placed me on.

I took hold of Sophia's hand, squeezing it gently. "I don't want you to worry. It's more or less all over with. There are just two members of the gang for the police to round up, although hopefully, they'll be miles away from Milan by now."

"Well, I'm sure the polizia will catch them soon. As for Inspector Romano and your husband, from what you told me, they're nothing less than heroes."

I stared at Sophia suspiciously. "You and Sherlock appear very cosy all of a sudden. You seldom have a good word to say about my husband."

"Why, ever since that business last year with Luigi and Renata Amato, I'm practically his number one fan." Sophia gazed at me with a warm twinkle of affection in her eyes. "You're so brave, Nene. I don't know how I would cope if someone took either of my children."

"If you don't mind, Sophia, I prefer not to dwell on what

happened. Come, tell me about your holiday. I trust Charlotte conducted herself in an orderly manner."

Sophia laughed as we retired to the drawing room, arm in arm, for what was to be a lengthy heart-to-heart conversation as we caught up on our news. Sophia proceeded to fill me in on all the salacious details about Rhodes and Stephanato's anniversary party, even throwing in a little gossip about her parents' next-door neighbours, the Contis, who were rumoured to lead a chequered, unconventional love life in what Sophia described as a *marriage of convenience*.

"At least they have a love life," I mused, smiling wistfully. "Sherlock and I are barely on speaking terms. I think deep down he blames me for Nicco's abduction."

Sophia turned to me with a puzzled expression. "You and your husband have been to hell and back lately. What you need is a welcome distraction to help reignite the flames, and I, your guardian angel, have thought of the ideal solution, something that will lift everyone's spirits, even the celebrated detectives." Sophia took my hands in hers. "My darling, it's plain to see that you have lost all your vigour and high-spiritedness in only a few days. It needs to be revived."

I rolled my eyes. "Tell me, what madcap scheme have you come up with now?"

"A picnic," Sophia triumphantly replied.

"Sophia? Why, I'm sure that's going to drive Sherlock wild with desire. You know he's not one for dinner parties or social gatherings," I said sarcastically.

Sophia furrowed her brow. "I know what I'm proposing may appear like a sorry substitute for romance, but I need you to trust me on this one. Wanting more from your relationship is only natural, but any fool can see that Sherlock loves the bones of you. He just needs reminding."

I nodded. "Yes, I know he does. Sophia, I adore him, but simply loving someone does not guarantee they will be by your side forever."

Sophia rose from her seat, kissing me on both cheeks. "Remember, Nene, I'm always here for you. But I need to go now. There is much preparation to do."

Without uttering another word, I could only watch out of the open window as my best friend ran out of the villa and approached her waiting cab. Reflecting momentarily on our earlier conversation and Sophia's words of wisdom, I leaned out the window and called her.

"Wait, Sophia, please wait for a moment."

She gazed up at me, furrowing a brow. "What is it, my love?"

"You haven't told me the date and venue of the picnic."

Sophia flashed a wry smile. "Why, it's this Sunday, silly, the first of July. Have you forgotten it's your birthday?"

"Yes, but where?" I laughed.

"Monza. Be ready to travel by train on Saturday. Be sure to pack enough for the weekend." Then, without further ado, Sophia jumped into the cab and headed home, waving to me with a silk handkerchief until the carriage disappeared.

Feeling lightheaded from the wine, I decided on an early night. I popped around Charlotte's bedroom door to find her sleeping soundly like a baby. She stirred softly as I kissed her goodnight, planting a kiss on the top of her head.

Then I checked in on Nicco, surprised to see the light under his door reflected from a taper candle. Helen was lying at the foot of the bed curled up in a ball, and she raised her head, gazing up at me, wagging her tail, before rolling over onto her side and continuing her doggy slumber. Nicco was lying fast asleep on the bed with a book in his hands. I gently removed the book, *The Man in The Iron Mask*, before settling on the bed beside my son, stroking his hair and face, and covering him with a fallen blanket. Then, gently cradling his delicate hand in mine, I felt the wondrous sensation of my son's soft skin, his long tapering fingers brushing against the palm of my hand, transfixed by the familiar sight of my sleeping child. Except, Nicco was no longer a child. Blowing out the taper candle, I quietly left the room, closing the door behind me.

After a leisurely breakfast the following morning, on what was a warm, tranquil summer's day, Charlotte refused Hildegard's invitation to accompany her on a shopping trip into town. Instead, she asked to play in the garden with Helen while Nicco retired to his bedroom to resume his studies.

I would have preferred Nicco to get some fresh air like his sister before getting lost in his books, but I decided not to push him on the matter. We had all enjoyed a delightful afternoon at Parco Sempione the day before, where the children ran around together without a care, frolicking in the familiar tranquillity of the park, offering much-needed light relief after our recent upheaval.

I reminisced about my son's eyes alighting with happiness as I busied myself with some paperwork in the study while Alice and Ginevra cleaned the villa in preparation for Sherlock's return later that afternoon.

An hour or so passed when I heard a noise from the inner hallway. The door opened, and I glanced up from my desk, expecting to see Sherlock. Instead, I found my daughter's lovely face beaming at me with an air of maturity that didn't quite fit the bedraggled child standing before me with flushed cheeks. Her face, dress, and shoes were muddied from rolling around in the sand pit with Helen.

Charlotte indicated the tin of fudge she held. "These are for Nicco. I bought them in Rhodes, as I know they're his favourites, may I take them to him? My brother's tired, so I promise I won't stay long."

I beamed at Charlotte. "Yes, of course, but first, we must clean you up. Alice will have a fit if you get mud all over the house."

I led my daughter upstairs to our en-suite bathroom, sitting her down on a chair. I washed her, patting her hands, face, and knees with a towel to ensure she was dry. I then brushed her wayward curls into submission before refastening the pink hair ribbon that had fallen loose. Charlotte wrinkled her nose, making faces in the pier glass as I dressed her in a change of clean clothes.

"Nicco was cross with me this morning," she said. "He refused to come out to play with me and Helen. He said we were too distracting and that I should pay more attention when people are talking to me instead of always having my head in the clouds. He told me many children will never have the things we have and take for granted." Charlotte gave me a wry smile. With unflinching honesty, she quietly admitted, "Nicco's right. I do get distracted sometimes, especially in lessons. It often gets me into trouble with Ms Achen."

I looked down at my beautiful little girl, observing the wisps of hair curling on her forehead, the dimples in her chin, the blue eyes bright as a button, the strange way her lip curled when she was troubled, so reminiscent of her father.

Taking her by the hand, I said, "Charlotte, it's true you appear preoccupied at times, but you noticed Nicco was tired. When Francesco came to visit recently, you saw him sitting alone in the garden nursing a cut lip, and while the other children continued playing, it was you who came and asked for the medical supplies and comforted him. But let me tell you something, my darling girl, Father, Nicco, and I don't ever want you to stop noticing. There's a kindness within you, Charlotte, burning bright . . . never let it go out."

As my daughter gazed up at me, her skin glowing and smelling of olive soap, her face broke into a wide grin. I hoped she realised, even at such a vulnerable age, that her remarkable empathy towards others had the power to make a difference in this cold, unpredictable world. It was a poignant reminder that in our darkest moments, we were not alone.

You see, we were all searching for that exceptional person, someone who was conscientious, thoughtful, sensitive, and kind. Yearning for them to notice our pain, insecurities, hopes, and fears because those who do, like Charlotte and my husband, were a wonder to behold.

That was a lovely, poignant moment with my daughter. With the grace of God, there will be more to come in the future. I sincerely hoped that in years to come, when Nicco and Charlotte remembered their childhood, they would recall that their father and I did everything in our power to give them the best possible start in life. We worried too much, sometimes failed, and did not always get things right. But as loving, devoted parents, we tried our hardest to instil the importance of strong morals, ethics, empathy, integrity, kindness, honesty and love in our children.

Martina Schockomohle arrived at 7 P.M. the following evening, joining us for pre-dinner drinks in the drawing room. She was briefly introduced to the children, who, having already eaten, were now safely ensconced in their rooms. Charlotte was fast asleep while Nicco continued studying. Although the children hadn't said much, I believe they were upset about Hildegarde's imminent departure, and as a consequence, regarded Martina with some disdain.

Martina Schockomohle, a dignified, beautiful, striking woman, was immensely popular in her heyday as an accomplished concert pianist until a sudden illness cut her brilliant career short after the death of her husband, Karl Achen. Although it was never divulged in the papers what illness had affected her, some say she was suffering from a broken heart. Still, whatever the reason, she never returned to the stage professionally. Still an eye turner, in her mid-fifties, Martina was attired in an olive-green silk dress embroidered with cream lace. Her ash blonde hair, be-sprinkled grey, was tied up in an elaborate updo.

The resemblance to her daughter was extraordinary. They were like peas in a pod with the same clear blue eyes, lips, nose, exquisite jawline, and swan-like neck. Their verbal exchange was a little strained throughout dinner, leaving me to pre-empt most of the conversation as my husband observed Frau Schockomohle with a fixed and curious gaze.

Sherlock had asked to speak to Martina earlier in his study, a private conversation that lasted at most five minutes. When Martina eventually emerged from the encounter, she appeared somewhat flustered, but she managed to compose herself before we retired to the dining room.

After dinner, sitting at the piano, Martina entertained us with a repertoire of classical music, including beautiful renditions of some of Chopin's Preludes, before Sherlock and I discreetly returned to the lounge, leaving mother and daughter free to speak confidentially.

Sherlock poured us both a glass of brandy before lighting a cigar. It was a tranquil evening, so we decided to take our drinks outside to the garden. Things were still strained between us. My husband occupied the guest bedroom as he had done since Nicco disappeared. His excuse then was that he was barely sleeping and had no wish to disturb me. We sat in silence for a while, taking in the night air, with the sound of the night jars and the muted noises of the servants going about their chores in the background.

Taking a sip from my glass, I stared at my husband with an air of curiosity. "Martina appeared a little perturbed after your private conversation earlier. I hope you didn't upset our guest?"

Sherlock smiled, leaning back in his chair and stretching his long legs. "I merely questioned the lady on her earlier life at The Royal Academy of Music in London, where she was awarded a full scholarship. Nothing sinister, I can assure you. I was merely showing a friendly interest in our esteemed guest."

I quirked a brow. "I'm not buying that for a second."

Sherlock laughed. He was about to say something else when we were disturbed by Hildegard and Martina coming to join us in the garden, and from the smiles on their faces, they were now far more relaxed in each other's company. Sherlock ushered the ladies towards a seat.

"I hope you don't mind," Hildegard said. "But my mother and I have reached an understanding, so if it is acceptable to you, Signor and Signora Sapori, we plan to travel back to Germany tomorrow. Under the circumstances, I think it would be best for everyone. This way, I will have the chance of a fresh start. I will miss you all, especially the children, but I promise to stay in touch and visit whenever possible."

I rose from my chair and hugged Hildegard, delighted that she was finally reunited with her mother and close family.

Sherlock nodded, turning his attention to Martina. "It has been an absolute pleasure to meet you, Frau Schockomohle. The Sapori family wishes you and your daughter all the best for the future."

Martina's face broke into a wide grin. "Thank you, that is most kind of you, Signor Sapori. I would like to thank you and your wife for your kind hospitality this evening and for taking such good care of my daughter. After my husband Karl died, life was lonely at times. So this reconciliation means a great deal to me and my beloved daughter. Hopefully, we can both learn from our past mistakes."

"I'm sorry for your loss," I said. "You and your husband were together for a long time?"

"Indeed, we were," Martina said, a whimsical smile appearing on her face at the memory. "We married in my hometown of Frankfurt after what my mother described as a whirlwind romance. It was a beautiful ceremony on my twenty-first birthday at Saint Paul's Church, the same year I returned from The Royal Academy of Music."

She laughed. "Karl and his parents were old friends of the family. My late mother, God bless her soul, couldn't help but play matchmaker. So my parents invited Karl to dinner, hoping that a romantic liaison might develop between us. Having not seen him for three years, I was a little apprehensive. He was even more handsome than I remembered, and I saw him in a new light. Indeed, our first meeting, to my mother's delight, was akin to love at first sight. Karl was eight years older than me and quite a catch as a successful criminal defence attorney. He was a good husband and a wonderful father to Hildegard, our firstborn child, and our two sons." She sighed.

Sherlock rose from his chair. "Pray, allow me to replenish your drinks."

I stared at my husband as he approached the drawing room and went to fetch the wine. "All will be revealed later. Trust me," he whispered, with a glint in his eye that was all too familiar.

Sherlock returned a few minutes later with a silver tray holding two glasses of wine and an envelope that he handed to a puzzled Hildegard. "Your birth certificate and references," he explained. "You will likely need them should you decide to accept another position. I have included a reference from me and my wife in the hope it will stand you in good stead for future employers."

Hildegard nodded gratefully. "Thank you so much. Your kindness and generosity have touched and humbled me. I'm excited about returning to Frankfurt, but Milan will always hold a special place in my heart."

Sherlock raised his glass. "A toast, ladies, to new beginnings!"

Chapter Forty-Five: Nene Adler
Fantasmi del Passato — Ghosts of the Past

The following day, I awoke early and came downstairs to discover Sherlock napping on the Chesterfield in his study. I gazed at my sleeping husband, resisting the urge to touch his handsome face, pondering if he would ever kiss me again.

Sherlock opened one eye as he noticed me approaching.

"Ah, you're awake then. When was the last time you got a decent night's sleep? Perhaps you might rest easier in the matrimonial bed," I cuttingly remarked, placing a cup of coffee beside him.

"I wasn't asleep . . . just resting my eyes," he answered sheepishly, pointing to an unfinished letter and pen on the bureau nearby. "I have some letters to post this morning, and I owe my brother a telegram. It's such a splendid day," he said, gazing at the sun streaming in through the open window. "I thought I would take the children to Parco Sempione at the same time. It's a place that never fails to delight."

I smiled at him through gritted teeth. "That would be lovely. I shall ask Ginevra to prepare the children for the outing. It will be a welcome distraction for Nicco and Charlotte. They have been rather quiet since Hildegard and her mother left yesterday. Who's the letter for?"

"Why, it's for Martha Hudson," Sherlock abruptly replied. "It's merely a note to keep her abreast of events and set her mind at ease. You know how much she adores the children."

"Oh, sorry, I didn't realise Martha was aware of Nicco's

abduction." I stared at him, perplexed, feeling somewhat aggrieved.

Having agreed to keep Nicco's abduction a secret, I was somewhat surprised at my husband's declaration. At Sherlock's insistence and for our son's safety, I hadn't even been able to confide in my dear friends, Violetta, Ava, Sophia, and my cousin Estelle, at a time when I really could have used a close female confidante.

"I asked my brother to inform Mrs Hudson. After all, Martha and I go back a long way. Why, I have known her longer than you." Sherlock paused for a moment, observing my shocked expression. "Are we to have an altercation?" he asked as a deep furrow etched on his brow.

I shook my head. "No, not at all, but perhaps you should have married Martha instead of me. Why, the woman is practically half in love with you." As I turned on my heels and headed towards the door, seething inside, I turned, determined to have the last word, only to find my husband, seemingly unfazed by my outburst, doubled over, quivering with laughter.

"You are jealous of Mrs Hudson?" He paused momentarily as those penetrating eyes twinkled with a look of amusement I hadn't witnessed in a while. "Admittedly, she does serve a rather stellar breakfast," he said, smiling.

"You're not funny, Sherlock." I fumed, although I couldn't help laughing, observing his ludicrous expression.

"I fail to see why Martha Hudson would be interested in me. I'm not in the least interested in her, well, certainly not in a romantic way."

I nodded resignedly. "All right, I may have exaggerated. I find it disconcerting that you pay your London housekeeper more attention than your wife." I heaved a sigh. "You know how much I admire Martha. The poor woman deserves a medal for looking after you and Doctor Watson all those years."

Sherlock smiled, raising a brow. "You raise a valid point, Nene. As for my infidelity, well, I hope you know that's a ridiculous notion. Cheating on you would be tantamount to committing grand larceny. Anyway, I need you by my side. Who else is going to remind me of my shortcomings? You and I are destined to grow old and fat together."

"I refuse to do either," I said, staring at him in mock indignation.

My husband's face softened as he gazed at me. "Your presence in the marriage bed has sorely been missed, Nene."

"Likewise," I answered shyly, fighting a blush. My heart beat wildly as the fervour of my feelings, my deep abiding love for this man, claimed mastery over my emotions.

"I'm sorry if I've been distracted lately, but there has been much to attend to." He sighed. "To be honest, I don't think I could survive another night in the guest room. That lumpy mattress has seen better days."

"You sure know how to flatter a woman, Mr Holmes."

My words were caught short as my husband suddenly strode purposefully towards me, drawing me to him in a sweeping gesture. His hands circled my waist as he leaned in for a lingering kiss that left me breathless. Our loving embrace was suddenly interrupted by Charlotte calling out to us from the inner hallway.

"Later," Sherlock whispered, his eyes crinkled as he tenderly placed his hand on my face, stroking my cheek, chuckling over my look of frustration. "You need to know that I consider you my equal in every way. I have never hidden the deep regard I hold you in. So, if I have done or said anything to make you feel otherwise, please forgive me. You have my word that I will find a way to make amends."

"You'd better," I whispered, my eyes misting over as I kissed my husband on the lips.

With the assistance of the servants, I organised an intimate dinner for later that evening, to be served after Nicco and Charlotte retired to their rooms, both utterly exhausted from their exertions earlier at the park. While Sherlock was busy in his study, Alice prepared a splendid joint of lamb, rosemary potatoes, and parsnips. The food smelled divine as it roasted in the oven.

Sherlock uncorked a bottle of Valpolicella, a prestigious wine from the Veneto region we'd been saving for a special occasion. This evening was special for both of us for obvious reasons I won't dwell upon.

Over dinner, Sherlock and I chatted at length. We agreed that Nicco's abduction had been complex, terrifying, and unpredictable. The experience brought us face-to-face with our vulnerabilities in a way that had previously been alien to us, giving us a fresh perspective on life. Above all, the experience reminded us to reflect and be grateful for the simple yet essential things many of us often take for granted.

And with that in mind and the safety of our beloved children, Sherlock and I agreed to bring forward our trip to America. We would leave Milan the second week in August, giving the family time to settle in and adapt to our new surroundings. We asked Ginevra to accompany us, leaving Alice to look after the villa and Helen until we returned the following summer. I hated the thought of leaving our family pet behind, but according to my cousin Estelle, many cases of rabies were reported in the USA that year, so I decided to err on the side of caution. The children would be distraught if anything happened to their beloved dog.

Estelle had written to us a few days earlier with good news to convey. She had discovered a private tutor, experienced in the rigours of the Harvard entrance exam, with a 99% success rate for admissions—not that our son needed such help. But I figured it was better to be safe than sorry. Nicco was hell-bent on being accepted into the prestigious institution. It meant everything to him, and after all our son had endured these past few weeks, how could we deny him that? It was the least he deserved.

After much deliberation, Sherlock and I agreed Charlotte was far too young to be sent away to boarding school. So, we enrolled her at a private day school in Trenton, New Jersey. The Woodlands School for Girls, which Estelle advised, had an exemplary reputation, where she was certain Charlotte would continue to thrive and be able to see her brother during weekends and the holidays. I knew the children would be excited when we explained our trip had been expedited. Like me, they looked forward to starting our new life and reuniting with Estelle and their cousins.

After dinner, we retired to the drawing room. The house was deadly quiet, the children both fast asleep, while Alice and Ginevra, having waited on us earlier, had now left for the evening. Sherlock poured us a glass of port as we listened to the French composer Delibes' opera *Lakme* playing on the gramophone. We danced, our bodies swaying in rhythm to the beautiful, haunting melodies of the music. The wine, the general ambience, my husband's subtle cologne, and the feel of his body so close to mine were intoxicating.

"I know, it's late," I said. "But can we go outside? I'd rather like to see the sunset."

Sherlock smiled, nodding in agreement. "Whatever you want." He took my glass and ushered me outside onto the balcony. We sat comfortably in two wicker chairs.

Sherlock gently took my hand. "I'm unsure what I've enjoyed more this evening, the wonderful food or the stellar company. My goal is to ensure your happiness. I would do anything in my power to do that. So I need to know how you feel about our relationship. What do you need from me?"

I stared at him searchingly, meditating for a moment as I chose my words carefully. "First, I want my life back with you and the children. Remember how we were before all this madness? I miss that. I miss us. So I want slow dances to Strauss and Chopin, moments like this together under a moonlit night and a starry sky. I want all of that. But, more than this, I need to know if you still love me."

Sherlock sighed as I stared at him anxiously. "You know I do. In the same way, I'm certain you feel the same about me. I know I wasn't your first, but you are mine in every way that matters. Although, after what I'm about to tell you, you may feel that I am no longer worthy. Promise me you'll hear me out before you jump to conclusions?"

"Oh, my love, I'd promise you anything. Pray tell me what's on your mind? What's troubling you?"

"When Martina Schockomohle came to dinner that night, you asked me a question, which I failed to answer. As I was not entirely certain of the facts." Sherlock sighed. "But now, a telegram I received from my brother earlier today only confirmed what I already suspected."

"And what did you suspect?"

Sherlock hesitated for a moment, and his voice sank almost to a whisper as he said, "There is no easy way for me to tell you this, but Hildegard Achen is Jack Stapleton's daughter."

I fell back in my chair, staring at my husband aghast. "But surely that cannot be. Hildegard even considered marrying the man until she came to her senses."

Sherlock topped up my glass, squeezing my hand as he continued his narrative. "Thankfully, Hildegard Achen has no clue who her biological father is, and I think we should keep it that way. Can you imagine the fallout if she discovered her real father was a narcissistic murdering psychopath, immortalised in one of my most infamous cases?"

"But, Sherlock, surely Martina Schockomohle must have

been aware of Stapleton's real identity before she embarked on a personal relationship with him and later discovered she was with child?"

My husband shook his head. "No, Nene, on the contrary, the man she knew and fell in love with back in her university days was a fellow student from the University College of London, where he was studying botany under Professor Daniel Oliver, who just happens to be an old acquaintance of my brother. At my request, Mycroft got in touch with Professor Oliver, who, having checked the academic records, was able to confirm that Jack Valderlour enrolled at the university in eighteen-sixty-nine, graduating three years later in eighteen-seventy-two, the same year as Martina Schockomohle. Although they studied at separate learning establishments, Professor Oliver remembered Valderlour very well. He described him to my brother as an exemplary student but a man of a singular mind, willing to do anything to get to the top of his class, even if it meant ostracizing his fellow students in the process. It was rumoured that he cheated on the final exams, although that was never proven, and Valderlour subsequently graduated from the college with a two-point-one."

"But how can you be sure it was him? His relationship with Martina appears tenacious at best."

Sherlock looked at me grim-faced. "Stapleton and Martina Schockomohle were seen together at public events, student gatherings, and similar places. It was well known they had embarked on a love affair that only ended when Martina's father travelled to England shortly after his daughter graduated to take her back to Frankfurt, and in doing so, likely saved her from a fate worse than death."

"But how can you know if the child was Stapleton's? Martina told us she and Karl married later that same year?"

"The lady in question graduated in June eighteen-seventy-two. She arrived back in Frankfurt in July of that year and married a month later in what appeared to be a rushed affair, akin to a union compelled by circumstance. I took the liberty of inspecting Hildegard Achen's birth certificate before handing it back to her. The young lady was born on the 1st of November eighteen-seventy-two, only four months after her mother returned from London. There is no doubt in my mind Martina was carrying Stapleton's child. Of course, it was all hushed up by Martina's parents, who hurriedly married their daughter off to a friend of the family, the legal advocate Karl Achen, who had always held a torch for their daughter.

"With the added incentive of a large dowry, Achen agreed to claim the child as his own. Consequently, no one was the wiser. Martina Schockomohle, of course, had no way of knowing the true identity of her lover, the father of her child."

"What did you say to her during your private conversation the other night?"

"I merely asked her if she had come into contact with Jack Valderlour while she was at university, explaining that his father was an old friend of the family. I hated having to lie, but I needed to get to the truth."

"And how did Martina respond?"

"She admitted they were friends but nothing more. But I could tell from her expression that she was concealing the truth, and to be honest, who could blame her? The Schockomohle family's reputation would be in tatters if the public and press ever got wind of the sordid affair."

"And that's why you decided not to mention anything to either of them?"

"Exactly," Sherlock said. "Stapleton has ruined enough lives. May his dirty secret march with him straight to hell. I'm sorry I couldn't tell you before, but I had to establish the facts, which were all there if only I had noticed them earlier. I can't believe I misread all the signs."

"Such as?" I pressed.

"The look of astonishment on Stapleton's face when he met Miss Achen in the library wasn't contrived. He was genuinely shocked by the staggering likeness to his ex-paramour Martina Schockomohle and the young lady he had just met in an extraordinary twist of fate.

"I don't believe that meeting was premeditated in any way. And, of course, Stapleton's interest in our newly appointed governess suddenly piqued after discovering her mother's identity. He realised without a shadow of a doubt and by merely asking a few simple questions that Miss Achen was his daughter. Discovering her impending employment with the Sapori family was the icing on the cake. I'll bet Stapleton could hardly believe his good fortune. Of course, that's why his ardour cooled, and he refused to make love to her. Thank God Stapleton didn't add incest to his list of crimes. He spared his daughter that at least, although he did callously use the poor girl to play out his cruel deception."

I froze for a moment, my breath catching as Sherlock's words settled like a whetstone in the stillness of the room. My grip on the back of the chair before me, my knuckles whitening, as though the sturdy wicker beneath my hands could anchor against the sudden torrent of emotions. A shiver passed through me, and I sank into the chair with a grace that belied the turmoil within. My head bent, looking at the floor, brow furrowed, lips parted slightly as if forming questions I could not yet voice. For what seemed an eternity, I could not raise my head, with thoughts racing through memories of the quiet, composed governess, now reframed in the shadow of this revelation.

"Hildegard? Jack Stapleton's daughter?" I whispered, the words scarcely audible, as if by speaking them aloud, I risked empowering them. Then, almost imperceptibly, I raised my head, turning my attention back to Sherlock, my eyes now wide open with incredulity and disbelief. "Hildegard confided she almost became intimate with him. It does not bear thinking about. It's almost too horrific to contemplate such an action."

Ever composed, Sherlock observed my reaction with the calm of a man accustomed to delivering earth-shattering truths. Yet even he seemed to pause due to my sudden shock at what had been revealed, his steel-grey eyes softening for a moment as he looked at me so tenderly and lovingly, almost as though he was trying to calm me hypnotically before he replied.

"Yes, he had some kind of feeling for her, his one show of remorselessness, no doubt triggered by his impending death. He begged me to protect his child because he knew I would figure it out given time."

"Sherlock, I think what you did was an extremely kind and noble gesture. You have been nothing less than spectacular throughout this madness, and I love you for that."

Sherlock smiled at me with a light in his eyes that spoke volumes. "You know I'm no expert on the affairs of the heart, but I have learned that a woman can't change a man no matter how much she cares for him. A man changes himself because of his love for the woman. Perhaps Stapleton should have taken heed of Oscar Wilde's quotation. *Be yourself. Everyone else is already taken.* Not to mention the situation could have been avoided."

I took his hand. "Come, let's go upstairs. I've missed my empty space. Let me show you how much you mean to me."

CHAPTER-FORTY-SIX: NENE ADLER
Giornata Perfetta — Perfect Day

Two deliveries arrived the next morning, shortly after breakfast, both from Enrico Caruso. The first was a parcel addressed to Nicco wrapped in brown paper, which I later discovered from my excited son, was two of the maestro's recordings, including a signed copy of Enrico's celebrated duet with the baritone Antonio Scotti.

The second delivery, addressed to me, was a dazzling bouquet of pink roses. Each delicate bloom was perfectly formed, creating a harmonious blend of pink shades. Sprigs of baby's breath were also beautifully wrapped in satin ribbon.

I read the handwritten note attached to the card.

Greetings Nene,

A little bird told me you will not be at home this weekend to celebrate your birthday. So I'm sending these flowers early. I hope you like them. I'm sorry I can't be with you to celebrate. Instead, to mark the occasion, I shall light a cigar and pour myself a large glass of the finest Tuscan wine while playing my favourite recording on the gramophone, a piece very close to my heart, **Mi Par D'udir Ancora** *from Bizet's* **The Pearl Fisher,** *which I'm sure you'll remember I recorded in April 1904, accompanied by my dear friend Salvatore Cottone.*

Then, singing along in my native Italian, I shall raise a toast for the Sapori family. I salute you all.

Buon more,
Enrico.

Ginevra and I had just finished putting the blooms in water

when we were disturbed by a knock at the front door. Alice ushered Salvatore into the drawing room, carrying a box of books for the children, a gift from him and Caterina. I kissed Salvatore lightly on the cheek, inviting him to take a seat and join me for morning coffee.

"Sherlock went to the library earlier this morning with the children, but he won't be there long if you want to wait for him."

Salvatore shook his head. "No, thank you, Nene. I'll catch up with your husband later. I just came to deliver the books and say goodbye. Sadly, I can't make the trip your friend Sophia organised. I'm caught up in what may prove to be another difficult case."

"Oh, that's a shame. I hope Caterina and the children are still coming. We're all looking forward to seeing them."

"Yes, of course, they wouldn't miss it for the world." Salvatore leaned forward in his seat, staring at me curiously. "Your husband told me your trip to the USA will be brought forward?"

"Yes, that's right, but we're not going until the second week in August. I will return to Milan next summer to honour my commitment to La Scala. You don't get rid of me that easily." I laughed.

Salvatore nodded, giving me a forlorn smile. "That's good to hear, although I'm unsure if I'll still be here. This could be my last roll of the dice."

"Why? Where are you going? Please tell me you are not moving away?"

Salvatore shook his head. "No, nothing like that." He paused for a moment. "I have a heart condition. Angina. I take medication, but the symptoms have been steadily getting worse. The doctors told me I need to take it easy and cut down on the drink and tobacco."

"Does Sherlock know?"

Salvatore laughed. "Of course he does. I didn't need to tell the great detective. Working together in such proximity, he noticed all the tell-tale signs . . . shortness of breath, restlessness, and unexplained sweating. Apart from my doctor, you, your husband, and Caterina are the only ones who know. So I have decided to take early retirement, citing health grounds. I was about to give notice to my superiors when your son was kidnapped, so I've been putting it off until I knew Nicco was safe. I would love to travel and see more of the world before I meet my maker. You never know, I could bring Caterina and the children to visit you in America. My wife always had a penchant to visit New York."

"I'm so sorry, Salvatore. I had no idea. Sherlock never mentioned anything."

"That's because I asked him not to. We both agreed you had quite enough to deal with."

Blinking back tears, I stepped forward and threw my arms around this remarkable man who had been prepared to put his life on hold to find our son.

"Don't worry. I'm not dead yet. There's still life in the old dog," Salvatore said, his mood suddenly turning sombre. "But when the inevitable occurs, I want you to promise me that you will keep in touch with Caterina and the children. They all adore you."

"Yes, of course, Salvatore, you have my word. But you'd better not go yet. When you roll the dice, sometimes you get two sixes."

"I will do my best." He smiled. "The doctors said I'm not in any immediate danger, and who knows, with rest and a healthier lifestyle, I could still be around to annoy people in years to come. So, I intend to make the most of the time I have left."

"I pray you do. I insist on it."

"Thank you, Nene. Before I go, I want to let you know that

I love you."

"Yes, I know." I beamed. "I love you, too, you and your wonderful family."

Salvatore stared at me with a burning intensity. "I don't think you quite understand, Nene. *Ti amero per sempre*. I'll love you forever." Salvatore held up his hand as I was about to protest, chuckling at my shocked expression. "Please don't be concerned. This is no indecent proposal. I realise that nothing could ever happen between us. For one, I have too much respect for your husband, and two, I love my wife dearly. I would never dream of being unfaithful to Caterina."

"Then what is this declaration?"

"I'm unsure." He shrugged. "But what I do know is that it's not a physical thing. I've never been a particularly sexual animal, but one day in another life, one where your husband and Caterina don't live, perhaps something might develop between us?" He raised a brow, staring at me searchingly.

I slowly shook my head. "Oh, Salvatore, I'm so sorry, but I would never want to live in a world without Sherlock and my children. They have brought so much joy into my life. They are my everything, but in the future, if such a world exists, then who knows what might happen. In the meantime, I hope you and your family can be as happy as this cruel world allows. Before you go, I want to thank you again for your loyal friendship and service, which were instrumental in finding our son. You have been a godsend to me and Sherlock."

Salvatore pulled a handkerchief from his pocket, wiping away a tear. "Thank you for trusting me. This means I retain your friendship, and that's the most important thing to me."

We held each other in a poignant moment between two close friends. And then I kissed him gently as though I never expected to see him again. I could sense he knew it. At that moment, I wanted to bundle him and Caterina up in some Dickensian liberation and convey them far away to a safe and illness-free place.

I waited until Salvatore left the villa before retiring to my bedroom. I sat on the bed, trying to come to terms with our conversation, finally allowing the tears to flow, my sobs shaking my whole body, praying to God that our dear friend would somehow survive his ordeal. Sherlock and I would miss Salvatore hugely should the unthinkable happen.

Later, managing to compose myself, I washed my face and applied a little make-up before Sherlock and the children returned. I was busy packing in preparation for our weekend away in the beautiful city of Monza—a sixteen-mile trip by train from Milano Centrale. We would embark on our journey late Saturday afternoon, arriving at our destination in time for dinner at one of the oldest and most historic hotels in Monza. The Eden Savoia Hotel.

Apart from our travelling arrangements, that was all the information I was privy to. I was intrigued about what to expect, especially since Sherlock was collaborating on some sort of surprise for me with Sophia's help. I was pleased they were getting along much better and wondered where my birthday picnic would occur. Still, it was a welcome distraction from Salvatore's grim prognosis and the past few days' events, and I was looking forward to spending time with Sophia, Caterina, and their families. Little did I know what delights were to come.

We eventually arrived at our destination at 6 P.M. on Saturday. Sherlock insisted on footing the bill for our entire party. After an early dinner, the children retired to bed, tired but happy and supervised by Ginevra, who had accompanied us on the trip. Sophia, Caterina, and I entered the plush grandeur of the hotel cocktail bar, where the hotel manager invited me to play the grand piano, to which I happily agreed.

Accompanied by Sophia, we got through a treasure trove

of catchy melodies from Carmen, one of our favourite operas. Judging by the applause from the appreciative audience, it appeared to be theirs, too. Afterwards, we laughed and joked, putting the world to rights. We quaffed several glasses of champagne while entertained by Sophia, who could always be relied upon for salacious gossip. How we laughed at her outlandish stories. I was glad to see Caterina enjoying the evening. We had a private conversation earlier, during which I offered my unwavering support and told her Sherlock and I would always be there if she needed help in the future.

As gracious as ever, Caterina, wearing a black silk evening gown that enhanced her slender figure, hugged me tightly, thanked me for our support, and said it was good to see me smile again. During this time, Sherlock and Robert Moon excused themselves away from an excitable gaggle of women, indulging their bohemian tendencies in the more congenial and amenable space of the hotel smoking lounge.

We slept well that night and awoke to a bright new day on Sunday morning.

After showering and changing into a yellow bustle dress and a feathered-topped hat, we took the children downstairs to find the hotel already thronged with visitors. Having consumed an early breakfast of freshly baked bread, pastries, and seasonal fruits, our party of twelve, making good use of the horse-drawn trams, ventured out to explore the beautiful city of Monza.

Our first port of call was the cathedral, the Basilica of San Giovanni. We arrived in time to join the morning service, which was about to start. A seminarian ushered us down the centre aisle towards our seats in the chancels.

The priest gave a stirring sermon about the church's allegiance to the poor and the sick. We sang along to the hymns *Adoro Te Devote* and *Te Deum*. After the service, Sherlock placed some silver into the collection plate, and we continued to explore the cathedral's treasures, which were famous for its frescoes and bell tower — the Duomo of Monza.

After taking in the historical side of the city, I was thrilled to discover that Sophia and my husband had organised my birthday picnic in the beautiful grounds of Monza Park, with food and drink provided by a local restaurant. The park, Parco di Monza, steeped in history, was commissioned by Napoleon's stepson, Eugene de Beauharnais, during the French occupation of Northern Italy as an extension to the garden of his royal palace, and it was quite an extension. The Royal Villas of Monza was the true jewel of Lombardy, where locals and tourists alike relaxed in nature, enjoyed sports, and visited the many cultural treasures in its vast green space.

As we approached the picnic area, all eyes were drawn to three figures emerging from the woodland area. I gasped in shock at the familiar sight of my dear friends Ava, Violetta, and Francesco Espirito as they strolled towards the picnic area, beaming from ear to ear. I ran towards my friends, embracing Ava and Violetta in a warm hug, chuckling as Francesco quickly pecked me on the cheek and then suddenly bolted.

"Nicco, Charlotte, you are here!" an excited Francesco exclaimed as he spotted both of them.

Violetta, Ava, and I laughed and chatted together. "But how did you know?" I asked.

Violetta took my hand and smiled at me. "Sophia and Sherlock invited us. We know you have all been through a great deal recently, but today is a celebration as your close friends join you in this enjoyable social gathering. Happy birthday, my dear. Ava and I have your gift at the hotel. We will, of course, present it to you later. But for now, I think we should celebrate this wonderful event with a large glass of wine. What do you say?"

"Absolutely," I said, linking my arms around both ladies

as we made our way to the picnic area. I gazed up at my husband as he handed me a flute. "Thank you for organising this and inviting my friends. Why, it's perfect."

"You're welcome," he said, kissing me gently.

We sat on the picnic benches and blankets, chatting while consuming the delicious freshly baked loaves, cold cuts, cheese pastries, sweet bread, and fresh fruit on the glorious afternoon. The ladies shielded themselves with parasols as the afternoon sun beat down.

As a special treat, Sophia had organised the hire of bicycles for the children to explore the grounds. Sherlock told them to keep their eyes peeled to spot the wildlife known to populate the area. The children set off with skittish energy like pigeons being released from a coup, calling out to each other as they peddled furiously around the area, pointing out the various squirrels, rabbits and ducks they spotted along the way. We erupted with laughter as Charlotte's short legs were pumping as fast as they could, struggling to keep up with the others, her face rosy-red from her exertions, and she had a determined expression, always unafraid to compete with any boy. My heart melted as Francesco, this fine young man of charming character, turned his bicycle around, patiently waiting for his friend, a broad smile of affection and empathy infused on his handsome face.

"Come on, Charley, follow me. We'll soon catch up," he said.

"How wonderful to be that innocent and carefree again," Sherlock said, smiling wistfully at the scene.

Later that afternoon, we bid farewell to our stunning historical location and made our way back to the hotel. After an early dinner, we headed to The Teatro Manzoni. Unbeknown to Nicco and me, Enrico Caruso had reserved complimentary tickets for us in the front stalls to celebrate an evening with the lyric baritone Giuseppe de Luca, who was giving a recital of operatic arias and Neapolitan songs.

A happy party returned to the hotel with seven exhausted children at the end of a perfect day. Ginevra took them to bed while the adults retired to the cocktail bar for a nightcap of brandy and liquor.

When we eventually arrived back in our suite later that evening, while my husband took a shower, I noticed an unopened present in the locker. I stared at the parcel, wondering who it was from. I thought I had opened all my presents earlier at dinner. There had been candies from the children, a pearl necklace from Violette and Ava, a collection of the complete poems of Ernest Dowson from Sophia, and from Caterina, an exquisite bottle of Fiori di Capri perfume. I stared in surprise at this last present from Sherlock, wrapped in elegant silver paper, furrowing my brow as I carefully unwrapped the delicate paper.

After the beautiful weekend, which I knew must have cost a small fortune, I wasn't expecting anything else from my husband. Although an exceedingly generous person, it wasn't unusual for him to buy me presents, but he rarely wrapped them. I sensed this was Sophia's doing, as the parcel was beautifully presented with a large bow and a gift card on what was simply written, *All my love, Sherlock.*

I opened the parcel to reveal a silver plaque engraved with the words of one of my favourite poems, splendidly depicting old ties of love and friendship. The author was Dinah Craik, the English novelist and poet. Even after everything that had transpired between us since our son's abduction, I still wasn't entirely sure if Sherlock had wholly forgiven me. There was no way I could change what had occurred, although I would have given anything to do so. The words on the plaque finally cast all doubt aside.

Oh the comfort
The inexpressible comfort of feeling
Safe with a person,

Having neither to weigh thoughts,
Nor measure words, but pouring them.
All right out just as they are
Chaff and grain together
Certain that a faithful hand will
Take and sift them
Keep what is worth keeping
And with the breath of kindness
Blow the rest away.

I placed the plaque on the bedside locker, poured two liberal glasses of port while sitting on the bed, and waited for Sherlock to finish his shower. I will never forget the precious hours spent with my family, close friends, and beloved husband. Here in Monza, I felt a rejuvenating energy, a new sense of belonging in what was a time for reflection, healing, love, and compassion, but most of all, new beginnings.

For Sherlock and me, the delightful joys of the weekend, after the challenging lows of the past few weeks, had played a significant part in our re-bonding as a couple, reminiscent of the delicious heady stage of our relationship in Fiesole and our second honeymoon in Venice, reminding us that we must stop and be thankful for those most important in our lives. The people closest to us, who we chose to spend time with, because one day, when we look up from all our distractions in life, they may no longer be around to hear you tell them how much you care.

A tall shadow hovered over me, interrupting my thoughts. I looked up to see Sherlock looking down at me with a tender expression, a towel draped around his shoulders, his hair wet and tousled from the shower.

"I hope you enjoyed your special day," he said.

"It's all been rather wonderful, thank you." I sighed as his lips softly brushed mine.

In each other's arms, we embraced the glorious survival of our shared intimacy and an enduring love that could never be tarnished.

I had no idea what the future might hold, but no matter what life throws at us, our family will meet it head-on, embracing life and any future adventures. We Saporis sing from our own hymn sheet, and woe betide anyone who had an issue with that.

Little did I know then that our new adventures would arrive far sooner than expected.

Epilogue

The air was warm, a tranquil breeze gently blowing as we stood on the SS *Moltke* of the Hamburg America Line deck. While Sherlock lit a cigarette, appearing deep in thought as he gazed into the distance, the children watched in wonder and giddy anticipation as the ship slowly moved out of the port of Genoa. We finally embarked on our fourteen-day journey to New York.

There was much to reflect on that journey as the ship gathered speed at a rate of knots, gliding effortlessly over the crystal blue ocean.

Jack Stapleton's body was finally released by the coroner, who, with the assistance of the Newton Abbot Police, acquired his medical records, identifying him by a birthmark on his torso. A verdict of homicide by arsenic poisoning was duly recorded. The body was later claimed by John Gregson from Birmingham, England, and shipped back to the UK.

The fate of the other known felons involved in our sons, abduction and related crimes were as follows.

Guardia Giarcosca was sentenced to five years for causing severe injury and grievous bodily harm, plus an additional two years for participation in the abduction of a child, less than two years for his cooperation in bringing the ring leaders to justice, a total of five years imprisonment.

Connie Gallagher, the person responsible for sending Jack Stapleton into his long twilight, was never found. Despite the best efforts of the police, the femme fatale was still at large. After a sighting in France, it was rumoured that she had once again cunningly outwitted the police and the armed forces and fled to the continent disguised as a false identity. Nevertheless, despite all of this, she was convicted in absentia. She received a whole life sentence at the Milan Courthouse for a multitude of offences. Murder, kidnapping, extortion, endangering life, terrorism, criminal damage, theft, fraud, and attempted horse doping.

Peppo Barbieri proved another elusive fish, and while his family was traced to Rome, there was no sign of Bob Barrett's accomplice and former henchman. Just like his partner in crime, Connie Gallagher, Barbieri was convicted in absentia, receiving a sentence of twelve years. The charges were kidnapping, extortion, endangering life, terrorism, criminal damage, theft, and fraud.

Just before we left Milan, a parcel with a Swedish postmark arrived for Nicco. It contained an elaborate ivory chess set with a card attached. The brief message, signed by G, simply said, *Have a good life, little soldier.* That note brought a wry smile to our son's face, leaving a lasting impression and finally bringing closure to his horrendous ordeal.

The perpetrators involved in the attempted horse doping scandal were each sentenced to two years of hard labour at San Vittore Prison.

Eduardo Balducci received two years imprisonment for child abduction.

Rodolfo Abbati stood trial at the Milano Courthouse. Entering into a plea bargain put forward so eloquently by his defence attorney, Abbati avoided a whole life term by pleading guilty to involuntary manslaughter and perverting the cause of judgment. The judge took Salvatore's testimony and mitigating circumstances into account. Showing mercy to the man standing before him in the dock, he sentenced the agent to ten years' imprisonment.

The Eel, Raoul Bengini, pleaded guilty to attempted arson

and criminal damage with intent to endanger life recklessly and terrorism, receiving a sentence of nine years.

Roberto Santini was tried for aiding and abetting the procurement of a stolen painting and handling stolen goods. He was sentenced to four years.

Gerard Francescone, also known as Mr X, was found guilty of attempting to procure a precious work of art by unscrupulous means for mercenary gain and handling stolen goods. He was sentenced to four years' imprisonment.

Gustav Bauman, the German chemist, stood trial at The Moabit Criminal Court, Berlin, where he was found guilty of unlawfully supplying a cholera vaccine to a criminal organisation for financial gain and sentenced to five years imprisonment.

As for Il Vecchio Cigno, the haunted house, neighbours reported that despite the property remaining empty, strange noises could still be heard during the night hours. The house was eventually sold at public auction for way below the market value, reaching its modest reserve. The new owners, most notably Sergente Ferraro and his new bride, instructed builders to renovate the property before finally moving in, after which no further disturbances were reported.

At Sherlock's request, Inspector Lestrade attended Jack Stapleton's funeral at Saint John the Evangelist Church, Bovey Tracey. The service was a quiet, sombre affair.

Lestrade reported that only a handful of mourners attended. The executors, amongst them two representatives from the Peaky Blinders and the Masons, and more notably, sitting quietly at the rear of the church wearing a black silk dress and veil sat Laura Lyons, accompanied by a striking youth of eighteen years or so, a shy looking boy of average height, slim, with piercing blue eyes, that were alert and intelligent, his blond hair coloured every hue from—spun gold to golden browns, all marinated into shoulder-length flowing locks. The very image of Jack Stapleton. They say the sins of the father are visited upon the children.

At the graveside, under an old oak tree, the priest began the committal service, offering prayers up to God and waving incense over the coffin. Laura dabbed her red-rimmed eyes and threw a single red rose onto the casket, sobbing uncontrollably as her ex-lover was laid to rest, reunited at last with his dear departed Beryl.

We can only hope and pray for a better life for our loved ones. So, whatever your battle, be brave and face your demons. Our son's abduction and life had taught me that every single day was precious. Although the past can never be changed, our perception of it can. What was important was the future, and it was up to every one of us to determine how that future was shaped.

Later that evening, I put the children to bed in their stateroom, leaving them in the care of Ginevra, who had happily agreed to accompany us to the States as a companion for the children.

The ship's band performed on the promenade as Sherlock and I made our way to the dining suite at 6.30 P.M. to join the other guests for a sumptuous dinner.

They say one's past never leaves us and can return at any time in unusual forms, as I was about to discover. We had barely sat down, having been ushered to our table by the chief steward, when I felt a light tap on my shoulder. I turned around, half expecting to see Ginevra come to tell me something was amiss with one of the children.

Instead, I found a vaguely familiar, attractive-looking woman of middle years smiling down at me, her blue eyes twinkling. A pile of beautiful titian hair arranged in an array of elaborate curls hung loose on her shoulders. She was dressed immaculately in a black satin evening gown, a string of pearls, and a silver tiara completing the outfit.

"Hello, my dear." She beamed, greeting me like an old friend as she took hold of my hand and kissed me tenderly. "How lovely it is to see you again."

I gazed at the woman, perplexed, trying to recall where I'd seen her before.

"Ah," she said, observing my nonplussed expression. "You don't remember me, do you?"

To be continued.

Dramatis Personae- List of Characters

Adamo — A gondolier.
Agata — Waitress/barista.
Alberto Patrese — Mason and friend of Ludovico Galli.
Alberto Romano — Father of Salvatore Romano.
Aldo Cardinale — Tic-Tac man at the Milano Racecourse.
Alejandro Rodriguez — Father of Emilio Rodriguez.
Alice Bergamaschi — Cook and general housekeeper at the Sapori residence.
Alfred Adler — Father of Irene Adler.
Alessio Muratori — Tenor
Alexio Claudio — Son of Inspector Claudio.
Andrea Romano — Son of Salvatore and Caterina Romano.
Antonio Selva — Designer of La Fenice opera house, Venice.
Arturo Toscanini — The principal conductor at La Scala.
Attracta Sweeney — Midwife and sister of Jim Sweeney.
Atty Parkinson — A horse trainer from Sandyford, Dublin.
Ava Espirito — The principal soprano at La Scala. Friend of the Sapori family.
Beatrice Shaw — A pseudonym used by Connie Gallagher.
Beryl Stapleton — Deceased wife of Jack Stapleton/Bob Barrett.
Bruno Conte — Alias Dominzia Santora.
Camoni Cannoni — A fictional character created by Nicco Sapori.
Captain Marco Lipati — Genoa Police Inspector.

Carlos Romano — Son of Salvatore and Caterina Romano.
Caterina Romano — The wife of Inspector Salvatore Romano
Charlotte Sapori — Daughter of Sherlock Holmes and Irene Adler.
Christine Upton — Wife of racehorse owner John Upton.
Cipriano Esposito — Front desk sergeant at the Milano polizia station.
Claudia Furmagalli — Equestrian riding instructor. Friend of Irene Adler
Colonel James Moriarty — The brother of Professor Moriarty.
Connie Gallagher, nee Rosenbaum — Works for Bob Barrett. Second in command.
Daniel Oliver — Professor of botany at the University College of London.
Dante — Head waiter at Lafayette Ristorante.
Dario Bergamaschi — Deceased husband and father of Alice and Ginevra.
Denis Rafferty — Secretary at Shire and Allen, an Irish holding company.
Derek Hamilton — A colleague of Mycroft Holmes-Works for The Foreign Office.
Doctor John Watson — A medical practitioner in London, friend of Sherlock Holmes.
Doctor Pease — Psychologist and doctor.
Dominzia Santora — Fugitive, wanted for suspected murder.
Eduardo Balducci — Driver employed by Rodriguez.
Egidio Capo — guardia at the Milano polizia.
Eliana Sanju — Pseudonym of Connie Rosenbaum/Beatrice Shaw.
Emilia Giordano — Nanny/governess to Robert and Sophia Moon.
Emilio Rodriguez — Member of the Italian Mafia, extortionist, and money launderer.
Enrico Caruso — World-famous Italian tenor.

Enzo Guiliano — doctor from Legnano.
Ernest Angelino — Esteemed Italian horse trainer and proprietor of Liguari Cars.
Fabrizio Gallo — Romany gypsy and fraudster.
Father Joseph Mancini — Catholic priest. Friend and mentor of Emilio Rodriguez.
Fergal McCabe — An Irish horse trainer.
Francesco de Sousa — Italian jockey.
Francesco Espirito — Family friend of the Saporis. Son of Violetta and Ludo.
Franco Mizzia — Notorious Mafia leader.
Fredrik — Maitre di Lafayette Ristorante.
Gabriella Moon — Daughter of Sophia and Robert Moon.
Ginevra Bergamaschi — Housemaid at the Sapori villa in Milan.
Georgiana Romano — Mother of Salvatore Romano.
Gerard Francescone, Mr X — Art dealer.
Gina Boccaccio — Ernest Angelino's private secretary.
Gina Ronci — Sister at The Policlinico Hospital.
Gina Stephanato — Mother of Sophia Moon
Gianni Moon — Son of Sophia and Robert Moon
Gino, also known as Peppo Barbieri — Member of the abduction gang.
Giorgione — Painter, pupil of Bellini.
Godfrey Norton — A lawyer and Irene Adler's first husband murdered in London.
Gormo Sanju — Pseudonym of Robert Barrett/Jack Stapleton.
Guardia Colombo — An officer at the Milano polizia.
Guardia Russo — An officer at the Milano polizia.
Gustav Bauman — German chemist based in Berlin.
Helga Rosenbaum — Mother of Connie Gallagher-nee Rosenbaum.
Henry Hodgson — A stockbroker from Southampton, an old friend of Irene Adler.

Hildegard Achen—Live-in nanny/governess at the Sapori residence.
Ilfranco Dachil—Journalist and deceased husband of Hildegard Achen.
Inspector Carlos Montalabo—Former colleague of Inspector Romano.
Inspector Lestrade—A law enforcer based in London.
Irene Adler—An acclaimed contralto, married to Lucca Sapori, Aka Sherlock Holmes.
Isabella Anka—Mother of Javier.
Isabella de Soto—Neighbour who comes to Irene's aid after the kidnapping.
Jabez Wilson—A character from Conan Doyle's The Red-Headed League.
Jack Valdelour—A persona of Jack Stapleton.
Janus—God of new beginnings. Pseudonym for the two faces of Jack Stapleton.
Javier Anka—The husband of Ava Espirito.
Jim Sweeny—A Kildare horse trainer and Bob Barrett's second cousin.
John Gregson—Member of the Peaky Blinders in Birmingham.
John Upton—Christine's husband and racehorse owner.
Karl Achen—Father of Hildegard and late husband of Martina Schockomohle.
Laura Lyons—A character from "The Hound of The Baskervilles."
Lina Mascagni—Wife and manager of Pietro Mascagni.
Ludo Espirtio—Close friend of the Sapori family.
Ludovicio Galli—Mason and proprietor of The San Siro Stables.
Luigi Amato—Protagonist in *Meet Me in Milan*.
Luigi Ambrosio—Musical Director at La Scala.
Luigi Giarcosca—Guardia at the Milano polizia

Luis Bandiero—A former barber and murder victim, along with his wife, Rosetta.
Madame Emily—Dresser and seamstress at La Scala, a friend of Irene's
Maggiore Ferraro—A high-flying Sergeante at the Milano polizia station.
Marco Anka—Father of Javier.
Mariette—Housemaid in Venice.
Mario Renaldi—Deaf-mute employed as a security guard at The San Siro Stables.
Marissa Hoffman—Fiancée and subsequent wife of Henry Hodgson.
Martha Hudson—Sherlock Holmes London housekeeper
Martina Schockomohle—Acclaimed German concert pianist.
Matilda Rodriguez—Daughter of Emilio Rodriguez.
Mattia Greco—the Saporis' coachman.
Mimi Gallo-Romany gypsy, an accomplice in the kidnapping of Nicco Sapori.
Mycroft Holmes—Older brother of Sherlock Holmes.
Niamh O'Doherty—The wife of Paddy, joint owner of the racehorse Olmo.
Nicco Sapori—Sherlock and Irene's son
Oisin O'Flaherty—Equine Vet based in Ireland.
Orlando Fontano—Stable lad at The San Siro Stables.
Oscar Wilde—Irish wit and dramatist.
Otto Rosenbaum—Father of Connie Gallagher-nee Rosenbaum.
Paddy O'Doherty—Husband of Niamh, joint owner of the racehorse Olmo.
Peppo Barbieri—Also known as Gino- Works for Bob and Rodriguez.
Pietro Mascagni—Italian composer of notable works, including Cavalleria Rusticana.
Ric Ricardo—Member of the Italian Mafia.

Raoul Benigni — An ex-army explosives expert employed by Rodriguez.
Robert Barrett — Known as Bob and various aliases — Aka Jack Stapleton.
Robert Moon — The husband of Sophia Moon. Art director at La Scala.
Roberto Santini — Fine art expert employed by Rodriguez.
Rodolfo Abbati — Flamboyant Letting Agent with a shady past.
Rosetta Bandiero — A murder victim, along with her husband Luis
Rosemary Adler — Irene Adler's first child who tragically died at birth.
Salvatore Romano — Inspector at the Milano polizia- A trusted friend of the Saporis.
Sam Perkins — Original arranger of the inaugural Walden Stakes, Baltimore.
Samuel Delori — Pseudonym of Robet Barett/Jack Stapleton.
Sal Claudio — Inspector at the Busalla Polizia. Colleague of Salvatore Romano.
Samuel Delori — Pseudonym of Robert Barrett/Jack Stapleton.
Seamus Gallagher — Deceased husband of Connie Gallagher.
Sergio Stephanato — Father of Sophia Moon.
Sherlock Holmes — Aka Lucca Sapori — The World-famous consulting detective.
Signora Alameda — Pseudonym used by Connie Gallagher.
Sir Charles Baskerville — Character from "The Hound of The Baskervilles."
Sir Henry Baskerville — Character from "The Hound of The Baskervilles."
Sophia Moon — A Mezzo-Soprano- Irene's close friend.
The DeTorres — Ex-tenants of the haunted house.
Thomas O'Flaherty — Retired doctor, father of Oisin

O'Flaherty.
Tom O'Connor — Groom to Jim Sweeney.
Turridu Cannio — Lead character in the opera Cavalleria Rusticana.
Ugo Lamaro — Local Mafia leader, father in-law of Emilio Rodriguez.
Victoria Bennett — Ex-fiancée of Sherlock Holmes.
Violetta Espirito — A close friend of the Sapori family
Virna Rodriguez — Wife of Emilio Rodriguez.
Victor de Soto — Neighbour who came to Irene's rescue.
Virna Rodriguez — Wife of Emilio.
Wilhelm Ormstein — The hereditary King of Bohemia, an old paramour of Irene Adler.
Wyndham Walden — Maryland-based racehorse owner and trainer known as Wink.

An Index of the Four-Legged Supporting Players

Beauty — A black mare.
Break The Bank — Racehorse owned by Ric Ricardo.
Caesar — Rodolfo Abbati's dog.
Carlos — Jack Stapleton's dog, referred to as The Hound of The Baskervilles
Duchess of Tuscany — Racehorse owned by John and Christine Upton.
Helen — A chocolate-coloured labrador rescue dog owned by the Saporis
Keepsake — Racehorse, winner of the Gran Milano 1903 and 1905.
Leeroy — Racehorse, a runner in the Champagne Stakes.
Lorenzo — Racehorse.
Messana — Racehorse, winner of the Gran Milano 1906.
Olmo — Racehorse, owned by the O'Doherty's, trained by Jim Sweeney.
Princess of Lombardy — Racehorse owned by John and Christine Upton.
Rathrea — Racehorse trained by Angelino.
Riptide — Racehorse, brother to Rahrea, who Angelino also trained.
Rosallion — Racehorse trained by Jim Sweeney.
Sandura — Racehorse trained by Angelino.
Speculator — Racehorse trained by Jim Sweeney.
Tobia di Lombardia — Dapple grey pony, a favourite of

Charlotte Sapori.
Touch and Go — Racehorse.
Viscusi — Racehorse, trained by Bob Barrett.
Willo The Wisp — Racehorse.

Acknowledgements

Sir Arthur Conan Doyle's works inspire this fourth book in the multi-award-winning Sherlock Holmes and Irene Adler Mysteries, featuring characters recognisable from his original stories.

"The Whistle of Revenge" has been a dedicated labour of love, and this book would not have been possible without the assistance of my good friend development editor, Tony Waslin-Ashbridge. His astounding knowledge of the Victorian era and the period's historical and musical nuances is phenomenal. I shall be forever grateful for his thoughtful insights and invaluable advice.

I wish I could say that modern technology's allure has transformed me from a typical procrastinator into a computer guru, but sadly, it has not. So, additional thanks are also due to Abigail McIntosh, Ryan Hale, Jayne Leahy, Gayna Dagnal, Lesley Williams, Benedetta Cinquini for her invaluable help with the Italian translations, my son David and daughter Katie for encouraging me to write, and my husband, John, for his continual support.

Others to thank Barbara Waslin-Ashbridge and my amazing ARC and Beta readers.

The fantastic team at eXtasy Books, the ever-patient EIC Jay Austin, Martine Jardin for the stunning covers, and Tina Haverman for removing my manuscript from the slush pile and taking a chance on my debut novel, 'Song for Someone' a recent Finalist at The Chanticleer International Book Awards—The Chatelaine.

Special mention to the late Alan Johnson, Annette Tarpley from The Passion of Poetry, Steve Thorpe, Lee Benson, John Cheetham, Sean Ryan, and Nish Hindocha for their extraordinary kindness.

A massie thank you to the readers and everyone who embarked on this incredible journey with me.

I hope Sherlock and Irene's exploits continue to fire your imagination and leave an indelible mark on your memories. God willing, more adventures will come from the celebrated detective and the acclaimed contralto.

Author's Notes

If you enjoyed *The Whistle of Revenge*, please consider leaving an honest review on Amazon or Goodreads. Reviews are the lifeblood of any aspiring author and are always appreciated.

To learn the latest about the Sherlock and Irene Mysteries, you can follow me on Facebook, Instagram and X.

https://www.facebook.com/KDSherrinford

Or why not check out my new Website:

https://emilydanie116.ag-sites.net

Or just email kdsherrinford@gmail.com.

OTHER BOOKS IN THE SHERLOCK HOLMES AND IRENE ADLER MYSTERIES

Book One: Song for Someone
Book Two: Christmas at The Saporis
Book Three: Meet Me in Milan

The above are all available on Amazon and at most leading outlets.

About the Author

KD Sherrinford is an award-winning author of the Sherlock Holmes and Irene Adler romantic mysteries. She was born and raised in Preston, Lancashire, and resides on The Fylde Coast with her husband John and their children. As an avid reader from an early age, KD was fascinated by the stories of Sir Arthur Conan Doyle and Agatha Christie. She read the entire Doyle Canon by age 13. A talented pianist, KD played from the age of six. The music of some of her favourite composers, Beethoven, Schubert, Stephen Foster, and Richard Wagner, all strongly feature in her writing.

KD had a varied career, working with thoroughbreds, show jumpers, and racing greyhounds. She and her husband, John, won the Blackpool Greyhound Derby in 1987 with Scottie.

Then, to mix things up, KD joined Countrywide, where she worked for over twenty years and became a Fellow of the National Association of Estate Agents.

After a demanding career, retirement finally allowed KD to follow her dreams and start writing professionally. In 2019, KD's daughter Katie inspired her to write *Song for Someone* after visiting the Sherlock Holmes Museum on Baker Street.

Writing about the iconic character Irene Adler has always been a passion of KD's. She felt disappointed when Irene failed to appear in any further Doyle stories after *A Scandal in Bohemia*. She waited years for someone to write a pastiche about the celebrated detective and the acclaimed contralto; others merely hinted at it without exploring its depths and endless possibilities. So, encouraged by her daughter, KD began her adaptation.

Song for Someone was published in November 2022 by eXtasy Books.

The book is a proud recipient of The Editor's Gold Seal and also made the finals of The Chanticleer International Book Awards for romantic fiction, The Chatelaine. Described by the Historical Fiction Company describes as, *An evocative masterpiece and a tale that stands out in Contemporary Literature.*

The first three books in this stylishly addictive series, *Song for Someone, Christmas at The Saporis,* and *Meet Me in Milan,* were shortlisted at The Ciba Series Book Awards for Genre Fiction and are available at most leading outlets.

Printed in Dunstable, United Kingdom